Looking Good

Tracy CULLETON

POOLBEG

Published 2003
by Poolbeg Press Ltd
123 Grange Hill, Baldoyle
Dublin 13, Ireland
E-mail: poolbeg@poolbeg.com

Typesetting, layout, design © Poolbeg Group Services Ltd.

1 3 5 7 9 10 8 6 4 2

A catalogue record for this book is available from the British Library.

ISBN 1-84223-155-3

Typeset by Patricia Hope in Palatino 10/14
Printed by
Litografia Rosés S.A., Spain

www.poolbeg.com

About the Author

Tracy Culleton lives in a little granite cottage in County Carlow, with her husband and seven year old son. When taking to the country life she had great plans for growing organic vegetables and generally living 'the Good Life'. But the reality was all too much effort so she decided to write a novel instead. She describes writing when it's going well as being 'the most fun you can have with your clothes on', but when it's not going well it's 'like pulling your own teeth with red-hot pincers. Blunt ones'.

Acknowledgements

I would like to thank my husband Peter for supporting me (both emotionally and financially!) in writing this novel, long before we ever knew it would be published. My further thanks to him for his suggestions for improving the content of this book. Sorry, Peter, but there are still no F16 aircraft, laser guns, or beautiful Russian spies, and not a single tank or submarine.

My thanks to Tadhg for being so gracious about his mammy being unavailable for large swathes of time, and for being totally underwhelmed by all the excitement surrounding its publication. Put me back in my box!

My thanks to my sister Frances, and to friends Elaine, Cindy, Maura, and Helen for reading it in manuscript form and coming up with both encouragement and good advice.

Thanks to Dan Feehan and Peter McConnon for information about the legal system.

And to others who helped me with information but who do not wish to be named.

To Paula and all the staff at Poolbeg. It's an author's dream to find a publisher who'll take them and their 'opus' on . . . to find a publisher which will do that, *and* manage to be professional, interested, friendly, accessible and helpful - that's beyond dreams! Thanks to you all.

To Gaye Shortland. I've often read acknowledgements where authors have thanked Gaye. Now I know why. She approached editing this book with such vision, such sense, such clarity, and also a great sense of humour. It was wonderful working with you Gaye. Thanks for your major part in making *Looking Good* the book it is.

To Peter
who believed I could do it

Chapter 1

Dr Bourke told me, with compassion on her plain face, "You have another six months." She leaned forward towards me, resting her hand on my arm. "Look, Grainne, you're only just gone thirty, and as you've told me yourself you've only been trying for six months. Honestly, that's no time. We don't even start considering there might be a problem unless a year's gone by. There really isn't any point in giving you a letter for the fertility clinic – even if I did so against my better judgement, they wouldn't entertain it, they really wouldn't."

I looked at her, full of determination. "Well, what if we told *them* in the letter that Patrick and I'd been trying for over a year? They wouldn't know any different."

She pursed her lips a little, and there was a flicker of amusement in her eyes. "No, they wouldn't. But I'm not going to do that. Quite apart from the fact that it wouldn't be ethical for me to lie to them, Grainne, I'd be doing you no favours. The fertility investigations are *horrendous*. They're undignified and demoralising – and that's the best it gets. If they find nothing wrong from those first tests – which they probably won't, seeing as there's almost certainly nothing wrong – you'll move further into the process, and those tests are both invasive and painful. I'm serious, Grainne, fertility tests and treatment put both finances and marriages under severe strain. It's not something to be gone into lightly, and I'm not going to put you through all that for no reason – I simply wouldn't be doing my job as your doctor if I did. It would be like you coming in with an ingrowing toenail, and me sending you off to get your leg amputated!"

She laughed a little at her own wit. In return, I produced a weak stretch of my lips which was *this* much short of a grimace. Easy for her to be taking it so lightly, with her photograph of three children on her desk. She didn't know what it was like to wonder, day after day, each month, and to be disappointed each month.

"Right," she said, recovering quickly from her fit of mirth.

She began tapping her pen on her blotting-pad, and I found myself wondering why it is that doctors always have blotting-pads even though they never use fountain-pens. And why they always tap their (ballpoint) pens when they talk to you.

2

"I think the best thing is if you go away and keep trying, without getting worked up about it, for another six months. And if that doesn't work, come back to me then. But I bet you won't have to. Especially if you remember the number-one trick for conceiving . . ."

"What's that?" I asked eagerly.

"Relax about it all."

Relax! Easy for her to say.

And she was insisting I wait another six months!

I felt like wailing at her, 'It's not fair!'. A mature reaction, I know. But honestly, it didn't seem fair. All around me, everyone we knew was getting pregnant at the drop of a hat. Well, the drop of trousers more like.

Okay, I'd better qualify that. To be honest, not everyone we knew was getting pregnant. Certainly a lot of our friends – mostly the female ones – were getting pregnant and admitting when I challenged them that, yes, it had happened quite quickly, thanks. However, once I thought about it, plenty more couples our age had neither any children nor any gushing, coy news. Maybe that was by choice, but equally, how did I know they hadn't also been trying for ages, that their cheery, bright 'We're great thanks!' wasn't hiding a deeper pain?

I had originally thought I'd get pregnant straight away. You know: you stop taking the pill, you get pregnant. Otherwise, what was the bloody point in taking the bloody thing all those years, for God's sake?

I mean, I knew rationally that not everyone conceived first time out, of course I did. I had read enough magazine articles and listened to enough Gerry Ryan shows not to be in any doubt about that. But that was them, this was me. Big difference there, I felt. The old it'll-never-happen-to-me mentality. Except that now it seemed that infertility *was* happening to me, when everyone else was conceiving easily. Except those women in the magazines and on the radio, of course – but, in a sleight-of-hand-of-thinking, I conveniently forgot about them whilst I was bewailing my fate.

So, after the first month, there I was, lying on the sofa numb with disappointment.

Patrick sat down awkwardly, perching on the tiny edge of sofa I wasn't occupying. "Poor you," he said, taking my hand and holding it tight, "but sure, you'll conceive no problem next month."

But I didn't, nor for the months after that. The whole thing became a constant low-grade hunger. It was like a background symphony to everything else in my life. I was constantly aware of this lack in my life, this constant niggling emptiness. It wasn't centre stage or anything, but below, behind and above all other aspects of my life – surrounding, almost embracing everything else.

I hate to admit it, but I was behaving slightly irrationally. Haunting the baby book section of bookshops, feeling like a priest in a porn shop, always looking guiltily around me for fear anyone I knew would see me. I hovered, with my metaphorical collar well up, behaving in a shifty manner, sneaking quick reads of a page or so of different books. I didn't dare

4

buy one, because that was tempting fate. But I was certainly looking at them. I'm amazed I never got stopped on the way out on suspicion of shop-lifting. Either the staff and security guards weren't doing their jobs, or they were used to the pathetic sight of childless women reading pieces of their childcare books.

And I had the nursery designed in my head. Now, I like strong colours – confident, vibrant. Well, that's what I call them. Others have said 'loud, raucous'. My best friend Sinead, on being invited to view my purple and red dining-room, said, "You know what, Grainne? If your taste were a person, it would be Ruby Wax." I must admit she had a point – I keep waiting for the fashion police to declare that fuchsia is the new black. I had read somewhere that babies don't actually like pastels – they can only see strong colours. So the nursery was to be in primaries: the floorboards, the doorframes and the window frames painted a nice rich red, the walls in a vibrant blue, and the accessories would be in yellow and green. I could imagine it now, but again, I didn't dare start putting it into practice until I was pregnant.

Patrick was getting fed up with me. Sure, having a baby was his idea too. When I say his idea, it was in fact me who had broached the subject, who'd mentioned that we'd been together seven years already, that I was hitting thirty, that we had the house mostly bought and mostly furnished, that surely we'd *been there, done that* with the partying and holidaying that comprised our twenties: in short, that it was time. But he had agreed. Enthusiastically.

Yet now he seemed to be getting a bit tired of it all. I'd even heard him muttering something one day about not appreciating being treated as a sperm factory, although when challenged he said he'd merely been remarking on the weather. I could kind of see his point. As soon as day twelve of my cycle came along I turned into a mixture of Mata Hari and Mae West, dragging him upstairs as soon as we were both home and basically not letting up until around day sixteen. Then I ignored him, pretty much, for the rest of the month. Partly because I somehow suddenly didn't see the point of sex that couldn't produce a baby, and also because I had read somewhere that it helped for men to store up their sperm, so that they had a grand collection by the time the fertile period rolled around again.

He did say, gently and kindly, obviously struggling for empathy, that he felt I was getting too obsessed, and that carrying the colour cards for the nursery everywhere so that I could match accessories was going a bit far for a baby that not only wasn't born yet, but wasn't even conceived yet. I had cried, at his insensitivity and his cruelty. I wouldn't like to give the impression that he's insensitive and cruel, far from it. But I was a bit emotionally challenged at this stage, and if someone said hello to me in the wrong tone of voice I'd be almost threatening pistols at dawn.

"Grainne," he continued, "I've heard that if you get too tense about it, it actually makes conception less likely – so maybe you could try and relax about it all?"

"Oh, yes," I muttered, between post-crying sniffles,

"easier said than done, and anyway, what do you know about it? You're only a man."

He sighed and said, "I'm just worried about what this is doing to you, and to our relationship. Look how long it's been since we've had any fun – any passionate and abandoned lovemaking. And, no, before you say it, it's not just a typical male reaction that I'm missing the sex – although I am. But what I'm missing is you, Grainne, and how we used to be together."

And I thought back over the previous years, how happy we had been. And still were, I told myself fiercely. And I know, I know, it's easy to be happy when you have no problems, when you aren't challenged. We were both in perfect health. We had tons of money, seeing as Patrick had a huge salary from his European bank, and I had my teaching salary, and we had only a small mortgage. We holidayed twice a year, ate out whenever we wanted, socialised regularly with our friends, never panicked when bills came in the door.

It was an idyllic time, and although we both enjoyed and relished it, I don't think we appreciated how lucky we were.

This infertility thing – or, to be honest, this taking-longer-than-we-had-anticipated-to-have-a-baby thing – was the first problem we had encountered, and the cracks were beginning to show. Often in a house you have settlement cracks and you simply paint over them, and I think that if I hadn't met a man called Darren Brogan this would have proven to be the settlement-crack period in our marriage, regardless of whether we had gone on to have a baby or not. We were just having to learn how to deal with each other about issues more real than what colour to paint the sitting-room.

It all began innocuously. Patrick and I were sitting at the kitchen table after our dinner, his lean torso lounging back in his chair as he sipped coffee, his long legs stretched carelessly almost the whole length of the table.

"Oh, by the way," he said, carefully casual, an air of suppressed excitement about him, "I just heard today – I have to go to Zurich again, for two weeks this time."

"Two weeks? But that's longer than you've ever been away!"

"I know." He shrugged. "But it's a very important trip – it's more responsibility than I've ever been given. I'll be working with some of the very senior people over there. Listen to this: Michael told me, unofficially, that it's to let them see what I do, how I work – that they have me in mind for serious promotion."

"That's great news! Well done! Well, it's about time they recognised how wonderful you are!"

"Ah well, wouldn't you say you're a tiny little bit biased?"

"Only a tiny bit," I retorted, laughing.

"Anyway, you know nothing about how good I am at what I do. You don't even understand half the jargon I use!"

"Still," I said stubbornly, "I do know what you are good at, and if you're half as good at banking as you are at bonking then you're surely due for a big raise!" And we both collapsed into laughter. "Sorry, sorry," I said eventually, "I am taking it seriously, I promise. And it's great news."

"Steady on!" He laughed his deep throaty laugh. "It's not in the bag yet. It hasn't even been officially mentioned. But still," he paused and grinned at me, his teeth white against his generous mouth, "yes, it is great news."

I stood up then from the table, walked towards the wall-calendar and picked up the pen velcroed beside it. "What dates are you going to be away?" But when he told me, and I found the correct squares, I said, horrified, "But, Patrick, my fertile period is right in the middle of that!"

"Oh no! Is it? I hadn't realised." He came up and stood behind me, putting his arms around me and resting the underneath of his chin on the top of my head, as he often did. "So it is," he said, seeing the row of asterisks ranged around the middle of the dates he'd be away. "Oh God, what bloody bad timing! But there's nothing I can do – I really have to go on this trip. But look, there'll always be next month."

I twisted in his arms, faced him, not sure whether to scream or cry.

"But next month is *ages* away! *This* might have been the month I conceived! We can't take anything for granted, we can't assume that next month I'll conceive!"

"But we can't assume that you would conceive this month, even if I was here."

"No, but I might!" I whispered and, pulling myself

9

free from his embrace, I stalked across the room and flung myself back onto my chair.

He turned to watch my progress, his dark angular face inscrutable now.

Deep down I realised that he wasn't being deliberately callous. He genuinely thought that one month was as good as another. He truly didn't understand why I was so concerned. Although he wanted a baby, that wanting was in his head. It wasn't in his heart and his body, feeling the empty womb, the breasts with nobody to nurture from them, the arms with no baby to hold, the shoulders with no baby to tuck its head into.

There was silence for a few moments, and then he said softly, "I'm so sorry, Grainne. But I do have to go to Zurich, even if so much didn't hang on it. You know it's part of the job."

I thought of a possible solution to the dilemma. I said, "Well, why don't I fly over for the weekend? That's the crucial time."

"Ah no," he said. "I'll be busy for the whole weekend, getting to know these people better, semi-business dinners and all that. And don't you think it's a little beneath us both for you to be sitting in some hotel room waiting for me to come back and service you?" And his mouth was twisted with a kind of disgust

And then he quietly left the room.

I sat in the chair. Leant my elbows on the table and rested my head in my hands. Patrick was right, I let myself realise. This baby thing was taking us over. Was taking all that was good about us and turning it into some kind of mission. Our glorious exuberant sex life was now, as he'd said, a mere semen-extraction process. A mutually demeaning process. Our laughter and sharing and love was being subsumed into this all-encompassing (on my behalf at least) need. And was the baby thing worth losing everything we'd shared for all this time? No, I realised. I want my husband, I need him. I need his touch, and caress and laughter and quirky-eyebrow raising. I need him, all of him, not just his sperm.

Wearily, like an old woman, I got to my feet and went in search of him, found him in the sitting-room, channel-flicking, a closed-up expression on his face. I went and sat beside him on the sofa, snuggled into him.

He immediately switched off the telly, a subtle but welcoming signal. Then he raised his arm and put it around my shoulders, pulled me close to him.

"I'm sorry," we said together.

I said, "You're right. I have become too obsessed about it."

"But it's important," he interrupted, wanting to meet me halfway.

"I know. But it's not the only thing. There's still us. We still need us."

"We still need us," he echoed, and he shifted slightly in the chair, lowered his head to mine, and kissed me. I had a brief thought: but there's no way I'll conceive now, pushed it away, and kissed him back with more passion, deliberately focusing on nothing but the sensation of his hard, soft mouth on mine.

His kiss deepened, and I gave myself up to the sensations, to all that I had always enjoyed about his lovemaking. How he managed to balance dominance and gentleness, demanding and supplicating at the same time. How he touched me and made me melt, mouth on mouth, mouth on breast, on stomach. How he breathed deep when I touched him with mouth, tongue, hand, breast. How I never knew, beginning, how it would end. Would I end up straddling him, or he me? Would it be quick and furious and passionate, or slow and thoughtful and still passionate? And each time we made love it was like a dance, which, after this many years, we knew the steps to. But in each case I never knew which particular version of the dance we'd share, and that kept it fresh and enticing over and over again.

Right there on the sofa we made love. And still I thought, as he climaxed powerfully into me: but there'll never come a baby of this. And it seemed a waste, and I remonstrated with myself that I should think that this sharing could ever be a waste. But still, I thought, no baby can come of this. And even as I was lying afterwards on the sofa, and listening to the beautiful sound of my sated husband's ragged breathing as he lay with his head in the crook of my neck, even then I thought: no baby can come of this.

When we finally made our way to bed, we slept curved together, like silver spoons in a drawer, my bottom against his groin, his hand cupping my breast.

Life resumed its course after this, and we both

tacitly avoided the subject of his trip to Zurich, and its unfortunate timing.

And the time came when he packed his case, and the taxi arrived. He stood in the hall and kissed me hard, gripping his strong large hand to my bottom, and then he held my chin and gently moved my face up till we gazed, blue eyes to blue eyes, and he said, "I'll be back before you know it. Look after yourself."

And I was left in an empty house, at a loose end.

And if there was one thing I hated, it was my own company. I was like the moon: I needed the reflected light of others to shine. In company I was great: brilliant raconteur and teller of jokes, laughing and joking, and somehow validated. When I was with people, I knew that I existed. Being alone, for longer than it took Patrick to get the Sunday papers, scared me. How did I know I existed, if there was nobody to hear me?

Chapter 2

On Thursday, which was, although I didn't know it, the last day of my old life, Sinead and I were invited to dinner by my friends Stephen and Richard. Richard was a top chef, so that was always a treat. It wasn't until I arrived that I realised there was another guest. My heart fell a little. I had, selfishly I admit, wanted to spend the evening with old friends, with history and in-jokes taken for granted, not making small talk with strangers. Oh well . . .

Stephen said, "This is Justin – we met him recently at the gym. He's just moved here from England, and doesn't really know anybody yet."

"Oh, Stephen," laughed Sinead, "and you've started him off on me and Grainne! What are you trying to do, scare him back home?"

We all laughed, and both Sinead and I shook hands with him.

We sat ourselves down and nodded grateful, if not frantic, thanks at Stephen when he offered us a glass of wine.

I said to Justin, "You're in for a treat. I suppose you know Richard's the head chef at The Place, one of the premier restaurants here in Dublin?"

"I didn't!" He raised his eyebrows and gave a brief whistle of appreciation.

"Exactly!" I told him.

The meal was as brilliant as advertised: a delicate garlic soup and home-made bread to start, then home-made spinach and ricotta ravioli with a delicious salad, and finally a deceptively light pavlova. All washed down with several bottles of excellent wine.

As the evening passed we all relaxed more and more into each others' company. We fell into chatting about how we met our respective partners, past and present, and eventually it was my turn.

"I met Patrick in Greece," I told Justin. "I was working in a bar for the summer, and he came in. I couldn't believe it, though, when he picked me. He's so gorgeous! He's tall, just about six feet, with black hair and blue eyes. His face is quite angular – no fear of him losing his cheekbones! And he's got a fabulous body, quite lean, but beautifully proportioned. I don't know what he saw in me at all!"

"Oh, come on," said Sinead, "you're gorgeous too."

"Yes!" echoed Stephen and Richard loyally.

I smiled my thanks at their words. I suppose I'm not too bad. Fairly average really. Medium height, medium build, quite pretty. And I'm lucky in that I've got really nice hair, long and thick. Brown, mind, but you can't have everything. And blue eyes which everyone says are my best feature.

"And," went on Sinead, slightly undermining her previous words, "you've got so much personality! And a wonderful sense of humour!"

"You mean," I said tartly, "that I don't need looks seeing as I'm so much fun to be with?"

This issued forth another round of denials – which may well have been the idea.

"Mind you," said Stephen, "Patrick was lucky to get her. I nearly got there first! Apart from the minor detail of being gay. Having said that," he added musingly, "maybe I wouldn't have taken her on, even if I was straight. The thought of having Grainne's mother as your mother-in-law would put the most stalwart suitor off, I'd imagine. I don't know how Patrick manages."

"Oh, she thinks the world of Patrick," interjected Sinead. "His background suits her social-mountaineering ambitions perfectly."

Once the laughter had died down, Stephen said reflectively, "The thing I really have against her is the fact that she talked Grainne out of coming to art college with me." He turned to Justin. "Grainne's a brilliant watercolourist and she's a genius at drawing faces – honestly, she could meet someone once, and draw them perfectly. She used to make great pocket money at school, doing pencil-portraits of the pupils and caricatures of the teachers. And she was quite keen on going to art college. But no, that wasn't good enough for her mother! Not nearly posh enough. What *would* she tell her friends?"

"It wasn't just her," I said. "It was my dad too. He wasn't worried about the image thing, more about the insecurity. I remember," I laughed a little, "he told me he didn't want to see me starving in a garret. And I said, 'studio', and he was really confused. I had to explain to him that it's poets who starve in garrets; artists starve in studios. I thought it was quite witty myself, but it just went over his head. He said worriedly that he didn't want me starving anywhere. So it was hard to stand up against the pair of them. But as well, maybe I was just as glad – not having to prove myself as an artist. Maybe I was scared. I always admire you so much," I said directly to Stephen, "having the courage and commitment to keep at your sculpting, even during those years before you became successful."

"You could have done it too," he said. "I don't think you even paint any more, do you?"

"Haven't the time," I said and, realising that it sounded like such an excuse, I added quickly, "Anyway, I love teaching. And I'm good at it too."

"I know you are," said Stephen, the few glasses of wine he'd had making him tenacious, "but it's such a waste, it really is."

Justin interjected then, recognising, as did we all, that a change of subject might not come amiss. He turned quickly to Sinead, asking her, "And do you have a partner?"

"No," she said lightly, "too busy being a super-career woman." And if her voice was too bright, a little brittle, Justin found some tact from somewhere, and didn't comment on that. He changed the subject again, and we all just chatted light-heartedly for the rest of the evening.

I've often wondered whether I would have enjoyed it more, or less, had I known the cataclysm the very next night was to bring.

Of course, had I known that, I would have done things very differently, would have ensured a different outcome. As Sinead often says, the retrospectograph is a great thing.

Chapter 3

Kate phoned the next day. "Hi," she sang into the phone as she always does, "I heard you were free this week! I'm going out on the town tonight with Mags, Ann and a few others – fancy coming?"

I was immediately tempted. I always had a laugh going out with Kate and her friends. I met her while working as a waitress at some forgettable summer job, and we clicked immediately. Kate was my good-time friend. We never ever had a serious conversation; in fact I don't think I've heard her say anything abstract, ever.

I've often had occasions with other friends, in those 3 a.m. moments after the third bottle of wine, when we, maudlin, start Solving The World's Problems, and find that we can't understand why it wasn't done before, it's so simple, and the UN and other world leaders should have come to us in the first place.

Well, those conversations never happened with

Kate. No, those three o'clock in the morning conversations with Kate turned to Great Shags I Have Had. Or, Favourite Sexual Positions. Current affairs, to Kate, are about who's cheating on who. A State of The Union Address means which house you're shagging in.

Patrick liked her, despite himself. But I don't think he approved of her, or her lifestyle. So I knew that he wouldn't like me going out on the town with her and I said weakly, "Oh, I don't know, Kate, I'd better not."

"Oh, come on," she said. "I know Patrick's away and you're on your own. You haven't had a night out with the girls for ages – you'll get middle-aged if you're not careful. It'll be great fun, you know it will!" She paused and then delivered her strongest argument: "After all, Grainne, he'll never even know."

Isn't it amazing how easy it is to persuade people to do something they want to do in the first place? Especially since I added a couple of arguments of my own: yes, well, he was quick enough to go away, wasn't he? And he turned down your offer of flying over to Zurich for the weekend to meet him. It's none of his business what you do.

And I did have nothing planned for that night, and its vast wilderness had stretched before me, with just the telly for company, and me alone in an otherwise silent house.

I said, "Fine, I will! Why don't you all come around to my place to get ready?"

So at about eight o'clock six young, beautiful, healthy women descended on my house, and for a wonderful, giggly two hours the white and yellow bathroom creaked under the demands made on it, the old walls heard squeals of delight over some new outfit, pleas to borrow some fabulous eyeshadow, casually tossed gossip about mutual acquaintances. In short, the essential beginning to a night out with the girls.

And then we hit Dublin. Was Dublin ready for us? Oh yes, this city needed fodder such as we seven young women to fill her bars, her restaurants, her nightclubs. And in return she gave us glitter, glamour, exciting people to meet, wonderful fleeting laughing encounters, the sound of enjoyment and music from all corners. And how we laughed – everything was funny! I had forgotten how much simple fun this all was. I loved Dublin so much – its buzz, its atmosphere, the huge numbers of people.

All this, and I was sober! Knowing how difficult it is to get a taxi late at night, I'd driven into the city centre. But I laughed with the rest, drunk on the innocent fun, the laughter, the camaraderie.

Eventually the pub closed, and we spilled out onto the pavement.

"Right," said Kate authoritatively, "where next? That new nightclub, Coronation, is supposed to be great."

"I'll pass," I said. "I'm an old married lady now, not able for all this partying."

This was greeted by a chorus of comments, entreaties, commands:

"Oh, come on," said Kate, "you must! You can't wimp out now!"

"Grainne, you have to!"

"It's not even midnight yet! Come for just a short time!"

"Ah, no," I said, "I'm really tired, and I'm in no mood for drinking over-priced warm mineral water, and shuffling to tuneless music, unable to talk with the noise level – and fending off the incoherent attentions of men with ten pints of the black stuff under their belts."

"Would you listen to yourself?" said Kate, and she quoted me, mimicking my voice: "'Over-priced', 'tuneless music', 'the noise level'!" She then delivered her knock-out blow: "You sound like your mother!"

That did it. "Right, I'll come," I said. And to a chorus of fair-play-to-you's, and maybe-there's-hope-for-you-yet's, we turned and walked towards the nightclub, paid and entered.

After fighting my way to the bar, and competing for ages for the barman's attention, I managed to buy a round of drinks. We stood in a circle, sipping them, and shouting comments into each others' ears.

After some time the DJ put on some slow music, and one by one the women I was with were approached by men, and were led onto the dance-floor where they swayed together. A couple of men approached me and waved an invitation; in each case I smiled and shook my head. It got a bit boring though, just standing there sipping my drink, trying to look nonchalant.

And then another man approached me, asked me to dance. I opened my mouth to refuse, but then I looked at him, and I liked what I saw. He was tall, surely topping six feet, and a lean body and long legs were shown off well by his black jeans and shirt. His face was handsome, angular and topped with thick black hair. That, coupled with the boredom of just standing there, decided me.

So I nodded yes, and we carefully made our way through the packed crowds until, at the far side of the room, we found a bare fraction of floor. I went loosely into his arms and we shuffled around together.

He leant forward, shouted in my ear, "Hi!"

I smiled and mouthed "Hi," back at him.

He shouted in my ear again, but I couldn't make out what he was saying. He made another couple of attempts and eventually I got it: "Are you enjoying yourself?"

I nodded, yes, but didn't attempt to say anything back to him; there was nothing I needed to say badly enough to go through that performance.

He gave up then on conversational attempts, and in lieu of conversation we just smiled inanely at each other from time to time.

And suddenly I was sharply aware of all the sensations around me: the dark, the cacophony of noise, the mingled smell of beer, sweat and stale perfume, the feeling of being squashed close to strangers' bodies, as we all moved together on this crowded space. What am I doing here, dancing with this stranger, I asked myself? The answer came: he vaguely reminded me of Patrick. You wouldn't mistake them for each other, but they were the same type: long, lean and dark.

And what was I doing dancing with this man when I had no intention of taking it further? Oh sure, I thought, a dance isn't a promise of anything else, so he'd have no right to be disappointed when that was as far as it went. But still, he could be forgiven for thinking I was single, that I might be amenable, in theory at least, to exchanging phone numbers and/or bodily fluids at the end of the night. Since I was not, I was wasting his time when he could be meeting someone available.

And I thought to myself, I'm tired, I have to go home.

So, as soon as the dance ended, I shouted in his ear, "I must go now, goodbye!"

He mimed, "What?" so I shouted again, louder. He nodded understanding, and we gave each other a brief wave goodbye.

I turned and plunged into the crowd, and eventually found Kate and some of the others. Got them to understand, with a mixture of shouting and mime, that I was going home. Goodbyes were waved. Mags said something unintelligible, with a cheeky grin. I just smiled at her and nodded in what I hoped was a way that would make sense regardless of what she'd said. I turned, desperate to get out, experiencing sudden claustrophobia at the dark, the crowds, the noise. I battled my way to the cloakroom, retrieved my coat, and suddenly, blessedly, I was in the cool of the night, the relative quiet of the city. Oh, the peace of the hum of cars and distant sirens, compared to the cacophony inside! It had been raining, and the streets were the rich and sombre colours of reflected lights.

I passed some pleasantries with the bouncer and went down the steps onto the path and began walking down the street.

Just then a voice behind me said, "It's wonderful, the quiet, isn't it, after the noise inside?"

I turned around and it was the man I'd been dancing with.

He continued, "You were the best thing there, and when I saw you were leaving, sure there was no point in staying. There's only so much you can stand – shouting monosyllabic statements at each other."

I said, "God yes, what a way to communicate! After however-many years of evolution, and we've come to that!" I smiled briefly at him, and turned to resume my journey.

He fell into step beside me. "Did you enjoy the evening?"

"I did," I said. "It was a night out with my girlfriends, a thing I haven't done in ages, and it was great fun."

"I was out with two mates of mine, but they disappeared ages ago – we'd a good laugh though, earlier." He paused and then said, "Er, are you off home now?"

"I am indeed," I assured him.

"Right," he said casually, "and you'd be getting a taxi, or one of the NightLink buses, then?"

"Well, actually, no. I drove into town tonight, so I'm driving home."

"Wow, that was well organised," he said in tones of admiration. "I'm getting a taxi myself – whoops, watch out there!" And he reached out a hand and put it on my shoulder, just in time to stop me standing in a pile of recycled beer-and-God-know-what-else.

"Thanks!" I said. "I would not have enjoyed cleaning that off my shoes!"

He laughed. "No problem. So, where are you parked? Have you far to walk?"

"Not far, just to Stephen's Green."

"Oh, that works out well – there's a taxi rank there. I'll walk with you if you like. Make sure you get there safely. You can't be too careful these days. Dublin might be one of the safest cities, statistically, but you don't want to take chances."

I thought, well, I can hardly stop him walking in the same direction as me, so why not welcome it? I was glad of his company. It's one thing saying you're a modern woman with the right to walk where you want when you want, it's another to actually do it, at two in the morning, with the city a mixture of quiet and tendrils of party noise, and the occasional drunken group staggering past.

"Thanks, I'd like that," I told him then. "By the way, I'm Grainne."

"And I'm Darren," he told me.

As we walked it began to rain again. Just the lightest and gentlest of drizzles, but deceptive, the kind that breaches the defences of coat and jacket and hunched shoulder, and could have you soaked before you knew it.

"So," he said, making conversation, "seeing as it's after midnight, it's Saturday now, officially. And we're going back to work the day after tomorrow. The weekend goes so quickly, doesn't it?"

I agreed that indeed it did.

"What do you do yourself? I'm an accountant – and we'll have less of the jokes please!"

I laughed and answered him, "I'm a teacher."

"Wonderful. And where do you teach?"

"It's a small school in Lucan – St Fiach's," I told him.

"Oh right. Do you know, I've a cousin who lives in Lucan – would her children go to your school? Name of Murray?"

I said, "Well, there's a Hannah and James Murray who have two children in the school – Clodagh and Mary. In fact, Clodagh's in my class this year. Would they be your cousins?"

He laughed with delight. "Well, isn't it true what they say – that in Ireland, everyone knows everyone! How are the girls keeping? I'd be embarrassed to tell you how long since I've seen them."

"They're doing well. In fact, Clodagh's showing quite a talent as an artist."

He laughed, "Ha! We should have seen that coming! I remember her, aged about two, two and a half maybe, in my mother's house, coming to call us, to show us proudly the beautiful picture she'd done – all over the bedroom wall! We couldn't be cross with her!"

I laughed. "That sounds like Clodagh, all right. She's a great girl, though."

"She is indeed," he agreed, in heartfelt tones. And then: "Have you children yourself?"

27

"No," I said, "no, not yet." I think he picked up on this, because he glanced sharply at me.

"You are married, though, aren't you? I saw your wedding ring earlier. Does your husband not mind you going out and dancing with other men?"

"Well, he's away on business at the moment," I said, "but even if he was here, he wouldn't mind – sure it was no harm, just a night out with the girls, and a harmless dance with one or two guys. Nothing for even the most jealous husband to worry about."

He laughed. "No, indeed."

As we continued our journey through the streets he said reflectively, "Maybe it's my age, but I found that the music they played in there was very hard to dance to."

"I know what you mean," I laughed. "I know I sound like my mother, but music was better in my day. Having said that, I have to confess – now, you won't laugh, will you?"

"Wouldn't dream of it," he said.

"Okay, then, here it is: I actually quite like a lot of the music of the 70's."

"Me too!" he said in tones of amazement. "Oh, no, far from laughing at you, I have to agree with you! Who are your favourites?"

"Well, Queen, of course."

"Of course! How could anyone not like Queen?"

"And Bowie, especially some of his older stuff. And rock bands like Rainbow."

"That's amazing – I have all their CDs! Well-hidden,

though – ruin the image in no time if someone saw them!"

We both laughed.

"What about this," I said, and I started singing 'Bohemian Rhapsody'. "Come on, join in," I exhorted him.

"Well . . . " he said, looking embarrassed.

"What? Don't tell me you don't know the words? It's only Queen's most famous song – probably *the* anthem of the 70's!"

"No, it's not that," he said hurriedly, "I do know the words. It's just that I've got a dreadful singing voice, and I made a committment a long time ago never, ever to sing in public."

"Oh, come on! I won't mind, I promise!"

"Are you trying to get me arrested for disturbing the peace?" he laughed.

So I gave up on it, and we continued walking, and chatting lightly.

We discovered that we had an amazing amount in common, in addition to the Murrays and 70's music. For example, we had both hated skiing the one time we'd tried it and had sworn never again, give us sun, sea and sand, and we both loved Terry Pratchet's Discworld series of books.

"And what do you think of what's happening on *Big Brother*?" he asked me then. The current series was on, and as usual the media were taking it very seriously.

"Oh, I don't watch it! In fact, I've made it a point of pride that I've never seen any episode of any series of

Big Brother! It's my claim to fame – I want it engraved on my gravestone – although not for a long time, of course!"

He laughed, said, "I don't watch it either, although I must confess not to have your perfect record – I did watch about twenty minutes of the first series. But I know what you mean – it's a waste of space, isn't it?"

I turned to him in mock-delight and amazement. "Oh, do you think so? I feel like everyone in the world's a fan except me. We could start an anti-fan club!"

All too soon we reached Stephen's Green. It had been a pleasant interlude, laughing and comparing notes through the late city streets. I was glad to see my car – first of all that it was still there! But also the rain had got heavier, and I was looking forward to shelter.

As we walked towards it, Darren said, "I hope that the taxi queue isn't up – or down – to its usual standard. Two or three hours in the rain is all I need."

I wondered if I could offer him a lift home. It seemed the least I could do, when he'd escorted me to my car. I never took lifts from strangers, but could I offer a lift to a stranger?

I thought about it, trying to be sensible. I do have a tendency to be impetuous – I remember Sinead saying to me once, in tones of indulgent frustration, "Grainne, you rush in where even fools fear to tread!"

But then I thought, why not? Isn't he Hannah Murray's cousin, and a nicer, more respectable woman you couldn't hope to meet?

"Where do you live?" I asked him. "Maybe I could drop you home?"

Quickly he said, "Well, where do *you* live? I don't want to bring you out of your way."

"I promise," I laughed, "that if you live too far out of my way, I'll tell you."

But he insisted, "No, you tell me first."

I thought, at this rate we could be here all night. So, anxious to get on my way home, I told him, "Ranelagh."

"Well, that's amazing!" he said. "I live there myself, just off Chelmsford Road. So I can take a lift with a clear conscience, if you're offering. I must admit I'd be glad not to wait for a taxi."

So when we reached my car, we got in, and sped off through the silent and almost-empty streets.

"You'll tell me the turning when we reach it?" I said.

"Ah no," he said, "you drive straight to your house, and I'll walk from there. That way I'll know you didn't go at all out of your way, and I'll also have the security of knowing you got home safely."

"I'm a big girl now," I said, feeling just a smidgen of irritation. "I usually manage to get myself home."

"Ah now, I didn't mean any harm by it! It's just the way I was brought up – I have three younger sisters, and my mother and father always made sure I knew how to look after them. Call it chivalry."

Yes, I told myself, get off your feminist high horse.

So I drove to the Victorian redbrick terrace in which I lived. I parked and we got out.

He paused, hesitated. "Don't suppose you'd offer a chap a cup of coffee?" he asked, half-joking, wholly in earnest.

"No, Darren, I wouldn't," I answered. "It's late, and the night is over. It was lovely meeting you though. Good luck."

I held out my hand to shake, to pre-empt any ideas of even a kiss on the cheek, never mind a fully blown snog, that he might be entertaining. He took my hand, accepting what I'd said with good grace.

"Ah well, you can't blame a man for trying, especially with such a beautiful woman . . . but so it goes. Good night, and good luck to yourself."

He turned and walked away, waving a hand over his shoulder. I went up my short path, and opened the door. It was such a relief to get home. I had enjoyed the evening with my girl-friends, but I was seriously out of practice, and the evening had been long enough – I was glad to call it a night. My bed beckoned. All I had to do now was to tear off my clothes, and wrestle with my conscience about whether or not to remove my make-up.

I climbed the stairs wearily, debating that issue. In the end conscience prevailed, and I did the full remove, cleanse, tone and moisturise. I didn't get as far as putting my clothes in the laundry though – beside the bed was enough for that stage. I'd tidy in the morning. I put on my old comfy sleeping T-shirt, and climbed into bed. My ears hummed with the residue of the nightclub music, and disjointed images of the evening spun around my head, making it difficult to fall asleep immediately, even though I was exhausted. Just then the doorbell rang.

Chapter 4

What? I thought, irritated. Who could be knocking on the door at such an hour? I was tempted to ignore them, whoever they were. But then I thought, I'd better not, it must be fairly important for someone to be ringing now. Maybe Lucy next door had a problem with one of the children, and needed me to baby-sit while she and Gordon took the sick one to hospital, or something. Although, why wouldn't she just phone?

Even as I was thinking this I struggled to my feet and went to the window. Opened it and leaned out, calling "Yes?" The caller backed away from the door, came into view. It was Darren.

"I'm sorry, Grainne," he said, "but I've just been home and I can't find my keys anywhere. I think I must have dropped them in your car. I definitely had them leaving the nightclub, because I remember feeling them when I was looking for my cloakroom ticket. So either they're on the street somewhere, which would be the bad news. Or they're sitting nice and safe on your car floor, which would be the good news."

"Okay," I called, feeling guilty for my earlier irritation. The poor man, locked out on the street, in the rain!

I unearthed my handbag from under the pile of discarded clothes, and got my keys out of it. I went to the window, ready to throw them out, with the instruction that he post them back through the letterbox when he was finished.

But then I thought, I don't even know this man. What am I doing giving him my car keys? What's to stop him just driving off with the car? Wouldn't I be the right twit trying to explain that to the Guards? Well, yes, I'd be saying in my statement, he did steal it, but yes, I must admit I gave him the keys first. And the insurance company probably wouldn't be falling over themselves to reimburse me.

So instead I called out the window, "Hang on a sec! I'll be right down!"

I grabbed a pair of jeans out of the laundry basket, and dragged them on under my sleep-shirt, and a sweatshirt. I added a pair of yesterday's socks from the same source, and slid my feet into my slippers. Hardly the epitome of sartorial elegance, I thought, but it made me both decent and warm. I went downstairs and opened the door. Darren was standing on the doorstep – obviously trying to keep out of the rain.

"I'll just come out to the car and look for you," I said.

But he said, "Don't bother."

"What?" I asked him, puzzled.

Suddenly he pushed me back into the hallway, stepped in himself and closed the door behind him. He grabbed the keys out of my hand – I was too shocked to protest – and turned the mortise-lock. He left the keys dangling invitingly in the lock, but I couldn't see any way of getting past him to get at them.

A surge of anger replaced the initial shock. "What the hell's going on?" I demanded. "What the fuck do you think you're doing?"

"What the fuck I think I'm doing," he mimicked, "is making sure that this evening ends the way it was supposed to!"

"What? You're not making sense, and you're to get out of my house right now!"

"No way," he said. And he smiled. And his smile was not gentle or kind. "Don't you get it? You can't dance with a man, flirt with him, get him all turned on and horny and just leave him to it. You especially can't tease him by offering him a lift home, getting his hopes up, and then just dropping him. You women are all the fucking same, you cockteasers, and I'm sick and tired of it, and I'm going to make sure that you give what you've promised!"

A trickle of fear joined the anger. "I didn't flirt with you," I said, and despite myself my voice squeaked slightly. "I didn't promise you anything. All we did was have one casual dance. And yes, I gave you a lift home, but there was no promise involved in that. You'll have to go now."

35

"Oh, I'll go," he promised, and smiled again. "I'll go – after I've come."

Fear was now a wave, taking over from all other emotions. Okay, okay, I thought to myself, trying to damp down the panic that was threatening to engulf me. I'll reason with him. He obviously thinks I had been promising all sorts. I'll just explain it to him, and then everything will be alright.

"Look, Darren. I'm sorry if we misunderstood each other. I really am. But I honestly never intended, meant, anything except a dance. A dance isn't a commitment or a promise, don't you see that?"

"No?" he sneered. "And what about the way you were rubbing yourself against me? You know you could feel my erection – you were loving it, I could see you were. And then inviting me home with you – you think that's not a promise? Especially when you carefully told me your husband's abroad – what was that if not a hint?"

"But," I said, and my voice was quavering, "none of that happened. You followed me out of the nightclub. I gave you a lift because it was raining. It was only a lift home. And I just told you my husband was away for conversation, no other reason."

"You fucking lying bitch! You made a promise and by God you're going to keep it!"

"Noooooo!" I screamed, and turned and lifted the receiver off the phone on the low cupboard, stabbing furiously at the numbers. But he grabbed my hand, slammed the receiver down as I was still holding it, then lifted his other hand and grabbed my hair, pulling my head backwards.

I gasped with the pain and the shock. Tears came to my eyes, my vision blurred and my neck hurt from the whiplash effect. My hips slammed against the table, the sharp edge cutting into me.

I thought, this is a nightmare. This is *not* happening, I'm asleep and I'm having a nightmare, all I need to do is to wake up. I struggled to waken, unable to accept that I was already awake, that this was reality, that I was in the cold hall with a madman, not in my warm bed with a nightmare.

All this was in an instant, and the next instant he'd grabbed the front of my sweatshirt and pushed me against the opposite wall. With his two hands he held my hands against the wall above my head, and rubbed himself against me. Oh God, I could feel his penis hard against me! I felt a surge of nausea.

He was muttering, "Oh yes, this is nice, this is what you wanted, isn't it? This is what it was like when we were dancing – you're loving it!"

"Stop, stop!" I sobbed, but I don't think he even heard me. He transferred my left wrist to his other hand, leaving me equally trapped but giving himself a hand free, and started kneading my breasts violently.

I screamed with the pain, but he just kept doing it, pushing and prodding, bruising. "Oh nice," he said, spittle spilling out of his mouth. "Nice tits – you're not even wearing a bra – you wanted to be ready for me – I knew it!"

I tried to lift up a leg to knee him, but my legs were pinned by his.

"Don't fucking try it," he said. "Don't you fucking think about hurting me, you bitch – you're all the fucking same – or I'll hurt you worse! Do you hear me?"

"Yes, yes," I sobbed weakly.

Abruptly he let me go and stepped back a pace or two. I lowered my aching arms, and wrapped them around myself, tears coursing down my face. Thank God, I thought, maybe he's come to his senses.

"Take off your sweatshirt," he said.

No! My mouth made the movement, as my head turned from side to side in refusal, but no sound came.

He hissed, menacingly, his quiet voice totally intimidating after the previous frenzy: "Take off your sweatshirt!"

"No," I whispered, then, gathering all my strength, more loudly, "No, no, I won't."

He stepped towards me, reached out one hand to my breast, grabbed my nipple and twisted with a strength and a fury that left me feeling faint with the pain. I reached out my hands to push him away, to slap him, but his longer reach had me flailing impotently. He laughed shortly, enjoying my powerlessness. And all the time he twisted. I tried to kick him, but dizziness, pain and fear conspired to mean I couldn't connect. He laughed again.

Abruptly he released my breast, but grabbed the back of my hair again and yanked backwards so my face was reaching up towards him. He moved in close again, leaned against me. I could smell him, sharp and feral. His clothes were wet from the rain, and I could feel dampness seep into my own clothes.

He put his face against mine, and said, slowly and clearly and softly: "You and I are going to have sex. We are going to have a good fuck. Long and hard and satisfying. Yes. Now, that's not a choice for you. But I'm a nice guy – I'm giving you a choice. The choice is, we do it the easy way, or the hard way. Now, I'd prefer the hard way. The longer it takes to get you naked on the floor under me, the more I'm going to enjoy it. I'm going to enjoy pulling your nipples off, or maybe burning them with my lighter. I'm going to enjoy slapping your face and your breasts until they are red like my hunger. I've got all night, and if it takes that long, and all your pain, to get you ready for me, that's fine. But like I said, I'm a nice guy. And besides, I'm horny now, so I don't mind having it now. So what is it to be? Your choice."

He stepped back, and folded his arms casually, the very picture of relaxation. There was silence for a moment or two. Then he said, still softly, "Take your sweatshirt off."

My mind raced – I thought, I can't, I just can't move my arms enough to do this.

He said, "I'm waiting. Don't try my patience."

Some uncountable time passed, probably only a second or two. He spat out, his anger hot with his breath, *"Do it!"*

Sobbing, I reached for the hem of my sweatshirt, pulled it over my head. My sleep-shirt still kept me decent, but not for long. He didn't say anything, just jerked his head towards it. God no, I thought, please, please stop this happening! But nothing changed – I was still in my hallway with this rapist looking at me.

He raised an eyebrow at me, and said, "Okay, you're making the choice for the hard way. Good. I'm going to enjoy this."

He reached into his pocket and pulled out a disposable lighter, flicked it on and moved towards me.

"No – no!" I said, and in one movement peeled off my nightshirt. I embraced myself with my arms, to cover my breasts, but he shook his head, amusement in his face.

"Oh no, that's defeating the purpose. Put your arms by your sides."

I did.

"Oh, nice boobies," he said, looking at them. I felt I would *die* with the shame. He walked towards me, around the side of me, viewing them from differing angles. "Oh yes, indeed." The cold air had made the nipples go hard, and he noticed this. "Oh yes, you're hard for me too. You love this – I knew you would when I saw you in the nightclub."

He reached out a hand and softly cupped a breast, hefting it gently, feeling the weight, stroked his thumb across the nipple – in a parody of the gentle lovemaking Patrick and I shared. But suddenly he squeezed the nipple, digging his nail in. I screamed, my knees

40

buckling with the pain. He released me, laughing slightly.

"Okay, now your jeans."

Numbly I unzipped my jeans, and hesitated there.

"Take them down," he said.

I did.

He moved his hand across my belly, down and shoved his fingers inside me, roughly. Dry as I was, it was excruciating, agony. His breathing became ragged, his eyes misted over slightly, as he moved his fingers inside me. He tweaked my nipple with his other hand; it hurt, but so far had I come that I was grateful for the fact it only hurt slightly.

"Okay, take off your jeans and lie down," he said, indicating the hall floor.

I said, "Darren, please, let's put a stop to this –"

But before I could say another word he hissed, "I warned you! You are so pushing your luck. Any minute now I'm going to choose the hard way, since you're not taking the easy way." He paused to let his words penetrate, and then said, "Do as I told you."

I did, taking off my slippers and jeans, and I stood there, defenceless, in only my socks.

"Lie down."

I did.

The tiled floor was cold and hard on my back and buttocks, and the soles of my feet.

"Spread your legs," he said, looking down at me.

I can't believe it, but I did.

He stared at me, a half-smile on his face, an almost

indulgent expression on his face. "Well," he said, consideringly, "I've had nicer, but you'll do."

His hands went to his own jeans button and zip. I turned my head away. I felt a damp warmth as he lay down on top of me, the roughness of his shirt buttons on my bare chest. And then a stabbing, invading pain as he thrust into me. And again, and again. Tears were rolling down my face, but apart from that I was quiet – what was there to do, or say, but just to endure? All the time he thrust he spoke in time with his movements: "You bitch – you fucking bitch – you piece of shit – you cocktease – well – I hope – you're satisfied – now – you bitch– you got – what you – were looking – for – you bitch . . ."

On and on it went, and to this day I can't even guess how long it lasted. A minute? Ten? In one way it lasted a lifetime.

Eventually his motion quickened, until he paused, grunted, and collapsed on top of me. I couldn't breathe – I flailed at him, trying to push him off. After a moment or two he lifted himself off. I took huge juddering breaths, my face still averted. I heard him stand up, the sound of his zipper closing, the whisper of the key turning in the door, and then the front door opening and closing again.

I lay there, stunned, shocked. My brain had switched off, unable to accept the enormity of what had happened. Sure that it had been a dream, I struggled to wake up. But you can't waken from reality. The cold November tiles soaked the heat from my bare skin, and still I lay there. After a while I began to feel warmer, comfortable, sleepy.

I thought, I'll just have a little doze here, and when I wake up I'll feel better, and I'll know what to do. I felt myself easing into the pleasant state of sleep.

But just before I went to sleep, the lazy thought came to my head that maybe I was suffering from exposure. Or heading that way. You could die from that – they said it was a pleasant death, a slipping away.

Sounds good, I thought. Really, if this is life, you can keep it. It will be so much easier just to slip away now. I didn't rationalise any further than that, but my feelings were such that I knew that there was going to be a lot of pain, and lots of complications, arising from what had just happened. My old life was ended, and a new, uncertain one was to begin. If I didn't die of exposure first.

Chapter 5

A few minutes later I heard myself muttering out loud, "Oh, bloody hell," and I pulled myself slowly, carefully, reluctantly, to my feet.

Fuck this, I thought to myself. If this is life, it looks like I'm choosing it. Then, panic. What if he came back? Don't rapists often murder to avoid witnesses?

I turned towards the door, saw to my relief that the keys were still in the lock. I lurched towards them and turned the mortise-lock key. I stood there, breathing heavily, feeling a little reassured to have the locked door between me and him.

What would I do now? Without further thought I lifted the phone, pressed the hang-up button to re-establish the connection, and began to dial Sinead's number, a number I knew so well I didn't usually have to think of it, just let my fingers dance a choreography across the buttons. But now my cold-numbed fingers were clumsy and I kept misdialling, more and more frantically. Eventually I stopped this useless exercise, and took a deep breath. I recited her number to myself as I pushed the buttons slowly and carefully. It rang for ages as I just stood there, still naked in the cold hall. It was oddly soothing, listening to the ringing tone. And I couldn't think of anything else to do.

Eventually, though, Sinead answered, said sleepily, "Hello."

"Sinead, it's me." Then I added, "Grainne." It seemed as if all my certainties had been brutally swept away, so that I couldn't even depend on her to recognise my voice. I paused. What was I going to say to her now that I had her? To tell her would be to make it real. Although, bruising quickly, and aching all over, how could it be more real? Just then a cold, wet, clammy trickle made its way down my leg. My stomach contracted in reaction and I retched dryly.

"Grainne," said Sinead, sounding irritable now, "what is it? I hope you're not waking me at – what –" there was a pause as she probably peered at the clock, "– three o'clock in the morning to tell me as usual that you're at a great party and to join you?"

"No," I said, "no, it's not that." And then, in a great rush I said, "I've just been raped."

I stopped there, couldn't think of what else to say.

But Sinead was instantly awake, her sleepiness banished. "Oh God, Grainne, what? Where are you? Is he still there? Are you okay? I mean, are you injured? Have you phoned the gardaí?"

Her volley of questions confused me. I said, grasping at the questions I remembered, "He's gone. I haven't phoned anybody, except you. And I'm not injured, not really. My chest hurts, and – and, inside."

"Okay, okay," she said, obviously pulling herself together with an effort. "Look, don't do anything, I'll be there as quickly as I can. Okay? Where are you?"

"Here," I said, surprised at her question.

"Where's that?" she asked patiently but urgently.

"Home."

"Right, just hang on, I'll be there in ten minutes."

"Okay," I said, and then a small decision came to me. "While I'm waiting, I'll have a shower. I feel so dirty, his hands were all over me, his – his *stuff* is still inside me. I have to clean myself."

"No!" she said, sharply, imperatively. "Grainne, my love, you must not shower! The state you're in now is evidence – you have to wait until you're examined. Do not have a shower!"

"Okay," I said, willing to do whatever I was told. My autonomy, my ability to make my own decisions was totally gone.

While I waited for her I climbed the stairs wearily, hauling myself up by the banisters. Got my towelling dressing-gown from the bedroom, wrapped it around me, holding myself tight, as if to comfort myself. But there was no comfort there, no comfort anywhere. I went back to the hall, sat on the stairs to wait for her. Time seemed to have stopped for me, so it seemed only seconds later that there was a ring on the doorbell. I went to the door and called, "Who is it?"

"It's me."

I opened the door and Sinead came in.

I was shocked: I'd never seen her less than perfectly groomed. Now her shoulder-length blonde hair was ruffled and messed, and her clothes didn't co-ordinate. It seemed yet another sign of the madness of this night.

But if I was shocked, it was nothing to her reaction.

"Holy Mother of God," she said, "are you okay?"

I shrugged.

"Okay, stupid question, I know." She came towards me, holding her arms out to give me a hug, saying, "My poor Grainne!"

But I hurriedly stepped back, holding up my hands to ward her off. "No! Don't touch me! I'm dirty."

She dropped her hands – they hung helplessly by her sides.

"Okay," she said after a few long moments, her usual efficiency coming to her aid. "First thing is, we'll phone the gardaí – they'll know what to do. And an ambulance – you have to get checked out."

"No!" I said again.

"What? You have to! You've just been raped – you have to report it, let the Guards catch the bastard!"

"But, Sinead," I said earnestly, "it was all my fault that he raped me. The gardaí would laugh themselves silly if I reported it."

"I don't understand! How can it be your fault if you were raped?"

"I was out at a club, and I danced with him. Just once, and loosely, but still . . . And I did give him a lift

47

back here – he lives off Chelmsford Road. I didn't invite him into the house," I added hurriedly, "he forced his way in – but I did give him a lift. So nobody's going to think I was raped." It all seemed very logical to me.

We were still standing in the hallway, the open door blowing gusts of cold night air through it. Sinead seemed to make up her mind about something, turned and closed the door. She said, "Come on," and led the way into the kitchen. She pulled out a chair, and came to me to put her hands on my shoulders and ease me down into it.

"No!" I said, yet again. "Don't touch me."

"Sorry, I wasn't thinking."

She put on the kettle without saying any more and in silence we listened to the sound of the water's increasing temperature. When it was boiled, she made tea, adding sugar to mine, handed me my mug and sat down.

"But Sinead," I said, and I was surprised to hear that I was sounding querulous, like a whingey spoilt child, "I don't take sugar in my tea. You know I don't."

"It's for the shock," she said. "Drink it, you need it."

So I drank it, forcing myself past the cloying sweetness, and I have to admit that its warmth hitting my stomach did feel good.

"Now, let me ask you something," she said. "Did you agree to have sex with him?"

"No!" I said, shocked. "Of course I didn't! You know I didn't."

"Of course I know. I was just asking in order to make

you say it, make you realise it. Okay, if you didn't agree to sex, and he forced sex on you, that's rape, regardless of the circumstances leading up to it. That was rape," she repeated, emphasising the words. "That's a crime, both legally and morally. You did nothing wrong – he did everything wrong."

"Yes, you're right, but I still can't phone the gardaí," I said again. "They'll say I was asking for it."

I could see that she was holding onto her patience with an effort.

"No, they won't. Look, Grainne, you have two choices here. You either phone the gardaí, and get that evidence taken, or you go upstairs now and wash him off you, and forget it ever happened. Except," and her voice was very gentle, "Grainne, you won't be able to forget it. It happened, and the best thing you can do, for yourself, is to be proactive now, to take your power back and make sure he pays for it. Otherwise, if you just 'forget' it, you're saying to yourself that it was okay what he did. And you'll have this with you for the rest of your life. I mean, you will anyway, in one way, but you'll regret doing nothing, as well as all the other stuff."

I shook my head.

"Look," and her voice was coaxing, "why don't I phone the gardaí for you, and let them take the evidence? And if you decide afterwards that you don't want to pursue it, you'll have that choice then. But it's not a choice to make now, when you're still in shock. And we have to move quickly – I have no idea how long the – the evidence stays in you, to be collected."

I shook my head mutinously, terrified of the consequences of reporting this, of making it official. If some stranger had dragged me into a hedge, then I would be an innocent victim, but I had danced with this guy, talked with him, even laughed with him, and I kept coming back to it: I offered him a lift. Tears began to trickle down my face. Sinead put out her hand to wipe them gently away, then halted, and dropped her hand.

"Okay," she said, "here's what I'll do. I'll ring the Rape Crisis Centre, and see what they say. Okay? Now you sit there, and drink up all your tea, like a good girl, and I'll be back in a second."

She went into the hallway, and in a few moments I heard her talking on the phone. I couldn't hear what she was saying, didn't want to. Oh, God, this was making it so real! Sinead came back.

"Right, I was talking to a really kind woman on the phone. She says what you do is totally your choice. But she strongly suggests that we go to the hospital, get you checked out. The doctors there won't report or anything, without your say-so. But Grainne, she also said that this kind of rape, where you have already met the guy, is amazingly common. The gardaí are used to it, they understand it, they really do. She promised that they will be sympathetic – they won't dismiss you because you gave him a lift. They even have specially trained gardaí, women, who'll deal with you. And there'll be someone from the Rape Crisis Centre at the hospital to meet you, to be with you. Everyone will be kind. But, I repeat, she says that everything is your choice, that I can't just ring the gardaí for you. But, do, please, let me." She added, "She also mentioned that if he gets away with it, he's quite likely to do it again, to some other woman."

I dimly heard the words – 'sympathetic', 'specially trained', 'kind,' 'do it to some other woman'. I nodded numbly.

"Great," she said.

She went back into the hall, and I heard her voice again. I sat there, nursing my half-empty cup of sweet tea.

She came back, said, "They're on their way. They want me to pack you some clean clothes, toothbrush and stuff. Okay?"

I nodded. Off she went, and came back sometime later with an overnight bag, into which she put my handbag and keys. When she came back she asked softly, "Can you tell me what happened?"

I shook my head, not wanting to speak the words aloud.

She nodded understandingly, and we sat in tense silence until the doorbell rang. She went to answer it, and I heard murmurs as she spoke to whoever was there, and then she came back into the kitchen with a woman garda, clean and pristine in her uniform. She exuded kindness and calm, and I could feel my heartbeat slow perceptibly just being in her presence.

"Ms Quinn? Grainne? My name is Sergeant Ger Reilly, and I'm here to help you. Your friend has already told us the man is long gone. Tell me, do you know him?"

"No, no, I don't know him. I never met him before."

"Okay so." She fished a small notebook out of her shirtpocket. "Before we go any further we need you to make an official complaint. And then we'll bring you to hospital, get you checked out, and get more details afterwards. Okay?"

I nodded.

"So can you tell me briefly what happened?"

Dully I said, "I met a guy at a nightclub. I – stupidly – offered him a lift home, and he forced his way into the house and he raped me here. In the hallway," I finished on a sob, as though that detail made it all worse.

Dimly I noticed her writing this down.

"Do you know his name? Any details about him?"

"His name is Darren – I don't know anything about him apart from that. Oh yes, I forgot – he lives off Chelmsford Road."

"Okay, that's all we need for now. Come on with us and we'll get you to the hospital, get you looked after."

When we went into the hall I saw a male garda. He was holding a clear plastic bag in which I could see the clothes I'd been wearing when I answered the door to Darren, and which had been still lying in the hallway until now.

Sergeant Reilly said, "Grainne, this is Garda John Moore."

He nodded at me, not engaging with me much (which suited me just fine, which may have been the idea), but his nod was gentle, sympathetic.

Sergeant Reilly said, "Shoes? Coat?"

"My coat's there," I said, nodding towards the coat-rack.

"I'll go and get her a pair of shoes," said Sinead.

She ran upstairs. While we waited for her I carefully took my overcoat down and put it on over my dressing-gown. Sinead returned with a pair of slip-ons, which I put on.

Careful not to touch me, they issued Sinead and me into the back of the waiting garda car, and off we sped, through the dark silent night. Slowly, tentatively, I inched my hand towards Sinead's. She took my hand, squeezed it once, briefly, and then held it gently for the remainder of the journey.

Sergeant Reilly twisted around in the passenger seat and said, "We're taking you to the Rotunda hospital. They have a special sexual assault unit there. You'll be well looked after, I promise."

There was a welcoming committee waiting for us: a young woman, soft and gentle, came forward. "Hi, I'm Grace Foley, I'm from the Rape Crisis Centre. And this is Dr Lynch, she's going to examine you."

Although Dr Lynch was kind, and gentle too, the examination and sample collection was a further humiliation, a horrible echo of assuming the same position on my hall tiles some unknown time ago. They took photographs of my bruised breasts, and the bruise on my hip from where I had banged against the hall cupboard. There were, it transpired, small internal lacerations, consistent with rape.

"You've been lucky," said Dr Lynch laconically.

"Lucky!" I sputtered.

She seemed taken aback. "Well, no, not lucky, of course. But I meant in a medical way. Those bruises will heal fine, and there's no broken ribs or anything, or worse. Now, I'm just going to take some blood. To test whether or not you have contracted any STDs. There's a few of them we can check for straight away. You'll have to come back in six weeks to be tested for syphilis, and in about three months to be tested for AIDs and hepatitis."

Oh God, I hadn't even thought of all that! I could have contracted *anything*. It was all too much. I could feel tears begin to fall, and I moaned in grief and fear. The doctor flashed me a sympathetic look, but didn't say anything, or touch me.

It seemed impossible, but worse was to come. She went on, "Now, I have to ask you this: is there any chance you might be pregnant?"

I shook at the thought. "God yes, there is! It is *that* time of the month, and I'm not using protection."

She must have heard guilt in my voice.

"Well," she said soothingly, "why would you use protection if you weren't planning sex? We'd better give you the post-coital pill – the morning-after pill, it used to be called." She handed me one, which I dutifully popped. "That's great. There's another one to take, twelve hours after the first, so we'll give you that then."

When they had finished they told me I could take a shower, and showed me to a beautifully kept bathroom, with clean, fluffy towels. I stood in the shower and frantically washed and washed, trying to wash away every trace of him. I felt so incredibly dirty, I can't describe it. I washed, and scrubbed, particularly between my legs, scrubbed my breasts, washing away his touch with the water and soap, but his touch seemed permanently engraved – wash and wash as I did, it still was there. Even after the water ran cold, I still washed, welcoming the discomfort as some sort of atonement (although I didn't articulate to myself what I was atoning for) and some sort of displacement from everything else.

Then I heard a nurse knocking on the shower screen, holding up a towel, calling kindly, maternally, above the sound of the falling water, "Come out now!"

Already? I thought, Jesus but they're tight with their water – I pay my taxes, don't I?

As I left the shower, and the nurse handed me the towel, she said, "You've been showering for an hour, you know. It's common, we see it all the time, but you can't stay in there forever. Unfortunately."

An hour? And it still hadn't been enough. I dried myself. My fingers and toes were pink and wrinkled, my skin raw and tender from the washing and abrasive drying.

I dressed in the clothes Sinead had brought for me, washed my teeth, combed my hair, and then, when I could delay no longer, went back outside, to the interview room.

Sergeant Reilly was there, notebook in hand. I sat. She asked gently, "Do you think you could tell us what happened? Everything, from the very beginning. Tell me every detail you can think of, no matter how irrelevant."

So I did, shaking and sobbing, feeling sick as I relived it. When I got to the part of the story where the actual rape had taken place, the nausea overwhelmed me, and I ran off to the toilets, hand over mouth. I didn't even manage to excuse myself. I stood in the cubicle and puked and puked. I hadn't eaten in hours and only bile came up, but still my stomach heaved and heaved, the physical pain somehow comforting, something to cling to, to briefly replace the emotional agony.

When I got back, still shaking, I told her, "I've just remembered – there's a way to contact him. He's a cousin of Hannah Murray, a parent at my school. The principal, Sandra Moloney, should have their address. And he's an accountant."

"That's interesting," she said calmly. "We'll certainly check it out." She took the details of how to contact the school principal, but said, "Now, don't get your hopes up. He may have given you false information."

"No," I said, "he definitely knows the Murrays – he knew all about them, all about the children, their names and everything."

She said gently, "Well then, we'll get him through that. Now, one other thing. Do you feel up to talking to our Identikit artist, and trying to get a likeness of him."

"I'll do better, I'll draw him for you. It's a talent I have always had, to draw accurately from memory."

My hands shook as I was drawing. Remembering

his face was torture. I tried to picture him as he had been while we were dancing, or walking to my car. But I kept picturing images from the rape. The disgust on his face, the hatred, the dead look in his eyes.

However, when I was finished, I was very pleased with the result. If you knew him, you'd recognise him.

"That's great," she said. "We should definitely be able to get him with this. And other good news – I was talking to the doctor while you were in the shower, and she said that they got a terrific sample. We'll be able to get him through the DNA."

I was delighted. My initial inertia was gone, replaced by a towering rage, and I wanted him caught, tried, convicted, and with a long prison sentence. Well, actually I wanted him castrated with a blunt knife, prior to being pulled apart by horses, but failing that . . .

After Sergeant Reilly had left, Sinead came in. "Have you got Patrick's number in Zurich?" she asked. "I rang his company but only the security guard is there, and he can't help."

Oh, God, Patrick, I thought. What am I going to tell him? It'll break his heart. And he'll be so angry with me . . . I don't think I can deal with him and his reaction, on top of everything else.

So what I did was, I lied. I told Sinead that I had no contact details in Zurich for him, and that we'd have to wait until Monday, until the Dublin office was open again. She looked at me a little bit oddly, but didn't pursue it, just promised to look after it then.

Dr Lynch came to me then. "We're finished all we

need to do. You're physically fine, we don't need to keep you in – unless you'd feel better staying for the rest of the night."

"I want to go home," I said.

"Grand, so," she said, scribbling on something which was presumably my de-mob paper. She gave me a brown envelope. "This is the second dose of the post-coital pill. Take it twelve hours after your first – so in another," she consulted her watch, "ten hours."

Grace Foley, the Rape Crisis Counsellor, came into the room then.

"Do you want to talk now," she asked, "or will you give us a ring tomorrow?"

"Tomorrow," I said. I didn't feel I could deal with anything else that night.

Sinead phoned for a taxi, and asked the driver to go via her house. When we got there she said, "I won't be a minute – I'm just going to pack an overnight bag," and she started to get out of the car.

I squealed, "No!" and grabbed her arm. She looked at me in surprise, and I went on, rushing my words, panicking, "No, Sinead, don't leave me in the car, on my own with –" I gestured towards the taxi-driver, "I'll come into the house with you, wait for you there."

Her face lit up with understanding and she said, "I'm so sorry, I never thought. Come on then."

I stood in the hall while she went upstairs and packed. Then we got back into the taxi, and went to my house, my home.

Chapter 6

When we reached there, she rummaged in my bag, got my key, and opened the door. I walked into the hallway, stumbling and with my hands in front of me, feeling as if I couldn't believe the information my eyes were sending me. There's a famous optical illusion picture, where if you look at it one way it's two heads in profile, facing each other; and the other way, it's a vase. Well, everything seemed to me like that – I could see two images of the same scene, at the same time, and it was making me dizzy and disorientated.

Here was the hallway in my house, scene of thousands of innocuous situations: picking letters off the floor; reading good news and holiday postcards; saying hello and goodbye to Patrick, and being said hello and goodbye to in my turn; greeting and seeing off thousands of visitors over the years; chats on the telephone, laughter and giggles. But also the scene of the rape: the exact part of wall he'd slammed me against, the piece of floor he'd laid me on before raping me.

I went into the sitting-room. At least he'd never been here, and the only memories of the room were my normal-life ones. But I was still disorientated: here was Sinead, my best friend, and when I saw her I saw the years of history between us – the girls we were, giggling and experimenting with our first make-up, the talk of boys, and later men, as we grew into women together.

But now, overlaid with this image, was another, unfamiliar one: that of rape-victim's friend and support. She hovered, uncertain, wanting to help me but unsure how best to do that, how to act. Trying to hide it, to be strong for me. It upset me, seeing her like this. I'd never seen her at a loss before, and it was disconcerting.

And me, what about me? My image of myself was shattered. I was no longer the strong, competent woman I had been. I was weak, totally unable to protect myself, nothing but a piece of meat for that man's gratification.

I sat down on the sofa, immediately got up again, wandered around, picked things up and put them straight back down again, always aware of Sinead hovering anxiously. What did people do with time? I wondered. How did people spend their days, their hours, their minutes? What did I used to do, all day every day?

I suddenly yawned, realised that I was tired.

Sinead noticed and said, "Come on, we'll get you to bed for what remains of the night."

She led me upstairs. Obediently I went, content to let her make decisions. She led me into my bedroom, said, "I'll leave you to get undressed and pop into bed – I'll be back in a minute."

Quietly, discreetly, she left the room and closed the door after her.

I stood there, uncertain. Only hours ago I had been in this bedroom, my most pressing issue being whether to take off my make-up. It now seemed like a dimly remembered image of something I had seen happen to someone else in a film.

Slowly, moving stiffly like an old woman, I took off my clothes, down to T-shirt and knickers. It was good to take off my own clothes, on my own say-so, with nobody to tell me.

Wearily I pulled back the duvet and climbed into bed, thinking that this was the first time in my adult life I hadn't brushed my teeth first, and not caring.

Sinead must have been listening outside for the settling of the bed-springs, because no sooner was I lying down than she knocked on the door, called "Can I come in?" and entered. Although I appreciated this, it was still another reminder of how things had changed. Sinead and I have shared so much, normally we'd undress in front of each other without a thought, but here she was making sure to give me privacy.

She pulled up a chair beside the bed, sat in it, and took my hand. She said calmly, "I'll stay until you fall asleep, and I'll sleep in the spare room tonight. If you need anything overnight just call me. And when you waken, either I'll be here again, or in the next bedroom, or certainly no further than downstairs. You rest easy now – I'll be here."

And I lay, looking at the shadows on the ceiling thrown by the streetlight coming through the gaps in the curtain, conscious of the touch of her hand on mine, and her voice lulling me and soothing me.

When I woke the room was bright with daylight, and Sinead was still sitting in the chair. Still? Or again? She smiled when she saw me, and I saw that her hair was wet, and she had fresh clothes on: she must have already showered and dressed.

I murmured, "What time is it?"

She smiled. "Four o'clock in the afternoon – you've slept for hours and hours. How do you feel?"

The question startled me, in a kind of passive way. Feel? What does that mean?

I answered, "I feel numb. I don't feel anything. I don't know."

"Hush, hush," she said, "it doesn't matter, I don't need an answer – I just wanted to show concern. Maybe I'd do that better by getting you a cup of tea?"

"Yes, please," I whispered.

"And breakfast? Or should it be lunch?"

At the thoughts of food my stomach clenched, my throat closed over. "Just tea," I said.

"Okay," she said. "I'm going to leave the bedroom door open, so you can hear me downstairs, and you'll know I'm here. And I'll hear you if you shout for anything." She smiled, reached over and squeezed my hand, and quietly went out.

I lay there, thinking, so this is the first day of the rest of my life. But I didn't know what to do with it, so I did nothing. Just lay there.

Sinead brought up a pot of tea, and some toast "just in case" I changed my mind.

"And," she said, almost embarrassed, "here's your second dose of the morning-after pill." She proffered it to me, along with a glass of water.

I swallowed it, feeling, somehow, somewhy, deep shame about it.

Then we both had a cup of tea, and I nibbled at the toast to please her.

We were silent. There wasn't much to say, or rather, not much that we felt able to say.

After this meal Sinead took the tray from me, and I lay back down again.

"Oh, no, you don't," she said. "I want you to get up, washed and dressed."

"Oh, no," I moaned, "I don't want to! I'm tired – I think I'll go back to sleep."

"No, Grainne, if you're tired you can have a nap later, but you'll do yourself no good just lying there. I am telling you: get up, get washed, get dressed!"

It seemed far beyond me, the energy to do this. These tasks seemed like huge mountains blocking my way.

I shook my head wearily.

She laid the tray on the top of the chest-of-drawers, sat on the edge of the bed, and took both my hands in hers. She looked straight into my eyes, and said, "Okay, we'll do this one step at a time. I want you, Grainne, to get up now. Just pull back the covers – or I'll do that for you if you like – and stand up."

I wanted to, I could see the sense of what she said, but this wanting didn't translate into being able to do it, to being able to work out the steps necessary to do all this.

"Okay," she whispered, softly, kindly. She released my hands, pulled back the covers and the cold air rushed in. She took hold of my hands again, and pulled, gently but inexorably. It would have taken more energy than I had to resist her – so I allowed her to pull me, and suddenly I was standing.

"Well done," she said, cajoling me like a child. "Well done," even though she'd done it all.

"Now, come on into the bathroom, and we'll have a shower. Oh God," her voice changed from being soft and gentle to pretend-shocked, "it's happened! I've only been minding you for a couple of hours and already I'm using 'we' when I mean 'you'. No wonder nurses do it all the time! It comes on you sneakily, and suddenly that's it! Your speech pattern changed forever." She was being melodramatic about it all, her hand pressed to her forehead, wild gestures. Despite myself I let out a little giggle. She smiled to herself, slyly.

While all this was going on she was leading me to the bathroom.

"Now," she said, "I'll leave you to it. Promise me you'll have a shower now, not just stand there?"

I nodded.

"Good. I'll be listening for water, you know. Wow, this is going to be such good practice for having children, all these techniques!" She was trying hard and I appreciated her efforts, even if some of it was a little bit overdone and belaboured.

She left me in the bathroom, and slowly, because I couldn't think of anything else to do, I pulled off my night-clothes, and stepped into the shower. Years of habit came to my aid then, as I switched on the shower and reached for the soap.

However, once I started washing, I couldn't stop. I scrubbed and scrubbed myself, till my skin was red and hurting, and still I washed, desperately trying to wash away the mark of him. All I could see, feel, was my ugly, dirty body, and maybe I was trying to wash it away. Unlike the hospital, we had an electric shower, so the water remained warm throughout.

After some time I heard Sinead knock on the door.

"Grainne?" Her voice sounded concerned. "Come out now."

"I'm nearly finished."

"Grainne, you've been showering for over half an hour. Come out now!"

Slowly, sadly, I turned off the water, and stepped out. Reached for the towel, and rubbed myself with it, hard, abrasively.

I wrapped the towel around myself and left the

room. Went into my bedroom, put on clean clothes, and felt a tiny bit cleaner than I had done. I went downstairs, into the kitchen. Sinead looked sharply at me when she saw my red face and arms, but she didn't comment on it. She just asked, "Do you feel better for that?" as she turned to fill the kettle.

I do, I thought, surprised. Only a little bit better, mind, but still. I still ached when I moved – between my legs, bruised and ravaged. My hip was a thudding pain where I had hit it. My breasts ached. And the ache in my heart hurt with every breath.

Sitting at the kitchen table, over the second pot of tea, she said, "You'll have to tell your family, you know."

I groaned, "Oh God, no!"

She smiled ruefully. "You know you have to."

I nodded, said, "Tomorrow, I will. I promise. I just couldn't face it today."

"Okay," she agreed willingly. "And what about Patrick? Have you thought of any way of contacting him?"

Clever, I thought, you're letting me gracefully 'find' his number rather than admit I had it all along.

But I said, "Sinead, I've been thinking about that. I don't want to ring Patrick at all. I don't want him told. He has another week to go in Zurich, the trip is important to him and there's nothing he can do here about what's happened. Just let him finish the trip. He'll be home on Friday – he can be told then. There's no advantage to telling him now. It'll only upset him unnecessarily."

She looked at me steadily, her bullshit-radar on full belt.

So I finished up with, "And besides, I'm scared of his reaction. He's going to be furious with – with that bastard who did this. But he might be cross with me – you know he doesn't really approve of Kate and her crowd, or me going out on the town with them. And he might be cross with himself too, in some macho-bullshit way believing that he should have been here to protect me, and upset about it, and worried about me. And I really don't think I can deal with his issues now, I haven't the strength."

She was still looking seriously at me.

"Please, Sinead!" I said.

And she capitulated. She's never been able to refuse me anything, which is why I'm always so sparing with my pleas to her.

She said then, "What about Stephen? He'd want to know."

I nodded my agreement, and she rang him. He was there soon, with Richard.

It was like there had been a death, my death. As Sinead answered the door to them, I heard my name and other murmurs, in discreet, respectful whispers: "How is she?" "Not great, still in shock, I think."

It was worse than a death, in some ways. With death, at least everyone knows their roles, not least of all the dead person. I don't mean to be flippant. It really seems to me that, sad and often tragic as death is, there is a routine, an etiquette. In this situation, none of us knew what to do, or say, or even feel.

This image of death resonated within me. I am dead, I told myself, there's just my body walking around, wondering how to fill the next forty years. My spirit is dead, the essence of me is gone. And this seemed, then, a greater death to me. The death of the body, and the spirit living eternally, that's not death at all. But the death of your soul, your spirit, your essence – leaving just a pile of flesh and bones and tendons and veins walking around – that's truly death.

For I felt then that this rapist had done this to me, that when he had left the house he had taken the real me with him, leaving just this empty body. I had no sense of the soul of me being anywhere – it had just disappeared. Perhaps it was in a cave, licking its wounds, waiting to heal and return to my body, but if it was, I didn't know this.

Stephen, visibly nervous, came into the sitting-room, where I sat aimlessly.

He said, "Can I hug you, or could you not bear the touch of a man?"

I said, "I'll be brave." And although I tried to say it as a joke, it came out flatly, as the literal truth it was, that I would have to be brave for even my beloved friend to touch me.

He pulled me to my feet off the sofa, and stood there, his arms open, letting me initiate the touch, the depth of it. I leant against him, body to body, and he folded his arms gently, loosely, behind my back. Rested his chin on the top of my head.

I waited to feel claustrophobic, scared, trapped. But

instead I felt – to my huge relief – the joy of his body, his strength that would never hurt me, that would only ever protect me. I felt secure, safe, cherished, loved. I stood for an age, with my head against his lovely chest, listening to his heart, feeling his hand caressing the back of my head, as he murmured to me.

It was a tiny drop of healing.

When Stephen and I drew apart Richard came towards me. He took both my hands, each in one of his huge ones, and looked deep into my eyes.

"Grainne," he said, in his deep voice, "what happened had nothing to do with you. Nothing. It was all to do with that – person –" (and such disgust and contempt he put into the word 'person'!) "and his neuroses, his problems. You just happened to get caught in the crossfire of whatever's wrong with him. It's hard for you, and I'm not dismissing anything you're feeling, but it was nothing about you that caused this."

"But why did he ask me to dance, of all women?" The question burst out of me. "A nightclub full of women – why was it me he chose?"

"I don't know," he answered, "perhaps even he doesn't know. But it doesn't matter. He doesn't know you, or anything about you. Therefore it is nothing about you that caused it. He was looking to vent his problems on someone, and you were just unlucky. That's all. Not guilty, not at fault. Just unlucky."

He continued looking into my eyes for a moment or two and then, apparently satisfied that at least some of what he had said had penetrated, nodded, squeezed my hands, once, briefly, dropped them and stepped away from me.

But it was sad. Here were my best friends, Sinead, and Stephen and Richard, and we should have been having a laugh, maybe cooking a Saturday-night dinner together, or going out for a quick drink in the pub – or anything, except sitting around, painfully quiet, not knowing what to say to each other.

Stephen said, "I won't ask any questions. If you want to talk about it, we'll listen, but I'm not asking any questions. But this isn't lack of interest, you understand – it's just that we don't want to pry. Is that okay?"

It was. But I didn't volunteer any details. I didn't want to talk about it.

They endured a couple of hours of this, bless them: of painful silences, and strained conversation. Eventually, with well-disguised relief, they stood up, hugged me gently again, begged me to call if I needed anything, and left.

"I'll go and make some tea," Sinead told me and I heard her bustling in the kitchen, and after a while she came out with plates of omelette and salad, and a French-stick which had seen better days. I ate as much as I could.

After this we sat, silent, gazing at the television, with nothing to say to each other.

I said, "Sinead, this is torture. If you want to go, please do – I'll be fine, honestly. You don't have to stay and watch me mope."

She flashed me a wide grin. "Grand – as soon as I want to go, I will."

But she didn't. And I was so grateful. I thought, I'm incurring a debt that I'll never be able to repay. And as quickly realised that this kind of debt, between friends such as Sinead and me, would never need repaying.

Eventually it was nine o'clock, and I felt I could justifiably go to my bed. I said goodnight to her, went upstairs, and got into bed. I was surprised at how quickly I fell asleep, and how deeply I slept.

Chapter 7

The next thing I knew, it was morning. Sunday morning.

Well, that's good, I told myself, pleased. That's one whole day safely got through. Only another forty-years' worth, give or take, to get through. This time I got up, washed and dressed by myself, albeit slowly and laboriously. Progress was being made.

After breakfast Sinead reminded me, "You were going to let your parents know."

"Will you ring them?" I pleaded. "I know it's a lot to ask, and I'll be your slave forever, and let you borrow any of my clothes or make-up in perpetuity, if you will."

It was a weak attempt at normality, at banter, but the way she beamed at me you'd swear I'd been really funny.

Later that morning she rang them. I was sitting

curled up on the sofa, staring mindlessly at the telly (it wasn't even on, but that was as good as most Sunday-morning viewing).

I was numb, but through the numbness, blunted as if it were viewed through a cloud, were raging emotions waiting their chance to engulf me. Pain, grief, shame, fear. And a huge, healthy dose of anger. How dare he? How fucking dare he? There was no way anybody could have construed what I did and said as an invitation to sex. Unless they were determined to do so, to justify to themselves what they were going to do anyway. God, I hate him, I told myself.

Mixed with the healthy anger, was some not so good – at myself. How could you be so stupid, I told myself unceasingly, giving a stranger a lift home? Have you learned nothing through your years on this planet? How could you have been so naïve as to let him con you?

I could hear Sinead's voice as she spoke on the phone, soft and low, coming from the hallway, but I couldn't hear what she said. I was glad. To hear the words about it would have been hard, made it more real somehow, which was strange, because it couldn't feel more real to me. I felt as if the situation, although real, was somehow fluid, swirling around inside me, both physically and metaphorically. To hear it spoken, to have it in the public domain would make it hard, set, unchangeable.

She came into the room, said dryly, "They're coming around."

Being Sunday morning, the traffic was obviously light, because they arrived in no time.

"My poooor baby!" sobbed my mother, concerned, as ever, more about her role in the situation than my actual suffering. Enjoying the drama of being the heroic mother flying to her chick's side, to help. "Cry, cry, do, get it out!"

Despite her insincerity, however, she did help me. In the midst of the shock, the grief, the physical pain, the fear, I was still able to smile wryly at the way she never changed, at the predictability of her reaction. I thought, universes might rock, novas might blow, black holes might be born, but my mother is the one constant in life.

My father didn't say anything. His face was crumpled, as though he'd been crying, or was trying hard not to cry. He took my hand, held it, hurting me, but I didn't mind. I was getting used to hurt, what more did one bit matter? And I knew it was a measure of his grief for me.

Eventually they left, and I had to face the rest of the day, of my life.

I was living and breathing moment to moment. If I let myself rise one inch above the moment-by-moment time-line, I was engulfed by so many stormy emotions: rage, disgust with myself, disgust with him, shame – oh God, the shame, knowing that that man had forced his way inside me, into the secret sacred core of me, the place kept just for me and my beloved Patrick. I felt dirty, soiled, spoiled.

There was also a huge measure of fear – the realisation that I was so helpless, unable to defend myself. I always had been, I realised; it just took until now for any illusion of safety to be brutally wiped away.

Around two o'clock there was another ring on the door-bell. Sinead went to answer it, and I heard Gordon's voice. Gordon? What does he want, I wondered? I heard Sinead's voice, soft, serious.

Then she popped her head around the sitting-room door.

"Gordon's here – Lucy sent him in, wondering had you forgotten you were supposed to be going to their house for lunch."

"Oh God, yes – I had forgotten. Oh, please tell him sorry, I'm so sorry!"

"It's okay," she soothed. "I told him that you're not well, and he understands."

He left, then two minutes later there was another knock. I thought we should get Sinead one of those concierge uniforms, she was spending so much time as a doorman. She came back in a few moments later with two foil-covered plates.

"Lucy just dropped these around, isn't she kind? Hang on till I get knives and forks."

Sinead and I ate, and it was good – at least I managed to eat more than a few mouthfuls. We were making desultory conversation. It was so difficult – we didn't feel up to just chatting about ordinary things, but we didn't want to talk about the rape. So having the meal was good – it gave us things to comment on.

"Nice potatoes."

"Yes, Lucy always does them this way, they're lovely."

"And broccoli, I love broccoli."

"Mmm, me too."

It was painful.

Afterwards, I said again, "Don't forget, I really wouldn't mind if you left."

"Grainne, I'll go when I want, don't worry. I don't want to hear another word about it, okay?"

Okay. Yet another topic of conversation denied to us, then.

Just then the phone rang. Sinead leaned over and answered it.

"Oh hi, Patrick," she said in a high cheery voice, waving madly at me. "Yes, grand thanks. How are you getting on?" She pointed towards the phone, and then towards me with a question in her eyes: do you want to talk to him?

I shook my head. She was still carrying on the conversation with Patrick. "Oh that's great, well done," and then she covered the receiver and mouthed, "You have to – there's no reason for me to be here without you!"

"Laryngitis," I mouthed at her.

"So is the weather in Zurich good?" she said, then grimaced at me, asking 'What?'

"Laryngitis," I mouthed, enunciating very carefully.

"Right, I'm glad it's going well. Oh, Grainne? You want to talk to Grainne?" She cringed as she realised

76

how stupid she must sound – why else would a man ring his own house? "The thing is, Patrick, poor Grainne has a bad case of laryngitis – she can't actually speak to you. That's why I've answered it. She's after writing me a note to ask if you'd e-mail her, and she'll answer you that way . . . you will, that's great . . . oh, of course I will. Bye for now – enjoy the rest of your week!"

She hung up the phone, and collapsed back against the sofa. "God, that was no fun. I hate lying to poor Patrick."

"Well, what was I going to do? Chat to him, say: oh, me, I'm grand, got raped on Friday, but sure you know yourself these things happen?"

"Don't be so cynical, Grainne!"

"I'll be as cynical as I want, actually, Sinead," I told her. "I think a nice dose of healthy cynicism wouldn't be out of place here, do you? Seeing as I've just had my faith in human nature brutally ripped away from me, seeing as I've just gone through the most horrible experience of my life!"

"Okay, okay," she said soothingly.

"And don't patronise me," I said, my voice rising. "I don't need that either."

She sighed, leaned forward and put her head in her hands.

"I'm sorry," she said then. "I want to do whatever's right for you. But this is a new one for me too. We're both making this up as we going along. If you know what you want me to do, to say, tell me, and I'll do it.

77

Otherwise I'm just flying blind – and I don't mind doing that, but please don't lose it with me if I get it wrong."

I felt deep shame inside me. "I'm sorry too, you don't deserve that. I think I was taking all sorts of stuff out on you, and that's not fair."

"It's okay." She lifted her hands and smiled weakly, wearily at me. "This is a tough time for both of us, and it's not surprising it's going to get a bit strained at times."

"Thanks for being here with me. For putting up with me. It's a tough time for me because it's happened to me. But you could walk away from it."

"Oh, Grainne," she smiled at me, half-amused, half-impatient, "of course I can't walk away. Friends are for the hard times as well as the fun times, you know."

She held her arms out to me, and I went over to her, and we hugged.

"Oh, by the way," she told me then, "Patrick sends his love."

That evening I rang my school principal, Sandra Moloney.

"Sandra," I said, "I hate to do this to you, but I won't be able to be in for the next week or two – I'm dying with some sort of bug."

"That's okay," she said in her precise way, that you would call pedantic if she wasn't such a kind woman, loved by staff and children alike. "Thank you for telling me. We'll see you when you get back, okay?"

Later Sinead cooked some food and I chased it around the plate.

"Please eat," she begged, "you must eat."

"I can't. I'm trying, but my throat is closing over, and my stomach is heaving at the thought of food. I will tomorrow, I promise."

We spent the evening staring mindlessly at the telly, side by side on the sofa, and her hand gently holding mine.

It wasn't long after nine o'clock when I began yawning. I suppose it wasn't surprising that I was exhausted, physically and emotionally.

"Come to bed," said Sinead gently and, standing up, offered me her hand and pulled me to my feet.

We went up the stairs, and outside my bedroom door she hugged me gently. "Will you be okay, getting yourself to bed?"

I nodded. At that stage I craved space, privacy, sleep.

As I got ready for bed, climbed into it, I heard her making going-to-bed noises also. Poor Sinead, I thought, she must be exhausted too, looking after me the way she has must have been a near impossible task.

I slept immediately, exhausted, and the next thing I knew, it was the next morning, Monday.

When I went downstairs I saw that Sinead was at the table, tapping away on her laptop. When she saw me in the doorway she immediately stood, came and gave me a good-morning hug and kiss, and then turned to switch on the kettle, saying, "Did you sleep well? You certainly slept for a long time – it's gone ten o'clock!"

I was puzzled, confused, still half-asleep. I asked, "Shouldn't you be at work?"

"I rang them this morning, got them to courier this" – she gestured towards the laptop – "over to me, and told them I'd mostly be working away from the office this week. There's a few meetings I can't get out of, but Stephen's going to be here then. I don't answer, mind you, for the state of your phone bill!"

I smiled. Sinead lives and dies by the phone, in both her business and personal life. An increased phone bill was well worth it, to have Sinead stay with me. Before I could say that, the doorbell rang.

It was Sergeant Reilly, and her colleague, Garda John Moore. They looked strict, formal. I led them into the sitting-room and they sat down.

On the night of the rape it had been the Sergeant who had dealt with me, kindly and gently. But now Garda Moore spoke, and his voice was severe. Good cop/bad cop, I thought. But why? I wasn't long finding out.

"Ms Quinn," he began.

And I thought, oh-oh, Sergeant Reilly calls me Grainne. This is serious. But behind my flippancy was serious fear, made worse because I didn't know what to be afraid of.

"Ms Quinn, we've been interviewing everyone who might be able to shed any light on the events of last night. And your friend," he consulted his notebook, "Margaret Dolan, has told us that you left the nightclub with a man. And we have showed her your drawing of the rapist, and she's convinced that that is the man you left with."

I shook my head, confused. "But ... I have no idea why she would say that man was with me. He wasn't." My voice rose slightly, with panic and frustration. "Honestly, I was dancing with him, as I told you, then said goodbye to him and left him, said goodbye to my friends, and then left. I didn't see him again until he spoke to me outside the nightclub."

He consulted his notes again, and said, "Ms Dolan says that when you were saying goodbye to them, and she saw you, as she thought, with him, she said to you," again he bent and consulted his notebook, and quoted, "'You've obviously got lucky, then – off for a night of passion?' and you nodded and laughed."

"What! God, no! I never heard her say that, and I certainly never answered yes to any question like that!"

I was angry now, the anger of fear, and panic. If the gardaí thought that I had said that, then I was in trouble – they'd never believe the rape was real. But surely all my injuries would make them believe me?

Yet I had a feeling of sick, nauseous dread inside me, dread that had as its source a dim memory, a small sense of recognition, that there was something familiar about what they were saying, there was something ...

"Oh, God," I said, "yes, I think I remember! When I was saying goodbye to them, Margaret did say something to me, but I couldn't hear her, with the loud nightclub noises. And it seemed more trouble than it was worth to ask her to repeat it. So I just nodded and laughed in what I thought, what I hoped, was a non-committal way.

I honestly didn't hear her, didn't know what she had said."

"A bit handy," he said, "you suddenly remembering that she had said something to you?"

Oh, God, I thought, I'm the victim here, and I'm being made to feel like a suspect.

"No," I said, and my voice was high, distressed. I thought I didn't sound a bit believable. "No, I didn't make it up. It's just that I genuinely hadn't remembered that little incident until now – it wasn't very memorable, or very important at the time."

Sergeant Reilly said, "We're not getting at you, even though I'm sure it feels like that. But we have to check everybody out, Grainne, and identify and sort out inconsistencies in all the stories."

And as for Garda Moore, well, I can't say he suddenly smiled, and flung his arms wide, and said, 'Of course! That makes perfect sense, I can see exactly how it happened the way you've described!' However, his posture became slightly less severe, and his expression softened slightly. He said, "We'll include your explanations as part of your statement." And he nodded at Sergeant Reilly, obviously indicating to her to carry on.

"Okay, here's how the rest of our investigations are going," she said. "We've contacted your principal, and she got the Murray's address for us. But, Grainne, he's nothing to do with Hannah Murray – she only has two male cousins: one lives in San Francisco, and the other in Sydney."

"But he knew all about them," I protested, "all about the children, everything!"

Sergeant Reilly shook her head gently. "No, if you think about it, I bet you'll find that you contributed all the facts, that he carefully pumped you for the information first."

I replayed the conversation in my mind. "It's true," I told her, slowly. "He only said the name Murray, and I provided both the parents' names and those of the children, and he fed them back to me. God, how stupid of me!"

"Not stupid," she said. "You were obviously in the hands of a pro. It's classic con man stuff – establishing something in common in order to establish trust. He chose a fairly common name, and waited for you to come up with someone of that name. If there had been no Murrays in the school, well, he'd have just been able to say he'd got the wrong school, all without rousing your suspicions. And, in any case, you probably found out you'd lots more in common."

I nodded. "It seemed like everything I had an opinion on, he had the same opinion."

She also nodded, gently, sadly. "Again, classic stuff – find out what your interests are, and pretend he has the same ones. We tend to identify with people who are like us, and therefore trust them. Don't feel bad –" (this as I pressed my fists to my stomach, and doubled over in pain), "they're very skilled, there's no blame to you."

I raised my head and looked at her. "Do you know, there was a split second when I didn't trust him. I was going to throw the car keys out the window to him, but it suddenly occurred to me that he might steal the car. I must have known that he wasn't to be trusted, but I was more worried about my car than about me! I wish he'd taken the bloody car!"

"You didn't care more about your car than yourself," she said. "You could imagine someone stealing a car, and that was the risk you considered. It never occurred to you that you would be raped – why would it? But it just shows you that your intuition was working, that you were getting a message. But most of us are programmed to dismiss intuition, and we do." She paused, then continued, "I'm afraid it looks like nothing of what he told you is correct. We've checked everyone on Chelmsford road, and on every road off it, and have got identification from every man on it, and there was no Darren matching your description. He was cute enough – he chose the name of a road that everyone in Dublin knows."

"Yes," I said, remembering, "he wouldn't tell me where he lived until I told him where I lived, all under the guise of not wanting to take me out of my way. But of course," I was bitter now, "it wouldn't have mattered where I'd said, would it? He would have lived in the same area and been able to take a lift home all without 'taking me out of my way'! If I'd lived in bloody Vladivostock, it would have transpired, *quelle surprise*, that he lived there too!"

She nodded. "That's about the height of it, Grainne, I'm afraid. Also we've checked all the memberships of the accountancy professional bodies, and there were several Darrens. But we've managed to interview them all, except for –" she checked her notebook "– three, who are out of the country, and again, none of them are remotely like your drawing. It's great having such a good drawing, such a positive identification helps us eliminate suspects quickly. As for the three who are out of the country, we've checked the airline records, and they genuinely are – abroad, I mean. We've also checked with the management and staff of the nightclub, and one of the doormen remembers you leaving, and he said that you did leave separately, and met again on the path outside. He says that the man was only a couple of seconds behind you –"

"Yes," I said, "that would be right. I'd only started walking down the street before he spoke to me, from behind me."

She nodded, and carried on. "And he says exactly that. He didn't hear the man speak to you, but he saw him come up behind you, and then you turning towards him; and he could see that you were speaking to him. He says that you didn't seem to be leaving together, but that neither did you seem that surprised to see the man, or distressed, or anything. Nor, he says, did you seem excited, or thrilled or anything like that."

"No, I wasn't – any of those things. It was, on my side anyway, just a chance encounter with a recent acquaintance – nothing to feel any strong emotions of any sort about."

She drew a deep breath and said, "However, the bad

news is that they don't know the man. He's not a regular they say, so they're no help with identification. But we needn't be so despondent – here's the good news: I've managed to arrange that this will be on *Crimeline* this week. And with such a good drawing, someone is bound to recognise him. And once we have identification, and arrest him, then we'll get him on the DNA evidence. So you see," she smiled brightly at me, "he doesn't have a chance. He picked the wrong woman to mess with in you, because you have this skill that'll catch him."

I felt vaguely cheered up by this.

But then I had a thought: "Won't everyone know? If it's made public, I mean?"

"Don't worry, none of your details will be mentioned. We'll just put his face on the screen and say we would like this man to help us with our enquiries – that covers a multitude! We won't even give details of the crime."

* * *

And so Sinead stayed in the house every night that week, and either she, or Stephen, was there for me during the day. They bullied me, cajoled me, loved and teased me into at least going through the motions of normality. It was great – I got to do all sorts of things I just wouldn't have done for myself, like eating, dressing, going out.

For the rest of it, I just mindlessly watched television, and mindlessly read books. My emotions were so near the surface it was silly. I found myself crying over even the feel-good news reports, such as the report on professional Santa Clauses. And although I sat turning pages of books, I found that I had to re-read each page several times before the sense of it would go in to my brain, and even then I promptly forgot it.

Bad and all as they were, I got through the days somehow, but the nights were different. For the first few nights after the rape I'd slept well, through sheer trauma and exhaustion, and looked forward to sleep each night, to a time when I would forget all and have blessed oblivion.

But then that changed. At night it began to haunt me. I had dark, twisting dreams, replaying the rape over and over. I kept reaching for some pause button, to stop the images, to change the outcome. I would say no when he asked me to dance; I would refuse to talk to him when he walked with me. I certainly wouldn't offer him a lift. I wouldn't answer the door to him when he claimed to have lost his keys. So many chances to avert the rape – I struggled to take even one of these.

But the tape played on, inexorable. I was raped again and again. I would wake, with a shuddering gasp, in the still blackness, heart thudding, and realise that I was here, safe in my bed.

I woke several times to Sinead shaking me. "Wake up, wake up, Grainne, you're dreaming!" Those dreams must have been especially noisy.

In either case, once I'd quietened, either by myself, or through the gentle touch of Sinead's hand caressing my forehead, I'd lie quietly, terrified to sleep again, to enter that dark door to the nightmare, determined to lie awake for the long hours until winter dawn eventually came, and it was time to get up, to drag myself exhausted through another pointless day. But tiredness would overcome me, and sleep would claim me despite myself, and the dreams would begin again.

And in the morning I would waken slowly, and there would be a few seconds of peace, but then a feeling of dread would settle within me, and then the awareness would flood back in a wave, pinning me to the bed.

And with all this going on I was living a lie in my contacts with Patrick. I answered his e-mails with bright, cheery, totally false content. Yes, I'm fine. No, I still have the layrngitis, it's a really bad dose, there's no point in ringing me 'cos I still can't talk. But I don't feel too bad apart from that. Glad to hear that the trip is going so well for you. That meal in the beer-cellar sounds amazing. I can't believe that the Swiss were singing 'The Wild Rover' in German!"

On the Wednesday of that week, the weather was beautiful: piercingly cold as you'd imagine in November, but a bright, still day. Stephen, who was on baby-sitting duty, announced that we were going to the beach.

"Oh, no," I protested mildly. My overriding feeling was still one of inertia, and I didn't want to go anywhere or do anything. But I couldn't even protest passionately, and this same inertia meant that Sinead and Stephen could, with persistence, make me do whatever they decided I should do. I was just glad they were on my side.

He paid no attention to my protests, as he pulled me off the sofa, pushed my shoes and coat at me. "Come on," he said, and led the way out of the house and into the car.

It was the first time I'd been out since the . . . since that night. Everything seemed so loud, so bright.

"I know," said Stephen brightly, "we'll go to Dollymount Strand. It's years since I've been there."

"Me too," I said, trying hard.

"Do you remember all those picnics we used to have with your parents or mine?"

I smiled. Yes, I remembered.

"And it was always sunny, wasn't it?" he asked. "And do you know what, I can hardly remember a bite to eat, in my whole childhood, that didn't have sand in it!"

I laughed mildly, "A high-fibre diet, that was," and he laughed uproariously in turn, far more than the mild joke merited, glad that I'd tried at all.

"And do you remember the time we hid in the sand dunes," he went on, "and your parents couldn't find us. We thought we were funny, didn't realise that they thought we'd been drowned or abducted or both!"

"Oh yes, and when we bounced out full of laughter we couldn't understand why they didn't seem to think it was funny at all."

"Wow, do you remember their fury? We were bundled into their car, no coke or ice cream or any treat

– remember how we felt so hard-done-by? – and brought home in a stiff silence."

"I suppose in those days we didn't realise what bad things could happen to people. I know better now," I said bitterly.

He reached over, his eyes still on the road, and squeezed my hand gently.

It didn't take us long to cross the city, and we drove north along the coast, and across the Bull Island bridge, and parked. We got out and wandered slowly down onto the beach.

This deep into the winter we had the huge expanse of strand almost to ourselves, and the view was glorious, as the sand swept its way in a majestic curve all the way to Howth Head.

Stephen followed my gaze. "I'll bring you to Howth for lunch, after," he promised, "if you work up enough of an appetite. And the way to do that is," he paused and then with a flourish he said, "to play noughts and crosses with me!"

"Oh Stephen, no!" God, it all seemed like so much effort! Had I ever had that much energy? "No, let's not bother!"

But he ignored me, drawing the grid with his feet, and then drew in an 'O'.

"Your turn," he commanded.

Again, inertia prevented me standing up to him, and I dutifully drew an 'X' in the sand.

He drew another 'O', and before long I was really into the game, determined to win. To my surprise I was actually enjoying myself, although the enjoyment was diffused, like sunlight through a muslin curtain.

After the game (which he won, natch), he then drew a hopscotch course on the sand, and found a shell to throw.

"I haven't played hopscotch since I was a child," I said.

"Well, now's your chance!"

Again he insisted, and I couldn't believe it but I got into it all. The physical exercise of hopping and jumping meant I couldn't but be involved. We laughed at our adult bodies' attempts at the one-legged bending to pick up the shell, and there were quite a few falls caused by a mixture of lack of balance and hysterical laughter.

And yes, I was laughing. Oh, nothing had changed, but for the first time I got a glimpse that I might possibly have some tiny space within me for emotions other than those surrounding the rape.

I hugged him tight, whispering fiercely into his neck: "Oh thank you, Stephen, thank you, thank you!"

And he grabbed me around the waist and spun me around with a shout of delight at my happiness, no matter how brief or ephemeral it was.

An elderly couple, passing by with their dog, looked at us fondly, and glanced meaningfully at each other, probably thinking 'young love', or something equally cute.

Stephen and I looked at each other, and I whispered, "Imagine what they'd say if we told them, no, we're not young lovers, but a homosexual man bringing his best friend out of herself after a rape ordeal – can you imagine their faces?"

Whereupon we both collapsed in laughter. I laughed and laughed, and the laughter became somewhat manic, somewhat hysterical, and eased inexorably into sobs, and I cried, huge, body-wracking sobs, tears streaming down my face, the salty taste sharp in my mouth. My legs buckled with the grief and pain of it all, but Stephen held me, braced me against himself, held me quietly as I howled my pain and anger and betrayal and sadness and fury and shame and hurt and guilt, howled it all into the crisp November sky.

The elderly couple had scuttled quickly away.

Eventually I quietened, and stood drooping in Stephen's arms, no more than the occasional tear and hiccup of a sob remaining of the storm which had engulfed me. I felt like a used tea-bag.

But, exhausting as it had been, it had been cathartic too. It wasn't that this weeping had cleared everything I felt about the rape, but it had cleared some. I felt a tiny corner of peace settle into me, digging in, clinging stubbornly to its place inside me, despite the swirling emotions still raging.

And I found that I was able to spend the rest of the day with Stephen, just as we had always done: just good friends together, not rape victim and the person minding her. The rape was still there, hanging over us, filling most of my mind, and I'm sure, of Stephen's, but I could squeeze some normality out of the tiny gap that was left over.

Chapter 8

On Thursday morning, after another bad night, Sinead said to me at breakfast, "I wonder have you thought about seeing one of the counsellors from the Rape Crisis Centre? Do you remember the woman we met at the hospital? She said that there would be someone available to do some counselling with you whenever you wanted. Do you remember?"

"Yes, I remember. Do you think it would be a good idea?"

"Well, Grainne, you can hardly go on the way you're going. And these are trained people, able to help people in your situation. I'll do what I can for you, but I don't have those skills. I think you should ring them, or I will, and see how it goes. You can always stop going if it's not working."

"Okay," I said, "I will. I'll ring them straight after breakfast."

As I ate my meal, I felt the warm glow of being able

to make a decision for myself. All week I'd been buffeted and pushed by Sinead and Stephen, for my own good, I know. But now I was doing something proactive. It felt like a huge step.

After breakfast I looked up the number of the Rape Crisis Centre, and phoned. The phone was answered by a warm, calm voice. I said, "I wonder if I can make an appointment to see a counsellor. I was – I was raped last weekend, and I'd like to talk to someone about it."

The voice on the phone said, "We can do some day next week, or, I have a cancellation for tomorrow morning, at ten o'clock, if that would suit you?"

"Yes, tomorrow morning would be great," I said. "I'll see you then. Thank you."

I put the phone down, and went into Sinead in triumph.

"I did it, I arranged the appointment. Tomorrow morning!"

"Well done!" she said, smiling at me.

That day was long – except for the day out with Stephen, they had all been long. I was bored without my normal routine, and not really feeling up to doing anything proactive. I could have painted the box-room as I'd been intending to do for ages, I could have done some gardening, I could have caught up on writing letters to friends, I could have read some of the many books I'd always intended to read. But I didn't do anything like that. I just sat, mostly watching television. God, there's so much rubbish on during the day! But it was suitably numbing.

Sinead and I shared meals together, but apart from that, although she was there, she was working, and I tried not to disturb her more than I had to. Her presence in the house was great – I didn't want to be a drag on her time also.

I got up early on Friday morning and, turning my back on the leggings and sweatshirts I'd been wearing for the past week, dressed carefully in smart black trousers, a sharply tailored red blouse, and a black cardigan. It seemed strange to be wearing clothes more formal than leggings and sweatshirts. I even put some make-up on.

I went downstairs. Sinead was already at the table eating her breakfast.

"Wow!" she said. "You look great! Is this because of the trip to the counsellor?"

"Yes, it is. I thought that it would be good for me to dress up a bit, a good discipline for me, you know. I don't want to start letting myself go completely, just because . . ."

"Oh right. It's not that they have some sort of dress code?"

"You mean bouncers on the door and all, not letting you in unless you're dressed smartly?" I said laughing. "No, I don't think so."

I got myself some cereal, and a cup, sat down opposite her and poured myself a cup of tea.

"Are you set for this presentation today?" I asked her.

"As ready as I'll ever be. Now, listen, are you sure

you're going to be okay then? I know you said not to, but it's not too late to ring Stephen and ask him to come over."

"Positive, Sinead, honestly. I'll be out all morning, and Patrick will be back this evening, so it's only this afternoon I'll be here on my own. But I'll be fine, I really will."

"Well, if you're sure . . ."

"I am," I said emphatically, crossly. "It'll be fine, honest."

"Sorry, sorry," she said. "It's just that I want to be sure."

"I know you do. I'm sorry I snapped. It's just been a hard week, for us both."

"It has, hasn't it? Well, Grainne m'dear, here's to us, for having got through the first week! And survived!"

And we toasted each other with our tea-cups.

After breakfast we kissed and hugged goodbye.

"Thanks again for all you've done," I told her. "You saved my life."

She smiled her thanks. "Ring me when you get back from the counsellor – let me know how you got on."

"I will," I promised.

"Good luck, I'll be thinking of you."

I had about an hour to wait before it was time for me to leave. It felt strange to be in the house by myself. But it was stranger still to go out of the house on my own. Apart from the trip out with Stephen to the beach, I hadn't been out at all, and now here I was doing it alone. The world seemed noisy, windy, big. I found it a little overwhelming, but put my shoulders back and walked on.

I'd decided to get the bus into town, rather than try and find parking. In retrospect (ah, that retrospectrograph!) it wasn't a good decision. I felt very uncomfortable being around so many people, so many strangers, all with their different conversations and/or thoughts. One young man tried to catch my eye, and smiled at me when he managed to do so. I looked away hurriedly, shaking.

He's only being friendly, I told myself, and even if he isn't, there's nothing he can do on a crowded bus. Calm down, you can't be reacting like this to every man who looks at you. But my thudding heart and frayed nerves said back: yes, we can, and we will.

I dealt with this issue by refusing to catch anyone's eye. When I got off the bus, and headed towards the Rape Crisis Centre, I walked looking down at the pavement, so that no matter what was going on around me, I wouldn't know. Battalions could be looking at me, trying to smile at me, and I wouldn't realise.

Eventually I made it to the Centre and, legs shaking slightly, pushed open the door. I approached the reception area and announced myself, my voice squeaking slightly. The receptionist, a warm, motherly, middle-aged woman, said, "Oh yes, Fiona's expecting you."

She tapped some numbers into a phone, spoke into it. "Fiona, Grainne Quinn is here." Then, to me: "She's coming out now," and no sooner had she finished speaking than a small, neat woman, with the kindest smile I ever saw, was coming towards me, smiling warmly, saying: "Grainne? I'm Fiona Sullivan, how are you? Come on in here, it's one of the nicest rooms we have, and I managed to net it for you!"

While she was talking she was ushering me into a small room, with two comfortable-looking armchairs in it, and a coffee table on which were placed some flowers, a jug of water and glasses, an ashtray and a box of tissues.

We sat ourselves down, and there was a momentary silence. I didn't know what to say, what to do. I toyed with the idea of getting up and leaving.

But Fiona, having left space for me to start, obviously decided I wasn't going to, and took the conversational ball.

She said, quietly and calmly, "You've been raped."

I looked at her, nodded, and my eyes filled with tears, little prickles of pain.

"This is about you, not me, so I'm not going to bore you with my life story. But, I do want to tell you that I know what you're going through. I was raped myself. When I was seventeen, by three youths living locally to me. It's an experience beyond words, isn't it?"

I nodded again.

"That's why it's so hard to talk to others about it – they can't imagine what it's like. But, me, I do know, so you can tell me anything. And I do hope that you'll find talking to me will help you – or to some other counsellor, if, for any reason you want that instead. I know it helped me, immeasurably, when I finally started going to counselling. For years I'd been a total mess. I couldn't function at all, I was just going through the motions – and not very well, either. But the counselling here made all the difference, really helped me. That's how I know it works, and also it's why I came back here and underwent training, to be a counsellor in my own turn. But enough about me. As I said, this is about you. How long ago did it happen?"

"Last Friday night – well, Saturday morning, really."

And I told her all about it, the words spilling out of me, falling over themselves. I was incoherent at times, and tears were streaming down my cheeks. (I now knew the reason for the tissues on the table.)

I just told her the facts, didn't try to explain the mixture of emotions that were engulfing me – didn't have to – she knew. And that was huge relief for me, it really was. She nodded often, sharing in my pain, taking some of it onto herself.

I said, "It's so great, being able to talk about it like this. I haven't been able to say anything to anybody. Only Sinead knows a little, you know – she's the one who came to the hospital with me, I think I told you that?"

"You did, yes."

"Well, she knows a little from being there with me, but even she doesn't know much. She wasn't in the room when I was being examined, or giving my statement. So, she doesn't know much of the detail, and nobody else knows any. I haven't been able to say anything about it to anybody I knew. I didn't want them knowing such horrible stuff, it would hurt them to know what I'd gone through. But as well I was ashamed, didn't want to talk about such intimate things to people. And also, Fiona, in a funny way, when I think of people – Sinead, Stephen, my mum and dad, my brother Gary, other friends – any of them knowing the details would be like being raped again. But still, still, it's been very hard to keep it all inside, not to be able to talk about it. So," I laughed a little embarrassedly, "I'm afraid you're getting this dumped on you. I'm really sorry."

"Don't be," she said placidly. "That's what I'm here for."

So I carried on, told her the rest, then sat, hunched over, crying. Fiona didn't say anything for a few moments, didn't do anything, just was there. Her presence, her – well, witness seems a strange word to use, almost biblical, but it's the only right one. She was witnessing my story, my pain, and honouring the former and easing the latter by doing so.

After a while she said, "Would you like a drink of water?"

I nodded, silent tears still coursing a stream down my cheeks.

She handed me a glass, and said, "That was tough, going through that. You're very brave."

There was silence for a few more moments, silence she left for me to digest her words. Brave, I thought. I don't feel brave. But I like the idea of being so. Maybe I am. I must be – this wasn't easy, as she said, going through all this. Yes, I was brave. I am brave.

And I wore that badge with pride.

"Now, I'm going to tell you something," she said. "I'm sure I'll have to tell you again and again, and I will do that. But I am saying this now – look me in the eye." I did, we stared at each other, and she said, slowly, clearly, emphatically: "Grainne, the responsibility for the rape is totally with the rapist, not with you. It was nothing you did, or said. Nobody asks to be raped, despite popular beliefs. Women do not say no when they mean yes. Women say no when they mean no. And if some man chooses to ignore that, the responsibility lies with him, him only. Never you."

This made sense, rationally, I could understand what she was saying. But a sharp internal voice played alongside hers, telling me: you were so stupid, you danced with him, gave him a lift, opened the house door for him.

"And you know, Grainne, it's important that you know this: rape is not a crime of passion, or of sexual desire. It's a crime about power, about hurting – and the weapon is sex. Of course, this knowledge is not popular, because it puts the blame for rape back where it belongs – with men. It would be much more convenient for men if they could say they were overtaken with lust, victims of their own sex drives. But it's not true, and you have to know that it was nothing you did or said or wore that caused this rape."

Her words flowed over me, soothing, healing. It made sense, and I really wanted to believe it.

She also told me: "Time does heal the pain, Grainne. But I'm afraid I must tell you: the rape never goes away.

Success is learning to live with it, putting it in a little box in the corner of your mind, moving it from the centre of your mind where you keep tripping over it. But it's always in the corner, where you can see it with your peripheral vision."

We sat in silence a moment, as I absorbed what she had said.

Then I asked a question which had been haunting me. "What if I have AIDS? Or one of the other STDs?"

"I don't know," she said gently, "we'll have to cross that bridge when we come to it. Most of them are curable, and even HIV isn't the death sentence it was. With proper management it can be prevented from progressing to AIDs."

I looked at that future, and it was bleak.

"You might be clear," she said. "You most likely are."

Small comfort.

And then I took a deep breath and said, "I should have fought harder. I gave in so easily. I feel so guilty about that. Maybe if I had fought harder it wouldn't have happened."

"Or maybe you would have been more badly injured. And don't forget, he used the most powerful weapons of all – intimidation and fear. Grainne, a lot of people come in here saying they should have resisted more, blaming themselves. But you did what you had to. There was no way you could have overpowered him. The fact that you came out of it alive and with no lasting physical injuries mean, in my opinion, that you handled it the best way possible."

And I felt a lump leave my heart, a lump I hadn't even been aware of until it was gone.

Then she said softly, "I'm afraid our session is over now."

I said dryly, "Time sure does fly when you're having fun."

Fiona laughed. "It surely does. And, although I've only just met you, I'll stick my neck out, and say that your sense of humour, your ability to laugh at yourself and situations affecting you, are going to be the saving of you. I'll make a prediction, which I don't often do: I feel sure that you're going to be fine, you're going to get over this, rebuild your life. But it will take time, and as much counselling as you feel you need. But mostly time, and on bad days sometimes the only thing is to endure, to go with the pain, accept it, and know that it will pass, to some extent, at some time. But, remember that powerful sense of humour – it's a strong weapon for you."

I felt exhausted after this session, but healingly so. It certainly hadn't wiped out, in one brief hour, the pain and the trauma I was feeling, but there had been such relief in talking about it to someone who understood.

I went home, spoke briefly to Sinead on the phone, told her how it had gone, and then went upstairs for a quick lie-down. For once, somehow, I didn't fear the nightmares.

I was woken with a shock by the bedside-phone ringing.

I lifted the receiver. "Hello?"

"Ms Quinn? This is Fidelma Harris from the Rotunda.

I'm just ringing with the results of your chlamydia and gonorrhoea tests. I'm delighted to be able to tell you, they're both clear."

"Thank God," I breathed.

"Don't forget, now, to come back in another five weeks for the syphilis test."

"I won't," I promised her. As if!

I then looked around me. It was dark outside – what time was it anyway? I peered at the clock, focused my eyes. Just before five o'clock. Oh, help, Patrick would be back within the hour. I sprang out of bed, into the shower, and washed and dressed in fresh clothes.

Feeling somewhat better, I went downstairs, grabbed a quick cheese and tomato sandwich and a cup of tea and ate standing up in the kitchen, not really tasting it, just needing the fuel.

I went then into the sitting-room, and sat, waiting for him. I didn't switch on any lights, or the television, just sat in the dark. It seemed strange to be alone, and I tried to let my mind go blank, not to think of what I'd say when Patrick came home, how I'd tell him, how he'd react. Oh God, how would I tell him? How would he react?

Different scenarios – none of them good – played through my mind. I sat and sat in a dark silent house, almost ill with nerves, waiting for my husband to come in the door. How many times previously had I awaited his return – either from a business trip, or even just at the end of the day – with joyful anticipation? And now . . . now here I was, with nausea in my gut and a dread like a stone in my heart.

Chapter 9

And eventually there was the familiar sound of his key turning in the door, the door opening, the light thud as he dropped his suitcase.

He called out, "Grainne, love, I'm home!"

I didn't answer, didn't rush to the door, to his arms as I normally would.

He came into the sitting-room, dropping his coat on an armchair, and came over to me.

"Grainne, what's wrong? Did you not hear me come in? And what are you doing sitting in the dark?" He reached for the switch on the table-lamp.

I said abruptly, "Leave it."

"Okay," he said easily.

Then he sat down beside me, put his arm around me and hugged me. Despite everything, it felt so good to be so close to him; his unique smell of clean healthy man, the specific contour of his body, his quiet strength, his love for me.

He bent to kiss me, and I turned my face so that his kiss landed on my cheek. I didn't feel able for an intimate kiss, either for its own sake, or, God forbid, if he would expect the kiss to move into lovemaking. It had happened before, many the time, as he kissed me hello on the sofa, and the kisses – on both our sides – grew deeper and deeper, and we ended up making glorious love on the sofa or the floor. I had welcome it then, and relished it; indeed, had often initiated it. But that was Before.

He pulled back a little then, said, "Sorry, forgot about the laryngitis in the excitement of seeing you again. How is it anyway?"

"Much better. How did the trip go?" Anything to put off the moment of telling him.

"Oh, great!" he said, and even though I couldn't see his face in the dark, I knew from the tone of voice that it was bright with enthusiasm. "I did great work, though I say so myself, and they all seemed to be very pleased with me. I spoke to Michael today on the phone, and he said that he'd been getting great feedback, so, hopefully we should have some good news soon. But you know, I've got something to tell you. I've been doing a lot of thinking over these two weeks. And I want to apologise to you, and to explain why I was so determined to go on this trip, even though the dates weren't ideal. I do know how important having a baby is to you – it is to me, too, honest. And I'm so sorry that I didn't give it priority, that

I was so dismissive about last weekend." He paused, perhaps waiting for me to respond. Then he went on, "I do want this promotion, I really do. It's partly, there's no denying, for the satisfaction of it all, an ambition thing. But also I was trying to get into a place in my career where I could provide for you and a baby. Where you could give up work if you wanted when the baby came." He took a deep breath. "But now, Grainne, I've been thinking, like I said, and I'm going to go to Michael, and tell him that I'm still as committed to the job as ever, and want to do well for the company and for me, but that I'm a family man, well, aiming to be, and that I'm not going to be as available for travel, or certainly I'll have to be consulted about dates before they're arranged. And I'll check with you before agreeing to anything, I promise. Is that okay? Grainne? Grainne, why are you crying?"

For tears had started trickling silently down my face as he was speaking, but he only became aware of this when I started to sniffle. But when I heard the concern and love in his voice, and felt his large rough thumb brush away some of the tears, they turned to huge wrenching sobs, literally hurting my chest.

"What's wrong?" he said, over and over again, totally confused as to what was going on. "Is it your mum? Your dad?" But I just couldn't answer him, just cried and cried. After a while he gave up asking me, and just gathered me tightly to him and held me as I cried.

All the tears since this had happened – on the beach with Stephen, in the Rape Crisis Centre with Fiona, during nights in my bed! I had often wondered if there was an infinite amount of tears inside me, if there would ever be an end to them.

But I cried and cried in Patrick's arms as if I hadn't used a tear up at all, as if it had all been waiting to come out with him there. I sobbed tears that were hot and acrid and bitter, and howled, cries of pure pain, and Patrick held me gently. It must have been about twenty minutes later that I stopped crying. I was exhausted, and I lay, feeling like a dejuiced orange, quietly in his arms.

There was silence for a moment or two, as Patrick calmly and silently stroked my hair and my back. Then he said gently, "Do you think you can tell me what's wrong?"

I whispered, "Patrick, it's very hard for me to say, but last weekend, this night week in fact, I went into town with Kate and Ann and Margaret and a few others, and I very, very stupidly gave a lift home to this guy I'd got talking to – well, I'd danced with him, but very chastely, I swear, and well, Patrick, well –" I took a deep breath, "– he raped me. Here, in the hallway."

He said on an intake, "Jesus." He was silent for a few minutes, then said, "What? Are you okay? Who, I mean, do you know? What?" He was incoherent with shock and a million questions.

I said, "I'll tell you from the beginning," and I did.

Patrick was quiet for a moment after I finished. Then he kissed the top of my head, and said passionately, "You poor, poor mite!" Then he stood up, and shouted out loud: "The fucking bastard, I'd like to kill him!"

Patrick's anger was rarely seen, but I'd always found

it magnificent on the rare occasions he expressed it. It seemed to me to be like a tumultuous storm, with pouring rain, and lightning, and thunder. I loved to witness it.

Of course, since his anger had never been directed at me, I was always aware that I was witnessing this storm from the metaphorical safety of a warm house, behind strong glass windows. Experiencing his anger from the perspective of its focus, that would be different. That would be the equivalent of actually being in the storm, running around trying to find shelter. I waited in trepidation for his anger to turn on me.

He hit his fist hard off the wall, obscenities such as I'd never heard from him gushing out of his mouth. "The bastard, I'd kill him, slowly – I'd like to cut him apart – how dare he do that to you, to anyone!" Then, and his voice was anguished now, he said, "Oh God, you bastard, you bastard Quinn!" And I realised that his anger had turned on himself. He groaned to himself, "If only I'd let you come with me to Zurich, this wouldn't have happened! But no, what did I do? Swan off and leave you! Grainne, I'm so sorry!"

He started crying then, clumsy tears and grinding moans, the crying of a man who doesn't cry. I listened to him in shock: I'd never ever heard him cry, not even when one of his best friends from school was killed in a motorbike accident.

Still crying, he came back to me, sat down, gathered me to him, and rocked us together. I clung to him, not sure who was comforting who.

I was still waiting for his anger to turn on me. It was

like waiting for the other shoe to fall. Eventually I thought I'd rather get it over than wait for it.

I said in a small voice, into his shoulder: "And me, Patrick? What about me? I was the one who was stupid enough to trust him. I danced with him in the first place. I gave him a lift home. Don't forget to give me my share of the blame."

He pulled away a little, gently wiped my cheeks free of tear-tracks. "There's no blame for you. You are perfectly entitled to go out with your friends, even to dance with someone without him raping you. You were possibly a little naïve to offer him a lift home, but it isn't a crime to be naïve. And you thought you knew him, that you had acquaintances in common – it's not surprising you trusted him. Why should I be angry with you? There's nothing to be angry about."

"Well, the same should apply to you. You're perfectly entitled to go on a business trip – it's not your fault, what happened."

"Fair point," he conceded, but I got the impression he was only humouring me. "Let's leave the blame where it belongs, with that bastard." Something then occurred to him. "But this happened a week ago – why didn't you ring me?"

I shrugged. "Fear, lethargy. It didn't seem the sort of thing you can say over the phone. I knew the trip was important to you. Lots of reasons, none of them very well thought out."

He said in an anguished voice, "Oh, Grainne!" Then, "Well, for a start, yes, this trip was important, but not more important than being with you if you needed me – although I can see why you thought it." He hugged me tight to him, rocked me as if I were a baby. "You poor, poor girl!" Then, "How are you now? Are you okay – well, physically? And how do you feel?"

"I'm grand physically, I think. The bruising is healing now. He only used his hands – no knives or anything, thank God – and those bruises are beginning to fade."

Patrick's face twisted, and I said, "I know, I know, being grateful for only being bruised sounds bizarre. But, Patrick, they said that some rape victims are slashed with knives, and end up permanently scarred, so I suppose if a rape has to happen, this is the way for it to happen." My attempt at humour fell flat for both of us. I went on: "They gave me the morning-after pill, so there's no fear of pregnancy, at least. But, Patrick, I need to get tested for syphilis in five weeks' time – and – and AIDS and hepatitis in three months' time –" I heard him gasp and I realised he hadn't yet thought of the possibility of infection, "and you and I must use safe sex for all that time. Assuming we even have sex. I've been trying to picture it, you know – healthy, loving, fun sex, to replace the rape, and I can't even imagine it. Even memories of sex feel strange, as though they're memories of a particularly pornographic film I saw, not memories of what you and I have shared." I started crying again, softly. "And, God, if I do have AIDS or hepatitis, what will we do then? I'm trying not to think about it, because they say the chances are I don't have anything like that, and there's no point worrying about it if it isn't going to happen. But it's hard not to think about it. This past week, I have been thinking about it a lot and it's really, really scary." I burst into huge tears again.

Patrick held me and caressed me and, when I felt wet on my hair, I realised that he was crying too, and shortly his body started juddering, and soon we were sobbing together, great racking cries from the soul. But it was good, it was sharing our grief, it brought us together in this. I thought, there's a long way to go before we can truly put this behind us, but our love and commitment is so strong, that we can never be parted, that nothing can ever come between us.

Eventually our tears ended, and we just sat, holding each other, for some endless time. Eventually he said, "I can't believe it, I still can't believe this has happened to you. I still feel so guilty, so angry –" he added hurriedly, "with him, not you. And so sad for you . . . I can't even imagine what it must have been like. I picture your terror while it was happening, your vulnerability, and it breaks my heart."

"It's been a week, and I still can't believe it myself. I know it's a cliché, but I really do feel as if I'm in a horrible dream, and I just want to wake up. But of course, I am awake. And I keep replaying the scene, keep having flashbacks, Patrick, like a film that's playing in my head over and over again, and there's no off-switch!"

He gave a short, mirthless, laugh.

I continued, "I had a session with someone from the Rape Crisis Centre, yesterday, and she said that it does get better, that a mixture of time and counselling will heal, to a huge extent. But it's such early days yet, I'm beginning to realise the only thing is to endure."

"That's horrible," he said reflectively.

"Yes. Yes, it is. The whole thing is horrible. But still, it's over now, we'll just get on with things. Show that bastard that he hasn't ruined our lives."

"Yes, we will," he said.

But we both knew that it was easier said than done.

The rest of the evening passed slowly; we spoke of trivialities.

Eventually, at last, it was time for bed. Although I'd slept that afternoon, I was still tired, ready for more sleep.

On Patrick's return from previous business trips, we had gone to bed early, and celebrated our reunion in passionate lovemaking. Now here I was, undressing in the bathroom, putting on my longest nightshirt, hoping so much that he would have the sensitivity not to make any approach to me.

We climbed into bed, and he gathered me to him, his arm under my neck. He turned and gently kissed my forehead.

"Good night, my love, my precious. Sleep well."

I silently thanked him for his gentleness, for showing the sensitivity I'd hoped for. I couldn't bring myself to say it out loud, to articulate the fact that I didn't feel able to make love to him. But I concentrated on sending him vibes of gratitude, and hoped he'd pick them up.

It felt strange, after only two weeks of sleeping alone, to be sharing the bed with someone else. Patrick's presence seemed like an invasion. The weight of him pressing down his side of the bed, the sound of his breathing, the heat from his body: it all seemed very alien.

But I closed my eyes, and slept.

And woke screaming some hours later, soaked in sweat, shaking, flailing my arms, hitting Patrick's arm as it lay across me.

"What, what?" he woke quickly, reached for me. "Grainne, what is it?"

"Oh, God," I sobbed, "I couldn't breathe, there was something pushing down on my chest, like he did, I could feel it happening all over again."

I sat up, looking wildly around me, searching for what I didn't know, in the dim light from the outside streetlight.

"It was my arm," Patrick said dully.

"What?" I was confused.

"In my sleep, I'd wrapped my arm across you. It must have felt too heavy, trapped you. Oh, Grainne," and his voice was anguished, "for all these years we've slept like this, with me wrapped around you, and you always said how safe it made you feel. Remember?"

I nodded.

"And now, that same position makes you feel trapped. Oh fuck!" And he angrily thumped the pillow.

"I'm sorry," I whispered.

"Don't be sorry – it's not your fault, you can't help

it. It's that bastard, yet another part of our life he's encroaching on." He hesitated. "Look, I can't promise that I won't wrap myself around you again, in my sleep. I'll sleep in the spare room tonight."

"No," I cried, "don't! We've never slept a night apart unless you were abroad – don't let this push us apart now. I need you, don't go!"

"God, I don't want to," he said. "If you're sure?"

"Yes, yes," and I lay down, gently pulling him with me, and we cuddled together, and slept.

And again I woke, screaming, trapped.

Patrick had, indeed, in his sleep, wrapped his arm around me again.

"Grainne," he said, despairingly, "this isn't fair on you. Look, I'll sleep in the spare room tonight – we'll sort ourselves out tomorrow."

I realised that we certainly couldn't spend the rest of the night like that, so I sadly agreed.

But the next night, and the next, it was the same story, and so Patrick continued to sleep in the spare room, and after two or three nights of this, we didn't even discuss it further, just slept apart. At least, I thought bitterly, it saved us facing up to the issue of sex.

And mostly, he managed to sleep the nights through. Except for those nights when I still woke him with my screams, as the horror movie that was on constant release in my head played over and over. And he would come rushing in to me, and hold me, rocking me gently, caressing my hair, until I quietened.

Chapter 10

Also during this time, the second week after the rape, and the first week of Patrick's return, my sketch of Darren Brogan was featured on *Crimeline*.

The next day there was a knock on the door. It was Sergeant Reilly – Ger, as I began to call her. "Can I come in?"

We went into the kitchen, I put on the kettle, shook biscuits onto a plate.

"There's been a development, on foot of the programme last night."

"Has someone recognised him?"

"Well, sort of. The fact of the matter is that he's given himself up. He turned up at his local garda station literally minutes after the programme ended. His name is Darren Brogan."

"Wow, brilliant! That's great!" I gave a little hop of joy.

"No, listen, don't get too excited. He's not admitting to rape. His story is that you did have sex, but it was consensual. Imagine his shock, then, he's saying, on seeing his own picture on *Crimeline*. He thought he'd better, he told his local gardaí, come in and get it sorted out straight away."

I was confused. "But isn't it still good news?"

She sighed. "Not really. Yes, it means that we've found him. But it also means that our DNA evidence is useless: after all, if he's admitting to sex, there's no advantage to proving that he had sex."

"But it was rape!"

"That's the problem. It often is with rape cases. If he was denying any sexual contact, and we could prove that sexual contact did in fact happen, well, that wouldn't look good for him. But he's obviously realised this, which is why he's admitting to sex. But since he's admitting to sex with you, the only question is whether or not that sex was consensual. You're saying it wasn't, he's saying it was. There are no witnesses, and so it's his word against yours. At the end of the day, it's up to a jury to decide who they believe. That's if the case goes to court at all."

"What! If? What's with this 'if'? The guy has come forward, you've just said so. What's not to take to court?"

"I'm sorry, Grainne. It's like this. We, the gardaí, have prepared our case. We've put it together in what's called a book of evidence. It includes statements from yourself, from Brogan, from the medical people who dealt with you, from anyone else, such as neighbours and the nightclub bouncers. It includes the photographs of your injuries, and details of the DNA evidence. With me so far?"

I nodded.

"Okay, we've sent this evidence to the DPP – the Director of Public Prosecutions," she explained, obviously seeing my blank look, "but don't get your hopes up. We don't know yet if he's going to prosecute. It depends on whether he feels the case is winnable, whether there's enough evidence."

"*He's* going to prosecute?" I echoed disbelievingly. "What about me?"

"Grainne," she sighed, "the rape laws are about a millennium out of date. Legally, you are only a witness of the State. Not a plaintiff or anything. It's the State which will prosecute. Or not."

"God, that's terrible! It's so unfair."

She nodded. "It is. Terrible, and unfair. But it's the system we have."

I sighed. "When will we know? Whether the what's-his-face will prosecute, I mean?"

"In a couple of weeks."

"And what happens in the meantime?"

"Nothing, I'm afraid."

"You're saying, though, that at the moment it's my word against his. But, Ger, what about the physical evidence?"

She nodded. "The DPP will certainly take that into account when he's making his decision. But as

118

corroborating evidence goes, it's pretty thin, I'm afraid. Any good defence lawyer could think up a thousand, credible alternative explanations for those." She was silent for a second, then said, "I'm sorry, I really am. The only thing I can promise you is that I'll keep you totally up to date on any developments, and that I'll be there for you in any way I can."

"But it's so unfair!" I said, as if saying this could change anything.

She didn't say she agreed. I suppose she was in an awkward position, being an agent of the system. But it was very clear that in the way she didn't disagree, that she thought so too.

"It turns out that most of what he told you that night is false," she said. "Not surprisingly of course. His name is Darren alright, but he's not an accountant at all, he's a business consultant, whatever that is. And of course, he lives nowhere near Ranelagh."

"So where is he now?"

"At his home. He's not charged with anything yet. But listen, Grainne, he'd be very stupid indeed to come anywhere near you with this hanging over his head. So don't worry."

So it was down to waiting to see what the DPP would do. I so wanted to see this bastard behind bars (failing the castration etc. option). One reason was to get justice – or revenge, I'm not sure which – for myself. I wanted him to suffer for what he did. I wanted him to feel a little of the fear I'd felt, a little of the loss of autonomy over your own body. Another more noble reason was that I truly felt that if he got away with it once, he'd be much more likely to do it again, and I didn't want any other woman to go through what I had experienced.

* * *

Slowly life got back to its normal routine. To judge by appearances you'd swear nothing had ever happened. Patrick and I both went back to work, we entertained friends, went to the gym, met people after work in some chrome bar somewhere. And always I felt as if I were acting a part, as if the real me was standing back looking at this woman with a drink in her hand and laughter in her voice. And the real me thought of this other woman: you have no idea, you truly have no idea. The real me stood back, assessed, was wary, didn't join in. And I acted for all I was worth.

That was partly because I swore, *I swore* that Brogan wasn't going to beat me, that I was going to get my life back, and if all I could do was to go through the motions, then by God I was going to go through the motions, over and over, until hopefully at some future date they started to feel as real and as natural as they'd always done.

It was also partly that my close friends really didn't need to have me moping around after them, not only raining on their parade but flooding it out entirely. There was nothing to say about the rape that hadn't been said, and we had to talk about something. So we chatted and laughed as we always had. There was also an amazing number of people – casual friends and acquaintances – who didn't even know about the rape and I certainly wasn't going to tell them. Pure conversation-stopper that'd be. Plus, I didn't want people knowing it; it was too intimate, too shameful.

So I acted the part of a happy carefree woman. And if sometimes a haunted look came into my eyes, only those who knew to look for it would be able to see it.

I was glad to be back at my job, back at school with the children. I found their innocence and joyous exuberance to be very healing. Except that sometimes, in my darker moments, I wondered, looking at the girls: which of you will grow up to be subjected to a man's whim, your body to be taken and used just because he wants it, and you powerless to do anything about it? And looking at the boys: which of you will grow up to be a rapist, to think that what you want you can have, to see women as so much meat for your satisfaction?

But mostly I held such thoughts at bay and, in the classroom, surrounded by these wonderful children, in a school with phones everywhere, and strong male colleagues only a shout away, and bright lights, I felt safe. And at home, with Patrick, I felt safe. And when I was with my father or brother, or Stephen and Richard, I felt safe.

But outside of those situations, I felt fearful. Always and forever scared. The illusion that I had any power, any way to protect myself, had been brutally and emphatically swept away, and I was so, so vulnerable.

Leaving school between three and four in the

afternoon, when it was already getting dark, I would either hang around until some male colleague was going to his car, and "happen" to fall into step with him. Or I would scurry, heart pounding, keys in hand, terrified, to my car, fall into it, lock all the doors and sit for a few minutes until I calmed enough to drive.

I could have explained my situation to my colleagues, and asked them to always escort me to my car. But I didn't. I didn't want them knowing what had happened. I was ashamed. Yes, despite all the talk about the shame being the perpetrator's, which I acknowledged rationally, I was shamed to my soul of what had happened, and hoarded it to me like a guilty secret. I knew that if I told my colleagues – all friends of mine – what had happened, there would be no judgement, only caring and help and support. But I just couldn't.

Or doing the shopping, going from the brightly lit supermarket to the car, was another ordeal. Usually I got Patrick to do it, or at least we would do it together. But sometimes, to prove that he hadn't beaten me, I would do it by myself. And pay for my pride in fear and terror and shaking hands and a thumping heart.

The irony of this, that I only felt safe with Patrick, or Stephen and Richard, or family and colleagues, did not escape me: that I was giving my power for my safety away to men. That Brogan had taken this power, and that I wasn't able to reclaim it. That the best I could do was to re-allocate that power to other men. Yes, to men that at the least I liked and trusted, and in the case of my family, loved too. But it seemed that the power of my safety was gone forever for me, and the only choices I had was which man would hold it.

It didn't help that I knew that Brogan was still at large, still free to walk the streets, still a threat to me and to other women.

It was about three weeks after the rape, towards the end of November, that Ger Reilly arrived at the door one rainy evening. "Good news," she said, in her bright way. "The DPP has said that he will prosecute! They have arrested him, but unfortunately he's been given bail. The judge decided he wasn't a flight risk, seeing as he gave himself up originally. But still, he has to be so careful when he's on bail, he'll be sure to keep his hands clean. He won't come near you, that was one of the conditions of bail. The trial is set for the 5th of July next year."

"So long," I said, dismayed.

She laughed. "That's actually a very short time – we were lucky to get that date." She grew solemn. "This might be a difficult one for you. You are only the witness in this situation. You will be called upon to give evidence, and you will be cross-examined, but you won't have your own lawyer to protect you if the cross-examination becomes too much. And seeing as it's his word against yours, the defence lawyer will be sure to attempt to discredit you.

"I hate to tell you this, but the judge may, or may not, direct the jury that they cannot convict on your uncorroborated testimony. The forensic evidence might be considered enough corroboration, but it might not. And, Grainne, the defence can – probably will – ask the judge for permission to question you on your previous sex life. The judge has total discretion as to whether to allow that line of questioning, and he doesn't have to justify his decision about that."

"Oh God," I breathed.

"As I told you, the laws are so out-of-date. The odds are stacked against you. I'm sorry to be so brutal, but it's best that you realise this now. You know, we gardaí hate rape – we see so much of it, and the pain and trauma it causes. Second only to murder cases, these are the ones we feel most about. And it's so frustrating for us. Officially I'm only allowed call this guy the 'alleged rapist', even to you, in case I ruin the case. And we put in all the work, helping the women concerned, searching for and collating evidence, presenting the case to the DPP. And then it's out of our hands."

"This makes me feel like pulling out of the whole thing."

"I can understand that," she said.

"But I won't. I'll go through with it, see him go to prison."

"Atta girl," she said, smiling at me.

* * *

Patrick and I tried to put the upcoming trial out of our minds, and carry on with our lives. Patrick was very busy with work, as usual, and I was at the time of the school year which is at once the most hectic, and also my favourite, the month before the Christmas holidays.

I was plunged into the Christmas-time school stuff:

the nativity play, the story of Jesus, lots of colouring of snowmen and making paper-chains. I always enjoyed this time of year – the children had had time to get into the rhythm of being at school, and were all settled by now, and yet they weren't as tired as the end of the summer term often finds them.

Add to that the excitement of Christmas for these young innocent children: the total belief in Santa Claus, the pure joy and excitement and anticipation, the empathising with Mary's being unable to find anywhere to stay, the joy of the new Baby Jesus – well, it was magical for me.

It was wonderful, but not surprisingly I didn't enjoy it as much this year as other years. The shadow of the rape, of course. But more than that. I was tired all the time. I, who had always had such wonderful energy, now dragged myself out of bed in the morning, dragged myself through the day, and collapsed gratefully into my bed at some ridiculously early hour of the evening.

And I had picked up some low-grade bug: I felt sick all the time. Not sick enough to actually get sick, and get some relief, oh no. Just feeling a slight nausea all the time, and a tinny taste in my mouth.

Oh God, I thought, maybe it's one of the STDs.

I got onto the internet and did a search on the symptoms of the various illnesses. The symptoms of syphilis were sores and rashes, which I didn't have, and a flu-like feeling, which, again, wasn't what I was experiencing.

Then hands shaking I typed AIDS symptoms into the search-engine.

I read: "Swelling lymph nodes", and reflexively my hand went to my neck. No swelling, thank God. I read on. "Headache." Well, yes, sometimes. I had put it down to the stress of it all. And anyway, doesn't everyone get headaches at some stage? "Fever." No, thank God. "Loss of appetite." No, I was eating fine. "Sweating and sore throat." No. I took a deep breath of relief. Only one of the symptoms applied, and that could have a million reasons. Of course, it didn't mean I didn't have AIDS – the symptoms could be waiting for me. But, so far so good.

Feeling marginally better I typed hepatitis symptoms.

Hepatitis A and B seemed to be okay. Although the symptoms included nausea and fatigue, they also included fever and diarrhoea, which I didn't have.

And so on to hepatitis C. I stared, horrified. There was a huge list of symptoms, and they all seemed to apply to me. Depression, anxiety, decline in sex drive, fatigue, indigestion, insomnia, irritability, mood-swings, nausea. Of course most of those could be attributed to the rape trauma. But still . . .

Dry-mouthed I pressed the page down button and began to read the rest. And as I did my heart-rate slowed slightly. Here were a list of symptoms from which I was not suffering: dizziness, dry skin, jaundice.

So I was none the wiser. I rang the Rotunda and they reassured me. There were a million reasons for the nausea I was experiencing. Yes, they admitted, it could be hepatitis C, but unfortunately there was no way of checking until the right time. Once that time arrived, they reminded me, I would have the results of the tests in five or six days.

But still, another two months to go . . . wondering, praying.

I was still seeing Fiona every week, and during the last week before Christmas, I spoke to her of an issue which had been very much playing on my mind.

"We're going to Tenerife for a week, right after Christmas," I told her. "I know – at least, I'm pretty sure – that he's going to want to resume our sex life then. I know he's bought condoms – you know, that safe sex thing, because of the . . . "

She nodded in understanding.

I went on, "He's been very patient, hasn't come near me, hasn't made a pass at me. But I dread it, Fiona. The thoughts of making love . . . " I shuddered at the thought. "You know, I've already told you, that Before we had a wonderful sex life, couldn't keep our hands off each other, even after all these years. And even when we weren't actively making love, there was this . . . this atmosphere of sexuality between us. He might pat my bottom, or grasp it, or come up behind me, and lift my hair and gently nuzzle my neck. Or he might cup my breast as we sat watching television. Or even more subtly, there was this expression on his face, sometimes, as he looked at me, and I knew that he would be thinking of sex with me, remembering some previous encounter, or looking forward to the next one. And

Fiona, I used to love all of this. I used to melt at it all. It was all like an ember that was constantly burning, ready to burst into flame at any time."

I said all this with wonder in my voice. Although I knew these words to be true, it seemed to me as if I was speaking of someone else, that maybe my memory was not of the events themselves, but of something I'd seen or read somewhere.

"He hasn't done any of this for ages, since the – the rape. Now he's treating me like I'm his maiden aunt. He's being so kind to me, so attentive, there're so many cups of tea made, and enquiries after my health and well-being. And although I miss where we were, I'm glad we're not there now. I don't think I could deal with his desire, his hunger. It would remind me too much of Brogan's desire. The act is the same, isn't it? It's only the intention which is different."

"Well, along with the minor point of consent," she said drily. "But, I'd suggest, don't dismiss the importance of intention. Sex with a man who has the intention of hurting, humiliating you, or lovemaking with a man who loves you and cherishes you: yes, the physical act is the same, but they are worlds apart."

I nodded. "Yes, I can see that rationally, but feeling it, knowing it here," and I lightly thumped my heart, "are two different things."

She nodded. "That's the trick, alright."

"And, quite apart from this issue of what's going on in his head, there's me. Fiona, I find it so difficult to think of myself as being a sexual person, having desires myself, wanting it. Rationally I want to get back to a proper sex life with Patrick. It was so good before, and it was such a sign of our love, or commitment. But now . . . oh God, I'm rambling, I'm not making sense."

"You are," she said placidly. "Look, it's not surprising that you don't have any sexual feelings now. Being a sexual being got you into trouble before. It's hard for your head to get around that conflict. But it will come back, sometime. Be patient. The other thing is, Grainne – about Patrick wanting to resume your sex life on this holiday – sometimes people who haven't been raped don't realise how deep it goes, they don't realise how long it takes to heal. They might be thinking, well, it's been two months now, why are you still on about it? They don't mean to be uncaring, they just don't realise. What I'm trying to say is, if during this holiday, Patrick wants to make love, and you don't want to, or just don't feel able, and he says something along the lines of how long it's been since the rape, and aren't you over it yet – well, I'm trying to say that he might say that, and it doesn't mean that he's selfish, or uncaring. He genuinely doesn't realise that two months is no time at all in this context."

"Really," I said, amazed, "it seems like no time since this happened, it is still so much with me, such a part of me. Does the time seem long to other people?"

"It can do. I just want to let you know that it's a possibility."

"Okay, I'll keep that in mind. But about Patrick. I don't think he'd throw that in my face. About how long it's been, I mean."

"No, he probably won't. But don't blame him if he does."

"But, Fiona, what'll I do if he wants to make love, and I don't?"

"It's up to yourself – I can't tell you what to do. But I suppose I'd feel that if you go through with something you don't want to, endure it, then, well, it's obviously not rape, as Patrick isn't forcing you. But it's hardly the ideal situation either, is it?"

I shook my head. "No, it's not. No, he'll have to wait until I'm ready. It would put me, us, back months, if I went through it without wanting to. But, Fiona, will I ever feel sexual again? Or has this ruined me for life?"

"You will," she assured me once more. "I was in a slightly different situation to you – I was only seventeen, and a virgin – so at the time, that was my only experience. I had no boyfriend at the time, which was good in a way because it meant I didn't have to cope, as you have, with a partner's needs and fears, and getting a sex life back on track. But it did mean that I didn't even have any good memories to compare with this experience, and I found it hard to trust men. For years I didn't go near men, but in my mid-twenties I met Martin. We got to know each other as friends first, so he kind of got under my defences. And the day he asked me out for a proper date, rather than just pals meeting, I told him about the rape. I thought I'd lose him for sure, once he heard that – I don't know why, but I was sure he'd run. But he didn't, just promised to woo me gently. And he did, and well, to cut a long story short, we ended up married, have been for ten years now and have two gorgeous sons. And a wonderful sex life. So, yes, there is sex life after rape. But it has to take its time. Be patient."

Chapter 11

I thought of all this now, as I sat in the aircraft seat, two days after Christmas, waiting our turn to take off.

I was nervous, and not just about the sex thing. I hadn't spent much time with Patrick since the rape, and certainly none without distractions. Up till now, we'd been both working hard, and even when we were home there were television programmes to watch, friends to visit or chat to on the phone, books to read.

I don't think we were deliberately avoiding each other. There just seemed to be this gaping hole between us, that neither of us could cross. We were so polite to each other, so kind, so attentive. It was all just a bit formal, a bit artificial. So the thought of spending a whole week with him, with nothing to do but be in his company, scared me.

And for the millionth time I thought bitterly, this is how things have changed. Before, I lived for the chance to spend time with him. Brogan, I thought, your few minutes of pleasure have thrown a huge shadow over my life. I wondered what he was doing just then, what kind of Christmas he'd had, whether he was nervous about the forthcoming trial.

"We're off," said Patrick, pleasure in his voice.

As I brought my mind back to the present I realised that the sound of the engines had increased as they do just before they start hurtling you down the runway.

"I love this bit," he said, as he always does, every time we fly. "The rush of speed as you're going down the runway, then the sense of being pushed back into your chair as the plane takes off, and seeing all around Dublin from the air as we climb."

"I know," I said. "It doesn't last long, though, before you're too high to have any sense of speed, or to see any more of Ireland. But those few minutes are fun."

We could have been any two strangers making conversation after chance and the arbitrary decisions of the check-in staff had thrown them together in adjacent seats.

The days of the holiday went as well as I could have expected. We both relaxed a little with each other, and found we could relate well on the level of casual friends. We explored the area together, and had plenty of polite stuff to talk to each other about, what with all the new sights we were seeing.

We walked, self-consciously holding hands, through the old town, ate together, talking at laborious length about our respective meals. We were still aware of the essence of our love for each other, there, as real as ever, but so much duller than it had been, with the shadow of the rape hanging over it.

But the nights, the nights were a different story.

On our first night there, we slept together in the hotel bed, each chastely clinging to our own side and, thank God, I had no nightmares, no night screams.

On the second night, however, he made his move.

As soon as we had switched off the light, and laid down, he raised himself up on one elbow, and looked down at me. In the muted neon light, I could see the dark planes and shadows of his face, the hard curves of his arms and torso. He was looking so good, but although I could appreciate this aesthetically, drinking in his beauty caused no answering leap, no sweet melting in my groin.

He gazed longingly, lovingly into my face. My stomach clenched.

He reached his free hand up, and gently pushed my hair away, half-caressing, half-massaging my scalp. This had never previously failed to simultaneously arouse and relax me; now I felt precisely nothing.

But that was good, I told myself determinedly. Feeling nothing is good. That means I'm not feeling panic, or fear, or entrapment, or anything else bad. Arousal, desire – well, they're optional extras, we can do without them. If I can go through with this, it will break that barrier – we can work towards the old sexual feelings later.

He said "Grainne?" in that dark, husky tone of voice which always sent shivers down my spine. But now he could have said, "And here is the news," for all the effect it had on me. And I heard the hint of nervousness hidden deep in his voice, and my heart broke for him, for the emotions he must be having: desire and hunger for sure – but also fear and nervousness. And also, I realised, probably also the realisation which I had, that the sooner we got this First Time over with, the better.

I thought hard about getting this First Time over with, and I answered the question in his voice, and I reached my hand up behind his head, caressed his strong hair, his muscular neck, and gently pulled him down to me.

He bent to kiss me, and I twisted away. "Can't," I said. "Remember, we have to practice safe sex. No exchange of bodily fluids. Not until I get the all-clear in February." (Not true, actually – they'd told me that kissing is fine unless there are open wounds in the mouth. But kissing just seemed too invasive.)

"Sorry, forgot," he muttered. And bent to kiss my neck, nibble my ears. Again, normally this would have had me writhing and begging him to fuck me now.

But now, nothing.

But I thought, okay, still nothing, still no panic. That's good. I can get through this.

But then I felt his erection pressing against my thigh, and his breathing grew deeper and more urgent.

I felt the first flickers of fear, of panic; fought them down.

His hands reached for my breasts, caressed them; he bent his head and nibbled, suckled. I lay there, enduring. But still not panicking. Just.

But then, with groans of lust, and whispers of desire, he climbed on top of me. Unlike Brogan, he supported his weight. But still . . . but still. He was on top of me, pinning me down, holding me helpless.

I panicked, flailed my arms everywhere, hitting him in my terror, unable to breathe with the weight of him on me, sobbing, "No, no, no!"

Immediately he flung himself off me.

"God, I'm sorry, Grainne, I'm so sorry! Did I push you too far? Too fast? I'm sorry, I'm sorry! My love, the last thing I want to do is to hurt you. I'm so sorry!"

Dimly I heard his repeated and anguished apologies, as I clung to myself, hugging myself, and shook.

We ended up sleeping uneasily, all thoughts of lovemaking abandoned if not forgotten.

The next morning Patrick said to me, "Grainne, again, I am so, so sorry about last night. I thought you wanted to. Or at least I managed to convince myself you wanted to. I've been wanting you so much, missing you so much, I think I rushed you. Please, please, I'm so sorry."

"I'm sorry too," I whispered. "I know you'd never hurt me, that you weren't . . . I just panicked, I'm sorry."

"It's okay, Grainne. I'm sorry for even trying it, it's obviously much too soon." He reached out tentatively and caressed my hair. This I could cope with. I sat, enjoying this gentle touch.

"I want you to know that I am as different from that bastard as two members of the same species can be. I will never ever force you, nor even try to persuade you against your will. That's a promise. And what's more, I'm telling you now that I won't make a pass at you at all. I'll wait until you feel confident enough to come to me."

"Thank you," I said. I felt huge relief, literally a lightening of a weight. But also a measure of sadness. I didn't want sex with anyone, but I could still regret the loss of our vibrant and passionate love life, which I had so cherished and enjoyed, and which I never could have imagined would end.

I looked into his deep blue eyes, hooded now, worry and nervousness and love entwined in them. And I reached up, and hugged him, but chastely, and I said, "That would be great, Patrick. And I promise, as soon as I feel ready, able, I'll come straight to you."

And he hugged me back, equally chastely, and our love was very present.

In a funny way the rest of the holiday passed better after we had got that abortive attempt at sex out of the way. Now that we both knew that sex was off the agenda, we could relax about it, and just be together.

So, yes, I think that I can safely say that we had a nice time that week. Not a great time, but a nice time.

I slept a lot. I was tired all the time, it seemed. My body's way of dealing with the trauma, I felt. I still felt ill every so often: it looked like I hadn't shifted that bug or virus or whatever it was that had been plaguing me before Christmas. Not surprising, I told myself, that with all you've been through, your immune system isn't the best, is finding it difficult to shake it off.

Or, I thought, deep in the hidden places in my heart, in the dark of wakeful nights . . . could it be AIDS? Or hepatitis. Or syphilis.

* * *

We came back from our holiday. Patrick went back to work and, a few days later, when the Christmas holidays were over, I went back to school, back to the pantomime of pretending everything was okay.

One good thing happened, though. I went for the syphilis test, and a couple of days later the result came: negative. So now I only had to worry about the other two. Only another six weeks until I could get checked for those.

They dragged, every day, every hour, every second of those six weeks. And always like a drum-beat my heart seemed to be asking: "Am I? Am I not?"

Eventually, though, the day came when it was time to go back to the Rotunda. Patrick took the day off, and we went in together. It was a bit of an anti-climax after all the waiting, all the build-up. They just took some blood, said they would have both results in about five days.

So, more waiting. The last few days. Soon I would know one way or another. And, I couldn't believe it but after all this waiting, suddenly I didn't want to know. What if either – or both – was positive? Dreadful as it was not knowing, knowing and having to deal with it would be worse. But at the same time, and equally strongly, I did want to know. It would be wonderful to be clear of this leaden cloud of fear.

And sure enough, the following Friday I got home from school to hear a message on the answerphone: "This is Fidelma Harris for Mrs Quinn. Could you please ring me when you get a chance?" and she left her number. I appreciated the equivocal message – anybody else hearing it wouldn't have had a clue what it was about.

But what was all this about "when you have a chance"? Yeah right, like I was going to put a clothes-wash on, then ring a friend for a chat, and then maybe get around to ringing.

I dialled the number, my mouth dry and my heart beating.

"Oh, yes, Mrs Quinn," she said when I had identified myself, "I have your results here – hold on a second."

And I could hear the rustle of papers for what was only a second or two, but seemed in my fear and terror to be forever.

"Mrs Quinn, the results of your hepatits tests came back negative."

I let out a huge breath, but she was continuing, "Unfortunately –" I thought my heart would stop beating right then and there, "the HIV results aren't back from the lab yet. It will be Monday or Tuesday now."

My heart started beating again.

So most of the hurdles over. Only one more to go. The biggest. Patrick and I hung around the house that Saturday and Sunday, cursing weekends.

When I got home from work on Monday I jumped on the answerphone, and listened impatiently to the messages. But the one I wanted wasn't there.

On Tuesday, again, I listened to the messages before I had even taken off my jacket. And yes! There was the neutral message to ring her.

With shaking hands I dialled the number. And to my horror got through to her voice mail. I left a message, telling her I had phoned and would be home the rest of the day to take her call.

And I sat there on the sofa, nibbling at my nails, willing the phone to ring. This was the worst. The results were there. They existed. The lab knew, Fidelma Harris knew. But I didn't know.

It was a long half-hour waiting, but eventually she returned my call. I only registered the words, "Great news," but it was enough. It was all I needed to hear.

When I hung up I stood there, a huge grin on my face. It was over, I had no long-lasting effects from the rape. No physical ones, anyway. I could get on with the rest of my life, picking up the pieces. Try to get back to a sex life with Patrick without worrying about infecting him.

And now that the stress of worrying about all that was over, the sick-feeling – which, I now realised was the nausea of dread, should clear up.

But it didn't. It had been going on for ages now, and now that I had ruled out any of the STDs, it was time to find out what was wrong, and get it fixed.

So, one afternoon after school, I went to the doctor.

She listened to my symptoms and her whole face lit up. "Well, my immediate diagnosis is that you're pregnant. When was your last period? Have you done a test? Will we do one now?"

It was like a blow to the chest. Pregnant. But I couldn't be, I had taken the morning-after pill. Although, now that I thought about it, I hadn't had a period since that night. I hadn't realised, hadn't noticed, with so much else going on. But no, that was the stress also.

"Oh, no," I hastened to assure her, "I couldn't be pregnant."

She was puzzled. "How are you so sure? The last time we spoke you were trying to conceive. Would it be so surprising if you're pregnant now?"

Oh God, I thought, I'm going to have to explain.

"Yes, Dr Bourke, I can see why you'd say that. But the situation has, well, let's say it has changed since we last spoke. The fact of the matter is – well, it's like this, I haven't had intercourse with my husband since my last period, so I can't be pregnant from him. However," I went on, breathing deeply, "I do have to tell you that I was raped, last November – "

She whispered, "Oh, God, no!"

I carried on. "But I know I couldn't be pregnant from that, because they gave me the morning-after pill. So whatever else is wrong with me, it can't be pregnancy."

"Oh, Grainne," she said, and there was a world of sympathy and sorrow in her eyes, "Grainne, I have to tell you, the post-coital pill is only 95 per cent effective – did they not tell you that?"

I shook my head, miserably.

"No? Well, I suppose they didn't want to worry you unduly. And that 95 per cent is only if you didn't get sick or have diarrhoea or anything."

"Oh God," I said, "I did get sick, just after taking the first one. The garda was taking my statement, and talking about it made me so upset that I had to go and throw up. But I never thought about the pill. I was all in a heap – my head was all over the place."

"Well," she said heavily, "there is, then, at least a chance that what's making you feel so ill is that you're pregnant. Under the circumstances I hope I'm wrong. I'd love to end up diagnosing some virus that rest and time will cure. However, let's do a pregnancy test, now, and then we'll know what we're dealing with. Here," she said, reaching into her drawer, and handing me a little plastic container, "will you give me a sample now, and we'll do it straight away. You know where the toilet is? Out the door and first on the left."

So I went and wee'd into the bottle, and after washing the outside of it and my hands, thoroughly, I went back into the surgery. She poured a few drops into the depression on a little white square. She said we should know in a minute or two.

There was silence while we waited. Talk about waiting for kettles to boil – this was the longest, most angst-ridden minute of my life. But eventually it ended, and she turned to me. "Well, Grainne," she said, "that's it. You're pregnant. I'm sorry."

I sat stunned. I felt as if I had fallen into an alternative universe, where everything was mixed up, or as if I were watching a film of somebody's life (and boy, what a mess they were making of it!).

"Grainne," she said, after a minute, "we'll need to

decide what we're – you're going to do. You pretty much only have three choices. One is to have the baby and keep it. Two is to have the baby and put it up for adoption. And the third choice is to have an abortion. When was the . . . when did conception occur?

"The third of November last," I said bleakly.

"Okay," she said briskly, taking out some chart and calculating. "Well, that means you're ten weeks pregnant now. You'll need to be making a decision soon, at least about whether or not you'll continue with the pregnancy. But it doesn't need to be now this minute. Do you want to go home and think about it?"

"Yes, yes," I said distractedly, "that's what I'll do."

"Look, are you going to be okay getting home? Will I call a taxi for you? Or Patrick?"

"No, no, I'll be . . . I'll be fine."

And I was, although how I don't know. I don't remember one bit of that journey home.

Chapter 12

When I got into the house I rang Sinead.

"Sinead? Look, I'm sorry, but is there any chance you could come around here now?"

"Grainne? Are you okay? You sound dreadful. Dear God, what's happened? Is it serious?"

"Well," I said, "I'm safe and alive and not hurt, but yes it's serious. I hate to call you out of work, but if at all possible, I need you."

Honestly, I thought, Sinead should get danger money for being my friend these days.

"Hang on," she said, and put me on hold. A couple of minutes later she was back. "Grainne? Look, I can't get away for about an hour. But I'll come around then, okay? Will it wait till then?"

"It will," I said, with grim humour, "it can wait for ages."

"Look, I'll be there as soon as I can, okay? Keep calm in the meantime, bye."

While I waited for her I just sat there. Numb of emotion, but thoughts swirling and ricocheting around inside my head.

A baby. That's what I had wanted. God, I laughed bitterly, it's true what they say: be careful what you ask for – you might get it. I didn't want a baby this way. I didn't want *his* baby. I wanted Patrick's baby. I wanted a baby conceived in love and commitment and passion and fun. Not one conceived in hatred and anger and hurt and abuse of power.

I felt so dirty. Bad enough him having been inside me, but now part of him was still there. It hadn't all been washed away. I was marked now, tainted, forever tattooed by him. But there was one way of washing this final residue of him away. The doctor had mentioned it. Abortion. God, yes, I thought in that moment. Like wiping chalk off a blackboard, leaving it pristine clean. Bringing everything back to where it had been before he'd raped me.

Except . . .

Except that abortion wouldn't make me un-raped. It wouldn't take away the fact of the pregnancy, it would only change the outcome of the pregnancy that was already there. And hadn't I, I told myself, always felt that abortion was not the solution. Hadn't I always believed that human life was sacred, and it wasn't up to any of us to end it. I had never been twenty and single and pregnant, so I had never had the opportunity of testing this principle.

Yet another ironic factor: now I had that chance. Did I live by everything I believed in?

Yes, I decided firmly. Yes, of all players in this drama, the baby was the only innocent. Why should it suffer because its father was a rapist and its mother a naïve fool?

But still, but still. To have to face up to the continued pregnancy. What a nightmare! I'd need to tell Patrick; the ramifications of that didn't bear thinking about. I, who thought I knew him so well, had no idea how he would react. And my job, what about that? And my family.

And the thoughts of living the next, what, six or seven months, with this baby, this interloper, this parasite, growing bigger and bigger inside me. The discomforts you'd bear gladly for a child wanted and conceived in love: heartburn, huge stomach, birth itself – having to do that for *his* child was beyond doing. And having his mark on me, the shame of what he did to me, growing larger and larger for the world to see.

Oh God, everyone would assume it was Patrick's baby – they'd be delighted for me. I'd have to suffer their congratulations. And then if I gave it away for adoption, they'd ask why. The whole world would then know I'd been raped. And yes, yes, I know it wasn't my fault, the shame wasn't mine. But it was.

I didn't want everyone to know about it, to have to explain: Oh yes, I'm pregnant, but please don't offer congratulations – it's not Patrick's child, it's a child of rape, I'm giving it up for adoption as soon as it's born.

My mind cringed from this prospect.

So, abortion. Nobody need know, not even Patrick. Sinead and I could go to London for a weekend as we'd done before – nobody would suspect anything. It would be much simpler.

But was it fair to balance someone else's very life against complications in my own?

No, but did I have any choice?

We always have choices, my conscience told myself.

A whisper said – it's half your baby, half the genes are yours.

Yes, and I'd wanted a baby . . .

But not *this* baby . . .

But this is the baby you have . . .

I don't have it yet . . .

Yes, you do, don't play semantic games!

Would it take after me, or him? Does anybody know why men rape? Is there a rape gene? Would I be bringing another rapist into the world?

Or could I consider this baby to be my triumph, my vindication over him? Yes, I would be saying to him, whether he knew it or not, you used power to do violence to me, and I couldn't stop you. But my victory over you is that I will not stoop to your level, I will not use my power to do violence to this baby. I am better than you. You perpetrated one act of physical violence on me – but you did not change me, you did not make me act in any way that was a reaction to your actions. I am proactive, I give you no power of mine. Yes, you took what you wanted, but that was a moment in time, that is all of me you have. You do not have any more power over me. I will win.

Yeah, right.

The doorbell rang, and Sinead was there. I threw myself into her arms. "Oh, Sinead, Sinead!"

"What is it? Tell me, for God's sake, Grainne, tell me!"

"Oh, Sinead, I just found out I'm pregnant!"

"Oh, sweet Jesus! Oh, Grainne, no, no! But you couldn't be, you took the morning-after pill – I saw you!"

"I know," I said miserably, "but seemingly it's only 95 per cent effective, even if you don't puke up half the dose. Which I did."

"Oh," she said.

"Oh indeed," I said, and started crying. "Oh Sinead, what am I going to do?"

She gathered me into her arms, steered me into the sitting-room and sat us both on the sofa. For some time I cried into her shoulder, relishing her small, soft, perfumed embrace.

At last she asked tactfully, "Have you thought about your options?"

"Well, yes . . . I can have the baby and keep it, have the baby and put it up for adoption, or go to England for an abortion."

"And, well, have you any idea which option seems best? I know you haven't had time to think . . . oh, God, this is terrible!"

"No, no, I haven't decided. Well, I have – on all of them, in turn."

We sat together on the sofa, and she held my hands. "You know I can't decide for you," she said, "or even influence your decision. All I can do is to be a sounding-board for your thoughts, and maybe point out some facts if you seem to have forgotten them."

"Yes, I know. Well, the three options . . . the last one first: abortion. I can't, Sinead. I always believed it was wrong, and I can't change my mind just because it inconveniences me."

She snorted.

"Okay, a lot more than inconveniences me, but still. There's only one totally innocent party in all of this, and that's the baby – why should it suffer?"

"But Grainne, look, I'm not trying to make you do anything, but listen – the baby will suffer anyway. The child of a rapist. Everyone will know. Maybe abortion is the kindest thing for it?"

"Nobody knows. Only you so far. I'll have to tell Patrick later. But if the baby is adopted, it'll never know. It'll never suffer because of the manner of its conception. And if we keep it – who's to say it's not Patrick's baby?"

"But . . . what about the trial? What if it comes up at trial?"

"There's no reason it should! I'm married! That probably makes it legally Patrick's baby – unless he says otherwise . . ."

She looked at me doubtfully.

I continued doggedly. "So I'll carry it and give birth to it. But then what? I don't know, Sinead. I suppose I have time to decide that. On the one hand, I wanted to conceive a baby and now I have. For all I know, Patrick's infertile and this is God's way of getting me what I wanted . . . God moves in mysterious ways and all that . . ."

"Oh yes," said Sinead drily, "a very benign God, to have you conceive like this!"

"Well, maybe it's a kind of a joke on God's behalf. You know, 'You asked for a baby, you didn't specify whose baby, so what are you complaining about?'"

"A sick joke, if it is," she interjected.

"I know, a very sick joke. I didn't want *this* baby, I wanted Patrick's. I don't want be to pregnant with Brogan's child, it growing like a parasite inside me, feeding off me. It makes me sick to think of it. Oh, I know," and I quoted myself, caricaturing myself, "'it's the only innocent party', but I still feel it's like a parasite, like he has put his mark on me, which will grow bigger and bigger for everyone to see. But yet, Sinead, it's half my baby too. Half its genes are mine. How can I hate it so much? I don't think I do – I hope I don't. I just hate the fact of its being. Does that make sense? No, not really, does it?"

She shook her head wordlessly.

"And, Sinead . . . what's Patrick going to say?"

We were both quiet. Although we both knew Patrick for all these years, each very well in our own way, neither of us could even begin to imagine his reaction.

"He probably won't be happy," she ventured at last.

"Of course he won't be happy! I'm not happy. Look, I'll just discuss it with him, see what he says."

150

"That's all you can do. I just don't know, Grainne – your marriage has been through so much already – how will this affect it?"

A good question. And one to which I had no answer.

Later that day, after Sinead and I had cried ourselves and talked ourselves into exhaustion, all without resolving anything, and she had left, I found out.

He came home, coming through the door warily as he did nowadays, not sure what he would find, what mood I would be in. I was in the sitting-room in the winter-evening dark, just sitting. Getting to be a habit, that.

He sat down quietly beside me, asked gently, "What's wrong? More flashbacks?"

"No, I wish it was. Patrick. There's no way to tell you but straight out. I found out today that . . . well, that I'm pregnant."

How often had I day-dreamed of saying those words to him. But in my dreams they had been said with pride, with joy, with love, with excitement. Never had I imagined it like this, saying them in a leaden voice, with dread, with fear, with sadness.

He said, "Oh."

And then there was silence for ages. I felt the tension building, wondering what he was going to say. And still the silence stretched.

In the end I could bear the silence no more. I said: "So, what are you thinking?"

"I don't know," he said, and his voice was emotionless. "I don't know what to think. I don't seem to be feeling anything. This seems like one shock too many. One thing to deal with too many."

With a visible effort he rallied himself enough to ask, "And how are you feeling about it?"

"Dreadful. Absolutely, totally and utterly dreadful. After the rape I tried and tried to wash him out of me, and now it transpires that I didn't succeed. He has left his mark on me. He is continuing to rape me through this pregnancy. I feel sick – both physically, with that 'virus' that I know now was morning sickness, and emotionally. I feel despair. I feel trapped. My mind is going around and around pointlessly, like a hamster-wheel."

He held me tight, and whispered into my hair, "My poor Grainne, so much you're going through! And poor me, too. And poor us – what is this going to do to us?"

And I felt a shiver of fear run through me. I had never thought that this would affect our marriage, our love, our commitment, long-term. It was bad enough that it was having this effect on us now. But it seemed that his words held knowledge, or foresight, that I didn't have. But I didn't have the courage to ask him what he meant, or to pursue that thought.

He said eventually, with a question in his voice, "You'll hardly have an abortion?" Patrick had always felt as I did, and must have known what decision I'd be coming to on that, even if I hadn't known it myself for a while.

I said, "No."

"Well, then. You'll bear the child. And then what?"

"I don't know. There are only two choices. To raise it ourselves. Or to have it adopted."

He kept his voice carefully neutral as he asked, "And which of those two choices are you favouring?"

"I don't know, I honestly don't know. Why, what would you think?"

We were circling each other like fighters, each trying to find out the strength of the other before showing our own position.

"It would be hard for me to raise another man's child. Especially that 'man'," and he sneered the word 'man'. "And would you really want to raise his child?"

"No, I can't imagine raising that man's child. But, Patrick, it's my child too."

He said softly, "But it's not mine."

"Define 'mine'. Is a child yours because you've contributed one sperm? Or is a child yours because you love it and rear it? Adoptive parents raise a child that isn't biologically that of either of the parents."

He said softly, "Yes, but adoptive parents get to make that choice."

I carried on, ignoring this, "And from my side, surely that child is more mine: he only contributed one sperm – my contribution is the egg, plus all the nutrition that grows it until it's born, plus the effort of carrying it, plus all the stuff parents do after it's born."

He muttered, "That's a nice bit of number-crunching – half the genes are still his. And God knows what's in the genes he has contributed."

"Yes, I know," I said dully, "I've thought of that. Tried not to, but still . . . but it's still my baby. Oh God, the situation is impossible."

There was silence for a moment, and then he said carefully, "It sounds as if you've made up your mind to keep it."

"No, I haven't. I'm just thinking aloud. I haven't had time to decide anything – my thoughts are all over the place. I deeply hate and resent the fact that this man has left his child in me, his mark on me. I have no feelings yet for the baby – I can't even believe that it's an actual baby we're talking about. But I *hate* this pregnancy."

"I can't imagine it as a baby either. Well, look," he said, "we're talking ourselves into circles here. We don't need to make up our minds yet. Once we know you're not having an abortion, we have until it's born. Let's just take some time to absorb the news – God, it's such a shock," and he placed his head wearily in his hand. "It seems like there's one blow after another. Maybe, though, you could make enquiries, Grainne, about how adoption works. So we have all the information to make a decision."

I agreed that I would and, in that inconclusive manner, we left it.

Chapter 13

The year limped slowly on. Patrick and I circled each other like polite strangers, each desperate to connect with the other, but unable to do so due to language differences. Each of us was going through a journey that the other couldn't even understand, never mind join in with.

One evening in late March, I was at Sinead's house. We were drinking coffee and chatting desultorily in the kitchen and I was relaxed, enjoying the time together.

"Will you have another cup?" she asked me.

"I'd love one. I'll get it, though – sit there."

"Oh," she laughed, "I'll definitely take you up on that."

I put on the kettle, and then reached into the top cupboard for the coffee jar. As I did so, my jumper must have ridden up, because I heard her say softly, "Grainne, you're starting to show. You have quite a bump there."

"Yes," I said dully, turning to face her but not meeting her eyes, "I know. I felt it kicking for the first time the other day. And it was just as they describe it, just like bubbles popping inside you. And for the first time I really realised that this is a baby, a real person, moving inside me, rather than just a pregnancy. It was wonderful. But at the same time as this realisation, there was the memory in me of Brogan hurting me, and I could see a parallel between that me and his child kicking me . . ."

"Poor, poor Grainne," she soothed, "this is dreadful!"

I came and sat with her at the table again.

"Sinead, what am I going to do? I haven't told anybody about the pregnancy, but I'm five months gone now – people will start noticing, as you just did. What will I say when they congratulate me? I don't think I can bear it. I could tell you the truth, because you knew about the – about Brogan. But what about neighbours, colleagues, the woman in the newsagent's? What am I going to say?"

"Let me think," said Sinead. There was silence for a few moments. Then, "Okay, here's a suggestion. When people congratulate you, why don't you put on a sombre expression, and say something along the lines of 'Thank you for saying that, but unfortunately there are some complications, and we don't know yet what the outcome is going to be – so we can't get excited just yet.'?"

"Brilliant!" I said. "Absolutely brilliant!"

"Well, that would be the truth – people will assume

you mean medical complications, but you haven't said so. And that way, if you come home with the baby, they'll just assume, or you can say, that the complications were resolved. And if you do give the baby up for adoption, people will just see you with no baby, and assume the worst, and, I bet, will be too embarrassed to ask you much, if anything, about it."

"Honestly, Sinead, you are amazing! You have no idea what a relief that is to me! Okay, I still have all the other issues, but this is one issue solved. Thank you, thank you!" I threw my arms around her, and she modestly insisted that it was nothing, that these strokes of genius were her normal lot.

* * *

The spring passed, and we moved into summer. I was going through the motions of daily life now and you'd never think, by looking at me, with my public face on me, that anything had ever happened to me.

There were good days, and better days, and bad days and worse days. On good days I could sometimes go hours without remembering the rape, until something would remind me, and then I would feel a wave of distress and fear all over again. On better days I would go those same hours without thinking of it, and even when something reminded me, I could pass it off.

On bad days everything seemed to remind me, it was pretty constantly in my mind, and I was down, depressed, weepy, short with people.

And on worse days I wouldn't even want to get out

of bed – in fact, literally wouldn't get out of bed if I could help it. I was overwhelmed by all the bad emotions: fear, stress, anger, fury, frustration, guilt.

But those worse days were appearing with decreasing frequency.

As this time passed, however, we headed inexorably towards two occasions: the trial, and the birth of the baby.

I was still seeing Fiona from the Rape Crisis Centre. As the trial neared, she said one day that we should speak about it, to prepare me.

"It's like this," she said softly. "The State is the prosecutor, not you. You're only a witness for the State."

I nodded. Ger Reilly had told me this.

Fiona went on, "For most rapes, there are no witnesses, so it comes down to her word against his. And it all hangs on who the jury believes. So in a strange sort of a way, you're on trial too, but without the benefit of a solicitor representing you. At least they can't ask you about your previous sexual history any more – they used to be able to do that – to try to make the victim out to be a slut. We haven't come far, but at least we've come that far. At least," she amended, "they can't automatically. If they want to, they'll have to request specific permission from the judge. And the judge can grant this request, or deny it, without explaining his or her reasoning."

"Oh no! Because if they do ask me about my previous sexual history, I'm in trouble. Because, although I've only ever had two lovers, which isn't much by today's standards, I did go to bed with a man on first meeting him. That man was Patrick, and I married him. But I can just hear a defence solicitor sneering at me that I wasn't married to him at the time!"

"That's a tough one," agreed Fiona. "It's ironic, because we know that Brogan's going to perjure himself every which way, since he's denying rape and swearing it was consensual. But yet, you are faced with the option of perjuring yourself on a minor detail, one which is not relevant even though they would try to make it so; or else, be honourable, tell the truth as you're swearing to, but maybe make people think that you make a habit of one-night stands. Which of course, even if you do, is totally your business. We'll have to hope that the judge doesn't allow this line of questioning."

"God, yes," I said strongly

"Do you remember me telling you, on our first session, that rape is about power, not about lust?"

I nodded.

"The problem is, though, that most people don't know this. They think it's about lust, about sexuality, maybe even about teasing. They might think that maybe the woman brought it on herself, maybe by wearing 'indecent' clothes, or dancing suggestively. The old 'she was asking for it' argument. So, although psychologists and such-like do know that it's all about men and their power issues, there is still a perception out there that it's about us women, and our behaviour.

And you have no idea what kind of attitudes the jury will be bringing with them."

My heart was sinking as I listened.

"The problem is, also," Fiona continued gently, "that the idea of date-rape, or acquaintance-rape as it's more properly known – which is the kind of rape in your situation – is only slowly being accepted in the public psyche. A lot of people still believe, without thinking about it, that stranger rape is the only kind, the 'attack you on the street and pull you behind bushes' kind of rape. And maybe some people on the jury will feel like that. The final problem is that, again, most people's perceptions of rapists are of bedraggled, foaming-at-the-mouth, unwashed, raincoat-wearing madmen. They don't realise that rapists come in all sorts. So they might have a problem with the fact that this guy – a 'nice, well-dressed, professional etc.' man – could possibly be a rapist."

"You're scaring me now."

She nodded. "I know. I'm sorry. But I want you to be prepared. It's good that you are a 'respectable' woman, from a 'respectable' family, with a professional-class husband. This will all stand to you. If the defence is claiming that it was consensual, and the jury is old-fashioned or prejudiced, then they will be expecting to see some sort of slapper, to fit neatly in with their prejudices. And you are patently not that."

"So what you're saying is, it's all about perceptions. Nothing at all to do with facts, or truth, or justice. Just an obscene beauty contest – which of us fits better the image of what we're claiming. Whether he's looking like a 'good' man, or I'm looking like a 'good' woman?"

"It could be like that, yes. I'm giving you the worst-case scenario. You could have highly educated people on the jury, people who do know a bit better. It's an absolute lottery with a jury."

I was very depressed after this particular conversation. But I knew Fiona was right – better to be aware of it before the trial than during.

Chapter 14

I was, of course, growing bigger and bigger with my pregnancy. People began to notice. It was kind of funny, actually, seeing them wondering, "Is she?", but not daring to ask in case I wasn't pregnant, just fat.

But after a while there was no confusing it: I was definitely pregnant. And so people began to comment.

"Er, have you good news then?" they might ask, gesturing vaguely towards my tummy. Or, "Are congratulations in order?"

And I took Sinead's advice and told them, "If you mean, am I pregnant, then the answer's yes, I am. But we aren't sure whether it's good news because," here my voice would drop to a whisper, and my listener would lean forward, agog, "there are complications." And just as she had predicted, people immediately became seriously embarrassed, and changed the subject with greater or lesser subtlety. Which suited me just fine.

As my pregnancy progressed my feelings about the

baby remained ambivalent. Sometimes in the early mornings, while I was still half-asleep, I would find myself affectionately rubbing my stomach as the baby kicked, with a half-smile on my face. But during the day the constant presence of the baby, the constant reminder of Brogan, was hard. I didn't know whether to love this baby, in anticipation of keeping it, or whether to hate it as Brogan's child, or whether to remain remote from feelings towards it, just carry it, (grin and) bear it and send it on to a new life.

I don't think that Patrick had any ambivalence at all. He never said anything much about it, and his face was carefully inscrutable as he looked at me and even that fact alone made it clear what he felt, but he never ever touched me, even in the most casual way, and once or twice I caught him looking at me when he didn't know I could see him, and his face was twisted with a mixture of hurt, pain and disgust.

The one thing he did say to me was, "Did you ever contact the adoption agency?"

He knew I hadn't, of course, but this was his gentle way of reminding me.

"No," I said, "I was going to. I will. I just haven't got around to it yet."

He nodded neutrally.

Okay, okay, I'd better, I told myself.

I got the number from the Fiona, and one day after school, before Patrick was home, I rang.

"Hello, Irish Adoption Agency, can I help you?" said a warm voice.

The words stuck in my throat and I said nothing.

"Hello? Hello?" said the voice. "Can you hear me?"

"I'd like to make enquiries about adoption," I said, and my voice was croaking, and it hurt me to speak.

"Grand, what would you like to know? We can talk over the phone, or if you are considering putting a baby up for adoption, we could arrange an appointment for you to come in and meet a counsellor – we usually find that that's the best."

"Okay, an appointment, please."

"Fine, when would suit you?" I could hear pages turning in the background.

We agreed a time and a date, and when the appropriate time came I was standing on the pavement outside the building. My heart was pounding, my palms were sweating. I really, really did not want to do this.

'Oh,' I asked my subconscious, 'does this mean that you know you want to keep the baby, then?'

'No idea,' was the answer I got back. 'I just don't want to go in there, and talk to yet another counsellor, and go through the story with yet one more person. And maybe there's something about not wanting to face up to adoption, yes.'

'Well,' I told it briskly, 'this is only a fact-finding mission, it doesn't commit us to anything."

And I forced myself to push open the door, and walk through.

"Hello," said the receptionist, young, pretty, looked like she didn't have a care in the world. She quickly glanced at the appointment book. "Are you Grainne Quinn? Agatha Cullen is ready to see you – would you like to come this way?"

I found myself sitting in another tastefully-but-innocuously decorated room, with another jug of water and another box of tissues, and another empathetic woman sitting across from me.

She had a form, and a pen, and once we got the basic questions regarding name and address and stuff out of the way, she paused.

"So, you're expecting a baby?"

I know she was only saying it to get the topic rolling, but I found myself thinking, 'No shit, Sherlock. A bit bleedin' obvious, that one, seeing as I've got a bump that arrives half an hour before the rest of me.'

But I just said, meekly, "Yes."

"And you're looking for information on putting the baby up for adoption after it's born?"

"Yes. No. I mean, yes, I'm looking for information. But I'm not sure about whether or not I'll be putting the baby up for adoption. I'm very mixed up, you see."

At which point my voice broke and cracked, and tears started rolling down my cheeks and I reached for the first tissue. Not bad, that, the first tissue when I'd only been in there five minutes.

But she was smiling at me, sympathetically, empathetically, kindly.

"I'm sure you're mixed up – it's an extremely mixed-up time. Having a crisis pregnancy, I mean. On the one hand, whatever reasons you have for considering adoption are there, are valid. But on the other hand, this is your baby, and you're carrying it, and the thoughts of giving it up are hard. Would any of that sound right?"

Sobbing, I nodded. And then, between spasms of sobbing, and sniffles and sniffs, I told her my story.

There was silence for a moment after I'd finished; silence, that is, apart from my trailing-off hiccups of sobs.

"Oh dear," she said finally, "you really have a dilemma, don't you? Well, needless to say, we can't make up your mind for you, or even try to influence your decision. But what we can offer is twofold: information, and someone to talk to. We offer counselling sessions, every couple of weeks or so – or however often suits you – talking through the emotional implications of having a baby adopted, going through your options, things like that. We also offer post-adoption counselling: you don't just give up your baby and be left in limbo."

"How does it work," I asked, "the whole logistics of adoption?"

"There's a social worker in each hospital, with whom we work. And when you decide you are pretty sure about placing the baby for adoption, you'll talk to her. You stay with the baby for as long as you're both in hospital – a couple of days barring complications – and then the social worker will take the baby to a foster-home. We always invite the mother to go with them: we find that it helps her to see where the baby is going to be staying, to meet the foster-mother. Okay?"

I nodded dumbly.

"Now, the baby will stay with the foster-mother for a minimum of six weeks, and then the birth mother will sign the consent to place for adoption. If she – you – are unsure at that stage, you can leave the baby with the foster-mother for longer, and sign the consent form when you feel ready. At the stage that the consent form is signed we'll start matching with adoptive parents. The birth mother is given details of the adoptive couple: ages, general area in which they live, profession, things like that. There's actually several different kinds of adoption. Closed adoption is the traditional kind, where all contact is severed between birth mother and baby. Semi-open is where the adoptive parents will send letters and photos every so often – probably twice a year – so the birth mother can see how the baby is coming on. And open adoption is where the birth mother can actually see the baby, again, maybe twice a year."

My head was reeling at this stage.

"Having said that, Grainne, I have to tell you that if you give a baby up for adoption, you are signing all rights over to the adoptive parents, and this agreement of letters or visits is not legally binding, and can be rescinded by the adoptive couple whenever they want; say for example, if they decide to emigrate. But we find that these agreements are most often honoured – they do work well."

She sat back.

All I could think to say was, "Oh."

"Oh, one more thing," she said, "since you and your husband are married, the baby will automatically be considered a child of the marriage. So, if you want to have the baby adopted, you'll both have to sign affidavits, in which you both swear that your husband is not the father. So, what do you think? Have you any questions about what I've said?"

"I'm more confused than ever," I told her. "Can I go home, and think about it?"

"Of course – you can do whatever you want. You have our telephone number, and you can contact us whenever you want. If you've any more questions, or you want to arrange some of the counselling sessions, call us."

She rose to her feet and I did likewise.

"Thank you for your time," I said. "You've given me plenty to think about. It's reassuring to know how much support there is for birth mothers – I guess, without thinking about it, I had this image that you were just left to your own devices. I'll talk to my husband, and be in touch with you."

"Great. I look forward to hearing from you."

Honestly, it could have been any business meeting. I was just short of telling her that I'd get my secretary to arrange a date with her secretary.

When Patrick got home that evening I told him, "I went to see the adoption agency today."

"Oh, great," he said, and he tried unsuccessfully to hide the delight in his voice. "How did it go?"

"Grand," I said, and my voice was carefully neutral.

"I certainly got a lot of information. But the main thing is, we don't have to decide until after the baby's born."

"That's good," he said neutrally. "How are you feeling about it now? What do you think you'll want to do?"

"I still don't know. Or, at least, I do know. I want to keep it *and* not keep it. I want to keep *my* baby and give away Brogan's; and that impossibility is sending me slowly mad. I don't think I'll be able to decide finally until I see it."

"I see," he said, equally neutrally.

I was going to ask him how he felt about it, but I didn't. I was very aware that I didn't want to know the answer.

I realised, with a heaviness within me, just how far Patrick and I had drifted apart.

* * *

Time was passing, the trial was coming closer and closer. This trial: I was dreading it, totally, gut-wrenchingly, head-swimmingly dreading it. Dreading telling the whole story in public, making it a matter of public record. But yet I was looking forward to it, looking forward to telling the truth, to putting on record exactly what this man had done to me, and seeing him go down for it.

And I was seriously looking forward to having it over and done with.

The end of June came, and the school holidays. I said goodbye to the children, wished them a wonderful summer. (They were probably going to have a less complicated summer than I was. Or maybe not – who knows what's going on in other people's lives?)

I spoke to the school principal, Sandra Maloney. "The baby is due about the 5th of July. And I just don't know what I'm going to do about coming back to work. When do I have to let you know?"

"Well, obviously you'll have your statutory maternity leave," she told me, "and that would be added onto the end of the school holidays just as it is for anyone else. But, as you know, you're entitled to five years' unpaid leave of absence, to be taken in whatever combination you choose. Now, you're supposed to have booked it long since, but if you can let me know by, say, the end of July, I'll stick my neck out and organise it."

"Thanks, Sandra," I said, thinking for the umpteenth time how lucky I was to have her for a boss.

So, school was finished, and with it the distraction from the worry about the trial and the forthcoming birth.

And a few days after that I got a phone call.

"Hello, my name is Sean O'Malley. I'm the Prosecutor for the State on your case. I wonder could we meet? To discuss the case, you know."

"Sure," I said.

So, we arranged a time and a place, and at the appointed date I went into the city centre, and met him.

He was kind, he was gentle, he was confident. He looked about seventeen, although he must have been more than that. Put it this way, he was a real advertisement for clean living.

170

He said, "We're going to win this case. This guy is going to be convicted as a man who raped you, and is going to be sent away for some years – depending on the judge – for doing this to you."

This is what I needed to hear.

"Tell me the whole story," he said.

And I did. Finally, I said, "The most important thing to tell you is that the gardaí interviewed a friend of mine who was there on the night. And it seems that when I was saying goodbye to her and my other friends, Brogan was standing behind me. I didn't know he was there – he must have followed me after I said goodbye to him. But she saw him, and she said something along the lines of was I off for a night of passion with him. And I didn't hear her, and I just nodded and laughed in what I thought was a fairly non-committal way – you know, as you do, so that no matter what she'd said, it would answer it. Well, it did answer her. More than I'd thought."

He nodded. "Yes, the gardaí told me this. So when I'm questioning you, I'll bring this up. I'll ask you about it, and you tell me about it, and when the defence later bring up this point, we'll already have answered it. We'll have to hope it's enough. To be honest, your explanation is totally plausible. I can really see how it happened. And it seems a lot, to hang a whole acquittal on this chance comment. Not that it would have mattered if you *had* gone off with him – rape is rape regardless. But certainly we need to get the jury to see how it could have been an innocent misunderstanding;

that you're not lying in contradiction of her story. I don't see it being a problem, but we'll definitely make sure to mention it, in a pre-emptive strike."

He told me a little bit about procedure, and then we shook hands, said goodbye, and told each other we'd meet again on the day of the trial.

And days passed, as they do. And time passed, as it does. And soon it was the night before the trial was due to begin. And then, after a sleepless night, the morning came.

Chapter 15

I dressed in a simple navy pinafore maternity dress with white blouse underneath. I couldn't have looked more nun-like if I'd worn a wimple – well, apart from the eight-month-pregnant belly.

In the run-up to the trial I had avoided dwelling on the fact that this would be the first Brogan would learn of my pregnancy. I had shrugged the thought aside – there was nothing to be done about it and in any case Brogan would surely assume the baby was Patrick's, would surely assume I had taken the morning-after pill or, if that failed, had an abortion. But now, I was not so sure . . .

I pushed the thought away from me and concentrated on the mirror. It's all about image, I told myself as I smoothed my hair neatly back, and put on the merest hint of blusher and light pink lipstick: it's all about looking like a good, well-behaved woman, the sort who'd never pick up a man in a nightclub.

Patrick knocked on the bedroom door.

"Be with you now," I called.

I came out, and he reached out both his hands. I took them both in mine. I felt a surge of shock, nearly like an electric shock, at the feel of his large, warm, hands on mine; it was so long since we'd touched each other even in such a superficial way.

"Come on," he said, "come on. It's time to go."

We drove into the city centre in silence, drove up to the courthouse. He managed to find parking, we got out. Walked up the steps.

Inside, it was all so confusing. People were rushing everywhere, all of them looking as if they knew exactly what they were doing, where they were going. There were smartly dressed be-suited people, people in long black cloaks and those white wigs, and people in torn jeans and greasy hair. There were gardaí everywhere, some of them escorting handcuffed prisoners.

We located a reception area, and went to it. Explained what we were looking for. The receptionist consulted a book, then said, "Oh, yes, court number 3. Down that corridor there, third door on the left."

We followed the directions. Patrick opened the door for me, I walked in. And stopped dead as if I'd walked into a wall. Sitting there was Brogan. He looked up and smirked at me. He was surrounded by people: family and friends, I surmised. One older woman who looked very like him – his mother, I thought – glared at me with a distilled fury.

Brogan looked wonderful. I wanted him to have

horns, and a tail and a smell of brimstone. But he looked great. He was wearing a well-cut grey suit, a pristine white shirt, and a discreet tie. His hair looked recently cut, sharp and black. His dark high-cheekboned handsomeness matched with a healthy wholesomeness which shouted 'Respectable!'. I realised with a shock that this was exactly the look that had taken me in. How could it not confuse the jury?

Patrick banged into me from behind, not having anticipated my sudden stand-still.

"What's wrong?" he whispered in my ear.

I shrugged, moved forward into the room. Patrick followed me, and also stopped when he saw Brogan. He had, of course, seen my portrait of him.

"Come on over here," said Patrick roughly, and guided me to a couple of chairs at the far side of the room.

We sat sideways on the chairs, so that we faced each other, rather than facing across the room to Brogan's faction.

But even so, I could half-see, half-feel, Brogan staring at my pregnant belly. And I knew he was bound to be speculating, perhaps counting months . . . I thought: I hate this, I hate him wondering if he fathered a child on me, if his effect on me went that far. I gave a mental shrug, more noncholant than I really felt: there's nothing I can do about what he thinks.

But suddenly I felt a surge of strength. Look, I thought triumphantly, look well! You might wonder if this is your child, but you'll never know! Live the rest of your life wondering whether there's a child of yours living, that you can't ever know or see!

Having said all that, the triumph was short-lived, as I realised I still had to go through this trial, still had to stand up and put into the public record all that he had done to me, still had to see him convicted and going to prison.

Stephen and Richard arrived. Richard always worked evenings, and of course Stephen, being the self-employed sculptor that he was, could work his own hours, so it was great that they could support me this first day at least.

Stephen whispered, "Sinead's here too. But she's not allowed be with us because she's a witness. She said to wish you the best of luck, and she would see you later."

And I felt warmed, and cherished by all their support.

After some endless time a door at the far side of the room opened, and a young man called us into the courtroom.

I waddled into the courtroom with my head held high, no matter that I felt like crawling under the nearest chair. Assuming I could have fitted, of course . . .

The courtroom was smaller than I expected. A little bit seedy, run-down. I think all I knew of court cases was based on American TV programmes, and I had subconsciously expected it to look like those.

The judge, Sean O'Malley the prosecutor, and a sharply-dressed, sharp-featured woman whom I assumed to be the defence lawyer were speaking together, and broke off as we came in. She looked extremely intimidating, very tall – perhaps six feet, with a brisk air and an I-mean-business attitude. They obviously knew each other well – I had the realisation that they had more in common with each other than with any of us, no matter whose side they were temporarily on. Cases, and the people whose lives they changed, came and went, but drinks in The Quill and Ink went on forever.

I took my seat, with my supporters, in the body of the courtroom.

Brogan and his cohorts took their seats at the far side of the room from me. The room was quite small, but it was crowded, and this meant that he seemed safely away from me.

Sean O'Malley approached me. I was reminded again at how well he came across: very ambitious, very enthusiastic, and very, very confidence-inspiring. Needless to say, I'd hoped all along that Brogan would be convicted, but now a kind of certainty hit me. I thought, we'll win this trial. Brogan will go to prison for a long time.

"Good news," Sean said. "The judge has ruled that you may not be asked any questions about your previous sexual history."

When I heard this I felt a lightening of my shoulders.

The jury filed into the room. I looked at them anxiously. There were five men and seven women. Surprisingly, most of them were older than average. Not too good for me, I thought – they might not approve of a married woman going out to a 'dance-hall' without her husband.

I said to Sean, "How come they're all older? I thought the jury service was done at random, to get a cross-selection of people."

"It is," he said wearily, "but people of working ages often get letters saying that they can't come for jury service, their job is essential or some such."

No matter about their age, they all looked like ordinary, decent people, sitting forward intently, obviously taking their duty seriously and wanting to do their job properly. None of them looked like people who would believe men couldn't help themselves and a woman was automatically a tart. But then, neither did they look like PhDs in psychology who could spot a rapist at fifty paces.

What did either of those kinds of people look like anyway, I asked myself impatiently.

After some time the judge banged her gavel, and everyone in the courtroom silenced themselves, and looked at her. She sat there on her podium, in the cloak and white wig, looking like everyone's idea of a grandmother. Little Red Riding Hood's grandmother. *After* the wolf had visited.

The indictment of rape was read out to Brogan, and he was asked how he pleaded.

"Not guilty, your honour," he said easily and confidently.

Then she spoke to the jury.

'Hello. My name is Maura Martin, and I'll be your judge for today.' Needless to say, she didn't say that, but my irreverent mind heard that. God, my irreverence is going to get me into trouble one of these days, I thought, but hey, what am I saying, I'm already in trouble! I've been raped, and I'm pregnant from it, my marriage is in ruins – how much more in trouble can I be in?

She said, "I would like to introduce you to our prosecuting counsel, Sean O'Malley."

And he got to his feet and acknowledged the jury.

The judge continued: "This means that he's in charge of putting the State's case. His job is to persuade you that the defendant did, in fact, do what he's accused of. And this is Mary Connolly."

The sharp-faced woman was on her feet now.

"She is representing the accused, and her job is to persuade you that the accused is totally innocent of what he's charged with. My job is to keep control of the proceedings, and at the end of the trial, to sum up for you, and to give you instruction on points of law, which you will be obliged to follow. It's your job to decide on the facts of the case: in other words, what actually happened. But don't worry about that now, we'll cover that at the time. For now, just listen, and take notes. If you have any questions during the trial, or anything that needs clarification, please let me know and I'll sort it out. Okay, over to you, Mr O'Malley."

Sean stood. He seemed relaxed, informal. As informal, anyway, as someone can be in an archaic outfit of long cloak and white wig. He smiled at the jury, some of them smiled back, a little nervously.

"Ladies and Gentlemen of the Jury, may I begin by

thanking you all, and I know I speak for Judge Martin, and for Ms Connolly also, for being here, for fulfilling your civic duty to provide fair trial to one of your fellow citizens. You have a very, very important job, the most important job in this courtroom."

The *plamas* seemed to be working: you could see them sit up a bit straighter, stick their chests proudly out.

"This job, ladies and gentlemen, is to decide on the guilt, or otherwise, of Mr Brogan."

Some of them deflated slightly at this reminder.

"My esteemed colleague's job," and he nodded politely in the direction of Mary Connolly who nodded politely back in acknowledgement, "is, as Judge Martin has said, to convince you that Mr Brogan is not guilty. And my job," he paused and smiled again, "is to place the facts before you so that when you go to the jury room to begin your deliberations, you will know that Mr Brogan did, in fact, commit the crime with which he's charged. And that crime, ladies and gentlemen, let us not forget, was the brutal rape of a young woman."

He paused and gave them a moment to digest that.

"The facts are as follows," he continued, "and we will prove each one during the course of the trial. This young woman was out for an innocent night's fun with her friends, had one chaste dance with a man in a nightclub, then said goodbye and left him, and headed for home. But he followed her, inveigled his way into getting a lift with her, and then took advantage of her kindness to brutally rape her in the hallway of her house."

Right on, I though. Succinct, but accurate.

But then the defence gave her opening statement, and her slant on things was frighteningly plausible.

She said, "My colleague speaks of a nightclub as a place where Ms Quinn went for innocent fun. I think we all know that nightclubs are not so much about innocent fun as they are about meeting people of the opposite sex. In many cases, nightclubs are resources for promiscuity and drugs. In fact, if it's innocent fun you're looking for, you're better off at the bingo hall."

There was light laughter at this, quickly quashed by the judge's glare around the courtroom, but Connolly gave a small satisfied grin at the effect of her little joke.

She continued, "We have a young man in his prime, who's offered a sexual encounter by a woman. Yes, he knew she was married, but she told him her husband was away. Was it honourable of him to take up this offer? Perhaps not – even though *he* is single, *he* was not committing adultery, or being unfaithful. But lack of chivalry is not a crime in this State, or any State. And it's understandable. We were all young once."

She smiled in complicity at the jury, and they smiled back – everyone, it seemed, fondly remembering their passionate youths. Hardly, I thought bitterly, you'd all have been young in the 1940's and 50's, before sex was ever invented in Ireland.

"It was not rape, and we will prove it. It was consensual sex – er –" it looked like some of the jurors were getting confused by the big words, because she went on, "that is, this night of passion was wanted by both of them – especially, since she suggested it, Ms Quinn."

When she had finished her opening statements Judge Martin said, "We'll adjourn for lunch now."

Surprised, I looked at my watch. Hard to believe it, but over two hours had gone, and it was now half past twelve.

Judge Martin said, "We'll begin again at a quarter past two."

It was difficult, passing Brogan and his cohorts as we filed out of the courtroom. There were thinly hidden smirks, and whispered comments to each other followed by submerged sniggers. Again, I could almost physically feel Brogan's eyes on my pregnant belly, could feel his speculation. In the run-up to the trial I had avoided dwelling on this aspect, had shrugged it off – there was nothing to be done about it and he would never know if the child was his or Patrick's . . .

We piled into this grotty local pub, and hit the mineral water hard. We ordered a mediocre lunch. Or rather, we didn't order a mediocre lunch, we ordered lunch and when it came, it was mediocre. I was glad, I couldn't begin to eat, and it would have been a shame to waste good food.

We were back in the courtroom for the designated time.

When we all got settled and had quietened down, Sean O'Malley said, "The State calls Dr Miranda Lynch."

Dr Lynch took the stand, and gave her credentials as a doctor at the Rotunda's Sexual Assault Unit.

Sean O'Malley, through a series of questions, took

her through the events of the night. She described how I had been brought in, giving all the appearances of someone in shock, how she had examined me, and collected swabs, and that the DNA evidence proved that it was Darren Brogan's.

"So," said O'Malley, "you have said in your report that there were internal lacerations."

"There were."

"And would they be consistent with enforced sexual contact?"

"They would indeed," she said warmly.

"And the bruising of her breasts?"

"That indicates rough treatment, also indicative of enforced contact."

"And the bruising on her hips?"

"That doesn't have a sexual context, of course," she said, "but my opinion is that those bruises occurred at the same time as the other bruising."

"And these photographs here," he waved them, "do you testify that these are the pictures taken of Ms Quinn at the time?"

"May I see them?"

He handed them to her, and she said, "Yes. My signature, along with the patient's name and the date, are on them."

Sean O'Malley said to the judge, "Your Honour, the State requests that these photographs be entered into evidence and shown to the jury."

"Any objection?" the judge asked Mary Connolly. She nonchalantly waved a go-ahead gesture.

And so the photographs were shown to the jury, and my face burned at the thought of them looking at pictures of my naked breast, my naked hip.

Sean O'Malley turned back to Dr Lynch.

"So, in your professional, expert opinion, the presenting condition of Ms Quinn was entirely consistent with her having been raped."

"Entirely," said Dr Lynch emphatically. We were left in no doubt as to her opinion of what had happened.

Sean O'Malley said to Mary Connolly, "Your witness."

Mary Connolly said pleasantly, "Dr Lynch, are those internal lacerations also consistent with rough consensual sex?"

Dr Lynch hesitated, and eventually said with obvious reluctance, "Yes, yes they could be. But it's far more likely –"

"Thank you, Dr Lynch," interrupted Mary Connolly swiftly. "It is, I think, the job of the jury to decide the likelihood of the different interpretations of the evidence. Now, let me ask you again, so as we all have it straight, are those internal lacerations *also* consistent with, shall we say, robust consensual intercourse?"

"Yes. Yes, they are."

"Thank you. And the bruised breast. That could have been caused by the same thing: enthusiastic sex?"

"Yes," Dr Lynch answered shortly.

"And, as you said yourself, the bruised hip could have come from any cause. All you know is that it dated from around the same time as the other bruising. Is this all correct?"

"Yes."

"Thank you. No further questions."

Sergeant Reilly and then Garda Moore came to the stand, and told how they had received the call, and come to my house, brought me to the hospital, and after my examination, had taken my statement. They detailed the fact that they'd taken statements from various people. Sean O'Malley didn't want them to read out the statements – he said that he would be talking to most of those people directly. The gardaí also told us about the incident being featured on *Crimeline*, and how Mr Brogan had come into a garda station within half an hour, and identified himself as the person featured on the programme.

Judge Martin then adjourned proceedings for the day.

We wandered out into the street, feeling a bit aimless, as though we'd been turfed out in the middle of a play or film.

We went home and ate, after a fashion, a meal which was lovingly cooked by Fusciardi's Take-Away. Went to bed early, slept, and got up the next day, washed, dressed, headed for the courts. Sat down, and waited to resume proceedings.

Sean O'Malley said, "The State calls Grainne Quinn."

This was me. Shaking, I stood up, and walked up to the top of the courtroom, turned to face the crowd. My experience with amateur dramatics had me used to the ice-cold fear that you feel before going on stage, but that was nothing compared to this dread. I really thought I would wet myself with terror. (Mind you, when you're eight and a half months pregnant, and the baby's bouncing around on your bladder, you tend to feel like you're going to wet yourself anyway.)

I swore to tell the truth, the whole truth, and nothing but the truth.

Sean O'Malley said to me, kindly and gently, "Ms Quinn, could you please describe to us the events of the 3rd of November last?"

I said, "My husband was away on business. And some friends invited me to go out with them, and I did. We went to a couple of pubs in the city centre, and then, when the bars closed, we went on to Coronation nightclub. My friends were dancing with different men, and I was at the bar by myself. And then a man, who I now know is Mr Brogan, the accused, asked me to dance. And I did. I had one, chaste, arms-length dance with him. And then I decided I wanted to go home. I said to him, shouted at him really, because it was so noisy in there, that I was going to go home, and I told him it was nice to have met him, and I said goodbye. I went off, back to my friends. I shouted at them, too, that I was going home. One of them, Margaret Dolan, said something to me, which I couldn't hear, so I just half-laughed and half-nodded in what I hoped was a response non-committal enough to cover whatever she'd said. This is important because I've since learned that she saw Mr Brogan standing behind me, looking as if he was with me, and she'd made some reference to me being off for a night of passion with him, and I had nodded to that. But," I said, putting it as sincerely and earnestly as I could, "I'm saying this under oath, and I swear that not only did I not know Mr Brogan was behind me, but that I never heard what she said to me."

I paused, took a deep breath, and then with a shaking hand took a drink of water from a glass that was thoughtfully placed nearby.

"Go on," said Sean O'Malley, gently, encouragingly.

"Well, I got my coat back from the cloakroom, and left the nightclub. Just outside I heard someone say something to me, and I turned and it was Mr Brogan. We were both going towards St Stephen's Green, so we fell into step. He said he'd walk with me to keep me safe," I said bitterly, "which is pretty ironic, and I feel pretty stupid about actually being grateful to him at the time."

"Your Honour," called out Mary Connolly in a bored voice, "could you please direct the witness to refrain from commentating – what we need from her is the facts."

The judge directed her gaze onto me, and said, "She's right, you know. Just tell us what happened, not what you feel about it."

I nodded. I continued my evidence, explaining to the court how he'd managed to convince me that he was Hannah Murray's cousin, and on foot of that I offered him a lift home, and how he'd managed to persuade me to drive to my house, so he knew where I lived, and then conned me into opening the front door for him.

"And then," I said, my voice shaking, "he raped me."

I stopped, and took a deep shuddering breath, and a delaying-tactic drink of water.

Sean O'Malley said, in the softest, kindest tones possible, "And could you tell us a little bit about that? What forms of coercion did he use?"

Oh God, this was worse than I'd ever imagined – and we hadn't even got onto the cross-examination yet.

"He was telling me that we were going to have sex, and I was telling him that no, we weren't. At first I thought maybe I could reason with him, but when I realised that I couldn't, I grabbed the phone, to try to ring for help. That was when he got violent and pulled my head right back by the hair."

I started crying, and the judge said to me gently, "Do you want to take a break?"

I shook my head, said to her, "I just want to get this bit over with."

She nodded sympathetically, but she also said, "I'm going to have to insist that you speak clearly, even though you're crying. Otherwise the court stenographer, and indeed the jury, mightn't be able to hear what you're saying. Okay?"

I nodded tearfully, and continued, being careful to articulate properly. "He told me to get undressed, and when I wouldn't he pulled my hair again. It was agony, I couldn't even think straight. Later when I was still resisting he twisted my – well, my nipple, and that was worse. And he threatened to burn my nipple. And the final thing, the thing that made me give in completely, was when he took a cigarette-lighter from his pocket, flicked it on, and walked towards me with it. He didn't say anything then, and he didn't actually burn me, but what he was doing, the look on his face, was so intimidating, the fear was literally overwhelming.

"Oh, another thing he did, he told me that he was going to have sex with me, that the only choice I had was how quickly and easily it would happen, and how much pain I would have to go through before it happened. That terrified me – I think that that helped wear away my resistance, the thought that I was only delaying the inevitable, that it might be better just to get it over with."

I looked at the jury then, briefly, and their faces were images of pity and horror. They seemed to be caught up in imagining what I was saying.

"No further questions," said Sean O'Malley quietly,

Mary Connolly jumped to her feet and began speaking immediately. "Ms Quinn – let's examine –" It seemed to me that she wanted to interrupt the moment, not to give the jury time to think too much about what I'd said.

But Judge Martin banged her gavel, and said we'd adjourn until after lunch.

Chapter 16

And after lunch I was called back to the stand, and reminded that I was still under oath.

Mary Connolly stood up. She started pacing, restlessly.

"Ms Quinn," she said abruptly, "let's go back over this 'story' of yours." And the emphasis she put on the word 'story' was very slight, too slight for Sean O'Malley or the judge to object, but it was there, and it used the word in the context of a work of fiction.

"You say that you went out on the night in question with some friends of yours, because your husband was away?"

"Yes."

"Are you in the habit of going out on the town, picking up men, the minute your husband's back is turned?"

"It wasn't a case of going out behind my husband's back. His being away was an issue only because I was at a loose end without him. I would go on a girl's-night out every so often, even when he's in Dublin. I wouldn't call it a habit, but neither is it unusual. And I don't pick up men, as you phrase it – I have never so much as kissed a man, apart from social kisses to the cheek, since my marriage."

"You say you don't pick up men," and her voice was incredulous, "and yet you admit to having danced with my client?"

"I'm telling you, and the court, as I've told everyone since it happened, that I danced with Mr Brogan. I'm not admitting it, in the sense of something shameful, something otherwise hidden."

So far I was answering her, holding my own, but the barrage of intensive, aggressive, scornful questioning was tiring. It was beginning to wear me down, erode my strength.

"So, if we're to believe your story, you had one 'chaste' dance with my client, and then, like Cinderella, you left for home."

"That's what happened, yes."

"And he followed you out of the nightclub?"

"Yes," I said miserably.

"And you're telling us that you walked off with this man, a total stranger, and gave him a lift home?"

Her incredulity-o-meter was off the scale at this stage. Put this way, my story did sound ridiculous. I could see the jury thought so too, all the former pity smoothed away from their faces.

"No," I said. "Look –"

But she interrupted.

"Ms Quinn, you said in your direct evidence, your sworn testimony, that you walked together to St Stephen's Green and you gave him a lift home. Are you now trying to say that that isn't so?"

"Yes. I mean no. I'm sorry, I'm going to –" and I started crying.

She waited patiently, but with the patience of one who's sorely tried, who's making a big point of being so patient. The courtroom was silent, except for the sound of my crying. Eventually I pulled myself together, took another drink of water, and said, "Yes, it did happen that I walked to my car with him, and gave him a lift. But not like that, in one decision. When I was walking with him, that was all I intended to do. There were enough other people around for me to feel safe with him, and he was helping me feel safe from any attack from anyone else. At this stage we were just two people whose paths were going the same way. Then, as we walked, I began to trust him more, especially when I found out, as I thought, that he knew Hannah Murray. I think that was the factor that made me feel safe enough to offer him a lift."

"Hmmm," she said disbelievingly. Then, "Okay, this lift: why did you drive to your house, and not his? Usually when Person A gives Person B a lift home, it's usually Person B's home that is referred to."

I thought: you really are one snide bitch! And I glanced over at where Patrick was sitting. He was watching, listening intently, his face sombre. Sinead, Stephen and Richard too looked as though they were listening with every fibre of their being.

"Because he wanted it that way – he said he wanted to make sure that I got safely home."

"Does it make sense to you that someone would take a lift to avoid having to stand in the rain, and then arrange to have to walk home in that self-same rain?"

"I didn't really think about it, I wasn't looking for holes in his story. But I suppose I thought that he felt a five or ten-minute walk would be preferable to a couple of hours waiting for a taxi."

She stopped, paused for a moment. Then: "Ms Quinn, nobody but you and my client will ever know what exactly went on in your house that night. But I put it to you, Ms Quinn, that given the absurdities in the story you're telling us, the huge inconsistencies in it, that your whole story is a total fabrication, and that therefore it's reasonable to assume that what happened in your house was not as you've told it. That in fact, Ms Quinn, to put it bluntly, you've made the whole thing up, and that all my client is guilty of is taking you at your word, at accepting some sex when it was offered but that he is not, I repeat *not*, guilty of rape."

I was shaking my head in confusion, in bewilderment.

"No," I said, "no. It all happened exactly as I've told you."

"Hmm," she said disbelievingly. "No further questions."

* * *

When we left the court I collapsed into the car seat and sat, shaking uncontrollably and so, so cold, tears rolling down my cheeks from the stress of what I'd been through.

Patrick got into the driver's seat, and turned to me, and the others crouched before the open door, and they all spoke over each other:

"It's over, Grainne, you'll never have to do it again."

"Grainne, that defence is totally preposterous – nobody, absolutely nobody could believe it – don't worry about it."

"Grainne, you were wonderful, you came across so well, so believable!"

And I just sat numbly, their words and the fact that they cared enough to say them comforting me, but the despair and the trauma of the day's events still washing over me.

Eventually we said goodbye to the others, and Patrick drove me home.

"How do you think it's going?" I asked.

"I don't know, I really don't. I think you did very well, but it's not up to me, is it? Oh, my poor love," and he reached over and squeezed my hand where it lay on my leg.

Although it was only about six o'clock when we got home, I went straight to bed.

Patrick brought me up a bowl of mushroom soup. As I drank it he said wearily, "One way or another, it'll all be over soon."

And I thought that no matter the outcome of the trial, it would never be over. And there was still the issue of the baby hanging over us.

But I just said, "Yes, yes, it will."

When I had finished the soup I lay back gratefully onto the pillows, and fell asleep.

And slept right through until the next morning – when it was time to get up, wash and dress, and go back and face the whole process again.

Sinead took the stand the next day and, in answer to questions from Sean O'Malley, described how she got the call from me, and had come over to find me, dressing-gowned and shaking; how I'd told her I had been raped, and she'd organised calling the gardaí and hence bringing me to hospital; how she'd stayed with me during the time in the hospital, and had stayed with me that night; how she'd given me the morning-after pill at the appropriate time the next day. How upset and traumatised I was.

Mary Connolly got up and surveyed her pleasantly for a moment.

"Ms Harking, you said in evidence that Ms Quinn was very upset on the phone, when she rang you."

"Yes," said Sinead pleasantly, "that's right."

"How could you tell?"

"She was crying. I could hear her crying. And kind of gasping when she was talking."

"And you said that when you arrived she was shaking."

"Yes, shaking, hugging and holding herself, rocking back and forth. Her face was tear-streaked."

"Hmm . . . I see," said Mary Connolly, still pleasantly. "Tell me, Ms Harking, am I correct in saying that Ms Quinn is involved in amateur dramatics?"

Shit, how did they find that out, I thought? Is there

anything about me that they don't know? And I could see where this was going.

"She is."

"And would you say that she's a good actress?"

"She's quite good, yes. But only as an amateur actress. She wouldn't be able to make it as a professional actress, she wouldn't be good enough for that. She knows that herself."

"But she could have been acting that evening, playing the part of somebody upset."

"In theory, she could," agreed Sinead. "In theory, anybody could be acting at any time. But I know Grainne for many, many years, and I know she couldn't take me in. I'd see through her in a minute. No, Ms Connolly, Grainne was genuinely distraught and distressed on that night."

Way to go, Sinead, I thought, delighted. You're well able for her.

"Indeed," said Ms Connolly. "Ms Harking, you've said that you know Ms Quinn for many years. Would you describe yourself as being friends?"

"Yes, we are very good friends."

"So you would not like her to lose this case?"

"Indeed I would not, since she is telling the truth. And, Ms Connolly, I don't know if this is what you're suggesting, but I can assure you that I would not perjure myself for anybody, even Grainne."

"Indeed," said Mary Connolly dismissively. Then: "No further questions."

And I took great pleasure in the slight frown on her face.

Chapter 17

Sean O'Malley said, "The State calls Derek Mooney."

A young man whom I didn't recognise stood up, went to the front of the court, and was sworn in.

Sean O'Malley said, "Will you state your name and occupation for the record?"

"My name is Derek Mooney, and I'm a nightclub doorman."

Ah right, now I recognised him.

"And you work, where?"

"At Coronation Nightclub."

"And were you in the employ of Coronation Nightclub on the 3rd of November last year?"

"I was."

"And were you on duty on the evening of the same 3rd of November?"

"I was."

"And do you remember seeing this woman," and he pointed towards me, "on that night?"

"I do."

Sean O'Malley said, "Let the record show that Mr Mooney identified Ms Quinn as being in the Coronation Nightclub on the night of the 3rd of November." He turned back to the witness. "And do you remember seeing this man," and he pointed to Brogan, "on that night?"

"I do."

Sean O'Malley said, "Let the record show that Mr Mooney identified Mr Brogan as being in the Coronation Nightclub on the night of the 3rd of November." Then, he said, "Can you tell the court, please, the situation in which you saw these two people."

"I was standing at the door – it was fairly quiet as most of the people who wanted to be in the club had already arrived, and it was too early for the club to close, so not that many people were leaving. This woman, Ms Quinn, came out on her own. She spoke to me for a moment, something about what it was like to stand there in the lobby when everyone else was having fun, and I said something along the lines of that I didn't mind, it was nice and peaceful. I distinctly remember that because there are very few people who will actually talk to you, unless they're trying to persuade you to let them in. She went down the steps, and began to walk down the street. But she had only gone a few yards when a gentleman – who I now know to be Mr Brogan – came out of the club, quite quickly. He pushed past me, and went straight down the steps, and came up behind Ms Quinn. I presume Mr Brogan must have said something –"

"Objection," called out Ms Connolly, "the witness is here to give us facts, not surmises."

"Sustained," said the judge. "That means that you, Mr Mooney, must only tell us what you saw or heard, not what you think happened."

"Okay," he said. "Well, I definitely saw Mr Brogan go up behind Ms Quinn. Then she turned around to face him and she said something to him. I couldn't hear what it was, but I could see her mouth moving. Then she turned back, and he fell into step beside her, and they walked off. I didn't see them any more after that."

"Thank you," said O'Malley. "So, they did not, in any sense, leave the nightclub together?"

"No. But they did walk down the street together, talking together."

"But your evidence is that Ms Quinn left first, and then Mr Brogan a few moments after that, and that they encountered each other on the street outside the club."

"It is."

Mary Connolly declined to cross-examine.

And that, it seemed, concluded the prosecution case. It was now the turn of the defence – after lunch, as per instructions from Judge Martin.

Sean O'Malley had told me that the defence had the absolute choice of whether or not to have Brogan testify. The theory was, he told me, that the defence had nothing to prove, that they don't have to prove the innocence of the accused, the burden of proof being on the prosecution. Therefore they might just concentrate on picking holes in the prosecution case, and not have the accused testify. If this was the case the judge would direct the jury that they were not to read any implications into the fact that the accused didn't testify.

On the other hand, the defence might, if they felt their client would come across well and help his case, have him give evidence; it was a judgement call for them.

However, once lunch was over and we were back in the saddle again, Mary Connolly said, in her crisp, clear voice, "The defence calls Darren Brogan."

And Brogan took the stand.

God help us, but he looked so respectable. Anybody looking at him would never believe he was capable of doing what he'd done.

He was sworn in, and was asked to give his name, and occupation.

"Darren Brogan, consultant."

Mary Connolly asked him to describe the evening in his own words.

"Well," he said, "I went out on the night in question with two of my friends: Sam Maher and John O'Hara. We went to Coronation – it's a new nightclub. John and Sam quickly picked up birds – er, women, met women, and I didn't see any more of them for the evening.

"I saw this pretty girl, who I now know to be Ms Quinn. I asked her to dance, and we danced. And well," he stopped, and blushing prettily, went on, "well, I don't know how to say it, she was very . . . interested in me." He stopped, apparently embarrassed.

That embarrassment's way overdone, I thought – carry on like that and you'll fool nobody.

"And could you tell the court which form this interest in you took?" asked Ms Connolly.

"Okay, if you say so." He cleared his throat (no doubt having read somewhere that throat-clearing was a sign of nervousness). "Well, she was, well, rubbing herself against me, and pressing herself hard against me. And I, well, I suppose I was enjoying it, and it was, well, I mean, obvious that I was enjoying it. If you know what I mean. And she was aware of – my – it being obvious that I was enjoying it, and she whispered to me, in my ear, that she'd like me to go home with her, and we could dance some more, in privacy. Well, I knew what she meant, and I was all for it. I mean," he said virtuously, "I'd much rather have a steady girlfriend, settle down, you know, I don't really like all this one-night-stand stuff, but I didn't have a girlfriend at the time, and, well . . ." he ran out of steam with a helpless shrug and a bashful smile.

"Go on, Mr Brogan."

"So I said I'd love to. And she said to me that she was married, and Sod's Law someone would see us leaving together. So she suggested that we leave the nightclub separately, and meet again outside. Which is what we did. Oh, yes. First she went to say goodbye to her friends, and we left after that. We arrived back at her house, and we went in, and we, well, we had sex . . ." Another shy, bashful smile.

Surely, I thought, the jury weren't taking any of this

on board, it was so obviously phoney? I glanced over at them, but their faces were impassive and it was impossible to tell what they were thinking. Beside me I could see Patrick, his mouth a thin line and his hands clenched in fists.

Ms Connolly spoke. "And how would you characterise this sex?"

"What do you mean?"

"Was it slow, and tender, or . . .?"

"Oh, right. I get you now. No, it was fast and furious. Quite rough, really. We were both so hot for each other, we just went for it. She kept asking me to give it to her really rough, said something along the lines of – she could get tender any time from her husband, she wanted something different. So I can see how the doctor said there were little internal injuries. I felt dreadful when I heard it, knowing that I'd hurt her, even a little, even though it was all happening at her instigation. After that I got up, and got dressed. I asked her for her phone number, but she said that no, we couldn't see each other again, that her husband would be back the next day. I felt a bit used, to be honest," he smiled self-deprecatingly, "but I suppose that's what women have felt for years, and it's about time it's our turn."

Nice touch, I thought begrudgingly.

"And that was it. I thought no more about it – well, I thought about her, but I knew I wouldn't be able to see her again – but – well, until a week or so later, I saw my face on the telly, on *Crimeline*." Huge indignation came into his voice then. "I mean, I couldn't believe it – my face on *Crimeline*! I was horrified! I was scared too, to be honest. And it was so obvious it was me, I mean, my colleagues and friends and family – everyone would recognise me! So I went immediately to my local garda station, to try and sort it out. I never thought it would come to this," he waved his arm around the courtroom, "but here we are. And all I can do is to tell the truth. And the truth is that we did have sex, but that it was entirely consensual."

"Your witness," said Mary Connolly to Sean O'Malley.

"If I may, I would like to reserve my cross-examination of this witness."

The judge and defence counsel agreed to this.

Mary Connolly then said, "The defence calls Margaret Dolan."

Margaret came up, visibly nervous, and was sworn in.

"Now, Ms Dolan, can you tell the court what happened in Coronation Nightclub on the occasion of Ms Quinn saying goodbye to you, and leaving you."

She sent me an anguished look. "She came up to us, and she said that she was going home now, and said goodbye to us." She stopped abruptly.

"And . . . ?" prompted Mary Connolly.

"And there was a man behind her, Mr Brogan, standing just at her shoulder. He was smiling at us, and kind of jerked his head sideways a little, to indicate Grainne, and smiled again. And I said to her, 'Oh, you've obviously got lucky then! Off for a night of passion?' And she gave a laugh, and nodded and said yes." She looked over at me again, an apology in her eyes.

"Thank you. No further questions. Your witness."

Sean O'Malley got to his feet. "Ms Dolan," he said kindly. "Did you actually hear Ms Quinn say goodbye?"

"Yes, I did."

"Think back, try to picture yourself there. Now, you obviously understood her to be saying goodbye, as indeed she was. But did you actually hear her – with your ears?"

"Oh, right!" Her face brightened with understanding. She thought for a second, then said, "No, I didn't hear her. The music was too loud to hear her. I could read her lips, and she was kind of miming it as well – she pointed to herself, and then to the door, and then raised her hand in a goodbye gesture."

"So it is very possible that she didn't actually hear what you had said either? That what Ms Quinn herself has said happened: that she didn't hear you, and was trying to give a non-committal answer? It's entirely possible that this is true?"

"Objection!" Mary Connolly was on her feet, "Your honour, this calls for speculation on behalf of the witness."

"Sustained," said the judge.

But I saw a tiny twitch of the lips on Sean O'Malley's face, and realised that he hadn't needed to hear Mag's answer, that he had got what he wanted out of the exchange, that the jury would hear this equally plausible explanation.

"Now, you've also said that Mr Brogan was standing right behind her."

"And a little to one side – yes."

"Was he the only person standing behind her."

"Of course not." Margaret looked at him as if he was stupid. "It's a nightclub! It was packed, there were people everywhere."

"And in Coronation Nightclub that night, with so many people, is it possible that someone might jostle you?"

"More than possible! It happens all the time, you wouldn't really even register it."

"So, anybody could be behind you, even touch you slightly, and you wouldn't take any notice?"

"That's right."

"Now, can you cast your mind back, Ms Dolan, and tell us to which side of Ms Quinn Mr Brogan was standing?"

She thought about it. "Her left side. That is, to the right of her as we were looking at her."

"And in which direction did Ms Quinn turn when she turned to leave?"

"To her right, our left. That's because the exit was that direction, from where we were standing."

"And what did Mr Brogan do then?"

"He waved goodbye to us, and turned and followed right behind her. I couldn't see them for long – they got swallowed up by the crowd."

"Has Ms Quinn ever gone off with a man she'd picked up, at any other time before?"

"No, she hasn't. I suppose it's with her being married and all."

"Thank you very much, Ms Dolan."

Judge Martin said, "We'll adjourn for the evening. Be back here at ten o'clock tomorrow morning."

We were.

Sean O'Malley said, "I would like to recall Mr Brogan to the stand, please."

Brogan went to the stand.

"Mr Brogan, may I remind you that you are still on oath?"

"Yes," said Brogan pleasantly, "yes, I understand that."

"I just have a few questions for you, regarding your testimony."

Brogan shifted a little bit uncomfortably. This, of course, was the downside for the accused giving their evidence: they were opening themselves to cross-examination.

"Mr Brogan, you claim no rape took place on the night in question. If that were so, *why* in your opinion did Ms Quinn call the gardaí and the Rape Crisis Centre that night?"

To my dismay, Brogan's face cleared a little. "I have no idea, " he said easily. "I've been trying to figure that one out myself and I've thought of all kinds of possible reasons, some of them fairly twisted."

Clearly this wasn't the response Sean had expected. "Thank you, Mr Brogan – " he began.

But Brogan cut across him. "I mean, women sometimes do make false accusations. Who knows what's in her head? Maybe she hates men? Maybe she's trying to punish her husband for something?"

My heart sank as I realised he had been primed to answer such a question. Sean O'Malley had erred by asking it and giving him the opportunity to air these speculations. And from the lengthening of Sean's face as he listened, it was clear he realised he had blundered. I looked at the jury. They were listening intently. Mary Connolly was looking smug.

Brogan was continuing. "Maybe her friend arrived unexpectedly and found her undressed and all that and she had to make a story up in case the friend told the husband? Maybe –"

"Yes, yes, Mr Brogan," Sean cut in, risking a reprimand from the judge, "we could come up with a hundred far-fetched theories, but the fact remains that Ms Quinn had no reasonable motive whatsoever to lie about the rape. And, as there was no previous relationship between you and Ms Quinn, there can be no question of a personal vendetta."

This last statement, of course, was what he had intended to elicit from his questioning of Brogan. But now he was hurrying on to safer ground.

"To return to your testimony: you say that Ms Quinn was rubbing herself against you in the nightclub?"

"Yes, that's right."

"But you have no proof of that? Nobody else saw her do this?"

"Well, no, the nightclub was dark. And crowded. But I felt it alright."

A brief, quickly suppressed snigger went through the courtroom.

"But she says that she didn't, so that it's only your word against hers. Right?"

"Yes."

Sean had by now recovered his equilibrium and was moving forward confidently in this line of questioning. "You say that she invited you home?"

"Yes. She did."

"But again, nobody heard her say this?"

"No, the music in the nightclub was very loud."

"Well, then, how did you hear her?"

"She whispered it into my ear."

"Oh really? How could you hear a whisper with all this noise?"

"What I meant was, she shouted in my ear – she had to, because the place was so noisy. But in comparison it was a whisper, because it was right in my ear and it was designed for only me to hear."

"Really," Sean said, his voice rich with derision, "that's what you *meant* as distinct from what you *said*."

"Yes, yes, it was."

"And how many other of your statements, I wonder, were not what you *meant*?"

"None of them."

"Indeed. Now, Mr Brogan, you say that you left the nightclub separately for discretion's sake?"

"Yes."

"Well, why, then, did you go with her when she was saying goodbye to her friends?"

This floored Brogan completely. He sat with his mouth opening and closing for a few seconds, doing a very credible impersonation of a goldfish. Then: "No, no, you see, it was like this: she said that the friends she was with wouldn't mind, that they were used to one or other of them going home with some guy, and that nobody would tell her husband. It was someone else – I mean, she was worried that someone else who knew her would see us leaving together, someone she didn't even know was at the club."

"Oh, I see," said Sean , his voice dripping sarcasm. "Here we have another thing that you *said*, that you didn't *mean*."

"I'm sorry?" said Brogan, confused.

"You *said* that Ms Quinn didn't want anybody seeing you together, but now we know that you *meant* that she didn't want anybody other than her friends to see you. Is that correct?"

"Yes."

"Another thing: when you saw the incident on *Crimeline*, you went straight to the gardaí."

"Yes," he said virtuously. "I needed to clear my name."

"Very commendable of you," said Sean dryly. "And would you say that this would contribute to proving your innocence: that you'd hardly have given yourself up if you were guilty?"

"Yes," said Brogan firmly. "Surely someone guilty wouldn't have given themselves up – not when nobody actually knew who I was."

"Well, a guilty person might do exactly that, as a double-bluff to 'prove' their innocence. However, leaving that aside, I'd like to draw your attention to something else you said in your evidence," and he made a show of consulting his notes, "'*And it was so obvious it was me, I mean, my colleagues and friends and family – everyone would recognise me.*'"

"What?"

"Do you not remember saying that? I can have the stenographer read it back to you if you like?"

"No, that won't be necessary. I do remember. That is what I said."

"Well, then, Mr Brogan, I put it to you that you had no choice about coming forward. The likeness of you was so good that it was only a matter of time before someone else identified you. In fact, I've checked with the gardaí, and they got seventeen calls identifying you as the man in the picture. I put it to you that in coming forward so quickly, you were simply making a virtue out of a necessity, and that in fact your coming forward has absolutely no implications for proving your so-called innocence!"

Brogan did his goldfish impression again.

"By the way," said Sean, "when you're claiming that Ms Quinn was asking for rough sex, are you also going to tell us that she asked you manhandle her breasts?"

"No, she didn't."

"Oh, right, you did that to her free, gratis and for nothing?"

Brogan paused, obviously thinking carefully, "No, I mean that when she asked for rough sex, I assumed that she would like that as well. She didn't object when I did it, or I would have stopped."

"Oh, come on!" said Sean. Then: "I have no further questions."

I felt hugely cheered after this. Sean had recovered beautifully from the disastrous opening question about my lack of motive and it seemed to me that Brogan had tripped himself up badly and was caught out on several lies. Surely the jury would realise this, realise that his whole story was pure fiction?

Chapter 18

Sean O'Malley got up to make his closing statements.

"Ladies and gentlemen," he said to the jury, "first of all I'd like to thank you all very much for your concentration during this trial. You have a hard decision to make, but a simple one. It is this: did a rape take place, or did consensual sex take place? Do you believe Ms Quinn, or Mr Brogan? Judge Martin may well tell you that that you do not have to convict – to find Mr Brogan guilty – on Ms Quinn's uncorroborated evidence. In other words, if there was no other evidence to support her story, if it was literally her word against his, you would not have to convict. But you could. Compare the two stories. And bear in mind that you do not have to *know* that Mr Brogan raped her – you just have to be sure beyond reasonable doubt."

He paused and let his eyes sweep over the jury. "Or, isn't it totally plausible, totally reasonable that it happened exactly as Ms Quinn has said. That Mr Brogan asked her to dance, that he followed her out of the nightclub, and she walked with him to her car, as you'd fall into step with anyone. But during this walk he managed, in classic con man style, to gain her confidence, to convince her that they knew people in common. And therefore she grew to trust him, and offered him a lift. Doesn't all this make sense, without having to undergo any mental gymnastics? And he managed, ironically by telling her that he wanted to see her safely home, to convince her to drive to her house. And then he conned his way into the house, and raped her. Intimidated her in various ways, including threatening to burn her. You can see this happening. It's plausible, it's believable." He paused and then said clearly, slowly, "Beyond reasonable doubt.

So, even if this was all we had to go on, we could convict. But we do have corroborating evidence. We have the vaginal lacerations which are a matter of fact; this has been accepted by the defence. How they were caused is what's in question. Yes, these can be caused by very rough sex, but they are also a classic symptom of rape.

"We do have the physical evidence of Ms Quinn's bruises. That's a matter of fact. Oh, I know," he said wearily, "that Mr Brogan is denying this, is saying that Ms Quinn wanted this kind of treatment, but, back on Planet Earth –"

"Mr O'Malley!" snapped Judge Martin

"Sorry, Your Honour," he said, and to the jury, "Sorry. It's just that this whole scenario is so crazy. One other piece of evidence corroborates Ms Quinn's statement. And that is that of Mr Mooney, the bouncer – sorry, doorman – of the Coronation Nightclub. He has told us that Ms Quinn and Mr Brogan actually left the nightclub separately. He has confirmed Ms Quinn's statement. Again, I know that Mr Brogan has come up with some sort of explanation for this, but it's nonsensical. He has even contradicted himself, in evidence, about this explanation. So, I submit to you, even without corroborating evidence, the logical step would be to find Mr Brogan guilty of rape. And when you add the corroborating evidence to that – well, there's no question – you will decide to convict, decide to make this man pay the price for his vicious abuse of this woman. And you have to ask yourself this: if the sex was totally consensual, why on earth did Ms Quinn call it rape, put herself through the ordeal of the hospital, gardaí interviews – indeed, this trial? What would have been the point? Isn't it much more likely that the reason she did this is because she, quite rightly, wanted justice for the horrible, perverted wrong which was done to her? Thank you."

And he sat down.

I felt so buoyed up. It seemed to make so much sense. Surely the jury would see this too?

But then, after lunch, Mary Connolly stood up to make her closing statement.

"My esteemed colleague has asked you why Ms Quinn would have accused my client of rape when it hadn't happened. I don't know. I'm sure you don't know. But you don't have to. Innocent men accused of rape are acquitted all the time, so obviously some women do this. Mr O'Malley would have you believe that the very fact that Ms Quinn said she was raped means that she was. That is not so. If that were the case we wouldn't bother taking up your valuable time with trials at all, we would just throw the accused man in prison. You are all intelligent people, you don't need me to point out the inconsistency of that argument."

They obviously did need it, the way she was over-emphasising the point.

But I was now very uneasy. She had chosen to grasp the thorny question of motive vigorously. It was a good move on her part.

"In order to convict, you don't even have to consider *why* she did what she did. You only have to consider *what* she did. Which is to accuse an innocent man of rape. Mr O'Malley has said that there is plenty of evidence with which to convict my client. This is absurd, as I will now show you. We have presented indisputable evidence that Ms Quinn knew that Mr Brogan and she were leaving the nightclub together. We have presented a witness – an actual friend of Ms Quinn's – who said to her that she, Ms Quinn, had 'scored' and was heading for a night of passion – and Ms Quinn said yes. Oh I know, Mr O'Malley tried some sleight of hand to try to persuade us that Ms Quinn didn't actually hear this, and answered a question she hadn't heard. Well, it's up to you, as the jury, to decide on the veracity – er, the truthfulness – of that statement, but I suggest to you that there is at the very least, reasonable doubt – which, as my esteemed colleague has told you, is the standard which you are to apply – that Ms Quinn would go around answering questions that she hadn't heard. I would suggest to you, that there is, at the very least, reasonable doubt that it's just coincidence that – on the very same night as her friend and herself had this disputed conversation about whether Ms Quinn had struck lucky and was off for a night of passion – that on that night, this so-called 'rape' happened. O'Malley has argued that Mr Brogan's version of events and Ms Quinn's version of events are equally plausible. Okay, okay – for a moment let's assume that they are. Even if they are, as Judge Martin will tell you, if there's an *equal* choice, you *have* to give the benefit of the doubt to the accused. But they are not equal." She paused dramatically. "I tell you – well, you don't need me to tell you, you are intelligent people as I have said – that the balance of evidence is totally on Mr Brogan's side. Ms Quinn agreed to dance with him – this is not in dispute. She left the nightclub with him. Again, this is proven by her friend's evidence. And yes, the bouncer's evidence showed that my client was a couple of seconds behind her, but that has been explained to us. Ms Quinn did not show surprise when Mr Brogan approached her. Again, that fact is not disputed by anyone. Ms Quinn did offer my client a lift. Again, this evidence is not in dispute. And I ask you," she leaned confidentially forward, towards the jury, "does anybody, in this day and age, offer lifts to total strangers?"

Oh, God, I swear, several of the jurors shook their heads.

"Exactly," she said, pleased. "Ms Quinn would have us believe that she, in all innocence, in all generosity and kindness, offered Mr Brogan a lift home, just as friends, even though he was a total stranger, with no suggestion of sexual encounter between them . . . well . . ."

Her face expressed enough derision to sink a battleship. The jury obviously agreed with her. At that exact moment, at least.

"And, as I've said, nobody except the two parties involved will ever know, with an absolute certainty, what happened in that house that night. But, knowing, as we do, what happened before they got that far, well, can any one of us doubt – reasonably doubt – that consensual sex took place? Ladies and Gentlemen of the Jury, given the evidence, there is reasonable doubt, and to spare, that Mr Brogan raped Ms Quinn. You *must* find him innocent."

Oh shit, oh shit! As confident as I was when Sean O'Malley was speaking, as sure as I was then that his – my – point of view was the only reasonable one, after hearing Ms Connolly speak it seemed that her version of events could be equally plausible.

Judge Martin then spoke to the jury.

"This is my summation," she said. "This is the bit where I, after sitting quietly for so long, get to shine."

She smiled at the jury at this, and several of them smiled back at her, appreciating the lightening of the atmosphere.

Glad you find it funny, lads, I thought, this is my life you're talking about.

"The first thing to tell you is that the burden of proof that a crime has been committed is on the State. So you are to decide if the State has proven, beyond reasonable doubt, that Mr Brogan did rape Ms Quinn. Now, what does reasonable doubt mean? It means doubt that any reasonable person would hold. And you're all reasonable people, right?"

She grinned at them, and there was slight laughter back.

"Also, as you've already been told, it is my job to tell you that you have no obligation to take Ms Quinn's uncorroborated evidence as fact. In cases where you have two totally contradictory stories, there's no way that you can *know* what has happened. Do take what both parties said, in their testimony, into account when reaching your decision. But a large part of your deliberations must concentrate on the corroborating evidence: in other words, the testimony that came from the other witnesses. Also, I would like to direct you that you are to read nothing into the fact that Ms Quinn offered a lift to Mr Brogan. Rape is forced sexual contact, there are no contributing factors. In other words, if, and I stress *if*, Ms Quinn did not consent to sexual contact, then that it so. The fact that she gave Mr Brogan a lift is totally irrelevant. You will now be taken to the jury room, to begin your deliberations. I need an unanimous decision from you. Take as much time as you need. If you need anything, ask the court official who will be there, just outside the room."

The jury got up and went out.

And the waiting began.

It seemed so strange, to be sitting there, knowing that a bunch of strangers were debating the most intimate details of my life, trying to decide the truth of the case. The tension was palpable. I felt a churning sickness in my stomach. We just sat there, and waited. Twelve o'clock came and went. One o'clock. Two o'clock. Three o'clock.

At about four thirty the judge called the jury back into the room.

"Are you near reaching a verdict?" she asked them.

"No, Your Honour," answered their spokesperson.

"Okay, then what I'm going to do is to direct that you be taken to a hotel for the night. You are not to discuss the case further with each other; nor are you to watch news on the television or read newspapers. This sounds harsh," she acknowledged, "but it's to make sure that you'll be able to continue debating based only on the information you've heard in this court of law, not on something else you might have picked up. Does that make sense?"

They nodded.

"Okay, for the same reason, don't talk to anybody else except the court official who'll be with you. You'll communicate with others, such as restaurant waiters, through him. He'll take names and phone numbers of your relatives, and phone them to let them know what's happening." She smiled at them and said, "And do enjoy your unexpected holiday. It's rare to get the government to pay for anything, let alone a night in a hotel. Relish it!"

They laughed, and filed out.

The judge turned to the rest of us then, her convivial manner totally wiped off her face, and said, "Please be back here at ten o'clock tomorrow morning."

And we were.

And we waited for more hours. Waited all day, in fact.

I kept saying to Patrick, "What can be taking them so long?" He could only shrug helplessly.

As on the previous day, the judge called the jury back at four thirty, and asked them if they were near reaching a verdict. This time, it seemed, they were.

"Okay," the judge decided, "we'll just keep going then, if that's okay with you, and try and get this thing wrapped up this evening."

The jury were pleased with this, probably looking forward to going home, back to their own lives. I wondered how strong the temptation would be, in that jury room, to say, "Come on, guys, let's just toss a coin, and we'll have time to hit the pub!"

At last the word came: the jury had reached a verdict. The tension, already high, now reached screaming pitch.

The jury filed back into the courtroom. The judge asked them if they had reached a decision agreed upon by all of them. The foreman said that they had. None of the jury would meet anybody's eyes. There were no clues forthcoming.

"And how to you find the accused, Darren Brogan – guilty, or not guilty?"

I concentrated very hard on the foreman, willing him to say guilty.

"Not guilty."

I heard suppressed cheers from the defence side of the court, with Brogan raising his arm in a victory salute to his friends in the visitors' gallery, a huge grin on his face.

Patrick said, "Oh, my poor love!" and took my hand, and held it hard.

I just sat, stunned. Sean O'Malley began gathering up his paperwork. He was probably disappointed, but on a professional basis. One loss on his scorecard. Not another wave in the total upheaval of his life.

I put a shaking hand on his arm. "Can we appeal?" I asked urgently. "This is so unfair – he's getting away scot-free with raping me!"

His eyes shone with sympathy for me as he shook his head. "No, one of the basic rights of our justice system is that nobody can be tried for the same crime twice. The only way would be if the judge ran the trial improperly – if, for instance, she had forgotten to tell the jury they weren't to take into account the fact you gave him a lift. But she ran this trial perfectly. Or, he could be tried again if new evidence were found."

"But there must be something I can do!" I protested.

"Well, the only other option you have is to take a civil suit against him. That's what happened after the OJ Simpson trial – the relatives took him to a civil court.

It's much easier to get a result as the burden of proof is much less. But the only thing you can ask for in a civil suit is damages. Money, in other words. He still wouldn't go to jail. And if you lost, you would bear all the costs. It could bankrupt you."

My shoulders sank. I didn't want his money. I wanted public acknowledgement of what he had done to me, and him behind bars.

Patrick then put his arm around my shoulders, pulled me tight to him, whispering, "I'm so sorry, I'm so sorry."

As we all left the court Brogan approached us, strutting. He said to Patrick, "Not much of a shag, your wife!"

Patrick clenched his fists, and went for him, and I'd never seen such fury, such hate, as I did in his eyes, as he went for the man who'd raped his wife, impregnated her, basically fucked up our lives.

I thought, yes! Get him, beat him to a pulp!

But before he reached him, before he could land even the first blow, Stephen had grabbed him, and ad was shouting, "Patrick, no!". But Patrick was stil! moving, his fury more powerful than Stephen's strength and Sinead's voice. And then two security staff rushed towards him too and grabbed him, and between them and Stephen they stopped him, encircled him, telling him, "No Patrick!" and from the security staff, "No, sir, you can't."

Patrick, thwarted, started shouting at Brogan, and they weren't compliments. "Let me at him!" he demanded of the security guards and Stephen, trying to push their arms away. "I'll kill him, I'll fucking kill him!"

But the men held him tighter. "It's for your own sake, mate," said one. "I'd like nothing better than to see him get his – the word is that he did do it. But listen, if you hit him, he'll sue you for assault, no doubt about it. That might be even what he wants, goading you. And you don't want to be in prison, do you, with him free? You'll be no use to your wife then, will you, mate?"

The words eventually penetrated Patrick's fury, and he calmed a little. He shouted, though, at Brogan, "Call yourself a real man! At least a real man doesn't need to use force to get laid!"

Brogan smiled beatifically from across the hall. "But I didn't. The law of the land says that I didn't," and he grinned gloatingly, triumphantly at Patrick before turning and leaving the courthouse.

The security staff released Patrick then. "Sorry," one of them told him, "but we had to stop you."

I turned to Patrick, saying "Oh Patrick, I'm so sorry, so sorry," over and over again, and he patted my back, saying, "It's not your fault."

At last Patrick calmed, and said, "Come on home now," and we all walked out of the court and down the steps. At least Brogan and his cohorts had disappeared. Probably gone to celebrate in some pub, I thought bitterly. There'd be no celebrating for me. At the bottom of the steps Sinead and Stephen hugged me, and their voices rained down on me like gentle rain, "Look, don't feel bad about the verdict, it wasn't your fault, the jury weren't there on that night, you were a great witness," they told me. They both promised to ring soon, and went towards their own cars, with my calls of thanks following them.

I stood, irresolute, outside the courthouse. The day was a true summer's day, the sort of day we Irish wait all summer for, the sort of day about which we say later, "Do you remember last summer – it was on a Thursday?". Even though it was now heading towards evening, there was still a delicious warmth in the air. I looked around, trying to take it all in. It seemed like so much of my life, for so long – forever it seemed – had been focused on this court case, and seeing Brogan sent to jail. And now it was over. Not as we'd hoped. But it was over. And it was on to the next stage of my life.

Although the pregnancy had been, of course, a huge factor the previous few months, somehow I hadn't really had to face it yet. I was pregnant, there was a baby growing inside me, I had to decide what to do. First, the court case. But now – now the time to think about the baby and our decision was next.

In two weeks, the baby would be here, I thought. Then what?

I stood rooted to the ground. It seemed, somehow, that if I didn't move, time wouldn't move either. That the next stage of my life wouldn't happen. That I'd never give birth to this baby, never have to decide on its – his or her – fate. That I'd never have to deal with the repercussions of Brogan's acquittal. Never have to think about how to get my marriage back on track.

Patrick said softly, "Grainne? Grainne, will you come home now?"

I turned a little towards his voice. But just then I saw a woman coming down the courthouse steps. She was about forty, but walked like an old woman, and there was a haunted expression in her eyes. I recognised her – she was one of the members of the jury.

"Hang on a sec," I said to Patrick, and I walked towards her, met her just as she reached the bottom of the steps.

We stood and looked at each other for a long moment, deep into each other's eyes, and I whispered, "Why?"

She said nothing, just looked at me.

I said, "Look, I'm not angry, or anything. I believe, I know, that you all did your job as best you could. And a pretty shitty job it was too, I know. I just want to understand. Did you really not believe me?"

More silence, and she looked at me, and there was sorrow and fear in her eyes.

"Please?" I said.

She seemed to come to a decision. "I'd like to talk to you about it. But not here." She looked around fearfully. "Can we meet?"

We agreed to meet in a pub further into the city centre.

"Thank you," I said, "thank you. We'll see you there."

Patrick and I went to our car, drove to a carpark, and went to the pub. And waited. Mostly in silence.

Nursing our drinks. After about fifteen minutes Patrick said reluctantly, "Grainne, she's not coming. Maybe she changed her mind, maybe she never meant to, just said this to get you off her back. Let's go."

"No."

He sighed, took another sip of his pint.

We waited another five minutes, anxiously scanning the door each time it opened. And again Patrick said, "Grainne, let's go." But just as he said it the door opened, and in came the woman, scanning the room. She saw us, came nervously towards us, sat at our table.

"I'm sorry I'm late," she said. "I couldn't get parking."

"That's okay," I said, just delighted that she'd turned up at all.

There was a nervous silence all around for a moment, none of us knowing what to do. But Patrick said then to her, "What would you like to drink?"

She looked at him gratefully. "Oh, I could kill a brandy," she told him. "It's been a tough time. I mean . . ." she paused, embarrassed, "I know it has been worse for you both, but it wasn't easy for us."

"I'm sure it wasn't," I told her as Patrick went to the bar. And for the first time I realised it was true. I had never considered the jury as actual people before, but if they took their civic duty seriously, how could it be anything but difficult? "What's your name?" She hesitated, and I said hurriedly, "If you want to tell me . . . it's okay if you don't."

"Denise," she said, "Denise Davis."

And we waited in silence until Patrick came back, and set the drink carefully in front of her.

There was silence for a moment longer, and then, "Well?" I asked her, as gently and softly as I could.

"Oh, I feel so dreadful," she said, and there were tears in her eyes. "It's like this. We all believed you. We really did. We were sure he'd raped you. But one of the men pointed out that we weren't being asked whether or not we believed you. We were being asked whether or not the State had *proven* that he did it. The judge had actually said that, he told us. And that made sense to us. We felt that our own individual opinions didn't really matter. It was as he'd said: whether or not the State had proven he'd done it. And we agonised over it, we really did. We really wanted to convict him." She took a quick gulp of her drink. "But at the end of the day we knew that the State hadn't proved it. How could they?"

"No," I echoed, "how could they?"

"And so, we acquitted him. We felt we had no choice. But we all felt dreadful about it, letting this rapist walk free. I mean, what if he does it again? How will we all feel then?"

And I felt compelled to comfort her. "No, no, you were right." Even though I didn't believe it. Yes, yes, I know about presumption of innocence. I totally agree with it. In principle. It's the difference between a democracy and a dictatorship. It's integral to our civil rights. But, I thought, anguished, how could they have acquitted him, when they all believed the truth of it?

But it was done now, and this poor woman didn't need my upset on top of what she was already feeling. They'd all done their best, decent honest people all. And it was done, nothing I said to her now was going to change it. And she had been so good to come and talk to me. So I said again, "No, you were right."

Her face brightened then, a little, and she quickly finished her drink. "So can I go now?" she asked us, as if we had the power to detain her.

"Of course," I said.

And she nodded at us, and got up and left.

I sat back wearily in my chair, passed a hand over my forehead. "Okay," I said to my husband, "let's go."

We got into our car, and drove away, back to our home.

"Are you glad you did it?" Patrick asked me. "Was it worth doing?"

"Yes!" I said emphatically. "At least I know that I did everything I could. And, God forbid, if he rapes someone else – at least I won't have any guilt for that. But, oh, Patrick, I can't bear to think he got away with it!"

"Nor can I," he said with feeling.

And we drove the rest of the way in silence, both thinking our own thoughts. I was replaying the trial in my mind, wondering if I could have said or done anything different to change the outcome. I didn't know then what Patrick was thinking, but it wasn't long before I was to find out.

Chapter 19

The next week passed as well as it could. Although the trial had brought Patrick and me closer together in our united aim, we now reverted despite ourselves to the distant strangers we had become. We were both aware that the baby was due in only a week or so, and the enormity of what that represented hung over us both. I still felt my huge ambivalence – I honestly didn't know what I was going to do. Patrick seemed to have said all he could say on the subject – he was waiting for me to decide, to decide the path of three lives.

One evening when he got home, I went again into his arms, needing comfort. But he held me me stiffly, holding me a little away from him. I lifted my head from his shoulder, puzzled.

He said gravely, "Grainne, we must talk."

He sat me down on the sofa beside him, and said, "Grainne, this is the hardest thing I've ever said." He paused, took a deep breath, "I can't live with you any more, not until the baby is born. The more and more the pregnancy has progressed, the more and more I've hated it – this visible reminder of that bastard. I've wanted to go for ages, but I knew I had to wait and be with you during the court case. Support you during it. I was sure you'd win, but now that you haven't . . . well, it doesn't change anything about us, and our situation. We have no relationship any more. We talk like polite flatmates, there's nothing of our previous way about us. This used to be a house of laughter and fun, now it's a house of shadows and sorrow. You know that that's true, don't you?"

I nodded numbly.

"I still love you more than I can say, but for now, I think we need some time apart. Time for us both to heal without having to deal with the issues of the other. You know, I'm a victim of this rape too – not as much as you, obviously, but in a different way I am. And there's been nobody for me – I can't talk to my friends about it – and you have, understandably, not been in the position to help me. I need some space, some time."

He sighed heavily, and then went on: "Kevin Dwyer is going to Zurich for about a year, and I'm going to live in his flat. It's just behind the Financial Services Centre, so it'll be handy for work." He came to a sudden stop.

I couldn't say a word. I was stunned into silence. Eventually, trying to find some sense in the fog swirling in my head, I grasped the one truth I knew.

I said: "I love you."

"I know," he said. "I still love you too, nothing changes that. But you know that everything else I've said is true."

I nodded.

"This isn't forever," he went on. "After the baby is born, and it's been given to parents who can love it, we can look at things then. It's just a break, some space. We're damaging each other by neglect, as we are."

"So you're giving me an ultimatum, the baby or you?"

He grimaced. "Yes, I am. I don't mean to, but I just can't live with that man's baby. I would, if I could, but . . ."

I nodded numbly again.

He kissed me, so gently, on the forehead, and stood up. "I'll just go and pack some stuff." And he left the room.

I just sat there, trying to process what had happened. My husband was leaving me. Patrick, the joy and soul of my life, was going. The marriage, in whose strength we had gloried, was bitterly wounded – perhaps fatally. This couldn't be happening to me.

And I was angry too. Angry at Brogan, for this final blow to my life. Angry at myself, for beginning the process of events which led to this. And angry too, at Patrick, although my anger at him was unfocused. I understood too. He hadn't asked for any of this, and it had turned his life upside-down.

Eventually, I heard him come back downstairs. He put his head through the door, and said awkwardly,

"I'll be off now. Just keep using the joint account as you always did, and if there's anything you need, let me know. I'll leave Kevin's phone number on the hall table." He hesitated as if he were going to say something else, but then just moved away and closed the sitting-room door behind him.

There was a pause during which I imagined him carefully writing the new phone number into the address book, and then I heard the door open, and softly close behind him. And a few minutes later, the familiar sound of his car engine as he drove away.

For the rest of the day I just sat there, except for visits to the toilet. I didn't ring anybody – what was I going to say?

This day, only two weeks after the summer solstice, passed, the long summer evening seeming an appropriate symbol of the endlessness of this day in my life.

I thought, I'll ring the adoption agency in the morning. Set things in motion. I still didn't know how I felt about the baby, but I surely knew that I couldn't live without Patrick. I told myself that it had all worked out for the best, that this had made the decision for me, took the pressure off me to decide. I thought this, but I couldn't feel it.

At least, I thought, bitterly, this fresh blow has overshadowed whatever I might otherwise have been feeling about Brogan being acquitted.

Eventually, moving like an old, old woman, I went upstairs, threw off my clothes, and went to bed. I lay there, and waited for my life to happen.

I must have dozed, because the next thing I knew I was woken by a sharp pain in my stomach, and I discovered that I was lying in sodden sheets. Oh God, the baby was coming! I rang Sinead – at this rate she was getting well used to middle-of-the-night calls from me.

She sleepily answered the phone.

"Sinead, the baby's coming – my waters broke – and Patrick isn't here. I'm going to ring for an ambulance – can you meet me at the hospital?"

She assured me she'd be there as soon as she could. I then rang for an ambulance, and dressed myself, and went downstairs to wait. Just as I reached the hall, I was gripped by another pain.

The ambulance came soon, and the men were kind and efficient. They brought me, and my pre-packed bag, to the hospital, where I was handed over to the care of the equally kind and efficient hospital staff. They brought me up to the labour ward, where Sinead found me about ten minutes later.

She hugged me, and said, determinedly, brightly: "The baby's coming, isn't this great?" She was nervous.

"Where's Patrick? Surely his company didn't send him away, at this time of all times?"

"Oh no," I assured her. "No, he's left me."

"What!"

Another contraction delayed my answer, while Sinead hovered uncertainly.

When the pain had passed, I told her what had happened.

She moaned, "Oh no, Grainne, oh no! You poor girl, it's all going wrong for you! God, I can't believe he would do this to you!"

"It's been hard on him too," I defended him. I meant it too. I understood why he had done what he had done. "Don't worry, though, he'll come back when the baby's . . . when it's all over."

But just now the concept of it all being over seemed like a strange, unreal idea.

Soon I was at that stage of labour when I told myself, 'I've changed my mind, I think I'll go home and have the baby another day, thanks all the same'.

Sinead was now playing her role as birth companion to the hilt, gently rubbing my brow and murmuring supportive comments. She was driving me mad!

Just then the obstetrician came in, and started doing obstetric-type things.

Sinead was looking at his name-tag. "Harry Moran," she said musingly. "I know a Colette Moran whose brother's an obstetrician."

He was nodding even before she'd finished speaking. "Yes, my sister. How do you know her?"

"Oh," said Sinead, "I met her through Finbar Whelan."

"Finn Whelan!" he cried. "God, I haven't seen him in ages. How is old Finn doing now?"

"He's grand," she said. "He's just after getting a new job with – Grainne, what is wrong with you? Why are you looking at me like that?"

"Because, Sinead," I said with dignity, "I'm the

reason we're all here, and you two are ignoring me! Would you mind doing your networking in your own time?"

She had been driving me mad, and the obstetrician's professional attentions had been somewhat lacking in anything comfortable or nice – but at least they'd been paying attention to me.

They did stop talking to each other, focused on me. But before he left, pronouncing me fine and healthy, a great fine big pelvis on me, hours to go yet, relax (relax? Easy to know he was a man!), I heard him murmur: "And are you still in touch with Colette, er – Sinead, is it? She'd have your phone number then? Grand, grand." And to me, "I'll be back to see you shortly."

The hours passed. I was dimly aware of the easing away of the night, the daylight coming softly in through the window. I did my breathing exercises for all the good they did. Inhaled gas and air until I felt like a balloon – even more than the average eight and a half month pregnant woman does all the time, I mean.

I fell into a kind of timeless pattern. Contraction, breathe around it, repeat. After some uncountable time, it all became more intense. The midwife explained I was going through transition, the changeover from the pelvis opening to the pushing stage.

She told me gently, "This is the hardest bit, just hang on for this, it doesn't take long, and then you'll be able to push and soon you'll have your baby."

Of course, time is relative. What isn't long to a clean, uniformed woman sitting quietly at the side of a bed, might not be quite so short to the woman sweating and grimacing her way through the process.

But yes, it passed, and then she said, "Now we're at the fun bit, the baby coming. This is what it's all been about."

The pushing sensation is funny. Not too painful, but strange. I've heard it described as, excuse my language, trying to shit a football, and that's pretty close.

And then the midwife and Sinead (who had, to my great relief, abandoned her birth-partner role in favour of excited observer at the business end), both said: "I can see the head!" At least, the midwife said it, Sinead squealed it.

A few more pushes and then a huge feeling of release, of rushing and flowing, and the midwife said, "Here it is, oh, it's a little girl, how beautiful!"

I raised my head to look. This ugly, blood-covered, squashed-featured, curled-up little yoke was my baby?

The midwife wrapped her in a blanket and handed her to me. I still stared in amazement. This old-woman-faced, bald-headed, dotey, beautiful, special, gorgeous baby was mine? I started saying over and over, "Oh my God, oh my God," as I stared at her and gingerly held her close. The midwife smiled benevolently, almost as if, I thought, it was all her own doing. And Sinead was just staring, much as I was, in disbelief and awe.

The midwife said, "It's a good idea to put her to the breast as soon as possible, within half an hour or an hour, if she's interested. Nature's designed it so the sucking instinct is strongest then, and once she's mastered that technique there'll be no stopping her."

Oh, I thought, I haven't even got the hang of holding her yet. But I gave it a go, trying to relate all those diagrams I'd seen to a real breast and a real baby's mouth, and figure out how they were possibly going to be able to fit together. My breast was as big as her whole head, for heaven's sake!

But we managed it, through a combination of my previous reading, the midwife's soft-voiced and well-timed comments, the baby's willingness, and Mother Nature. She latched on (the baby, not the midwife or Mother Nature) and sucked strongly. I felt the tugging, almost painful in the intensity of its emotion, go straight from my nipple to my heart, and the feelings of love almost burst me. And pride: this little mite, not five minutes old, could already feed herself! What a genius, was there ever a child like her? She nursed for about fifteen minutes, and then slept.

The midwife said, "I'll take her now, clean her, dress her and weigh her. Although, the amount she's had, I'll need to subtract about half a pound to get her actual birth weight!" She smiled happily and conspiratorially at me. "You did great, and she did great there."

And even though I knew there was an element of I-bet-you-say-that-to-all-the-mothers about it, I still felt so proud and such a wonderful mother, that I could do this for my baby, to feed her and nourish her myself.

I said softly to Sinead what I'd been thinking while the baby was feeding: "I can't believe she's mine."

And equally softly, Sinead said, "But Grainne, she's not."

I stared at her in horror. I had forgotten. I had actually forgotten. In all the emotion of the labour and birth I had lost sight of the fact that this was not to be my baby, my child. I had, indeed, forgotten that I didn't even want her to be mine.

When we were brought up to our room, I kissed Sinead and thanked her for everything. "Sinead," I asked her, "will you please tell nobody about the baby? Not even Stephen. And if you don't mind, don't come in to see me again. I'll ring you when I get out."

"Sure thing," she said quietly.

She kissed me and dropped a little kiss on the baby's forehead.

"Goodbye, baby," she said sadly. "I'll remember you always."

* * *

Later, after I had slept, I sat up and rang the bell. A nurse came. I whispered to her, all strength gone from my voice, "Can I see the hospital social worker, please?"

"Of course," she said, and went off.

About twenty minutes later the door opened and the social worker came in.

"Hello," she said to me, holding out her hand. She was quiet, calm, very, very understanding and kind. "I'm Sally Fleming. What can I do for you?

I said, whispered, my voice cracking and breaking, "I need to arrange the adoption of this baby."

She looked at me and nodded slowly. "Do you know much about how adoption works?"

"Yes. I had a meeting with Agatha Cullen of the Irish Adoption Agency – she explained it all to me."

"Grand. Okay, leave it with me, I'll sort it out. Now," as she pulled a form out of her briefcase, "I'll need a few details."

I answered the routine questions easily, but then she asked, "And who is the baby's father?"

"He raped me. I don't want his name to go on the form."

"That's fine, we can do it without his name. The only thing is, you're married, aren't you? You're wearing a ring, at least."

"Yes. I know I'll have to sign an affidavit, and get my husband to sign one.

"Great," she said. "You know that you've got at least six weeks before you sign the consent form? Well, if you could get the affidavits to us by then, it would be fine."

She went off, and came back a couple of hours later.

"Well, that's all organised," she told me. "I've arranged the foster-home for the baby, for the six weeks, or however long until you sign the consent form. And we've picked the adoptive parents from our list. I've met them myself, they really are lovely. They're both professionals, although the mother is going to work part-time, from home, in order to care for the baby. They are well off, having a good lifestyle, with a nice house right on a beach. And, even better, they were quite keen on the idea of semi-open adoption, so you'd get a letter from them twice a year, telling you how the baby's getting on, along with photographs. They don't know yet about this baby – you will make them so happy. And the baby will be so happy with them."

I only had two more days to spend with this baby, and I was determined to make the most of them. I called her Helen, and whispered her name to her a thousand times. I wondered, when she was safely adopted, and had another name, would the name Helen resonate deep in her brain, and she'd hear me calling her when she was asleep?

I spent this time giving Helen enough love to last a lifetime without me, gazing at her to memorise her face, her tiny fingers, her beautiful tummy, the perfection of her. I fed her as much as she'd take, to send her away replete with the life-giving colostrum which is the pre-milk.

I didn't even sleep. I know new mothers don't do much of that anyway. But I didn't even try to sleep. I knew I had a lifetime to do that, but only finite minutes with her, and I didn't want to waste any of them. So when she was sleeping, I just gazed at her.

I had no visitors – we were totally alone in our private cocoon. Apart from the interruptions by nursing staff and catering staff, of course.

So when the door opened at one stage, I didn't even look up.

"Hello," said a stranger's voice.

I looked up. There was a woman there, holding a clipboard and a pen.

"I'm the registrar of births. If you've picked a name, you can tell me, and I'll register it for you. It saves you having to go and do it later."

I've picked a first name, I thought bitterly, it's the surname that's going to be a problem.

But then I said, "Yes, I have. Her name is Helen."

"Your name and occupation?"

"Grainne Quinn, schoolteacher."

"And the baby's father's name and occupation?"

And out of my mouth came the words: "Patrick Quinn, financial consultant."

I expected the ceiling to open and a bolt of lightning to hit me. I expected the registrar to say, 'Ha, caught you out, you liar!'

But she just calmly wrote all this down, and then smiled, thanked me and left.

God, I thought, what have I done? Only lied on a legal document. But, I reasoned to myself, justifying my decision, when she grows up she may want to trace her birth parents. And I don't want to put that the father was unknown and have her think her mother was a right slappper.

And neither can I put her real father's name. Imagine her tracing *him* in years to come. I must protect her from that at all costs.

And the fact that I'd just perpetrated what I assumed was a major crime didn't bother me a bit. And it didn't occur to me till months afterwards that I'd already left a blank on the adoption form for the father's name, nor that Patrick and I were going to have to sign an affidavit swearing that he wasn't the father. So, the documents would be mutually contradictory. But, as I said, I didn't think of that for ages – at this stage I was so emotionally exhausted by all that was happening that there was no room left for fear, or guilt, or morals. Or even logic.

On the evening of the last day the social worker came to see me, to explain what would happen the following day.

"You'll both be officially discharged when the doctor does his rounds, and that's when we'll bring the baby to her foster-mother. Would you like to come with us?"

But I shook my head, "No, I'll give her to you here. I don't think I could bear to hand her over to someone." To myself, I didn't think I could know where in the city she was, without pounding on the door one despairing day, demanding her back. Of course, I knew, theoretically, that I could ask for her back any time up to signing the consent form, but it would still be much harder to resist this, if I actually knew where she was

Chapter 20

And so the last few hours passed, and I held Helen, and fed her, and kissed her, and changed her, and stroked her cheek.

And the next morning, time moved inexorably on. The doctor discharged us, and I dressed myself, packed my bag, dressed Helen for the last time. And a few minutes after that the social worker arrived to collect her. And I, tears streaming down my cheeks, handed my precious, unique, special baby into her caring arms, and saw them both go out the door. And I collapsed onto the bed, my legs not able to hold me, and sobbed and sobbed.

Wept for all the days and nights Helen and I wouldn't have. For all the birthdays I wouldn't see. For the first bike-ride, the first day at school, the laughter I wouldn't be able to share, the skinned knees I wouldn't wash and kiss better, and tears I wouldn't comfort away.

And even as my heart and soul were still sobbing helplessly on the bed, my legs dragged themselves to their feet, my hands wrenched open the ward door, and my legs were running, running, down the corridor, dodging the people who were looking askance at me. Running, running, don't wait for the lift, almost fall down the stairs, swinging around the corners, hanging onto the banisters.

I caught up with them in the carpark, as she was carefully placing Helen into a carseat. I didn't say anything, just stood and gasped for breath. The social worker straightened and looked at me. She didn't say anything for a moment. Then, only, "Are you sure?"

Still struggling for breath, I nodded. My hands held themselves out.

Wordlessly she unbuckled Helen and handed her to me. Took Helen's clothes bag out of the car and placed it on the ground beside me. I held Helen so hard that she squirmed feebly, my tears running over her downy head. I was shaking. I held Helen tight so that I wouldn't drop her.

The social worker got into her car, and reversed carefully around me, as I stood in the carpark, still holding my baby. Through the open window she said to me, softly and kindly, "Goodbye. Good luck," and she drove off.

I hefted the baby bag to my shoulder, and slowly Helen and I made our way back to the hospital entrance lobby.

When I was there the enormity of what I had done

overwhelmed me. I'd made my decision. Or rather, my decision had made itself. I didn't know, didn't want to think of what ramifications this decision would bring. For now it was enough to hold Helen close to me, to whisper over and over to her "I'm sorry, I'm sorry, I'm sorry". I'm not even sure what I was apologising for – for almost giving her up, for ever doubting her, for the whole mess of a life into which I had brought her.

I also now had a logistical problem. Knowing, as I thought I did at the time, that I wasn't bringing the baby home with me, I'd bought no equipment. My most pressing need was for a carseat to bring her home, and I'd need more clothes.

I felt that Sinead had performed well above and beyond the call of duty over the past months. So I rang Stephen.

"Hi! How are you?" he asked.

"I'm great. Listen, I've had the baby. A baby girl. She's beautiful, her name's Helen. She weighed 7lb 10oz!"

I felt wonderful. This was the very first person I had told about the birth, and I could tell with joy, knowing I was keeping her. I felt an unfamiliar emotion, excitement, bubble up inside me.

"That's great," he said mildly, "and are you well yourself?" His voice was carefully neutral, and I realised it was because he didn't know the rest of the news.

I said, "I'm great! Unbelievably good! Wait till I tell you, I'm keeping her!"

His shout of joy bellowed down the phone lines.

"Well, now, I'm delighted for you. Congratulations! You are wonderful! Can I be godfather?" Then he sobered up, and asked, "How did Patrick take the news?"

I said, "Ehh", and Stephen "Ahh"ed in understanding. "You haven't told him yet, have you?"

"No. To be honest, I only found out myself an hour ago. You are the first person I've told!"

"Well, I'm deeply honoured and privileged," he said, in a theatrical manner. But I sensed the truth behind the lightly delivered words.

"Well, don't be too delighted. There's an ulterior motive. I need you to do something for me. Something requiring great daring."

Oh, I was on great form now!

"Anything!" he promised, grandly, rashly.

"Can you go into a shop and buy me a baby carseat?"

There was silence, then: "Ah no, let me do something easy, like rescue a maiden from a dragon, or get a politician to deliver on a promise. Come on, Grainne, I'm a single man – a single, gay man – what do I know about baby carseats? Ask Sinead!"

"Well, Sinead's a single woman, she's never bought a carseat either – the knowledge of carseats doesn't come programmed in us along with ovaries, you know! It's easy, you go into the nursery section of a department store, and you explain to the woman there that you are buying a carseat for a newborn baby." I could sense he wasn't convinced, so I played my trump card, "And besides, Sinead's already done her bit – she was At The Birth!"

"She never told me!" He was outraged.

"Sorry – I told her not to. I wanted to get it all over with –"

He cut in swiftly. "I understand completely."

"So about the carseat?"

He said, "We-ll." He was wavering.

"Please, Stephen! I've had a hard time, you know, what with an eight-hour labour, and after four hours I was only three centimetres dilated –"

"Okay, okay," he agreed hastily.

I pursued my advantage: "Also, in the same place, and getting the same person to help you, can you get about a week's supply of baby clothes – she'll know the sort of stuff. Nothing too girly or frilly. And absolutely nothing that needs ironing. And a week's supply of nappies. Do you think you can do that?"

"Yes," he whimpered.

"And then, my darling Stephen, can you come and collect me from the hospital? I'm – we're due to go home today – now really, and I need a carseat to put her in."

"I'd love to," he laughed. "I'll be there as soon as I can. I look forward to seeing you, and to meeting the baby."

While I was waiting for him I rang Sinead.

"Sinead, I've got some news for you! I'm keeping my baby!" My voice squeaked with excitement.

"I'm so happy for you," she said, "if that's what's

right for you. But Grainne, are you sure? Did you tell Patrick yet? What did he say?"

"In order of your questions, yes, I'm completely sure. And no, I didn't tell Patrick yet," my voice grew serious, "and I have no idea how he's going to react. But I simply couldn't give her up, and well, I don't know what Patrick'll say. I'll ring him soon – we'll know then."

"My love, I support you in everything you do, you know that, and if you're delighted about the baby, then so am I. I'll send positive vibes to your telling Patrick. Let me know how it goes. So, when can I come and see you and her? Can I be godmother?"

After arranging that she would come the following day, we hung up.

I went back to my room, still carrying Helen – my baby! – and fetched my bag, then returned to the lobby to wait for Stephen.

He arrived eventually, with everything I'd asked him for, bless him.

He took one look at Helen, and fell in love. "Oh, she's beautiful, so beautiful! She's like you, you know."

I was interested to hear this, as I'd been trying to figure this out myself. The only time Sinead had seen her, she'd only just been born, and was too face-squashed and red to resemble anything other than an overripe tomato, so I'd had no opinion from that quarter. Needless to say I wanted the baby to resemble me, rather than *him*, and I'd spent ages gazing at our faces together in the mirror, but hadn't been able to get any likeness at all, to either of her parents.

Of course it did cross my mind that Stephen might be being tactful, but I preferred to believe him.

So we walked out of the hospital, back into the real world. Half an hour later we'd worked out how to attach the carseat to the car. I carefully placed Helen in, and fastened the seat belt. She was sleeping peacefully. Then Stephen put my case into the boot, I got into the car and we drove to my house.

I was so excited, and yet so tired. And terrified too, of the future. Stephen, bless him, spent ages with me that day, making me endless cups of tea (far more than I ever wanted), acting generally like a doting husband who'd brought his wife and new baby home. I kept thinking sourly: this should be Patrick.

Stephen was fascinated when I fed the baby. "So that's what they're for!" he camped. "I thought they were just for selling products to men and for their general gratification!"

"Oh, you know what they say, women's breasts are like toy train-sets – they're intended for the children, but the fathers play with them!"

He laughed hugely, and then returned to his fascination. "How does the milk come out? How do you know when the baby's had enough? How does your body know to make enough milk? Doesn't it hurt? Does it feel nice?"

So I gave him all the details I'd spent months learning from books, and he sat back, satisfied, and continued to look at me.

"It's beautiful," he breathed, "seeing it, and there are

249

wonderful shapes there – all curves – your head as you bend over her, the curve of your shoulder, your breast, and the baby's head, all flowing curves that run naturally together. Hang on! I feel a sculpture coming on!"

He went into the hall, and I heard him rooting in the hall cupboard. He came back in with a pencil and an old bill. "Do you mind?" holding up the bill, and when I shook my head he began sketching on the back of the paper.

Later he cooked me dinner, although I use the term 'cooked' in its loosest sense. 'Cooked' in the sense of 'opened'. He'd never been much of a cook, and since meeting Richard any little skills he previously had, had totally atrophied.

Stephen always explains his fidelity to Richard like this: "Why go out for hamburger, when not only can you have steak at home, but Sole Veronique, and home-made pasta, and Thai green curries – with fresh coriander and lemongrass – and pan-seared swordfish with a Mexican salsa, and –"

He might not be able to cook, but he talks a good menu.

Having him cook me a meal was almost more trouble than it was worth, except that the thought of it made me glow, that he cared enough to do this. He kept shouting questions from the kitchen.

"Grainne, where's the tin-opener?"

Tin-opener? I wondered. For pasta and tomato sauce out of a jar? But I just called back, "Second drawer down."

We had a fun meal, laughing and joking. It was great. But eventually he had to go. Kissed me hugely, and planted a reverential kiss on Helen's head. Promised to phone soon, and let himself out.

I then rang my parents. Got my mother. Oh joy . . .

"Hi, Mum, how are you? Listen, I've got some news for you. I had the baby, a baby girl."

"Thank God that's over then. And is she handed over to the adoption agency yet?"

"Well, no, I'm not going to have her adopted. I'm keeping her."

There was a silence, disapproval radiating clearly down the wires. Then she said, "Are you sure you know what you're doing? There's bad blood in her, you know."

"Oh," I said lightly, although my heart was pounding – trust my mother to go straight to my deepest, darkest fear, "our family's surely not that bad."

"Grainne!" she snapped, in that don't-you-take-that-tone-of-voice-with-me mode.

"Sorry, sorry," I muttered, "but seriously, Mum, on the nature/nurture argument, I always voted for environment being much more important – don't you worry about that."

There was something that may have been "Hmmph!".

"I'm sure you need time to get used to it, not being able to get excited about being grandparents during my pregnancy, so I understand that you can't be too excited now. But I'd love for you to see her," – I was crossing my fingers at this stage, that childhood protection against telling lies – "I'm getting out of hospital today, so maybe you could come tomorrow? Your first grandchild, imagine!"

"Well, now, tomorrow doesn't suit. I have my hairdresser appointment in the morning, and Betty said she might pop around tomorrow afternoon."

"Well, whenever suits you then." She was not going to ruin my joy. She – was – not, I told myself, ungritting my teeth with an effort. "Say hello to Dad for me, and give him the news. And do you mind telling Gary?" Not that my brother was likely to be hugely excited, but still.

"Of course I'll tell Gary," she sighed, as though I'd just presented her with the twelve labours of Hercules, "but not till after six o'clock mind – we must watch the phone bill."

"Yes, yes," I said, aware that my you-will-not-depress-me defences were crumbling, and that I was running out of time. "So I'd better go, she's crying – bye, bye."

And to the sound of my mother saying something about babies always crying and any pretence at normal life was over now, and I wasn't to spoil her, I hung up.

Chapter 21

Okay, I judged, looking at my watch. Patrick would be back from work now. I lifted the phone and dialled his number. I stood listening to the ringing tones, with my heart pounding painfully. I was terrified. Be tactful, I told myself. This is going to be a shock for him. Take it handy now.

His deep, mellow voice resonated as it always did as he answered. It was wonderfully painful, or painfully wonderful, to hear his voice as he said, "Hello".

I said, "Patrick, it's me. Listen, I've had the baby. A week or so early, but she's fine. It's a baby girl. But Patrick, I, well, I've decided to keep her. Not put her up for adoption, I mean. I couldn't."

There was silence for a moment or two. Then he said, and his voice was carefully neutral, "I see. Are you well? You got through the birth okay?"

"Yes, no problem. Bit tired, but that's to be expected."

There was more silence. I could hear his breathing. I wondered what was going through his head.

"This is very difficult for me," he said at last. "I don't know how to react. I'm delighted you're safe. But, Grainne, keeping the baby is a big problem for me."

"I'm sorry. I truly couldn't do anything else. I did try. I actually handed her to the social worker and she took her away, but then . . . then I couldn't. I just couldn't let her go. But, Patrick, can we look at this another way? We wanted a baby, and we got one. Not the way we wanted, true. But maybe this is God's way of answering our want for a baby. Maybe you're not able to have babies."

"Yes, a prospect definitely calculated to make a man feel good, the thought that he's sterile. Thanks for sharing that thought with me."

"Oh Patrick, come on," I said, "don't tell me you never thought of that before, yourself. Please, please consider it – coming home and letting us be a family, the three of us."

"It's not that easy. I just can't get my head around the fact that you are keeping this rapist's baby."

"Patrick," I almost shouted in frustration, "it's not the rapist's baby, except in the purely biological sense. It's my baby, mine! I conceived her, I carried her, I'm feeding her, I'm raising her – none of that has anything to do with him! And you could make her yours!" My voice dropped. "If you could only see her! She's beautiful – you'd love her immediately, I know you would. We could make this our victory over him, triumph in our lives despite him!"

"I doubt it," he said sadly. "Look, you've made your decision, and I respect that. Can't you do the same for me – respect my decision? You can't have everything all your own way, all your life, you know."

"Oh yes," I said, shouting in earnest now, "this past nine months has been just the way I wanted! I really wanted to be raped, to carry that bastard's child, to have my husband leave me!"

"Calm down," he said, in an infuriatingly calm voice, guaranteed to totally wind me up. "You don't need to get emotional."

"I'm fucking post-natal!" I shouted. "It's the one time in my life I'm allowed be emotional and, by God, I'll be as emotional as I want!"

"This conversation is getting us nowhere," he said wearily. "Look, I'll continue to support you, and the baby too. I won't see you stuck. But I can't see me coming back and playing happy families. I'm sorry," he went on in a gentler voice, "I wish I could – it would be ideal. But I can't."

"You bastard!" I shouted, and then to my horror I heard my voice say, "You probably *are* shooting blanks! Did you ever stop to think you couldn't get me pregnant in six months, and he managed it in one go?" Then I gasped, "Oh my God, I can't believe I said that! I am so, so sorry."

"Why be sorry? It's true," he said coldly. "Look, I'm going to hang up now, we're getting nowhere except upsetting ourselves. I'm glad you're safely over the delivery, and that the baby is well. Forgive me if I don't congratulate you, under the circumstances. Look after yourself, I mean that, and let me know if you need anything."

And he hung up.

"Fuck," I said, and kicked the hall table. Wow, you handled that one well, didn't you, girl?

I went back into the sitting-room. Helen was awake and crying – probably all the shouting. I picked her up and fed her, looking down at her. I said, "Well, it's just you and me, sweetheart. Let's have a wonderful life, and show them all." She just nursed peacefully. I wished life could be that simple for me, that someone could give me the adult equivalent of a nice warm breast, something that would give comfort and love and warmth and reassurance on demand.

Oh well, failing that I'd watch a good soap opera (if that's not a contradiction in terms). It would be nice to see people who were making more of a mess of their lives than I was. As Helen nursed herself back to calmness I sat back on the sofa and reached for the remote control.

* * *

Sinead came around the next day, lifted Helen up and pronounced her beautiful. "She's the image of you," she said, "no look of anyone else. Sit yourself down there, and I'll make us a cup of tea."

She did that very thing and as we sat hugging our mugs, she said, "And did you tell Patrick yet. About –" and she waved a hand at Helen, as if there were other things I was going to discuss with him, and this minor detail might have escaped my memory.

I said ruefully, "I did."

"And? How did he take it?"

"Do you mean before, or after, I accused him of shooting blanks and suggested Brogan was twice the man he was, to do in one night what he, Patrick, couldn't do in six months?"

She sighed, "Oh Grainne," and then, stifling a giggle, "You didn't! Please tell me you didn't!"

"I did." And I caught her eye and we both collapsed laughing, more in hysteria than humour. She carefully put down her cup, and then came over to me and hugged me tight. "It'll all work out, you'll see it will," she promised.

And, right there and then, for that instant, I believed her, even though I knew, deep down, that that promise wasn't in her gift to give.

The day after that my parents came, along with my brother Gary. I answered the door holding the baby, with her head tucked into my neck, and led them into the sitting-room.

"Well," I said nervously, "here she is," and I lowered her down and cradled her so they could see her. My father and brother both looked surreptitiously at my mother to get their cues. My mother looked at her sharply.

"Isn't she pretty?" I said nervously, annoyed with myself for being nervous.

"She looks sweet now, but really, Grainne, you've no idea how she'll turn out."

"None of us knows how our children will turn out," I said.

"That's true!" she said with a wealth of meaning. Obviously a reference to something (everything?) I'd done that didn't suit how she'd wanted me to turn out.

She changed tactics, attacked from another angle.

"How has Patrick taken the news that you're keeping that rapist's child?"

I took a deep breath. "Well, Mum, it's difficult for him –"

"Of course it is! You can't expect any man to take in some other man's bastard. I really wouldn't blame him if he left you if you insist on this course of action."

Since Patrick had gone I'd been waiting for a good moment to tell her that we'd separated. Not surprisingly, that moment had never come.

I jumped up, and placed Helen in her little carseat which was doubling as her house seat too.

"Would you all like a cup of tea?" I asked, and before waiting for an answer I escaped into the kitchen, and put the kettle on.

Right, I thought, my daughter's my priority. And if people won't accept her, that's their problem. And if my mother's going to cause a problem then I won't let her be with Helen. I don't want her growing up with this woman judging every childish tantrum as a sign of genetic evil. Scary, that, to cut off my mother for my child's sake, to even consider it. But right, and a painless decision. Wow, I thought, I'm a grown-up now! A mother now.

And the enormity of what I'd taken on, and the joy of the responsibility had me bawling my eyes out. Oh, those post-natal hormones – would they ever settle down?

My dad found me there, and he whispered, like an adulterous lover making an assignation, "Your baby's bonny, love. Don't mind your mother, she'll come around. Here, buy the little dote something with this," and he surreptitiously slipped some notes into my hand.

He helped me make the tea, and carried the tray back into the sitting-room.

My mother took a cup, and resumed her attack. "So, tell me how Patrick has taken this?"

Okay. Deep breath. "It's like this, Mum, Patrick and I are separated temporarily. It happened before the baby was born – it's just that we both need more space in order to sort ourselves out."

Her eyes were opening wider and wider as I spoke, and her mouth was open in horror.

"I don't believe you! Are you serious? You let that wonderful man go, all for the sake of this – " words failed her as she gestured at Helen.

"I had no choice. You're a mother, you must understand how your children take over your heart and turn you inside out, and nothing else can come before that."

"What?" She looked at me blankly, as if I'd suddenly started talking in Sanskrit.

"You really don't understand, do you?" I said, looking at her. "You've never loved either of us – you don't know what it's like to feel this total love for a baby!"

"Of course I loved you both," she snapped. "It's because I love you that I'm trying to stop you making the worst mistake of your life. For God's sake, use your head now rather than your heart as you always do. You simply cannot lose that wonderful husband of yours. I mean, in a few years he's probably going to be a vice-president of that company. And I see his name mentioned in the papers all the time! So what I'm going to say to you is this, and I'm only saying this for your own good: it's not too late to get that baby adopted. You're not fit to mind her on your own, and you can't, you just can't let Patrick go. If you get the baby adopted now, it'll all be over, this whole uncomfortable phase behind you, and you'll be able to start again. You can always have other babies."

"Mum, I'm not having Helen adopted. She's my baby, and I'm keeping her," I said, amazed that my voice sounded so cool, so in control, when my emotions were swirling around like the more vicious type of tornado. Fear of standing up to my mother, determination to do so, pride at doing so, panic at the consequences of standing up to her, all spun around, adding to the constant mix of exhaustion, grief over Patrick, fear over the future, hatred of Brogan, loathing of myself, anger at myself for loathing myself, etc. etc.

"Well, then, there's no more to be said." She put her untouched teacup carefully down on the floor, and stood up. "Come on, Barry, come on, Gary, we're leaving." She picked up her huge handbag and glared at the two men. Not daring to meet my eye, they stood too.

"Let us know when you've come to your senses," she told me and headed for the sitting-room door.

"Mum," I said. I stood too.

She turned and faced me.

I took a deep breath. "I've just come to my senses."

"Oh, that's great!"

"Yes, and my senses tell me that you are the most unfeeling woman I have ever met, that you've never been anything but miserable and begrudging. These last nine months have been the most horrendous, difficult time of my life, and where have you been? Nowhere. How have you helped me? You haven't. And now that I'm reaching to retrieve some good out of the horror, taking a gift out of the evil, you're being no help or support to me. You just sit there being judgmental and critical, without an ounce of love or compassion in you."

She was gazing at me in total horror, shock obviously preventing her from intervening or leaving. Dad and Gary were also gazing at me in amazement, maybe unable to believe that someone was finally standing up to her.

I was on a roll, years of hurt pouring out of me, as I continued, "And now, here you are, only concerned about my losing a man of Patrick's status. That's all that matters to you, all that's ever mattered to you. I don't think you even know him as a person, he's just a symbol to you, a good reflection on you that your daughter married 'well'. I am devastated that he's gone, and it's nothing to do with his status. It's him. I miss him, his laughter and his love and his company. But you haven't even expressed one bit of sympathy for me for having lost my husband. To you, it's all so easy! I'll just hand over my daughter – my daughter! – to some strangers to rear her. I'm not surprised you don't see why I can't do that, you've never had one iota of maternal feelings. How could you understand the dreadful situation I'm in, having to make a choice that was no choice at all!" I stopped suddenly, not because I'd run out of things to say, but because I'd run out of breath.

"Well!" she said, and then, again, "Well!"

We stared at each other in silence, the words I'd spoken overwhelming us both.

I felt a rush of exhilaration at having had the courage to say all this to her, but also a sense of horror at the enormity of it. Talk about burning bridges: this was nuking a country's whole transport infrastructure.

"I think you'd better go now," I said in a quieter voice. "You can come back when you're ready to accept my daughter, and in fact, accept any decisions I, as an adult woman, make."

Without another word she turned and walked out, followed by her shamefaced husband and son.

I looked at Helen in her little chair. "You're costing me everything," I told her, and then, in sudden fear that I was going to forever blight her self-esteem, "But don't worry, you're worth it. More than worth it."

It was true. I knew in the deepest parts of my psyche, she was worth the cost of losing Patrick and my family. I was sorry that I had to pay that price, but it was a price other people were putting on her. If it were up to me I'd have the whole family still together – I didn't choose this division. But in some primeval way it was very simple. Not easy, but simple. She was my daughter, I was keeping her. I'd have rathered other people could accept that, but if they couldn't, it wasn't going to make one bit of difference to what I was doing.

* * *

Lucy from next-door also came around, with hugs and kisses and congratulations. "Congratulations!" she said. "I'm delighted for you!"

"Mm," I said, "it's great. But you know, Lucy, you've probably noticed that Patrick's car hasn't been around. We're kind of separated."

Her face was a picture of shock. "What! You and Patrick! Oh, no, I can't believe it! You and Patrick were always so right together. Gordon and I used to laugh that you were our role models."

I shrugged. "You never know what's going on in other people's lives, do you?"

After a moment Lucy said, "Look, I've brought you these." And she held aloft the big black bin-bag she'd been carrying. I had noticed it – impossible not to – but I'd pretended not to.

"Oh, wonderful," I said, determined to lighten the

mood, "a black plastic bin-bag, just what I always wanted!"

"No, silly," she giggled, "it's a black bin-bag full of baby clothes! All the clothes that Jill had from birth until now. And there's a sling in there too, and a buggy for when she gets bigger. Not in the bin-bag, obviously! We got one when Daisy was born, but then we had to buy our double-buggy when Jill came along so soon. So you can have the single one."

"That's brilliant," I said, "really brilliant."

It was, too. Patrick was being so good about supporting me – us. But I wanted to spend as little of his money as possible, particularly on the baby. So this was great.

"Thank you so much." I said.

Her gift really helped. It meant that we were pretty sorted for Helen's needs. She had been sleeping in my bed until I could get a cot, with the back of a chest-of-drawers pushed along the length of her side of the bed so that she wouldn't fall out. However, it was so nice, not having to get up at night to feed her, that I kept putting it off. I felt, too, somewhere deep inside, that since she'd spent nine months so close to me, she might appreciate not being separated too soon. And for me, having spent nine months resenting her very existence, I was finding it very healing, to spend this time with her, relishing her presence.

I found myself often whispering to her, "I'm sorry I hated you, resented you. I didn't know it was you. I never hated you as a baby, as a person, just as a reminder of him."

I don't know if I was just conning myself, but I did my best to put Brogan's connection with Helen right out of my mind. She was, I decided, totally my daughter, and I never looked for him in her, refused to see any resemblance between them. And if I was conning myself, hey, if it works, what harm?

Another day there was a knock on the door, and when I answered it there was a delivery man, carrying a huge bouquet of flowers. I took them in, read the card: *With all best wishes from Jim and Moira.*

My heart went out to them, my beloved in-laws. This must be so difficult for them – obviously their first love, their first loyalty, was to Patrick. But they loved me too, and probably felt so caught in the middle.

The next days passed in a blur. I slept a lot, I know – but in what seemed like thirty-minute stretches. Amazingly, though, within about a week we were in some sort of routine. It was great, I could organise showering and stuff now.

I felt very lonely, though. I had lots of visitors, but there were many times when Helen and I were alone. This irony did not escape me, that I had gone out with Kate to avoid one evening at home by myself, and now I was spending most of my evenings in solitary splendour. It helped a little, having Helen there. But, wonderful and all as she was, even a devoted mother such as I couldn't describe her as scintillating company.

One thing I did do was to ring Sandra Maloney, my school principal. I brought her up to date with the fact that I'd had the baby, and I said, "Remember you said I could take a year's leave of absence? Could you arrange that for me?"

"Of course, my dear Grainne," she said. "I'll sort it out, don't you worry. You take your year off with your baby, and enjoy it. My congratulations to you!"

And the next day there arrived a big bouquet of flowers, and a card which Sandra had signed: *From all the staff.*

* * *

I remember with pride the first day I put Helen in her sling to bring her for a walk. Mrs Cummins from three doors down passed me. "Oh, you've had your baby, how lovely," she said, peering at her. "Oh, what a dote, she's lovely! And isn't she the image of her daddy?"

I looked at her sharply, but she had meant nothing by it. And I realised with a rush of relief that people see what they expect to see, and nobody would question that Patrick was her father. It helped, I realised also, that Brogan was superficially similar to Patrick – same height, build and colouring anyway.

I still missed Patrick with every breath. We hadn't spoken since the day I told him I was keeping her. I thought of him constantly, wondered what he was doing. Was he living a bachelor lifestyle, I wondered all the time. Please don't let him have met anybody else! The thought of another woman sharing that glorious body, that intent lovemaking, that melodious voice, that laughter and fun – it made me feel sick. But like someone picking at a scab, I thought of it constantly.

Why wouldn't he meet someone else? He was a great catch, for anyone. And he was single now. Or was he? We had never said we were officially separated. I didn't dare ask. I just waited, and agonised, on those long evenings on my own.

A couple of times people rang looking for him, business people, and each time I had to say, my voice carefully neutral: "Mr Quinn doesn't live here any more. Here's his new phone number." And felt a bitter maw of jealousy of those people who would soon be talking to him, no matter how dull their topic of conversation.

Chapter 22

Helen was ten days old now, and visibly growing. I was thrilled. All my own work, I thought to myself. That morning, about ten o'clock, I was feeding her as we lay together on our bed. She nursed herself to sleep, and I quietly extricated myself and stood up. Even though she was far too young to roll, I placed a pillow on the chest-of-drawers-less side of the bed, and went downstairs, fastening my bra as I went.

A cup of tea, I thought, and Gerry Ryan on the radio, that was the ticket. Just as I reached the hall the doorbell rang. Probably Lucy, I thought fondly, anticipating that now it would be a cup of tea for two, and Gerry Ryan abandoned for more immediate company.

But it was Darren Brogan!

He pushed his way into the house and shut the door in a horrible replay of the night of the rape.

"Hi," he said pleasantly. "Thought I'd just pop

around and see how you're doing." He eyed my waistline. "You've dropped the baby then? Thought so, I've been keeping an eye on the house. What was it, boy or girl? Where is it? I'd love to see it – my own flesh and blood and all that."

As he spoke he had been coming forward, until I'd found myself backed into the sitting-room.

"It's not your flesh and blood," I said. "It's my husband's baby."

"Oh yeah," he sneered. "I can count, can't I? And why has your husband left you if it's his baby? Well," he repeated, a bit more forcefully now, "what did you have?"

"A boy," I whispered, lying automatically.

"A boy," he repeated, visibly pleased. I swear, he preened a little, thrust his pelvis slightly. I felt a wave of nausea. "Well, they do say it takes a real man to make boys. Where is he? I'd love to see him."

"At my mother's," I said, which was the first thing I could think of.

"At your mother's?" he repeated, aghast. "What's he doing there?"

"So I could have a rest," I whispered. "It was a very hard birth, and I'm very tired."

"Oh, stop whinging," he said. "I don't care about your 'hard birth'," mimicking me, mocking me, "but I do care, very much, about you farming my baby out. What kind of unnatural mother are you anyway?"

He didn't seem to expect an answer, which was just as well, as I'd none to give him. None that wouldn't have had him furious anyway.

269

He sat himself down on a sofa, nodded towards a chair that I should sit too. I did. I debated making a break for it, calling for help, but I realised I'd never make it in time. Also, there was no way in this world that I could leave Helen alone in the house with him, even if he didn't know she was there. What if she woke up and he heard her crying? I felt shivers go over my body.

"I want to arrange regular access to him," he said. "After all, he is my son."

"No way," I said, "absolutely no way. He is not your son."

"Look, Grainne, I want to share in this baby. I am his father," he said again. This was obviously important to him. "I want, I need to have time with him, help raise him. I'd be a good father, I know I would. I'd love him, mind him."

There was yearning in his voice, which I ignored. I certainly wasn't going to start feeling sympathy for Brogan of all people.

"I'd be a good dad," he repeated, imploring. "Strict, mind, but fair. My father was always very strict with us – it was the lick of the belt if we stepped out of line. Never did me any harm, though."

I managed to swallow my gasp at this last. He's a rapist, for God's sake, and he thinks no harm was done to him! And he wanted access to Helen . . .

"No," I said shortly. "I repeat, he is not your baby."

His manner changed then, his voice hardened. "Well, if you won't do it unofficially, I'll just take it to court."

"Court wouldn't do you any good," I said. "My husband's name is on the birth cert. You'd have no case for custody." Thinking, thank God I put Patrick down as the father.

"I've consulted a solicitor and he said that, since you swore under oath that we had sex at the appropriate time, I'd be able to insist on a DNA test. And that would be fairly indisputable, wouldn't it?"

I felt as if I'd been punched in the stomach. Is it true? I wondered desperately. He might well be bluffing, I could well believe that. But if he isn't . . . I felt physically sick.

"No . . . no," I said, shaking my head in denial, "no, there's no way."

He smiled at me, and I knew that he was enjoying this, enjoying my powerlessness just as, albeit in a different way, he'd enjoyed it before. He continued, "He seemed to think getting access wouldn't be a problem. After all, I'm a respectable man, with a professional job, my own flat. And nowadays, he said, judges like to see children have both their parents."

"But they'd never give you custody," I whispered. "You're a rapist."

He shot out of the sofa, shouted, "Don't call me that!" and I couldn't help myself, I flinched, moved back into my chair. He stalked across the room towards where I was sitting and leaned over me.

"Listen," he said, softer now, but with menace in his voice, "don't ever ever call me that word again, if you know what's good for you. You got me in enough trouble once, by saying that. Have you any idea what it was like for me, before the trial, before I was acquitted? Everyone looking at me strangely – my neighbours and colleagues. My family and friends knew I hadn't done, couldn't have done what you said, but the others, they didn't know, and I'd see them looking at me, wondering. And they'd try to talk to me normally, but it wouldn't work – they'd be sounding strange, really artificial. It was hell." Then he smiled smugly. "Anyway, I'm not a rapist, I was acquitted."

A sense of fury overcame me, stronger than my fear. "How *dare* you?" I said. "How *dare* you? At least here, now, have the courage to admit what you did. Bad enough to force me, but not even to admit it to yourself! Go on, I dare you, admit it to me, now! There's nobody else to hear, go on, say it!"

And, incredibly, the force of my fury was such that he stepped back a pace. He looked at me consideringly for a moment, and then turned and sat down again on the sofa facing me. Knowing what I did about him, I found it hard to equate this tall, handsome, clean-cut man, well dressed in pristine jeans and a red polo shirt, with the man who'd forced me, who'd humiliated me, hurt me.

He said, "Look, it wasn't like that. You just misunderstood. I know we got off to a bad start, with you thinking I'd forced you, and all. But I didn't, you know, it was just that I wanted you so much. And Grainne," his voice softened into some travesty of seduction, "I've thought about you so much since that night we shared. I couldn't come near you before, when I was on bail, but now . . . now it's different. And I know your husband's gone, his car hasn't been here, and I rang up once, pretending to be from his insurance company," I took a deep in-breath of shock and realisation, "and you said he was living elsewhere. So why don't you and I give it a go?" As if it was the most reasonable request ever. "Like I said, I know we got off to a bad start. But we could start again, with dates, couldn't we? You know, dinner, theatre, things like that. And it would be wonderful," he crooned, "I could be a father to the baby – a child needs a father. And I could be a partner to you – a woman needs a man."

He stopped, looked at me, smiling expectantly.

I thought, he's mad. He's stone-crazy mad.

And he's in my house, and God knows what he's going to do next.

I said nothing, could think of nothing to say. I was shaking. Helen, don't wake up, I begged silently. And I kept trying not to think of her, in case the force of my thoughts reached her and woke her up.

He whispered, "Why don't we go to bed now? I've waited so long for you."

My stomach clenched, heaved silently. Oh, please don't let him rape me again, I couldn't bear it. Inspiration struck me, and trying to keep my voice calm, I said, "We certainly can't have sex now. I'm only ten days after giving birth. They told me no sex for at least six weeks. There were tons of stitches," I improvised wildly, "and they told me that those stitches would rub off a man and hurt him, if we didn't wait."

His face turned in disgust. "Well, not now then, but soon." He smiled at me – he probably thought he was smiling affectionately, kindly, but to me it looked feral, like a wolf.

He looked around the room then, examining it like a prospective purchaser. "Nice house," he said. "I could move in here, you know, after we have enough dates to make it appropriate. My place would be too small for us all. And the baby wouldn't have to move. What's his name, by the way?"

What? "Er, it's – John."

"Nice name. Good and plain. Now, this house, show me around, hm?"

"No!" I yelped. "No." Apart from the fact that as soon as he went upstairs he'd see Helen, I couldn't bear him to invade my house, see any more of my personal space. What would I do? How could I stop him?

Again, inspiration came just in time and I said, "In fact, I was just leaving to collect the baby. Why don't you come with me, and you'll see him the sooner."

"A great idea," he said, visibly pleased.

"Come on, then!" I got to my feet and headed for the door. Although my heart turned over at the thought of leaving Helen alone, I had no choice, and my heart began beating faster at the fact that I'd be soon getting him out of her vicinity.

He followed me, saying in a relaxed tone, "Hey, what did you think about my defence lawyer? Bit of a dog, wasn't she? Wouldn't have wanted to shag her."

On and on he drivelled about different players in the court case, as though he was recapping the events of a party we'd both been to.

With shaking hands I grabbed the keys and my handbag off the hall table, and went out, shutting the door behind us. A tiny measure of relief passed through me as I closed the door between him and my precious baby.

We got into the car. I started it and drove off towards the city centre, thinking: Great, Grainne, now you're stuck in a car with this insane man. Where to now? I could hardly really go to my parents' house. And God, what if he overpowered me, and brought me somewhere? Helen was so tiny, she'd suffer for hours – nobody would think to look for her. And what if he killed me? She'd just cry and cry for me, weaker and weaker . . . with a huge effort I pulled myself together. What was I going to do?

I said, "I'll just ring my mother and tell her I'm on my way." And I grabbed my mobile phone from my bag, still not knowing what I would do. With a thrill of relief I remembered Patrick's voice, on the night he left: "Let me know if you need anything," he'd said. I'd ring him.

As I held the phone I hoped that I'd be stopped by the gardaí for using the mobile phone in a car, but, of course, no such luck.

But: "Hang on," said Brogan. "How do I know you're not ringing the gardaí?"

"Of course I'm not," I said. "Look," and I tapped the

keys of my phone, "you can see that it's my phone address-book. Look, that number there: 'P' for parents."

"Okay," he said, "go ahead."

So I pressed the 'dial' button. Please, please let him be at his desk! With huge relief I heard his voice, brisk and businesslike, saying, "Patrick Quinn."

"Hi, Mum," I said brightly, "I'm just ringing to tell you I'm on my way to collect the baby."

His voice was amused. "Hey, Grainne, it's me. You dialled the wrong number."

"Oh, I know," I said, "that's what I wanted."

Patrick is always quick off the mark; often I've rued this particular tendency, now I blessed it.

"Grainne," he said, his voice serious now, "are you okay?"

Still in a determinedly bright voice I said, "No, not in the slightest!"

"Is it something to do with Brogan?"

"Gosh, yes," I said. "Listen, Mum, I should be with you soon, I'm at the Portobello Bridge now. And I've got a friend with me, for you to meet. He wants to see the baby."

There was silence for a nano-second – I could feel the waves of his concentrated thinking. Then he said, "Tell him your parents live in Clontarf, and go towards there. But instead of swinging around the normal way past the Customs House, take the road past Store Street garda station. If he questions that, tell him that you know from years of experience that it's quicker. I'll be waiting there, with some guards. Stop the car right outside the garda station, right in the traffic if there's no parking spaces."

"Thanks so much, Mum," I said. "We'll see you soon." And, my hands shaking, I hung up.

It was a bizarre journey, into and then through the city centre. Brogan chatted about this and that, God knows what, as if this was a perfectly normal situation, and I made noises in return.

As expected, he questioned me as I turned into the road leading to the garda station. I told him what Patrick had suggested, and he accepted it, merely passing a comment on the dreadful traffic in Dublin nowadays.

He didn't question the garda presence outside the station – they're always coming and going from there. There was a space right outside, and I pulled into it. "What the –" was all that he had time to say, before a burly guard pulled open the passenger door and ordered him out. Patrick ran around the outside and pulled open my door, as with shaking hands I undid my seat-belt and fell into his arms. "Hush now," he said, holding me tight. Oh the feel of him, the solidness of him!

But I said, "Quick, I have to ring Lucy, get her to rescue the baby – she's in the house!"

Brogan was looking at me, anger and horror in his eyes. "You lied to me! I can't believe you lied to me!"

And despite my relief at being safe from him, I felt a frisson of fear run through me at the look of hatred in his eyes.

I turned away from his gaze, and began to dial Lucy's number on my mobile phone. But I was stopped by Patrick's hand on my arm. "If you do that," he said, "you're leaving yourself open to having to give all sorts of explanations. Look, we'll finish here quickly, and get back. The baby will be fine, she's not going to starve in an hour."

I stopped dialling. He was right.

"Okay, let's go then."

But, "Hang on," said the garda, "we have to sort this out. What's the story?"

Patrick and I moved onto the pavement, where Brogan was flanked by two guards.

Incoherently I told them the story, aware of Patrick's gasp when I revealed that Brogan had been watching the house.

"You tricked him into getting into the car?" said the Guard. "Well, that means we can't get him for abduction. Did he break into your house?"

"No, he rang the doorbell, and I answered it, and he pushed his way in."

They conferred quietly among themselves, and then said to us, regret in their voices, "There's nothing we can get him on. If you want to make a statement about the threats, we'll look into it, but honestly, it's going to be his word against yours. Your best bet is to get an injunction against him, stop him going anywhere near you. And I'll get the boys in Ranelagh to keep an eye on the house, drive past it every so often. And you," he said sternly to Brogan, "do you hear that? Keep away from the lady."

Oh yes, I thought that's going to stop him. But right now I didn't care, I just wanted to get back to Helen.

"I'll make a statement," I said, "but not now – I must go get my baby. Can I go into my local garda station and make one later?"

"That'd be grand," said one of the guards. And to Brogan, "Now, you, clear off, and remember, keep away from this lady!"

Brogan gave me another look of such hatred, such menace, such promise of retribution, that I shivered.

"Come on," said Patrick gently to me, "I'll take you home."

And we got into my car, he driving, and we went home. I was shaking, and then, now that I was safe, the enormity of it overwhelmed me and I started crying, in delayed shock and relief. Patrick laid a brief, quiet hand on my kneading hands, and muttered obscenities under his breath.

"The fucker," he said, at one stage, hitting the steering wheel hard in anger and frustration. "Look, we can't have this. We'll organise something, I promise – we'll keep you safe."

His certainty reassured me, somewhat.

When we got back to the house, I ran frantically up the driveway, pushed the key into the door, and ran up the stairs, gasping, and into the bedroom. Helen, bless her, was still sleeping. In my fright I picked her up and cuddled her hard, and in the process woke her up. As I carried her downstairs she began crying – perhaps cross at being disturbed from her sleep, perhaps picking up on my upset.

Patrick was sitting in the sitting-room. I joined him,

nervous now to be alone with him, still shaking after what had happened.

"I need to feed Helen," I said, embarrassed. "She's crying, and a feed will settle her."

"Go ahead," he said. I looked at him, sitting back in the chair, and felt a sudden sense of awe at the size, the pure beautiful maleness of him. I also felt, with a sense of delight, the return of a familiar but nearly forgotten feeling: a surge of hunger for him. It was the first sexual desire I'd felt since the rape, and I had to laugh ironically to myself at the timing. But still, still, I was exhilarated at the stirrings of sexuality that I'd feared gone forever.

I drank in the sight of him, seeing him sitting there with his long lean legs stretched out, the shadow at his groin. He looked relaxed, but when I looked closer, there was a coiled tension about him. It couldn't be easy for him, being back in his own house in these circumstances, seeing the baby for the first time, and now to see me feed her.

Assuming a nonchalance I certainly didn't feel, I sat down some distance from him, and latched Helen on, looking only at her and what I was doing. But I could feel his gaze on me.

He said, and his voice sounded rough, as though something was catching in his throat, "You look beautiful doing that, like a Madonna."

I looked up.

He was gazing at me intently, his focus strong. "You always said you'd breast-feed, when we had a baby."

His voice broke slightly, so slightly I wasn't sure if I'd imagined the emotion in it. And then, with a light casual voice that he couldn't quite carry off, "So no regrets then, about keeping her."

"No regrets about that. But plenty of regrets about the price I had to pay."

"You made your choice. I suppose, when it came down to it, you didn't love me enough." He said it in a joking way, trying to hide his hurt.

"Oh Patrick," I said, "never, ever think that. I love you so much. And I didn't make any choice, in the end I didn't have any choice to make. I could no more have let her go than I could have torn out my heart if you'd asked me. If I had given her up, you still wouldn't have had me, you know. You might have had the shadow that was left, but it would have been a torn, shrivelled parody of me. The essence of me, the me you fell in love with, would have gone with her. There would have been nothing left for you, nothing worth having, anyway." I was only realising the truth of all of this as I was saying it. "Once she was born, she was more part of me than she had been when she was inside me."

He looked intently at me, his dark angular face expressionless. He didn't say anything.

"In fact, it's a measure of my love for you that I tried to give her up for adoption. I fell in love with her immediately, and I spent three days thinking I'd be losing her, feeling the pain of that. And anyway, the truth is the other way around: you didn't love me enough to accept me, once Helen and I came as a package. It was you who put conditions on our relationship. It was you who forced what you called a choice, which wasn't any choice at all." I said again, softly and wonderingly, "You didn't love me enough."

There was silence. I bent my head again to my nursing baby, caressed her soft head.

Eventually Patrick said, "It wasn't that I didn't love you enough – I love you so much it hurts. It was that I couldn't handle it, all of it. In fact, I am going to –" Abruptly he stopped.

He got up and began pacing the room. He said, "We have practical things to consider, now that we know this madman is going to stalk you. And forget an injunction, he's hardly the sort to let that stop him. Let me think this through. You can't stay here, it's the first place he'll look for you. And you obviously can't stay in Kevin's flat."

Why not, I thought, but didn't say.

"You could move back home with your parents, but I'm sure you don't want to do that." He flashed me a smile, the smile I loved, and for an instant it was as wonderful as it had ever been.

But he was back thinking now, wondering where to stash me.

Then he said, "I know – my parents' holiday home in Cilltubber." He caught my blank look. "You know, in West Cork – it's on the sea, it's lovely. The cottage is tiny, mind you, but that bastard'll never find you there, and you can stay there for a while. God knows what we'll do long-term, we'll have to sell the house and buy somewhere else for you, that he doesn't know."

I caught the mention of buying a house for me, rather than us, but didn't say anything. I didn't want to pursue that thought.

With Patrick, the thought is always the deed; he went to the phone and dialled. Then: "Dad, hi, it's me. Yes, grand thanks. But listen, we've got a bit of a problem." He stopped, took a deep breath, obviously struggling to keep calm. "Thing is, Dad, that bastard Brogan turned up at the house looking for the baby . . . yes, just today. I know, she was terrified. He's been watching the house, stalking her, really. Yes, I know. But she managed to get to a garda station, and escape from him that way. And he's furious now with her about that. God, Dad," his voice cracked slightly, "you should have seen the look of fury and hatred he gave her.

"So she can't stay here – she needs somewhere safe. And I thought of Fisherman's Cottage. I know it's a lot to ask, but could she stay there for a while? She can? Great, thanks, Dad. Talk to you soon. Bye – oh . . . of course I will."

He hung up and turned to me.

"Dad says it's no problem. He also said to tell you that he loves you, and is thinking of you. We'll pack your stuff now, and go straight away."

So we packed suitcases for me and Helen. I felt so safe with Patrick there, and so scared about going away on my own. We threw clothes and toiletries into cases, and picked up duvets and sheets. Got some basic foodstuffs together.

Casting a last glance at our house where we had once been so happy, I buckled Helen into her carseat, and we got into the car and drove off. I felt mixed emotions: in addition to sadness at leaving the house there was a remainder of fear from the day's earlier trauma, and a sense of unreality at the suddenness of it all.

But deep down, underneath it all, there was a bubbling excitement and joy at being with Patrick again, for the whole five hours or however long it took us to get there. Surreptitiously I looked at him. God, he was so handsome! I gazed at his strong dark profile, his long lashes, his solid hands confidently gripping the steering wheel. I felt a thrill whenever his hand came near me to change gear, and watched the play of muscles under his forearm as he did so. I thought, he's not even aware of my proximity.

Conversation, as might be expected, was stilted. We spoke a lot about his job, chat about different colleagues whom I knew. We spoke a little about our respective parents, and brothers, and how they were getting on. He told me a little about Cilltubber, where he had spent seemingly idyllic childhood holidays.

"It's a little town with a main street running parallel to the sea. There are several roads leading from this main street to the sea, and one of those leads to a small, busy, harbour. That's where Fisherman's Cottage is, on the little road leading to the harbour. So it's close to everything. I'll leave you the car – I'll get a taxi and the train back – but you can get everything you need there."

There was silence for a moment, then I took a deep breath, "Patrick. Patrick, I've something to tell you. I don't know how you'll take it, you'll probably be very cross with me."

He gave me a sharp, brief look. "What? It can't be that bad, surely, after all the other shocks?"

"Patrick, when I was in the hospital with the baby, the registrar of births came around, to fill in the details for the birth cert. And I, well, I put down your name on the birth cert, as the father I mean." I briefly explained to him my reasoning: that at that stage I had thought she would be adopted, and I didn't either want her thinking her mother was a slapper who didn't know who the father of her child was, or that she would ever try and trace Brogan. Then I stopped, and waited for his reaction. Luckily we were just coming into Cashel, so at least if he threw me out I wouldn't find myself literally on the side of the road.

But he surprised me. "You were right," he said. "If I'd thought about it, I'd have suggested it myself, especially since we thought then that she'd be adopted. I can't do much for her, but at least I can give her my name."

The wonderful journey, replete with the sight and sounds of my beloved husband, passed too quickly. We by-passed Cork city, and drove on through the scenic countryside, and eventually, as the long summer day was turning towards evening, we arrived in the village of Cilltubber. We drove up the main street, with its colourful shops, houses and pubs, and soon turned left down a small road. "This is called Harbour Lane, for obvious reasons," said Patrick.

There was a small row of tiny, traditional, cottages along the left-hand side of the road. At the end of the road, joined at a sharp right angle, so it was parallel with the main street, was the harbour wall. Fishing boats and rowing boats were tied to bollards ranged along either side of the wall, with stone steps leading to the sea. In the distance was a picturesque island, with what looked like a ruined chapel on it.

Patrick pulled up outside a little white cottage. The front garden was hardly bigger than an average dining-table – three steps would bring you up it. But it was entered by a gorgeous white wicket gate, and the garden either side of the path had gravel on it, with a few dead pots. "It's hard to keep plants, what with the salty air, and my parents only coming here every so often," said Patrick, following my gaze. He lifted one of the redundant pots, took a key out from under it, and opened the door.

We walked straight into the sitting-room. There was a staleness about the air, and a light covering of dust, but the room was painted a gentle white, and there was a wood-burning stove at the far end. There were two comfortable-looking sofas, covered with bright throws, and a table with four chairs. All in all, even taking into account the need for a good airing, it was a welcoming, relaxing room.

At the back of this room was a kitchenette, about half the width of the house, obviously an extension. There was a door from the sitting-room leading to, I saw as I opened it, a little yard with a bin in it, and a little shack which had logs in it. There was also a stairs leading directly from the sitting-room, facing the front door, and Patrick began climbing them, hefting the suitcases.

"The bedrooms are up here," he said. I followed him.

Directly above the kitchen, and also obviously a new addition, was a tiny bathroom, with room only for a toilet and shower: I'd be bathing Helen in the kitchen sink, I noted. The space above the sitting-room, sharply sloped by the roof, was divided into two small bedrooms, one leading off the other, the first one containing two single beds, and the second, a double bed.

He left the suitcases on the floor, and we went downstairs again. We stood awkwardly in the sitting-room.

He cleared his throat. "Money . . . do you have your cash card and your credit card with you?"

I nodded.

"Well then, just take out of the account whatever you need – I don't want you to be stuck for anything."

My voice was thick with emotion as I said, "That's – that's very good of you. To support me when I'm not earning my own money because of – " and I gestured towards Helen, "and to support her too. I really appreciate it."

He shook his head wearily. "No, no, least I can do. Actually, it feels to me like guilt money, nearly. I feel so bad about not being able to come back to you, not being able to accept," in his turn he nodded his head in the direction of my daughter, "it really is the least I can do, to support you financially even though I can't support you any other way." He shook his head. "Don't think it's good of me," he said again. "In a way it's a cop-out."

"It still makes all the difference to me," I said.

"Good, good. And look, don't see yourself short, or anything. I guess you won't be jetting off to Florida on the credit card, but don't feel you have to watch every penny, either."

He shifted uncomfortably, then said, changing the subject, "There's no central heating, but the stove warms the whole house wonderfully – it heats the water also. There's also an electrical immersion heater, so you can have hot water even when the stove isn't on. It's here," and he showed me. "The shower is electric too, so there's no problem with hot water. There's no phone – do you have your mobile phone with you?" He nodded, satisfied, when I said I did.

Eventually he ran out of things to show me, and we hovered uncertainly.

He said, "Well, I'll be off now. I'll go up to the pub – they'll have the phone numbers of the local taxis – and get a taxi from there."

"There'll be no trains from Cork by the time you get there. Do you – do you want to stay the night here, and I'll drop you back to Cork in the morning?"

Say yes, I pleaded with him silently, please stay.

But he was shaking his head, "Better not, work in the morning, and I've missed most of today after all. I'll either stay in Cork tonight and get the first train in the morning, or I might see if I can hire a car. I'll be fine, don't worry."

But it wasn't worry that had me in its grip, it was the need to hang onto him, to grab every minute of his company that I could. Maybe I was also thinking, somewhere deep inside, that if he stayed the night we'd end up sleeping together, and I'd win him back that way. Maybe that was in his mind too, and that was why he was so adamant about going.

He stooped as if to kiss my forehead, but stopped short. Said quietly, "Look after yourself, I'll be in touch. Ring if you need anything."

And he let himself out the door and left.

The house was so empty. Helen was sleeping. Any noises that might have come from the street outside were blocked by the thick stone walls of the cottage. Inside was total silence, not even the ticking of a clock. I felt so lonely, totally isolated. I had the strangest sensation that the rest of the world had disappeared from outside the door, and here we were, Helen and I, the only two people left alive. Or maybe we were the ones who had disappeared.

Wearily I trudged upstairs and made the beds.

At some stage in the evening I fed Helen and changed her. At another stage I opened a can of soup, half-heated it and ate it, not even registering what flavour it was. At yet another I gathered Helen into my arms, and went upstairs, and laid us both down on the double bed in the back bedroom. At least the sheets and duvets, unwashed since we'd slept in them in my own house the night before, were comfortable and familiar. As was Helen, the warmth of her, the little snuffling noises she made in her sleep.

I said to her, my own voice sounding startlingly loud, "Well, it's just you and me, baby. Fugitives, although we've done nothing wrong. Here for I don't-know-how-long. Starting a new stage of our lives, knowing nobody."

And, on that first night, I sobbed my heart out as I lay preparing for sleep to come and claim me, for the loneliness and the fear of the future, for fear of Brogan, for the thoughts of my beloved husband, gone from me.

But just as I was dropping off to sleep I thought: that's *it!* No more victim stuff here. This is the situation I'm in, and I'm going to make the best of it. I'm going to get a good life going here, for me and Helen, for as long as we're here. And as I reached over and capped Helen's soft head, I promised her, whispering fiercely, "I'll give you a good life, I swear. We will be happy."

When I awoke next morning I still felt this resolve, but yet it was hard to know where to start. Brave words are all very well, but what would I actually do? One day at a time, I promised myself.

I was soon distracted by the sound of Helen whimpering in a request for food. I sat up as I fed her, and studied the room. It was painted a rather pretty pink, with muslin curtains at the window. At each side of the bed was an orange-pine locker, on each of which stood an ornate brass lamp, topped with a flowery-frilly shade. An aged, and frankly awful, carpet (all purple and brown swirls, and so acrylic that you could nearly see the static electricity on it) covered the floor. But all in all, a comfortable, homely room. A good clean, I decided, would do both the cottage and me a world of good. After Helen had finished feeding, I got up. Changed her and dressed her. Had a shower and dressed myself.

When I searched the cupboards for cleaning stuff, I realised I'd need to go shopping. So I popped Helen into her pushchair and set off up the short street to the main street. My spirits rose marginally – the weather was glorious, even so early, with the sun a bright comforting yellow.

The first thing I did was to present myself at the local garda station, which was an annexe to the Sergeant's house, consisting of one little room with a counter dividing the 'office' from the public area. A uniformed garda asked if he could help me. "I'm Sergeant Farrell," he told me, "and I'm the garda presence in Cilltubber – it's not exactly the crime capital of Ireland!"

I laughed, and then became more serious, and introduced myself, and explained that I had come to make a statement on an incident that had happened in Dublin yesterday. He gravely took my statement about Brogan's visit, not making any comments on it, and promised to pass it on to the gardaí in Store Street.

"Could you pass a copy also to Sergeant Ger O'Reilly? She was involved in the original case, and I'd like to keep her updated." I told him where to send this copy, and he promised he would.

We said our goodbyes, and I made my way back onto the main street.

The town was beautiful, I found, with its painted shop fronts, and hanging baskets everywhere. There was an amazing arts and crafts shop, bright and colourful, its window artistically arranged. I stayed for ages looking in this window, not daring to go into the shop. The paintings were wonderful, all of local scenes, and there was jewellery, and candles, and turned wooden bowls. A cornucopia.

And there were bright, vibrant pubs, which later proved to be well stocked with business no matter the time of day.

There was a small park down the next side street after Harbour Lane, containing a small children's playground, and benches from which there were wonderful views. It backed, I realised, onto my own house, as I looked at the eight-foot wall which was Fisherman's Cottage's back boundary. Pity there isn't a gate in that wall, giving direct access to the park, I told myself, and then laughed: well, it was hardly a long walk to it: up Harbour Lane, along a little bit of the main street, and then a hundred yards down this road.

And everyone I met said hello, and commented on the fine day we were having, hope it stays this way. This was different from big-city Dublin, alright. I didn't know them, they didn't know me, but I felt I belonged because of their kind, casual words.

I went into the mini-supermarket (a contradiction in terms, now that I think of it – but probably no proprietor wanted to call his or her shop a fairly-average-market). I surveyed the shelves – there were certainly all the basics, we wouldn't starve. No balsamic vinegar, no pesto. The frozen puff pastry had a smug air, as if it knew that filo pastry would never be allowed across the door.

I collected what I needed to spring-clean the house, and went to pay. The woman at the checkout made the regulatory comment about the weather, and then, said, "You've come on holiday here, then?"

"No, no, I'm here to live for a while. I'm staying in Fisherman's Cottage."

She nodded sagely, "Oh yes, Jim and Moira Quinn's place."

"That's right. I'm Grainne Quinn, I'm their daughter-in-law."

The gossip antennae quivered, and it was fun to see her try to pick her words so as to extract the most amount of information whilst giving the least sense of inquisition.

"Oh, is that right? And your husband? Would he be Patrick, or Donal?"

"Patrick –"

"Ah right. I remember them well, boys they were then, coming on their holidays. My daughters used to play with them. I suppose we weren't exciting enough for them once they got bigger." She smiled to show she wasn't really upset.

"Ah well," I said feebly, "you know . . ."

"A wonderful place, Cilltubber. I've lived here all my life and the only way I'm leaving is in a box, but even I must admit it's a bit lacking in the bright lights. My daughters still live here, though. The eldest, Claire, she's the solicitor in the town. The middle girl, Laura, works as a receptionist in the hotel. And the youngest, Imelda, she works here in the shop with me – it's her day off today. It'll all be hers, one day. And – Patrick," she paused delicately, this was the crunch one, "he'd be coming down weekends so then, would he?" She looked at me from under her eyelashes.

"Whenever he can," I said. "Work commitments, you know."

"Ah right, sure don't I know? Everyone's so busy nowdays, all it is now is work, work, work. They have no time to be doing anything else. People don't even seem to have the time they used to, to talk to you."

You seem to manage it alright, I thought uncharitably, but then I softened. She wasn't being nosy. Well, she was, but in an Irish way. A way that wants to know all about you, without the slightest bit of malice about it.

Finishing the conversation, the shopkeeper took my money, gave me my change, and said, "Before I forget, I'm Dympna Doran. And you're very, very welcome to Cilltubber, for however long you live here."

My spirits buoyed, Helen and I went home, and I cleaned and dusted and polished the cottage, in between tending to Helen's needs. Eventually, towards the closing of the day, the house was done. It gleamed, and its inherent charm was now obvious. Also, cleaning the house had worked almost like an inverse dog-pissing-to-mark-its-territory, because this clean-fest had made me feel much better about the house. I felt that it now belonged to me (in an existentialist sense anyway) and I belonged to it. It began to feel like home.

I'd always loved the long bright summer evenings which Ireland gets, courtesy of its northern latitude. But now they seemed to mock me. All bright out, and nothing to do. I thought that I'd go mad – or worse I'd end up doing macramé. At least I had Helen to talk to, even though she didn't understand me, and wasn't too hot on the conversational front yet. But it saved me from talking to myself, or worse, the walls.

Just then my mobile rang. It was Patrick, and my heart leapt with joy to hear his voice.

"How are you going?" he asked. "Have you settled in okay?"

"Yes, I'm great," I told him, neglecting to burden him with the loneliness and fear.

"I'm glad. Don't forget, ring me if you need anything, okay?"

I need you, I wanted to say. But I just said, "I will, thanks."

Chapter 23

The next day dawned overcast, which suited my mood.
I stared, terrified, at the day before me. I had nothing
to do. I couldn't clean the house any more or the walls
would dissolve. Maybe I *would* make enquiries about the
Macramé classes. Oh God. I know, I decided eventually.
I'd ring everyone I knew, even people I'd been in pre-
school with – indeed, even people whose mothers had
been at ante-natal classes with my mother. But the
problem was – I daren't tell anyone where I was.

I rang Sinead.

"How are you?" she said. "And where are you? I've
been ringing the house, and I keep getting the
answerphone."

"Oh Sinead," I said, "you won't believe where I am.
I'm in Cilltubber – on Cork's south coast, of all places.
Me! Big-city Grainne! I'm a fugitive!"

"What?"

Quickly I brought her up to date. "God, the bastard," she said feelingly. "This is dreadful. It seems like you'll never be able to put this whole thing behind you."

"Look on the bright side," I said, with a trace of irony, "I'm getting to spend the summer in a beautiful seaside town. In fact, I feel sorry for you stuck in the heat and pollution of Dublin."

She laughed. "Fair play to you. It works out well for me, then – I'll have somewhere nice to spend weekends."

"As many as you like," I said seriously. "What about next weekend?"

Uncharacteristically, she hesitated. "Sorry, Grainne, next weekend won't be possible. Thing is, I've got a date on Saturday night, and I don't want to break it."

"Great!" I said. "Who with? Do I know him?"

"Well, sort of." Again she hesitated. "It's Harry Moran. Do you remember? Your obstetrician. He got my phone number from his sister, and rang me, and we went out a few days ago, and it was wonderful, and well," over the phone lines I could hear her blushing, "he's very nice, and I really like him."

"My obstetrician!" I squealed. "Oh no, Sinead, I absolutely forbid it. You simply cannot – cannot – go out with a guy who's seen my fanny! You just can't."

"But he's so nice!" she appealed.

"But if you go out with him, at some point I'd have to meet him! Oh, the shame of it! And come on, surely there's something strange about men who want to be gynaecologists! What a job, looking at women's bits all day. You can't do this!"

There was silence, and then her voice, sharp with suspicion came down the line: "Grainne, are you winding me up?"

"Could be."

"Oh you! You had me really worried there. Especially since . . . especially since I do like him, you know."

Wow, Sinead had fallen for a man! This was great news!

"Sinead," I said, "I am so, so happy for you. And if you can bear spending the rest of your life facing the embarrassment of telling people how you two met, then go for it, girl!"

"Hardly 'the rest of my life' after one date," she said, laughing, but something in her voice said that, maybe, possibly, this idea was not totally bizarre. Hooray, at least something good had come out of all that had happened to me! Two good things, I thought quickly: this romance, and – I glanced fondly at my sleeping daughter – Helen.

After promising to ring often, and to come down the weekend after next, and mutual virtual hugs and kisses, we hung up.

Then I rang Stephen. He wasn't there so I left a message on the answerphone with a quick explanation.

And that was it. I realised how few true friends we have in life, and thanked God for having Sinead and Stephen. I didn't ring Kate – with the best will in the world, I couldn't trust her with anything I didn't want the world to know. I might as well have taken a front-page ad out in *The Irish Times* as do that. Of course she wouldn't tell Brogan directly – assuming she bumped into him, I knew that she wouldn't even talk to him. But for sure she wouldn't be able to resist telling other people – the drama of it would be too much for her. Imagine, she'd say, he turned up at the house and kidnapped her, and she had to flee to Cork! Whereabouts? Well, I'm not supposed to say, but I know you won't tell anybody . . . And Dublin's such a village, it really is, that there would be some chance – a small chance, but even that was too much – that Brogan would get to hear it. Kate and I were only in touch spasmodically, anyway – she probably wouldn't ring the house, and if she did, she'd just have to wonder why I didn't return her call.

I debated ringing my parents, decided against it. Since their less-than-successful visit to my house they hadn't been in touch at all. So why should I? But then I thought about it, and realised they'd need to know where I was in case . . . well, in case one of them was ill, or something. So, reluctantly, I dialled their number.

"Hi, Mum, it's me."

"Oh." She was still frosty. So I became all business. "I'm just ringing to tell you that I've moved temporarily down to West Cork. So I can't be contacted at home, but you can get me on the mobile. Okay?"

"Okay. Have you got that baby with you there?"

"Yes. And will have for the forseeable future, until she leaves home of her own accord."

"Well, then, nothing's changed, has it?"

"No, Mum," I said wearily. "Well, look after yourself."

I felt down after that call. She hadn't even asked why I'd moved, she hadn't shown any thawing towards me, she was still more interested in her upset than in me. Fine.

Once I'd phoned everybody, it was still before noon. And the day stretched before me, long and scary and empty and terrifying. Helen still needed feeding regularly, but even that, once I'd latched her on, didn't take much of my energy or attention: she did all the hard work. And she needed changing every so often, but with modern nappies it wasn't often enough to distract me. She mostly slept, but on the occasions that she was awake we goo'ed and gaa'ed at each other, and I was flooded again with relief that I hadn't let her go. Having said that, she soon settled into a pattern of crying for no reason from about eight o'clock for about two hours. And as I exhaustedly walked the floor with her, which was the only thing that settled her, I thought longingly of Patrick, and how if it were his child he could have helped me with this.

But like all small babies, she slept a lot outside those times. Great, except, what did I do with myself in the meantime?

I took to going to bed with her, sleeping when she slept. It's okay, I told myself, I'm still recovering from the birth, there's no problem in all this sleeping. But I knew, deep in the heart of me, that I was sleeping to avoid reality. Sure, as any new mother would, I needed a lot of sleep. But this much?

It was terrifying, the spaces between sleep. Nobody

to talk to. Nothing to do. I didn't even have a television to distract myself. Sometimes I sat numbly on the sofa, either feeding Helen, or watching her sleep, and was overwhelmed with how much had changed. In an instant my previous life had been wiped out. I could remember how it had been: working hard and socialising hard, laughing and talking and making love with Patrick, living in our lovely house, painting it, even simple things like grocery shopping. But those memories seemed unreal somehow, as if they'd happened to someone else. Reality was, and in my more fanciful moments seemed always to have been, this silence, this enforced solitude. The evenings were the worst. Somehow the days dragged by, but the evenings . . . During the day, since I had the windows open, I could hear people passing, talking, and reassure myself that I still existed, that I was still in the real world. But at night-time I closed the windows, and then the silence was total.

I wondered if I'd go mad. If Helen and I would be found, dead, at some future date. Or maybe someone would notice, and call in the authorities, and they'd arrive, and judge me an unfit mother, and she'd be taken into care. Into the hands of foster-parents, which was a bit ironic, since she was destined for foster-parents before I changed my mind. (Or rather, my mind changed me). How ironic, to go through all this, and have her back where she started.

But instinct's a wonderful thing. No matter how down I felt, how black, how un-existing, I still washed her and fed her and changed her. Despite everything, she was surviving: more, thriving. I could see her growing from day to day, and that gave me strength. I don't exist, I whispered to myself. Nobody knows where I am (not quite true, but depression deals in absolutes) but Helen and I are doing fine. I even found myself eating well, not for myself but for her. How could I produce good milk if I didn't eat? And in this darkness it became an imperative that Helen should have the best.

And that best included fresh air, so during this week I walked the feet off myself, and the wheels off the pushchair, walking around the town and its surrounding country lanes. I found myself shopping for the bare minimum so that I had to shop every day, just for the human contact.

But things were changing. I was now greeted by name when I went into the shop, and Dympna Doran sometimes introduced me to others there I might meet again in the town, and it was wonderful to be greeted like a local. On my second time into the shop she introduced me to her daughter Imelda.

Imelda was a beautiful woman, although you didn't realise it straight away. She was, like her mother, wearing a shop-coat which would make Helen of Troy look plain, and her glorious long red hair was carelessly pulled back and roughly plaited. She had creamy skin, lightly dusted with freckles, over fine features.

But, I realised, she doesn't know she's beautiful. She doesn't carry herself proudly.

One day I said to her, "Your mother told me that

your sister's a solicitor here in town. Where would I find her? Do you have her phone number?"

"Surely," she said, and rattled it off as I wrote it on the back of the receipt.

I rang her, and we made an appointment, and met. You'd know that she was Imelda's sister, although she wasn't nearly as beautiful. But she had the same sunshine-red hair, although hers was short and carefully styled.

"I need to know that what I'm going to tell you will be treated as totally confidential," I told her.

"Don't worry, solicitors are used to that. We make priests look loose-tongued," she smiled.

"It's like this," I said. "My daughter, Helen, here, is the child of a man who raped me. And he wants to put in a claim for shared custody. This is the reason I came here to Cilltubber, so he can't find me. But what I need to know is, could he get custody?"

"Was he tried for this rape?"

"Yes."

"Was he convicted? Judges look only to the well-being of the child when they make custody rulings, and I can't see any judge letting a convicted rapist have custody of a baby."

"No. He was acquitted."

"Oh. That's not so good. You see, legally, if he's acquitted he's as innocent of rape as if he'd never been charged. The judge wouldn't be able to take your statement of rape into account. But it's not too bad. Well, before he'd be looking for custody, he'd have to prove he was Helen's father. He'd have to convince a judge that there was good cause to compel you to provide some of Helen's DNA, for comparison purposes."

"He said that since I swore, under oath, at the trial, that I had intercourse with him, and the dates match, a solicitor told him he would have good cause because of that. Although I'm not sure I believed him – he might have been bluffing."

"Oh." She played with her pen a little. "That's difficult. Look, I'd be very surprised if he could get a DNA test on only that, but I couldn't tell you definitively that he wouldn't. That's why we have judges, to hear opposing arguments from solicitors – and that's why we have different levels of courts, to appeal decisions made by other judges. That's how the whole legal industry works, by holding different viewpoints. I would say, though, that he could very possibly find a solicitor who would tell him he had the right to custody, and who would take it to court. And you, and your solicitor, would argue the opposite case."

I listened in growing apprehension.

"Where is your husband in all of this?" she asked suddenly.

"We're separated – he couldn't cope with the baby."

She grimaced. "You see, another factor in a judge's decision might be whether she had a father figure in her life. And since she doesn't . . . Okay, here's what I think. I think that legally it would be very unlikely, although possible, that he would get his way. But I also think that since you're here in Cilltubber – and I take it he doesn't know where you are?" I shook my head, "then nothing can happen. He would need to know where you were to serve the court papers on you anyway. As as long as he doesn't know your whereabouts, you're safe. And even if he does ever find you, and you get served with a court case, you and your solicitor could drag it on for years, to higher and higher courts, to the European court of human rights, even. It would cost a lot of money, but it would buy you time, time when Helen is growing up, until she's either legally an adult, or at least old enough to tell a judge what she wants. So, for those two reasons, I don't think you need worry."

Easy for her to say. So, now I have an extra fear about him finding me. And where would I get the money to fight these court cases? I could hardly expect Patrick to fund them. I had hoped that she would have laughed at the thought of Brogan being able to get custody.

But eventually I managed to put that worry, along with all my other ones, into a box at the back of my mind, from where it only came out to play on dark, sleepless nights, along with memories of the rape and longing for Patrick. I don't mean to go on and on about it, but they were always there, no matter what else I was doing.

On Friday evening I decided, enough! So, instead of feeding Helen in the quiet of our house, I sat outside on the front step. She nursed away peacefully – she didn't care about where her food was situated. But as I sat on the front step I could see and hear people passing as they walked to and fro from the harbour. And some of them saw me, seated low as I was, and called hellos, and I called hello back, and realised that I still did exist.

Just then my mobile rang.

"Hello," I said into it.

"Hi, Grainne!" It was Stephen. "I'm here in Cilltubber – how do I find your house?"

I felt my heart lift at the thought of seeing him as I gave him directions. Two minutes later his car pulled up, and out he hopped, full of his usual joy.

"Hi," he said, "I was away for a few days, but I got your message, and I thought I'd surprise you. Hope I'm not interrupting anything major!"

"Hardly," I muttered.

He had a huge parcel under his arm. "Happy birthday," he said, as he flourished it at me.

"But it's not my birthday," I said, laughing.

With a a wave of his arms he dismissed this irrelevancy. "Go on, open it," he said, so full of excitement you'd swear he didn't know what was in the parcel himself.

So, one-handed, the other holding Helen to me as she nursed peacefully, I opened the present, Stephen helping when he deemed my single-handed clumsiness too much for his patience. He wasn't hopping up and down in anticipation, but it was all he wasn't doing.

When the parcel was opened it turned out to contain all the necessary equipment for painting: lots of watercolour paper, a range of watercolour paints, every brush size you could think of, and an easel, and books.

I just stared at it all, wordless.

"Do you not like it?" he asked anxiously.

"I do. Beyond like." But that was all I could say.

"It just came to me, how you used to draw and paint all the time, and how you loved it, and how good you were at it. And how you let it go for all these years. And I thought maybe you could paint out your anger and hate at . . . well, your anger and hate. And you were saying, before, in Dublin, how you dislike taking money from Patrick, with things the way they are, and I thought you could sell paintings of local scenes to tourists, and maybe become financially independent. And I thought it might save you from being bored with nothing to do but look after Helen all day. Although," he smiled ruefully, "seeing as my mother gave a short sharp laugh of the type usually described as 'mirthless' when I told her this, maybe I was wrong about that last bit. But I thought I was right about the rest." His face fell and he said, "But I wasn't, was I? I was wrong about it all. You don't like it a bit. I'm very sorry. Look," and he started gathering up the arrayed riches, "you go and put the kettle on – and by the time you get back it'll be back in the car, and forgotten." He reached for the easel.

I said, "No." My tongue felt too big for my mouth, and I had trouble speaking. Needles were pricking behind my eyes, and I had a physical pain in my chest.

I tried again. Said, "Leave it. I want it."

He carefully placed the stuff back on the step around me, and sat beside me, our hips touching. We sat in silence for a while. Around us we could hear the gentle noise of the waves lapping against the stonework, and the strident caw-caw of seagulls, and the murmurs and occasional laughter of people walking up and down the street. But we were silent. Stephen gave me all the space I needed.

Helen's nursing slowed, and she slept. I unlatched her, straightened my top, and eased her into the cradle of my arms.

Eventually I said, and my voice was croaky. "Stephen, I'm sorry I sounded as if I wasn't pleased. I couldn't react because I was stunned. You have given me the gift of my past. And of my future. But I'm scared. I was scared twelve years ago, and I didn't have the courage. And maybe the fear is even greater now, having lived unchallenged, feeding off me for so long." But I said, realising it only as I said it, "Maybe the desire, the need to paint is stronger for having been denied for so long. I thank you for the perception you've brought to this."

Stephen reached out and took my hand. Helen stirred in her sleep and gave a tiny yawn, then settled again.

I smiled at Stephen, and said, "Never mind the cup of tea – it's a glass of wine I need. Here, hold your honorary niece," and I placed her in his startled arms, went into the house and came out with a bottle of wine, glasses and a corkscrew. And so, as the sun went down over the bay, and in between waving and saying hello to passers-by, we laughed and chatted the whole evening. And I kept looking at the painting materials still placed around me.

Later that evening, as we were turning into bed in

our respective bedrooms, I said to him: "I hope you enjoy your night's sleep – it'll be the last one you get there!" He looked at me enquiringly. I went on, "Yes, my boyo, it'll be the couch for you next time – that room will be taken over for a studio."

He punched the air, shouted (quietly, remembering the baby), "Yes!" and gave me a huge grin of delight.

* * *

When he left, among hugs and kisses, after lunch the next day, I settled Helen for her nap, and went and studied the painting equipment where it sat in the spare bedroom, circling it almost nervously. I reached out and tentatively touched the easel, caressed the rich paper, feasted my eyes on the glorious colours in the tubes, luxuriously rubbed my face with the soft brushes.

Nervously, tentatively, I set up the easel, filled a jar with water, laid out the paints. Said aloud the names of the colours: burnt umber, raw sienna, cobalt blue and ultramarine blue, alizarin crimson, phthalo green – even the sounds of these paints filled me with joy, and thrilled me. I taped the paper to the easel and then wondered.

What would I paint? Of course, the view out the tiny window – indeed, paint the window and its curtains as well, to frame the view of the harbour, and sea, and the distant Church Island with its picturesque ruined chapel.

I drew in the scene before me, and then began to paint, my fingers shaking with the forgotten joy of the familiarity of a brush in my hand.

And over the next couple of days I worked on this painting, and when it was finished I surveyed it critically. Not bad, I thought joyously, not bad at all. Of course, not great. But definitely there was potential there – all I had to do was to practise, and learn and refine techniques.

Now my days were full, and not long enough, as I painted and painted. Clumsily at first, throwing more away than I kept. I didn't paint therapeutic abstracts, as Stephen had suggested – it wasn't the time for that.

No, I painted the local scenery, and there was such a wealth of choices for my subjects, with the beauty around me. Many the day I put Helen into the car, and drove around until I had a scene that satisfied me, and spent hours and hours, pausing only to tend my daughter, as I gloried in painting. I experimented with different styles: precise drawings, painted in what was almost a painting-by-numbers way; or wild, almost impressionistic, very loose paintings. I liked both styles, I decided. I could do very different paintings of each scene simply by using these different styles.

It was still a very solitary existence, during the week especially. And I still missed Patrick with every breath. He hadn't phoned beyond that second day, and although I was disappointed, I understood. I had made my decision when I chose Helen, and for him to keep in touch would be like picking at a scab. What could we say? Where could we go? He knew I would ring him if I needed anything, which was more than generous of him.

Although I had visitors from Dublin pretty much every weekend, which was great, and wonderful reassurance that although I might be gone, I wasn't forgotten, during the week it was just me and Helen. And slowly I got used to it and realised that I was actually quite good company for myself. That I could live by myself, on my own emotional resources. That, to my surprise, I was a valid person, and didn't need to reflect myself off others.

It was a slow lesson, and one hard-earned, and there were still nights when I sobbed myself to sleep from loneliness – quite apart from the nights I cried myself to sleep with pain over the rape, and the loss of Patrick. But it was a rich lesson, and a happy realisation. I could be by myself, I still existed even when there was nobody else there to prove it to me.

And friends phoned often. Jim Quinn phoned one day. I'd always got on great with him and Moira, and it was wonderful to hear from him. He asked how I was doing, and Helen, and was she big now? We spoke about the safe subjects of the cottage, and Cilltubber.

Towards the end of the conversation, though, I cracked. "And, Patrick, how is he?"

"Good," he said neutrally.

I cursed myself. Jim might love me, but Patrick was his son, and his first loyalty had to be to him. I realised again what an awkward position he and his wife were in. "He's working hard," he said, obviously realising he'd been a bit abrupt.

Quaking, I asked, "And is he . . . does he?" I stopped,

311

I couldn't dare put into words my fear that Patrick might have met someone else.

But Jim, bless him, understood what I couldn't say. "I don't know," he said gently. "Not that he's told us, anyway, or that we've seen. But . . ."

And I in my turn understood him, that Patrick had a whole life away from his mother and father, and could have any number of girlfriends.

I bargained with God, that night in bed. Please don't let him have anyone, I begged. But if he does, please let it be lots of casual girlfriends, and not one special one. The thought of Patrick with a string of women pierced my heart, but not as much as did the idea of him getting serious with anybody else.

Chapter 24

After about two months, I had completed twelve paintings with which I was, if not happy, at least content. I went, terrified, late one afternoon, to the craft shop. A bell pinged as I opened the door. A richness of colour and scent welcomed me: paintings, Irish knits, hand-made soaps, crystal jewellery, candles, wood-turned bowls and candlesticks and pottery adorned the walls and shelves. I almost walked straight out again as I looked at the paintings, appalled at my arrogance that my work could keep such company.

Indeed, I was turning on my heel when from behind a bead curtain came a woman, a smile of enquiry on her face, and a warm and serene expression which immediately calmed me. She was small – little more than five feet, I judged, and elfin, with a gamine face topped by a short dramatic cut with a red hue never dreamed of by nature. She was dressed in a flowing purple crushed-velvet skirt, a velvet red top, and silvery jewellery everywhere that jewellery could be put – rings, bracelets, necklaces, two earrings per ear, and I noted as I caught sight of her bare, sandalled feet, even an anklet. She was, I thought, about ten years older than I, around forty, but you had to study her well to realise this. She moved, I noted as she came towards me across the shop floor, with a wondrous grace, with a dance in her step as though there was music only she could hear.

All this I noticed in an instant. It took no time before she was standing beside me and asking in a clear voice with an English accent and her beautiful smile, if she could help me.

I said, "I'm wondering how it works, selling paintings through this shop? I have some here to show you. Not very good, I'm afraid. I thought they were until I saw these" – I gestured around the shop. "Especially these," and I pointed to three that totally entranced me on a personal level, and intimidated me on a painting level, and awed me with their beauty, and made me long to have them to own and gaze upon forever. They were acrylics, bright and jewel-like scenes of the fishing boats in harbour, of the fishermen, happy and wrinkled of face, sitting mending nets, and of the nearby Cross Head – the beautiful scenes which I had also painted, but mine did not show such vibrancy, such surety, and such love.

"Well," she laughed, "you're off to a good start there – these are my paintings! We're always looking for new artists and crafters though – the more variety we can offer the tourists and other customers, the better. So do show me what you have. But first, let me introduce myself. I'm Magda Harrison, I'm from Manchester, I've been living in Cilltubber for three years now, and I've set up this shop." I nodded and she went on. "And you'd be the Quinn's daughter-in-law come to live in Fishermans's Cottage, wouldn't you?"

"Yes, Grainne Quinn."

"And who's this little work of art?" She looked into the sling at Helen. "This is my daughter Helen – she's eleven weeks old."

"Well, she's a pet – aren't you, my lovely? Now, let's look at your mum's paintings."

Nervously I handed her the portfolio and she drew out the paintings and looked at them. Time slowed. She looked at each one for a long time, her face in repose, no expression to give anything away.

I had included several obvious scenes – indeed, the same scenes as in Magda's paintings. The boats in the harbour, Cross Head and the sea, a street scene of Flanagan's bar, with its royal-blue paintwork, vibrant flowerboxes and traditional Guinness-ad signs. There was a beach scene, with children crouched, heads bent over their sandcastles, the late evening shadows long and dramatic. There was a scene of the whole village, as seen from the boat to Church Island. And finally, a scene of Cilltubber Crafts, the shop itself. I wasn't trying to be sycophantic – it truly was a beautiful scene, as Magda with her own artist's eye had already done the composition for me: with its red and green woodwork, and hanging baskets, and the name of the shop done with each letter a different Letterland character. And, although in real life you couldn't actually see the window contents from across the street, as the window was in shadow, I had taken artistic licence, and had painted in great detail all her wares – miniature paintings done of the real ones, rainbow candles, dots to represent the jewellery – a cacophony of colour.

She was silent for an eternity. Then she said softly, "How much?" I gulped and told her, cursing Stephen. This price was at his insistence, doubling what I'd tentatively suggested – after all, he'd pointed out, the shop's profit had to come out of that.

But she was nodding. "Grand, that means I can sell them for 40 per cent more – that's our standard mark-up." She lifted her eyes from the paintings and said, "We'll take all six, and you can replace them as they sell – which shouldn't take long – they're beautiful. Wonderful composition and excellent execution. You have an eye for scenes – it's amazing how often I've admired my shopfront – needless to say I've gone to a lot of trouble to make it look as good as it does, but I never saw it as a painting!" She looked at me appraisingly. "The tourists will love these paintings, and any like them you do. But I find a lack of passion in them. I look forward to seeing what work you produce when you have the confidence to paint passionately. Such paintings would hardly sell here –" she gestured with indulgent fondness around the shop, "but I predict that this talent, combined with the courage of passion, will go far, will appeal to real collectors, be sold in 'real' galleries. So we'd better enjoy selling your work for as long as we get the opportunity."

Before I could respond to this startling statement, Helen stirred and started whimpering.

I said apologetically, "I'd better go, I need to feed her."

Magda smiled her gentle smile. "Come into the back room and feed her there – there's a lovely comfy chair, and I'm sure we can run to a cup of tea for our new client!"

As I started to protest out of politeness she hushed me.

"Nonsense. Please stay. I'd love to get to know you better."

The room behind the bead curtain proved to be Magda's sitting-room – "I live above *and* beside the shop," she explained, as she busied making tea and Helen nursed hungrily. Her eyes kept flickering briefly, resting on Helen.

I said, drinking the tea, "Do you really think the paintings will sell?", still hardly able to believe it.

"Oh yes," she said. "I wouldn't take them on if I wasn't sure of it – it wouldn't be doing you any favours in the long run, and besides, I simply wouldn't have the space."

"How many, would you say, could I sell?" I asked nervously.

"Hard to say, and of course don't forget that it's essentially a summer trade – which suits me, I paint all winter and run the shop all summer. But probably about fifty a year."

The door pinged."Oh, that's someone in the shop," she said.

As she went to serve the customer I thought about it, and worked out the maths in my head. It came to about a third of my annual teaching income, after subtracting framing costs. Would I need to pay tax on that little? Hardly – must check it out. Say for now I didn't. It was still not a living wage. But it would take some of the burden off Patrick. I still wouldn't be able to pay rent on the cottage. But it would definitely feed us, and pay the bills. Maybe even get us some clothes.

And I, who not a year previously had probably spent that much money on clothes, make-up and other luxuries, was dizzied at the wealth of it all, the independence it represented.

Magda came back, and we sat and chatted. Nothing personal – I certainly didn't feel up to explaining my situation, and I thought I noticed a certain reticence about Magda also. Maybe it was my imagination, maybe it was just with her being English (not every race, I told myself firmly, tells their whole life story upon first meeting). We talked about painters we liked, about the joys and sorrows of being a painter (I felt simultaneously a thrill of joy at being able to discuss this, and a sense of fraud at calling myself a painter), places we liked around Cilltubber, harmless anecdotes about several of its citizens. We laughed quietly as the tea was drunk, and the rest of the afternoon passed, punctuated by Magda serving in the shop.

I noticed her gaze resting often on Helen, with a kind of hunger that I recognised, belonging as it does to childless women when confronted with babies.

At last I said, "Would you like to hold her?"

I've never been one for playing pass the parcel with babies, but I already realised that Magda was going to be Helen's honorary aunt. Her face lit up, "Could I?" And she took Helen, and tucked her safely into her arms, and gazed at her with a pure and perfect love, as we talked.

Eventually I stood up, reluctantly, to go, feeling as if I were being forced to leave some sanctuary.

Standing too, to let me out, she said, "Are you doing anything next Saturday evening? I'm having all the shop suppliers here, for a 'do'. It's something we do every so often, but this Saturday is going to be a bit special because there's something quite exciting in the pipeline, which I'm going to announce then." I hesitated, and she read it correctly. "Don't worry, you can bring Helen. I don't allow smoking in the house, and it's not going to be a riotous party. I know –" abruptly she stopped and started again, "I imagine that it's quite difficult, not being able to leave a baby that young, but honestly, she'd be welcome."

I smiled hugely. I might have to leave the sanctuary, but I was being given leave to return. I said: "I'd love to!"

* * *

319

So the next Saturday evening found me getting ready to Go Out. I was excited, because I hadn't been Out for ages. Not since, my hand slowed as it brushed my hair . . . not since the night I had been raped.

Oh well, I thought, speeding up the brushing again, this is the first night of the rest of my life and all that jazz – it's about time I started layering positive memories on top of those memories.

I didn't know what to wear – I even felt a thrill of fun and recognition at re-encountering this perennial female dilemma. I didn't have much choice, to be honest, as I had only packed very basic clothes, not being interested in fashion at the time. In the end I wore a plain black trousers, and a white cotton tunic. But I brushed my hair until it shone, and I wore make-up.

"This is one of the fun parts of being a woman," I told Helen, who was regarding me solemnly from her carseat-which-doubled-as-carry-seat. "The getting ready to go out – oh, you have it all ahead of you!" And she smiled at me.

However, when the last primping was done, and I was undeniably ready to Go Out, I found myself strangely nervous. It seemed that it was another person, in another time, who had had the confidence to blithely go into a room full of strangers with total confidence and self-acceptance. I was terrified, sure I'd never be able to remember people's names or make small talk with them. I regarded Helen in her little seat, and said to her: "Well, we'll just talk to each other, won't we?"

And something else occured to me. Nobody here knew me. I could re-invent myself. Be who I wanted to be. And I suddenly realised that I was tired, exhausted, of always trying to be the life-and-soul of the party. I'd still be witty, I decided, if I wanted, if something funny occured to me. But I'd allow myself to be quiet, too, if that's what I felt like. I wouldn't put on myself the burden of having to perform for the entertainment of others. And if they didn't like the new me, well, that was their problem.

And armed with that resolution, and the knowledge that I'd have Helen with me to talk to if all else failed, off we headed.

With all the beautifying, and angst-ifying, I was pretty much the last person there. Magda came to me as soon as I stepped through the door, led me into the sitting-room, and announced loudly: "Hey, everyone!" She waited a second or two for the buzz of conversation to cease – I thought I'd expire on the spot with embarrassment. When there was silence, and everyone was looking at her expectantly, she went on calmly, "I'd like you to meet the newest member of the Cilltubber Crafts family: Grainne Quinn. She does absolutely beautiful watercolours, so the rest of us had better look to our laurels!"

There was laughter at this.

She went on, "She's just moved to Cilltubber, so I'm sure we'll make her feel very welcome. And this" – she gestured – "is her beautiful daughter Helen, who's only eleven weeks old."

She turned to me and started introducing all her other guests: "This is Mary, who does the beautiful candles, and Sarah who does the jewellery."

The faces and names blurred until she said: "And this is Rory, who does the gorgeous wood-turning."

Chapter 25

And there in front of me was the biggest man I think I've ever seen – easily six foot three or six foot four. It was impossible to guess his age – anything from thirty to forty. He was hugely broad, with a chest it seemed you could build a house on. His checked shirt-sleeves were rolled up, revealing huge forearms, muscles sharply defined, and brushed with a generous coat of dark red hair. His head-hair, too, was dark red, as was his woodsman beard and moustache. I couldn't see much of his face under all the hair, but it all made his eyes even more conspicuous: a bright piercing blue, with a powerful gentleness gazing out of them, and humour-filled creases at the corner. Topped by, of course, bushy red eyebrows. In fact, he looked like nothing as much as an Irish Wolfhound which had been at the hair-dye. His whole body, his whole stance, radiated strength and power, all set off by a kindness and gentleness.

His voice, too, when he spoke, was deeper and richer than average. He clasped my hand hard, my hand disappearing in the vast expanse of his, and said in a rich Cork accent, "Indeed, you're very welcome, Grainne." Not inspiring words, perhaps, but as he said it he gazed at me, as if he could read my soul and found it pleasing, and I felt warmed and comforted. "And what brings you to Cilltubber?"

"Well, I –" I floundered. I should have anticipated this question, prepared for it.

But he saw my confusion, and kindly, gently, said, "Hush, now, it doesn't matter, I was just making conversation."

"I'll tell you sometime," I said, and realised, looking into his blue eyes that, yes, I really could.

He smiled at that, in a benediction, his smile saying that I was to tell him as much or as little as I chose, there was no pressure.

He said, "Well, I'm originally from Cilltubber. I was abroad for many years, though, playing at the big executive. But eventually I realised that I had to come home, to the land, and do work that involved something real. I have a house about three miles inland, with about ten acres. I keep horses, and I have my wood-turning studio there. And beautiful trees, and a view of the distant sparkling sea. Maybe you could come up sometime soon, and I'll show you around. You never know," he smiled again, "you might get more inspiration for your paintings from the views there."

"I'd love that," I said.

Then Magda clapped her hands and called everyone to order, and everyone turned to her, anticipation on our faces, waiting for the promised announcement.

"I've been talking to Emmett O'Mahony – most of you know him." There were almost universal nods, and she turned to me. "He's in the local Chamber of Commerce. Indeed, there are those who say he *is* the local Chamber of Commerce!"

There was a light sprinkling of laughter at this, and Magda twinkled at everyone as she went on, "And he has arranged for Emmett-Óg – his son," she explained in another aside to me, "to do us up a website: www.cilltubber.ie, it's to be called. And we're going to use it to showcase Cilltubber to the rest of the world! Mostly it's to be used for tourism – to show people the beauty of the area, so that they can't but come here! And to get details of the hotel, and the B&Bs, and the holiday houses for rent – Emmett-Óg is even arranging that people can book their accommodation on-line with it! But, and this is the reason Emmett was talking to me, he wants to know if we artists and crafters want our work featured also, and it can, it seems, be arranged that we can sell our work on-line too."

This announcement was greeted with great interest. It would offer, literally, a worldwide market for our products. And the crafters, who were making a living, certainly, but not about to get rich on the summer trade in Cilltubber, were delighted.

After all that chat had died down, Magda pointed us all in the direction of the food and the wine, and the party began. Quiet, by Dublin standards. But lovely. Everyone, it seemed, made a point of coming up to me, to talk to me. My head whirled with trying to remember names, who did what, who lived where, who was related to whom. But it was wonderful. For the first time in a year, I felt as if I belonged, as if I had found my place.

Rory didn't speak to me again, but when, as happened often, my eyes landed on him – conspicuous in his height and colour – his gaze was resting benevolently on me, and I felt a sense of – what? Of safety, that was it. Of being protected. Stupid, really, he's only eyeing me up at a party, I told myself, you don't have to read so much into it. But that was how it felt.

* * *

He phoned, about three days after the party. He'd got my number from Magda, he said. And then he wondered, would I like to go up to his house for lunch on Sunday?

"Come early," he suggested, "around eleven-ish, and I'll show you around, and then we can have lunch, and see how the afternoon goes."

Warmed, I said I would.

On Sunday morning I was frantic with nerves and excitement. Was this a date? I wondered. Or a casual invitation, such as anybody might offer? Did I even want it to be a date? I scurried away quickly from that thought, didn't even want to answer it.

I dressed carefully, casually. Jeans, shirt and jumper,

and low-heeled boots. Make-up or not make-up? I asked myself. The answer to that question depended on whether or not it was a date, and since I hadn't answered that, I didn't know. In the end I decided: mascara, a touch of eye-liner, and a pale lipstick. Sure I'd wear that anyway (no, you wouldn't), I'd wear that much make-up if I was going to lunch with Magda (no, you wouldn't) – there was nothing to be read into this decision.

Following his carefully dictated directions, I headed inland, up the steep hill which cradled and protected the village. Straight across the crossroads, for one mile, I read in my scrawled notes, then left at the next T-junction. Another mile, then, opposite a Lourdes grotto, the turn into his driveway. The driveway was rutted, grass growing in the middle, and I drove slowly and carefully down it. Eventually I came to a farmyard, and Rory's house. I pulled the car to a halt, and got out, entranced. It was a low, whitewashed house, with a thatched roof; the window frames and sills, along with the door, were painted a glowing red. The quintessential Irish cottage, I thought to myself in glee – this is wonderful! What a painting this will make! At right angles to the house was another building, with a stable door, the top half of which swung open. And in the open doorway was Rory, smiling a warm welcome.

"I heard the car," he explained. He swung open the lower half of the door and came out to meet me. "You're very welcome," he said formally, "yourself and your daughter also."

"Oh, my daughter, yes!" I laughed, as I remembered her, and turned to take her out of the back of the car.

"Come in," said Rory, almost shyly. "This is my workshop, it's nearly more my home than the house is." I went through the doorway, Helen in my arms, and looked around me. The stone walls were painted a bright white, and light flooded in from windows in the roof. On a big table was his wood-turning equipment, and everywhere around me were pieces of tree waiting to be worked on, and finished pieces, the beauty of the wood glowing in them: bowls, candlesticks, discs with clock faces attached to them.

There was an air of tranquillity in the room, along with the resinous smell of wood. "What a wonderful place," I breathed, and Rory looked pleased, and proud.

"Would you like to see how it works?" he asked.

I nodded. He sat himself with familiar ease at his table, and set the machine to work, turning the half-finished piece that was in it. His big hands were deft and gentle, his concentration absolute. For about ten minutes I just watched him, knowing, and content in the knowledge, that he'd forgotten us, so intent was he upon what he was doing. I looked again at his hands, so large, so gentle. Those hands would only ever be raised to you to cup your face, I thought, or brush away tears. And I felt a sense of safety, of security.

When he finished, he raised his head to me. "What do you think?"

"Wonderful," I said. "You are a true artist, a genuine craftsman."

He smiled shyly, proudly, and I was glad that I was able to please him.

"Come on," he said, standing and leading the way to the doorway. "I'll show you the rest of it."

He was so proud of what he had, so keen that I should like it too. I thought of some of the people I'd known in Dublin, never happy with what they had, although it was, surely, in money terms much more than this man had. They were always fretting for the bigger house, the better address. But Rory exuded contentment, and was visibly happy that I should find it to be good.

We began to walk through his land. I hefted Helen into a position more comfortable for me, and he said, "Will I carry her for you?"

Without a thought I handed my precious daughter into the care of this man, knowing I could trust him totally. He cradled her reverently, tucking her into the crook of his arm. She looked so comfortable there, so safe, so tiny! Like a baby bird on the side of a mountain.

He said, "I've no children of my own, but I have plenty of nieces and nephews, so I consider myself quite an expert with babies."

With Helen nestled contentedly into his body, we continued our walk. Rory pointed out things as we passed: "There's the paddocks, and my two horses, Minnie and Beauty." The horses trotted up to us as we passed, and with his free arm, Rory caressed their long silky noses and they snickered softly.

"And here is my beautiful wood – I tend to use only

trees that are falling – they provide me with my livelihood. And of course, people bring me, or tell me, of other fallen trees – everyone's happy that the trees find a new life after their original one is over. And those trees over there, that's my orchard. There's nothing like a fresh apple or pear that you've picked yourself."

Our path brought us back to the house, by the back door. As we neared it he said, "And here's my vegetable garden – I'm pretty much self-sufficient for vegetables. I get great compost from the horses."

I muttered what I hoped were knowledgeable-sounding comments. Of course I knew, in theory, anyway, that vegetables came from the ground, but previously I'd only seen them, sanitised and wrapped, in supermarkets.

I mustn't have sounded knowledgeable enough, though, because he chuckled amicably, "Oh, city girl, there's a lot for you to learn!"

We reached the back door, and he said, with a carefully ironic wave of his arm, "And welcome to my humble abode."

Inside there was just one room, with a kitchen at one end, a sitting area at the other, and a big dining-table between the two and, I noted as I saw a cat nestled on a rug with four tiny kittens, there was even room for a nursery also. At the far end of the room a narrow staircase led to, I assumed, the bedroom, or bedrooms, and bathroom.

The room was immaculate, carefully kept. The walls were a simple white, and the window frames, like those outside, were painted red. The low ceiling was also white, with ancient beams. From the beams at the kitchen end were hung strings of onions and garlic. The furniture looked simple, rough-hewn.

"I made most of it myself," he said, following my gaze. "You can probably tell."

There was a huge fireplace at the sitting end, ringed by three huge sofas, old and in need of re-covering, but which looked hugely comfortable.

As in his workroom, there was an air of deep tranquillity about this. I felt comforted and calmed simply by being there.

Rory handed Helen, sleeping peacefully, back to me, and said, "I'll just get the dinner sorted. Are you hungry?" I was, I realised, famished.

He cooked up a simple meal, with potatoes featuring heavily, and wonderful tasting vegetables. There was no wine to drink, simply fresh well-water. The meal was fabulous. I ate and ate, and he smiled at me in appreciation of my enjoyment.

No after-dinner cognacs, either. No, we repaired to the sofas with a good strong mug of tea each, the teapot resting on a small table, easily accessible.

"And how do you find Cilltubber?" he asked.

"Oh, I love it," I said, surprising myself even as I said it. "I found it hard when I first came here, I didn't know anybody, I was very lonely. Of course, friends came down from Dublin regularly, but still . . . But now that I know Magda, and the other crafters – and yourself of course, well, it makes all the difference."

He nodded. "Any place can be lonely if you don't know anybody. But in fairness to Cilltubber, the people are very easy to get to know, very welcoming. They're not a bit cliquey, not like some places. Mind you, here in West Cork we're used to lots of foreigners coming to live, English and Germans, other people from the continent looking for a quieter, simpler lifestyle."

I said, mock-crossly, "Last time I looked, Dublin was still in Ireland. That means that, technically, I'm not a foreigner!"

He laughed. "Of course you aren't. But you know what I mean – a newcomer."

"And you're from Cilltubber yourself, aren't you? I seem to remember you saying that."

"I am, one of that rare breed, a native Cilltubber man. I lived abroad for many years, but . . . ah, sure, sometimes you have to come home."

"Yes," I nodded my agreement, and wondered would I ever be able to go home. But I banished that thought. Live in the moment, I told myself, you're having a grand chat with a lovely new friend, enjoy this for itself. Leave the future to happen in its own time.

The tea finished, I got slowly and regretfully to my feet. Taking my cue, Rory stood also. It was quite an experience watching him stand – the whole process seemed to take ages, as he straightened up, and up, and up, until, long after the time you thought he should be finished, he was still straightening, until, at last, he was standing, the whole magnificent length of him.

"Thank you very much for a wonderful afternoon,"

I said and "Thank you for coming," he said at the same time , and we laughed.

"It was wonderful, I really enjoyed it," I said.

"Me too. Thanks for your company – and that of Helen, of course. Maybe we could do it again sometime?"

"I'd love that."

"Next Sunday?" he asked, carefully casual, a little tentatively.

"Next Sunday would be great," and we stood and smiled at each other, a smile of pleasure, of joy at having discovered each other, a smile of anticipation of another afternoon spent together.

He saw me to my car, and said, "When you come next week, if you wanted, you could bring your paints. You could paint for a couple of hours before dinner."

"That would be great!" I said. "As long as you didn't think me very rude, coming to visit you, and ignoring you for that time."

"Not at all," he said. "Sure don't we artists understand each other?"

And we laughed, and on that happy, relaxed, note, we parted.

I wondered if he would kiss me before I left, but he didn't. Social kisses hadn't made their way to Cilltubber, and he had the sensitivity not to try any other sort. Assuming he wanted to, of course, I thought, berating myself for my arrogance.

* * *

Apart from spending the wonderful time with Rory, in

other ways too my life changed for the better after that party. As I said to Rory, I was getting to know the other crafters. People I'd met began popping into the house when they were in the village, proffering gifts on their first visit. Mary brought a fabulous rainbow-striped candle, as a joint housewarming and welcome-to-Cilltubber present. Sarah came with a dainty pair of earrings. Aine brought a cushion covered in one of her handwoven tweeds (I wasn't too fond of that one, but I loved the thought).

And when I was walking through the village, it seemed that I knew every second person by name now. And often someone would say, "Have you half an hour? Sure why don't we pop into Flanagan's for a coffee – it won't be smoky at this hour – or we could sit outside?"

Or if it was someone who lived in the village, they might see me passing, and call out, "Grainne, I've just wet the tea, you must have smelt it – come in for a cuppa!"

And many was the lazy hour I spent in Magda's shop, chatting to her, and even, if she was busy, helping out behind the counter. Helen was still at the stage when she was usually happy if she was fed and dry, and often sat contentedly behind the counter with me, in her little carseat, and grinning gummily up at us when we smiled at her and passed a comment. And if she did cry, it was a simple matter to lift her up and tend to her.

And of course I was painting madly. To be honest,

after a while, it became a bit production-line, as I did the same scenes over and over. But they were what sold. Magda told me: "If you want to experiment, do it in your own time!" All we crafters and artists were trying to build up stocks, to have enough to sell when our website went on-line.

And through it all, I was minding and tending and loving Helen. With each day that passed, she grew and thrived, and was smiling and laughing now, and holding out her arms to be picked up.

And still I thought of Patrick, wondered about him, dreamt of him. I missed him every moment of every day. I certainly missed the relationship we'd had before the rape. But now I was even missing what had passed for a relationship after that. At least then I got to see his face, hear his voice, know what he was doing, be with him.

One morning the post brought a letter from him, my name and address written in his bold, assertive thick black scrawl. My heart leapt and a twin buzz of excitement and fear fluttered within me. With shaking hands I opened the envelope. Was it a love letter, a request to get back together? Or was it a request for a divorce?

It was neither. It was a car-tax disc. Nothing else, no note. I even, stupidly, turned over the disc to see if there was something written on the back of it. I only just stopped short of heating it with a candle to see if there was writing in invisible ink on it.

No message. Except this message: I am going to the

house regularly, collecting post. And I saw the tax renewal form for your car. And I care enough, at least, to organise getting the new tax disc and posting it to you.

Not much of a message. But I clung to it. I even kept the envelope. I put it to my face, trying to get some scent, some awareness of Patrick from it, where he'd touched it. But there was nothing. It was just a bit of paper. So after two or three days, realising that I was acting in a sad, sad manner, I binned it. Hey, maybe that was progress.

Chapter 26

All that week, also, despite missing Patrick, I was looking forward to seeing Rory on the following Sunday. I was aware that there was an inherent contradiction in those feelings. But they were both valid feelings, and I decided not to twist myself into knots over it, but rather to accept them both.

So, in a repeat of the previous Sunday, I strapped Helen into her carseat, and we headed for the hills. Again, Rory was waiting for us, having heard the car. I climbed out of the car, and we smiled at each other, looking into each other's eyes from across the yard, delighting in each other's presence.

"Did you bring your painting stuff?" he asked.

"I did."

"Well, would you like to get in a couple of hours of painting before lunch? I'll mind Helen for you, if you like. I could bring her out to you if she gets hungry, but, other than that, she and I could keep each other company."

"That would be great!"

So Rory took Helen into the house, and I headed for a spot I remembered from the previous week, which had a wonderful view over rolling fields, with the distant sea in the background. And I lost myself in the joy of painting, the constant challenge of trying to get scenery, already perfectly made by the Ultimate Artist, onto paper with some fraction of its beauty and majesty still intact. There was the usual frustration of it never quite being as you see it in your mind's eye (and I often think that it's that frustration that keeps you going back to the easel, the tantalising thought that, this time, it'll be perfect) but also the satisfaction of getting it close.

It seemed like no time before I heard Rory's voice calling my name. Looking at my watch I was amazed to find that over two hours had passed.

"Grainne, Helen's crying," he said, but as he walked towards me with her in his arms I could hear it for myself.

I took her and, awkwardly, as I was still standing, gave her a quick feed which seemed to settle her. As I was doing that Rory studied the painting on the easel.

"It's really lovely," he said. "You've picked the best view of the lot – but more, in enclosing it and framing it, you've made it more conspicuous. And the colours you've chosen – you've slightly exaggerated the real colours, and it makes it so vibrant. It works really well.

It's a little bit more daring than the stuff you do for the shop –" he shot me a speculative look.

I nodded, "Yes, this was just for me, for fun, I could afford to experiment a little."

"Well, it's worked – worked really well," and he handed the painting back to me.

"Would you like to have it?"

"Oh, I would, it's lovely, but no, no need for that at all, it's yours."

"But you've been so good to me and Helen, it would be lovely to give you something in return – I have been wondering what I could get for you."

"Nothing, nothing at all," he said. "Sure isn't the pleasure of your and Helen's company reward enough for anyone?"

"Okay," I said, deciding to myself that I'd get the painting framed, and give it to him, and refuse to take no for an answer.

Rory began tidying, washing my brushes and tidying away my paints, and when Helen was finished her feed we walked together back to the house, carrying baby, paints, painting equipment and the painting between us.

We were greeted by the most appetising aroma and my stomach growled in response, loudly enough, to my embarassment, for Rory to hear.

"Dinner'll be ready in two minutes,' he grinned at me.

We ate another lovely, simple, substantial meal, and just as we had done the previous week, repaired to the couches with our mugs of tea. I thought, already we're developing patterns, habits.

We made pleasant small talk, then I said abruptly, surprising myself, "You're not married?"

"No," he said, easily. "I never did. I had a long relationship when I lived in London, but we came to want different things. I wanted to come back here for a simpler lifestyle – she wanted to stay on the corporate roundabout. I remember asking her what her deepest dream was, and she laughed and said that she didn't have dreams, that dreams were for losers. What she had were goals. And that was when I knew we were finished." He gazed at me. "Do you have dreams? Or just goals?"

"Oh, I have dreams," I assured him.

"Go on," he said, looking at me expectantly.

To get back with Patrick, the thought came straight to my mind, as if there had never been any doubt. But that was probably not the most tactful of things to say to him.

So I said, "My greatest dream? Hmm – I think it would be to be recognised as a great artist. To make serious money at it, to have galleries queuing up to exhibit my paintings. To have critics say critic-speak things like 'the voice of a generation' and 'Ireland's greatest living artist' and 'her paintings show a sense of incredible latency overlaid by a post-modern membrane of reality'."

He was smiling at me, his eyes crinkled up.

"You know, Rory," I added musingly, "I don't even

know what 'post-modern' really means, but I'd like them to say it anyway."

He put back his head and roared with delighted laughter.

And I laughed too, with pleasure at his company, and enjoyment at the fantasy.

Then he said, "So that's my story. What's yours? You are married, aren't you?"

"Yes, to Patrick Quinn. Moira and Jim's son, do you know them?"

"No, I wasn't in Cilltubber when they used to come. But I know of them."

He said no more, didn't ask any questions.

After a few minutes I said, gesturing towards Helen, "She's not Patrick's child. And he can't handle that."

He said neutrally, "Aah."

"I wasn't unfaithful to him," I added hurriedly. "I was raped, and I got pregnant." I had said it before I knew I intended to.

He nodded in great understanding, totally undemanding of me, of any expectations of explanation.

But I went on, "And when she was born, I couldn't put her up for adoption, as he wanted, as he needed me to do. I was able to separate the fact of her conception from the reality of her, but he couldn't. It's not his fault, I wouldn't want you to think badly of him."

"Indeed I don't," he said, and I realised that here was that rare person, someone totally nonjudgemental. "It's harder for men, to relate to babies that are even their own. When a woman conceives, she's totally connected to the baby from very early on, she bonds with it even before it's born. But men find it very hard to imagine, even as they see their wife's belly getting bigger, and can feel the baby kicking under their hand. I remember my brother, Fionn, he came here in tears the night after Sive had their first baby, and he was so worried, and so ashamed of himself, that he couldn't connect with the baby – he felt excluded from them, she was so wrapped up in the baby. And intellectually he was delighted, and proud, and thrilled, but his emotions were different: they were fear, and rejection, and abandonment, and confusion. But after a couple of strong whiskeys, he went home. And as the weeks and months passed, and he did his share of caring for the new baby, he fell in love with her, and now they're great together. But men need that time after the birth, I think, and Patrick didn't have that. Add the reality of Helen's conception to the mix . . . well, it's not surprising he had troubles." He paused and said, "What's the situation between you now?"

"I don't know," I said miserably. "We're not officially separated, or anything. But he says he can't accept her and he hasn't phoned since he brought me here. I don't know," I said again.

"Things sometimes take their own time to be resolved," he said calmly. "Sometimes the best thing we can do is to do nothing. Although, of course, that's often the hardest."

"I had to come to Cilltubber," I said. "The – the rapist came to my house, was talking about us getting together, wanted sex again – the only reason he didn't was because I managed to convince him it was too soon after giving birth. And worst of all, he wanted access to Helen – God, that doesn't bear thinking about – I had to come somewhere safe."

"Well, you're safe here," he said, and I was comforted. Then he said, "You poor girl, you've been through the mill, haven't you?"

"Yes," I gasped, and suddenly I was crying.

He carefully put down his mug, moved over to the sofa where I was sitting, equally carefully removed my own mug from my clenched hands, and placed it down. Then gathered me into his huge embrace, and I leant against his wide chest, and sobbed and sobbed. He didn't say anything, just held me and caressed the back of my hair.

Eventually I gathered myself together. "Sorry," I hiccupped.

He didn't say anything, just smiled at me, with the kindness of giants in his eyes, and I realised that I had nothing to be sorry for. I smiled tremulously at him, and he said, "Would you like another cup of tea, before you go?"

I grasped it for what it was, a device to give us space from our recent intimacy. When he returned with the fresh tea, he sat again in the other sofa. I told him more about the past year, and he just listened, absorbed all the pain into his massive frame and his huge heart.

But sometimes it seemed to me that there was an infinite well of pain that I could pour and pour it onto people like Rory, but still the cauldron of pain within me remained undiminished. Fiona, my counsellor, had told me in one of our meetings that the cliché was true, that time really does heal all ills, that these months were still early days. But if I was recovering at all, it was so slow and subtle that I wasn't aware of it.

Chapter 27

Having said that, there seemed to be two layers to my life. Well, three actually. On one level there was the trauma of the rape and Brogan's stalking me. Mostly I was able to bury it all deep down and carry on. But it was always there, like a kind of dismal aura.

The second layer was my grief over Patrick, the pain of missing him in every moment. A dozen times a day, it seemed, I'd think, oh, I must remember to tell Patrick that, and the pain would hit me, as ferocious and intense as if for the very first time, that I couldn't tell him any bit of news, that I couldn't see him, talk with him, touch him. I would have a physical pain in my chest with the ache of missing him. Like picking at a scab, I replayed scenes from our life together, trying to remember them in detail, trying to conjure up the reality of him, the beauty of his dark face and strong body, the solidity of his muscle beneath soft skin, the earth-clean scent of him. And though I tried not to, my imagination conjured up images of him living happily without me: out drinking with friends, chatting with women, maybe his arm around some faceless particular woman. In these images he was laughing his strong laugh, head thrown back. I knew I was doing myself no favours putting myself through this, but the images came anyway, particularly in those slow moments before sleep. Bad and all as they were, they were still better than the images from the rape which were showing in Screen Two of my head during those last moments of the day.

So they were two of the layers of my life at this time, kept well hidden during the day. With the exception of Rory, I'd told nobody about what had happened to bring me to Cilltubber, and everyone had accepted me easily. Maybe there was speculation behind my back but if so, it never impacted on me. There was no sly questioning, no subtle hints that I should give more detail than I chose to.

And that leads me to the third layer: my life in Cilltubber. Slowly, without my realising it, it had become full and rich. At this level of my life, I was very content. I was painting each day; and now that autumn had come, I was simply copying those paintings I had done during the sun and warmth of the summer. But I was still enjoying it. Each painting still turned out differently enough for me to be proud of it, happy to sell it as an original. Each time I lifted brush in hand, I felt a sense of calm come upon me. I could literally feel my heartbeat slowing. I was relaxed, completed somehow. It felt so right to be standing there, brush in hand, glorious colours on palette.

Although the tourist season had ended with the summer, and sales went way down, I painted anyway, enjoying it, and stocking up for the following season. And even as I did so, I sometimes asked myself, did this mean that I would still be here the following year? Where else would I be? I still couldn't go back to Dublin: all the reasons why I'd left still applied. And somehow, knowing that I'd still be here next year no longer filled me with despair – in fact I was happy enough (in this third layer) at the prospect.

Apart from the painting, I had my friendship with Magda, which was strong and deep. We shared our past lives, although I certainly edited mine, and I still got the strong sense that she, too, wasn't telling everything. But that was okay. What we did share gave us a sense of each other. And we talked about current affairs, about painting. And we just chatted, and laughed together, in the way of women friends all over the world, all through the millennia. Now that the shop was closed except for Saturdays to sell to locals looking for presents, she had more time, and we spent a lot of it together. We went on shopping trips to Cork together, we went to the cinema in Bantry (Helen still being small enough to take), although mind you, I must be heading for a record for the number of films half-seen, as I often had to leave. Usually if she started grizzling I would just put her to the breast and it would settle her, but other times, it didn't.

We shared lunches in the Courtyard. We had fun together. And I mixed with the other Cilltubber-crafters, like Mary, Aine and Sarah, who'd made a point of visiting me after that first night in Magda's house. I wasn't nearly as close to them, but still, we were good pals, and it was great to have people who'd call to your house, and who you felt comfortable calling on in your turn.

And of course, there was, always, and totally, Helen. She was, there's no other way to describe it, a joy. Happy, waving her arms around now in exuberance. I couldn't begin to imagine life without her, life before her. And a thousand times a day I thanked God, or whoever, for the impulse that had led me to keep her. What would my life be like now if I hadn't gone through with the decision – the impulsion – to keep her? Living, perhaps still in Dublin (although, who's to say, perhaps Brogan would have come after me anyway). Wondering every moment, every second, of every day, about her with her new parents, wondering what she was like as she grew. But now I didn't have to wonder, I knew. And I relished each day with her, as she grew bigger and bigger, and became more and more aware of the world around her, and responded more and more to it. And I cherished each time she nourished from my breasts, one eye always hidden, and the other looking deep into mine, and seeming to have the answer to the mysteries of the universe. And her whimpering for a feed, and her quickly coming to recognise the action of my reaching under my jumper to release my bra, and her quivering excitement about it all, nearly chortling with glee about what was to come. And the gusto with which she tucked in, the energy and strength with which she suckled. And the pride I felt as she visibly grew and thrived and blossomed, that this was my own work. It was hugely healing, actually, after my body being so ravished, to realise it could provide such amazing nutrition.

In addition to all this I saw Rory regularly. We'd got into a pattern of meeting most Sundays in his house for lunch. I felt totally at home there now, and we'd even got into the habit of my cooking sometimes. I bought him a new cookbook one day, and we had many a fun afternoon cooking together, experimenting and learning. I thoroughly enjoyed my time with him; he was never less than cheerful, kind, confident and upbeat. And yet, never by look, word or deed did he show any interest in taking things further. Maybe he doesn't find me attractive, I thought, or maybe he's just happy to be friends. Whatever the reason was, I was glad and grateful that he never made a pass or anything. I was happy to slip into friendship with him, and to leave it at that. We never articulated what we meant to each other – but then, neither did Magda and I. So maybe it was just genuine friendship he was after, and he had no need to label things, to compartmentalise our relationship.

And so three or four months passed through a blustery autumn, into the beginnings of winter. My cottage was deliciously snug, with its wood-burning stove keeping us both cosy. Rory called often with wood for it, already chopped, and laughed when I thanked him: "Sure what's the point of knowing a woodsman if you can't get logs?"

One evening Magda called around unexpectedly with a bottle of wine under her arm, and another bottle under the other arm. It was, although she couldn't have known it, the first anniversary of the rape, and it had been a bad day, full of swirling thoughts of the rape, and the familiar hatred towards Brogan, and the huge sense of injustice about the acquittal, and the loss of my husband.

"Oh, hi," I said listlessly, when I saw who it was. "Come in, do."

"Is this a bad time?" she asked, obviously picking up on my mood. Well, that wasn't difficult to do – it was radiating out of me like a grey fog.

"If you don't mind me being less than my usual scintillating company," I told her.

"Of course I don't," she said. "Are friends only friends when they insist on good humour?" She rooted in the kitchen drawer for a corkscrew, and expertly fished out the cork, got two glasses from the cupboard, and sat herself down beside me.

"What is it?" she asked sympathetically.

And it all came pouring out, the black acid spewed out of me, and I told her the whole story, the words tumbling over themselves, and I finished with, "How can I ever be happy again, with all this?"

She murmured to herself, "I thought there was something."

But then there was silence for a minute. I guess I'd

expected her to gather me to her, and comfort me, because I found I was surprised when she didn't.

She said instead, "You ask, how can you be happy again, with all that inside you? Why, by deciding to be. It's that simple, and that difficult. And you let go of the anger and bitterness by letting it go, by forgiving Patrick for acting out of fear and upset, and his own issues with the rape. Did it occur to you that he also needed counselling?"

Shocked, I said, "No, it didn't. It was all about me. But, Magda, I was the one who'd been raped."

She nodded. "Yes, and your trauma was huge, I'm not saying it wasn't. But the fact of your trauma doesn't invalidate his. Can you see how difficult it was for him – his wife raped, and he not able to protect her? And the loss of his former relationship with you, as you were so upset and traumatised – how could he be expected to deal with that on his own? And then your pregnancy, that must have been so difficult for him, to see that man's seed growing inside you. And then to be expected to welcome the baby with open arms! Oh Grainne, his pain is real, too!"

It was the first time I'd realised this, accepted this. I know Patrick had tried to explain this to me, but I couldn't see it then. I felt a huge release of the anger and hurt I felt. "I can forgive him," I said wonderingly. "He was acting out of pain and confusion and upset, and yes, trauma, I can see that now. He has friends, but you know men, they don't share their feelings, only their golf handicaps."

She nodded. "You must forgive him. And the next thing you must do, Grainne, is to forgive the rapist."

I laughed in disbelief. "Are you mad? Forgive *him*? After what he did? No, I'm going to hate him every day for the rest of my life!"

Instead of answering directly she asked me, "Did you ever stop to think what I'm doing here? Why I moved to Cilltubber in Ireland, from my home in Manchester, at the age of thirty-eight? Did you ever wonder what I had done before that? What had happened in my life to make me abandon it all and start again, at an age when most people are with husband and children and house?"

Well, I had, of course, but Magda had never offered this information, and I didn't like to ask.

"Why did you come here?"

Again she didn't answer directly but said dreamily, "I was married once. To a man called Mark. Oh, he was wonderful! At his funeral – oh yes, he dies in this story – people came up to me and told me stories about him that I'd never even known. About how he had lent one guy a hundred pounds just when he needed it, and never asked for it back. And one of his colleagues told me he'd driven her on a ninety-mile round trip to visit her dying mother, when she couldn't get there any other way. And someone else would tell how he had listened to them for hours, at the lowest point of their life, and kept them sane. English funerals aren't like funerals here, they're much quieter, and they tend to be by invitation only. But his funeral was huge, and I didn't know half the people there. People came from all over, many of them openly crying, for a good, good man who had touched their lives for the better, and now was dead. But although I saw his goodness, relished and cherished it, there was far more to our marriage, our love. We laughed together – my memory of our life together seems to be all laughter. He had a wonderful sense of humour – I used often tell him he would make a great stand-up comedian. But he'd tell me he wasn't neurotic enough." She smiled at the memories. "My mother had a dog – Jessie. And Mark had what he called a hate-hate relationship with this dog – even though the dog adored him. He was always badmouthing her, particularly her stupidity. One day I said, laughing, that he was to stop saying such things, that he'd give her a complex. And he said, 'Complex? You couldn't give that dog a complex. A simple, maybe, but not a complex!'"

I laughed, but I don't think Magda heard me.

"And the same dog, she used to have a habit of chasing the shed at the back of my mother's garden. She probably wasn't chasing the shed – I'd say she'd come across a cat there, once, and kept checking it wasn't there. But it looked like she was chasing the shed, as she ran towards it, barking furiously. Once she had a leg operation, and couldn't run anywhere for a while. And then I told him she was getting better, that she'd had her first shed-chase since the operation. And he said, 'Oh joy! Yappy days are here again!' He was like that, full of quick wit. There was such an atmosphere of laughter, of love, in our house, in our lives."

She was silent for a some moments.

"And one day we were driving, back from my mother's late at night. And a car came around the bend, far too fast, was pushed by centrifugal force onto our side of the road. Clipped our car, and pushed it off the road, down a hill until it crashed into a tree. Mark died straight away. I knew that, could see his chest crushed by the steering-wheel column – we had an old car, no airbag. I could see his glassy open eyes, the staring eyes – I can still see those sometimes. We didn't even get the chance to say goodbye."

She was staring into the fire now, seeing her dead husband and his wide-open unseeing eyes, it seemed. But more than that, I learned as she went on.

"And I was pierced by glass in the stomach, and the baby I was carrying died too. I was eight and a half months pregnant. He died of suffocation – the umbilical cord was cut, and he couldn't get out to breathe the oxygen that he would have been well able for. He was perfect, when they cut him out, uninjured, except for his purple, oxygen-starved colour. Geoff, we would have called him."

She fell silent again. I sat silent too, transfixed, horrified.

Still watching the flames, she continued: "Of course, the glass and shrapnel cut my womb to pieces. They had to cut it out, no use to me any more, poor ragged tattered thing. No home, ever, for another child. But the worst, worse than all of that, was my daughter, Amanda. Amanda was just three years old. I had nursed her, just as you're nursing Helen, for a year and a half. All for her to die in a dark field. She wasn't badly injured. Just a deep cut to the top of her thigh. But no help came, as we sat there in the darkness, and she slowly bled to death. I couldn't move, couldn't help her, because the bonnet had crushed into me, trapping my legs. My handbag, with the mobile phone in it, was at my feet. But I couldn't reach it, for the same reason: the bonnet was in the way. And Amanda was scared, so scared. She was crying, 'Mummy, get me, get me!' And I said, 'I will in a minute, pet, Mummy's going to come in a minute.' And my heart was breaking for my dead husband and the worry about the baby I was carrying, and knowing I was lying to her – that I, who had sworn to protect her all her life, couldn't come to her to save her, or even comfort her. And she kept saying, 'Mummy, it hurts, my leg hurts!' And I was saying, 'In a minute, love, I'll get a plaster for it, and I'll kiss it better.' And she was crying. I couldn't even put my hand behind me to touch her, the crushed bonnet had me trapped so high in the body, I couldn't reach. And after a little while she said, and her voice was faint now, 'Mummy, I'm getting cold.' And I said, still lying, 'I'll get a blanket for you now, precious.' And then she didn't say anything any more. Ever."

I breathed, "Oh Magda!"

"Do you know," she said conversationally, "the guy who ran us off the road never told anybody. He could have summoned help – maybe my little boy could have been saved . . . probably not, but I always wonder. But Amanda . . . she took ages to die, she could have been saved. He had another minor accident about half a mile up the road – the police were called to that. And still he never said. He was totally drunk, it transpired. I don't know if he'd even noticed hitting us or not. He always said he didn't. But the police think that he did, that he was just scared, and thought that he figured we'd all die and there'd be no evidence against him. But when somebody did find us, not until well after daylight the next day, after I had lain there all night with my dead family, the paint marks matched up, and he was done for it. I had nearly bled to death myself, from the wounds in my abdomen. He never showed any remorse. He didn't care. He's probably out by now – this was eight years ago."

Her voice was still soft, still gentle, almost unconcerned.

I said, "Oh Magda, how you must hate him!"

But she surprised me. "Oh no. I forgive him. I forgive him totally."

"What! How can you?"

"Oh, for a long time I didn't. For a long time I was like you are now – full of anger and hate, so that it ate me up. I was killing myself slowly, with drink and lack of food. I wanted to join my family. I wanted to make him pay by the force of my hatred. And then somebody did for me what I'm going to do for you now."

"What was that?"

"Made me realise that forgiveness is not something you do for the other person, it's something you do for yourself. It liberates you. The transgressor doesn't know, or care how you feel – if they were the sort of person who cared about things like that, they wouldn't do the things they do. It was my godmother, Sarah – she was a good bit older than me, she's dead now. It's a pity because I'd love you to have met her, you'd have got on well together. Anyway, one day she came around, and she said to me: 'I am sick and tired of you slowly killing yourself. So I have two choices for you. Either you choose death, or you choose life. Mark would have wanted you to choose life, you know he would. I want you to choose life. Your family and friends want you to choose life. But you, you are choosing neither. You don't seem to have the courage of either path. You seem to be choosing a living death. Your body is still alive, barely, but you, Magda, are gone. And I'm going to force you to choose. I have here,' and she waved a little bottle at me, 'enough sleeping tablets to kill you, gently and painlessly. And here,' in her other hand, 'tickets for a holiday for you and me in Sardinia. And Magda,' she said, 'you must choose. Before I leave here tonight, you must have chosen one of them!' And she was relentless, forcing me to choose. Screaming at me, 'Choose, choose!' Waving the little bottle, and the envelope of tickets at me. 'Take one, take one!' I wavered. Reached out for the bottle. But her words hit me. Mark, my beloved Mark, yes, he would have wanted me to live. Why let that drunken youth kill all four of us, instead of just three? But God, to choose life, with all the ramifications that Sarah meant – that was frightening. And I knew that if I chose life, it was on her terms, with no half measures. And eventually," said Magda, in a calm melodious voice, "I chose life. I took the envelope with the holiday tickets in it. But then Sarah stopped me and seized the envelope and we both held it in midair. She said, 'Magda, my love, thank you, thank you for your choice! The rest of us are so bereaved as well, and we so nearly lost you too. But Magda, there's a price for those tickets. A hard price, a huge price. One you won't want to pay. But, a price that will liberate you, will set you free!' I looked at her. She said, 'Magda, in order to get these tickets, you must forgive that young man!'"

"But how? *Why*?" I whispered. "Why should you?"

"And I laughed at her. I reacted as you are doing now. I said, 'Forgive him! Are you insane? He killed my husband, my daughter, my son – all my future children. And you want me to forgive him? Forget your holiday, it's too high a price! In fact, forget your life, it's too high a price!' But she said, 'Magda, you're not doing this for him – you are doing it for you. If you want to live a full life, which, let me remind you, Mark and your children would have wanted, you must forgive him. Not excuse him, never that. But forgive him, let go of your anger and your hate and your bitterness. That's what forgiveness means, you know. Not that you're saying what he did is okay. Obviously we all know it was not. It wasn't then, and it will never be. But to forgive him, to tell yourself that you're not going to hold this anger any more. As long as you're hating him, you're tied to him by some sort of cord, you and he are still connected, he's still hurting you. But if you forgive him, you set yourself free. Do you want to be bound to him for the rest of your life, or do you choose freedom?'"

Magda paused and looked directly at me again.

"All through that long evening she kept up this theme, and eventually it penetrated, and I realised she was right, that I had to forgive him. Not for his sake, never that. For my sake. And I did. God knows it wasn't easy. I didn't want to forgive him. I wanted, as I've said, to make him pay for what he'd done by the force of my hatred. But I realised, eventually, as Sarah's words slowly made sense to me, that the force of my hatred wasn't even reaching him. It was staying, deep in my heart, the anger and the bitterness rotting me. But I certainly couldn't feel forgiveness for him. I said that. And Sarah told me, 'You don't have to feel it, you just have to decide it.' And that's what I did. In the end."

"But –" I said, and stopped.

There was silence for a long, long time. Thoughts ricocheted around the inside of my head. I was still thinking, forgive him? Is she mad? But yet some of what she was saying made sense. I had spent this past year wrapped in my anger and pain and fury and bitterness. It was like a constant taste of bile in my mouth. No matter that on the surface I seemed to be doing fine, everything I did always seemed to be coloured by the rape. Always, even as I laughed and joked, I was thinking of Brogan and what he'd done to me. On good days, as I laughed with friends, I'd be thinking, see, Brogan, you didn't defeat me. On bad days I felt that my laughter was a mockery. What right did I have to be happy? To laugh? I wasn't who I had thought I was, I was Brogan's plaything.

I tried to explain this to Magda, and she listened intently. And at the end she said, "So you're still measuring your life and how you live it with reference to him? You're accepting his estimation of you? You're accepting the label that he's put on you? That you're worth no more than this?"

I was silenced. I didn't like to think of it like that. I said, "No, no."

She said implacably, "But that's what you said."

"No," I said again, struggling now. "No. I don't accept his estimation of what I'm worth."

She looked at me compassionately, cynically. And I realised that she was right. That was what I was saying, wasn't it?

I suddenly realised, suddenly said, "The more I hate Brogan, the more I'm tied to him. Isn't that right, Magda? Tied to a brief hour of my life, to the past, instead of to the present, to the future."

"Yes!" she said, with satisfaction that I'd got the point at last.

"But how do I do it?" I asked wonderingly. "How do I possibly set about forgiving him?"

"By setting the intention to forgive him. By saying aloud, 'I forgive him'. Or even, picture him in your mind, see him before you, and say to him: 'I forgive you. I do not excuse or exonerate what you did, but I forgive you, because I'm a stronger, better person than you.' Whenever thoughts of hatred towards him come into your mind, say this. And if the thoughts are too strong for you, say 'I can't feel forgiveness towards you right now. But I set my intention to forgive you.' It takes a while, but the anger comes less and less, and eventually, one day, you are free. I know this, I'm not telling you any theory or idea. I know this, because I did it. And it did set me free."

Free!

The word resonated around the room, around my heart. To be free of the burden of the anger and hatred. It sounded wonderful, like a gift beyond price.

"I will," I said suddenly, "I will forgive him." And even as I said it I was thinking 'but I can't'.

"Good," she said to me, and beamed a huge smile. "I am so glad. Do it now."

I just sat there, and she told me, "Stand up."

I did.

"Can you imagine him? Picture him here?"

I gazed into the middle distance, and pictured him. "Oh God," I said, frightened, revulsed. "No, Magda, I'm sorry." I sat down again, took a nervous gulp of the rich red wine, studied my glass, its sombre colour reflecting to and from the fire and the side lamp. "Look at the beautiful colours," I said musingly, turning the glass a little. "I'd paint it using alizaron crimson, I think, with a hint of burnt umber."

She continued looking at me intently, her eyes always gentle. "Grainne."

"I can't. I would if I could, I see the sense of what you're saying, I really do. But I simply, physically, totally just can't."

She didn't comment directly. She said, "Sarah used to say something else. She used to say 'happy people don't do bad things'. It didn't really apply to my situation; that young man hadn't done something bad, just something totally careless and thoughtless and irresponsible. But Brogan did do something bad. And he did it to fulfil some lack in him. No, wait, let me finish," this as I opened my mouth to protest loud and long at where she seemed to be going.

I closed my mouth again. Went to take another sip of wine and noticed my glass was empty. With an unsteady hand I poured myself another glass, proffered the bottle to Magda, put it down again at the shake of her head, as she indicated her nearly full glass.

"Do listen," she said, "till you see where this is going. It's not to excuse what he did, honestly it isn't. Now, look. Sometimes people who are hurting think it'll make them feel better to make others hurt. It doesn't of course, which is why they have to keep on hurting others, hoping that this time it'll be different. But they have a choice whether to hurt others or not. We all have choices, and we're all responsible for the choices we make. A lot of people have suffered dreadfully, and don't take it out on others. It's not a given. I mean, did you, after what happened, go around mugging old ladies and kicking puppies?"

"No," I laughed a little despite myself, "of course I didn't. But then, to be fair, it never occured to me."

"My point exactly! You are a strong and wonderful person, you took your pain onto yourself, you didn't seek to turn around and bully – in whatever ways – anybody else. But weaker people do. And that's what I'm trying to say. Something happened to Brogan, somewhere along the way, to make him a weak broken person. And that's what I meant when I said happy people don't do bad things. So," she ennumerated on her fingers, "he's weak, broken, and unhappy. And I want you to see that so that you can feel superior to him. That you can despise him, look down at him even. Maybe even pity him, not in an empathetic way, but in a feeling-sorry-for sort of way. You are, in every way, a stronger, better person than he is. So why stay chained to someone so pathetic?"

I thought about it.

After a few seconds she continued, "And maybe we won't use the word 'forgive' if that doesn't sit right with you. Let's just say that you are going to – if you choose – release your anger and bitterness, let it go, free yourself from it. Think of those feelings like a huge weight that you've been carrying around for this time, and that you've no need of any more. So you're just going to lay them down. Mentally throw them out, with as little attachment as you'd throw out an out-of-date newspaper."

We sat in silence for about ten minutes, which is a long, long time to be silent. But Magda didn't rush me, just took placid sips of her wine and stared at the fire in the stove.

And I thought of all she'd said. It did feel like all of this was a weight that I hauled around with me in each second of each hour of each day. Could I just let it go?

"Is it really so easy?" I asked wonderingly.

"Simple," said Magda, "but no, not easy. You might find that these weights want to cling to you. That they jump back onto your back time and again – okay, okay, I know I'm mixing up my analogies here."

I laughed a little, appreciating her attempts to lighten the atmosphere, notwithstanding the seriousness of what we were doing.

"And when they do," she continued, "you'll have to – again, if you choose to – be firm, and put them down again. Firm like you would to a puppy who's chewing slippers. But like with a puppy, without too much emotion that he's doing it again. A little frustration maybe, that he hasn't learned the lesson yet. But no more than that. And again like the puppy, in time the message will get through, that you're not entertaining this behaviour – these weights, these feelings – any more. It's the work of months, maybe years. You have to be committed to it, because you're committed to your own wellbeing. It can be tiring, always being vigilant against those feelings sneaking up on you. But not nearly as tiring," and the sincerity in her voice was absolute, "believe me, I know, I do know, not nearly as tiring as carrying them around with you always."

I carefully placed my glass on the floor, and I stood up. "I'm going to picture him now," I said, and my voice shook.

"Steady," said Magda, "you'll be okay." And her voice, and her confidence settled me a little. "Tell him," she said, "tell him, as he stands there before you, tell him what you want to say to him."

Okay, I will, I thought. I said, my voice shaking and the words stumbling, "Darren Brogan, you are a nasty evil person, and you had no right to do what you did. But I release my anger and hatred towards you, because I will not be bound to you any more. I – I forgive you." And even though my voice cracked on the last three words, I had done it.

I looked at Magda in delight, and we both laughed with joy.

"Don't forget," she said, "you may have to do this again and again. But each time it will be easier, and eventually, it will be over. Now – here's one more person to forgive."

"Who?" I asked, puzzled.

"Yourself. I'm only guessing here, but if you're anything like I was, you're blaming yourself for what happened. I blamed myself for insisting we go to my mother's that evening – Mark didn't really want to go. And I blamed myself, so much, over and over, for staying longer than he wanted – I kept telling myself, if we'd only left that half-hour earlier . . . I tortured myself with the maybes of that. I hated myself for it, perhaps even more than I hated the drunk driver. That was a large part of the wanting to kill myself slowly. And once I forgave him, well, I had the space to forgive me, and that was hugely liberating. I say again, forgive yourself."

I stared at her. I felt as if someone had thumped me in the stomach. The truth of what she said overpowered me. Tears began rolling down my cheeks as I said, "I was so stupid, so naïve, to give a lift to a stranger. None of this would have happened if I'd been more sensible."

"Well, forgive yourself." She was compassionate, but implacable.

I stood up, and opened and closed my mouth a few times. Wiped away some of the tears. My voice cracked. I said, "Grainne Quinn, I totally forgive you for your naivety in giving Brogan a lift. You did nothing wrong, just something stupid. You were just being kind to someone who, you thought, had been kind to you. I forgive you. I forgive myself."

And then I cried in earnest, but they were freeing tears, liberating sobs, and those tears washed away so much of the bad stuff that had been burdening me. And Magda, then, did cross the room, and hold me, and croon to me, as I wept into her shoulder.

When I had quietened, we smiled at each other, a smile of love, of survivors. She picked up her glass, and handed me mine. "A toast," she commanded, "a toast to happy, free futures," and we both drank deeply.

Eventually I asked, "And did you go to Sardinia with Sarah?"

"I did, and while we were there, over a few bottles of wine, she confessed to me that there hadn't been tablets in the bottle at all, only mints! She had been taking no chances, she told me. Mind you, she had me convinced. We had a wonderful holiday together. She got sick about a year later, and died another six months after that, so I was doubly glad for that time spent with her."

"You've had a hard time," I said softly.

"So have you, so have lots of people. But I'm happy now. I never forget, however, that happiness is a choice, and sometimes I have to make that choice every day. But Sarah gave me a wonderful gift that long night, and I hope I'm now being able to pass that gift on to you."

"Yes. Thank you."

Chapter 28

Of course it wasn't always easy. Images of the rape came still, and feelings of hatred. And I certainly couldn't *feel* forgiveness towards him. There was many the night that those horrific memories overwhelmed me, and I could feel no release of anger. But I repeated to myself like a mantra, "I forgive you, I forgive you, I forgive you . . ." I certainly didn't feel the sense of the words, but I repeated them over and over, because it was all I could do. Because the alternative was to remain in my loop of anger and bitterness.

And after some unknown time of repeating 'I forgive you', the images would fade, for that occasion at least. And each time that I banished those dreadful images with those powerful words, I did indeed free myself of some of my anger. For the first time I could envision a future that was of my choosing. In which I could be proactive instead of reactive. In which I would no longer define myself by what had been done to me against my will.

And one thing I found, once the hatred and anger were being banished, was that my creativity blossomed. I was still doing the routine paintings for Magda's shop, but also I started experimenting. Wild abstracts, huge impressionistic pictures of flowers, semi-abstract pictures of angry seas (in the pictures for the shop, the skies were always blue and the sea always calm). I enjoyed doing them hugely, it was a liberation all by itself. I didn't do anything with them, though – I just stacked them against the wall in the second bedroom which I was using as my studio.

Soon after Christmas, which I had spent quietly with Magda, Sinead and Harry Moran came to spend the weekend, booking into the one hotel. She was effervescent with joy, and he was so attentive to her, watching her always with a look of love and wonderment in his face. I was so happy for them both that I even forgot to feel embarrassed on meeting him.

I shook his hand, introduced myself, "Hi, I'm Grainne. We *have* met, but you probably don't recognise me with my clothes on."

He didn't say anything, just put his head sideways and looked indulgently at me.

And I realised. "You've heard that before."

He nodded, smiling. "Lots of times."

"I've been collecting gynaecologist jokes, since I heard you were coming, but . . ."

"Heard them," he said succinctly.

"All of them?"

"Yep."

"Oh well," I said despondently, and we both burst out laughing, and Sinead, who had been watching our exchange with delight, laughed too.

I then said to Harry, "And this is my daughter, Helen. You probably don't recognise her with her clothes on either."

He admired her, then said, "You forget how big they get – I only see them when they're just born – and a lot redder and more wrinkled."

I said indignantly, "Helen isn't in the slightest bit red and wrinkled!" and everyone laughed again.

We had a fun, boisterous, meal of pasta together, and sat after it over a bottle of red wine. But about nine o'clock Harry lumbered to his feet. "I thought I might go out for a pint," he said. "Will you ladies excuse me?"

We assured him that we would, and off he headed, promising not to be late.

After the door had closed behind him Sinead said, her voice rich with love, "He's such a pet, giving us time together." She then looked at me, studied me, even putting her head slightly to one side.

"What?" I said. "What?" and laughed.

"You've changed," she said consideringly. "You've changed a lot in these last few months."

"How?" I demanded.

She paused, obviously marshalling her thoughts, "Well, it's hard to describe. I'd say, you've grown up. Got mature."

"You mean I wasn't mature before?" I asked, putting on a high-dudgeon that was only half-faked.

"Of course, of course," she said, floundering, and then, "but now you're even *more* mature." She beamed a bright smile at me. She then went on in a musing tone, "But it's more than that. You're calmer. More centred, if that doesn't sound too psycho-babble. You were always the, well, the drama queen. Always looking for attention, through the fun and laughter and drama that you carried like an aura around you. As if," and she was thinking aloud now, picking her thoughts and her words, "you felt that you were never enough, that you had to bring stuff to the party: this fun and laughter and drama. And now – now you're calmer, it's the only word I can think of. As if all that extra stuff has been stripped away. Stuff that, I might tell you, your friends never needed. You're still fun, don't get me wrong," she said hastily, "but now – now it seems as if this is the real you, that you no longer feel the need to amuse us or impress us, as the price of our friendship." She stopped abruptly, as if she thought she might have gone too far.

There was silence for a moment. I thought about what she'd said.

"Well," I said slowly, "I've been through a lot. And yes, I suppose it has changed me. You're right, for the first time ever, I've been able to be happy to be me. Even," and I gulped, in fear of what I was to share, even with this, my closest friend, "happy to be with me. I never could, before, you know. I was terrified of my

371

own company. But here, I had to. I had to learn how to be with me."

Sinead was watching me intently, taking in every word.

"And the rape, and dealing with that, and having Helen, and nearly losing her, and then losing Patrick – well, I suppose it's stripped a lot of stuff away. What's been important is surviving, living each day. And now that I'm a mother – that makes you grow up, being responsible for every breath your child takes. It's the most scary, empowering thing I've ever done."

"Hmmm," she said noncommittedly, an invitation to continue.

"And I had an amazing experience. There's a woman who lives here, her name's Magda. I'll introduce you soon, tomorrow maybe. And she has had traumas that put mine in the ha'penny place. And she, right here, one night recently, over a bottle of wine like we're sharing now, well, she changed my life. If that doesn't sound too melodramatic, too drama queen," I said, a touch of acid in my voice.

Sinead laughed.

I went on. "She told me about forgiveness. About forgiving Brogan. And Patrick. And even myself. And I did. God it was hard, but it was, Sinead, the most liberating thing I've ever done. Do you know," I continued, on a roll now, "I read recently that the Dalai Lama not only has forgiven the Chinese for his enforced exile from Tibet, he has said that he thanks them for it. Not that he excuses them or exonerates them, never that. No more do I excuse or exonerate Brogan for what he did, but he, the Dalai Lama, is grateful for the circumstances that have let him be able to bring his messages to a wider world, which he would never have done if he was safe in Tibet. And I suppose," I was thinking aloud here, "I can't thank Brogan, not being quite as spiritually advanced as the Dalai Lama – in much the same way as a snail isn't quite as fast as Concorde."

Sinead laughed, and took a sip of her wine.

"So I don't thank him. But still – if he hadn't raped me – I wouldn't have Helen. I wouldn't have discovered myself. I wouldn't be making money – not a lot, but some – doing my first love, painting. Yes," I said sadly, "I have still lost Patrick. But maybe our marriage was never that strong, to let this come between us. And it was mostly my fault. After the rape I just couldn't relate to him. He had to sleep in another bed because I panicked every time he was with me. And he had all these issues about the rape, which were never dealt with. I wasn't able to. I forgave myself for that. And I forgave Patrick – he was acting out of his hurt and pain, not malice or anything. If someone had said to me, before all this, 'Here are the gifts I'm offering you: a beautiful baby, a painting career, good new friends, finding your own strength and your own self. But, the price is that you are going to be raped, you will lose your husband, you will need to flee like a refugee from your home', I would have said no. But if someone said to me now, 'Okay, I can wave a magic wand and put it back the way it was. You're back in Dublin in your life, with your husband, your teaching job, your doubts, and there's no baby, no painting, no life in Cilltubber.' Would I choose that? I don't know, Sinead, I don't know. I've gained so much, I wouldn't want to lose it all, even to get back what I had. But I still want what I had – well, Patrick, mostly."

I stopped abruptly, having talked myself to a standstill.

Sinead said, "Wow." Then, "Are you happy here?"

"Yes," I said, surprised to find it was true, "I am. I have a good life here. And Magda said something else, she said that happiness is a choice, and I suppose I'm choosing to be happy. I didn't choose the circumstances that led me here, but I can, and do, choose my reaction to it."

She then said, "And you never know, Patrick and you might get together yet."

I just said, "Yeah, you never know."

* * *

Stephen and Richard came down for a few days not long after this. Despite my earlier threat to have Stephen sleep on the sofa, I gave them the two single beds in the spare room, carefully moving my painting stuff out of the way.

We had a nice meal together – I attempted to cook an Indian meal, which went quite well – and sat and chatted until the small hours over a few beers.

The next day Stephen came down for breakfast, with

a quivering excitement about him. He said, "I hope you don't mind, but I've been rooting through your paintings. Not the Cilltubber landscapes, although they're great. No, I mean the others."

"Oh," I said dismissively, "I was only playing, experimenting."

"I think they're wonderful!. Can I take them back to Dublin with me, show them to a few people?"

"Oh, no," I said, horrified, "they're not good enough!"

"Well, if they're not, we'll know soon enough. Please, please let me take them!"

I didn't want to, but what Stephen wants, Stephen gets. I'm only glad he's on my side. And when Richard and Stephen left, they did so with a half a dozen of my new paintings, placed carefully on the back of their car.

On a cold, rainy Sunday afternoon soon after that, I was up in Rory's house, as usual. We were companionably cooking dinner together, laughing and joking. I now knew his kitchen as well as my own. Helen was now eight months old, and sitting up well, and chattering away to herself, and everyone else who came near her. She adored Rory, would crow with delight whenever she saw him, bouncing up and down on her nappy with excitement, holding out her hands to him. And he never let her down – he delighted in her too, and would sweep her up and up into his stratospheric heights whenever he got the chance.

We ate together, for all the world looking like a family. Some weeks previously Rory had shyly produced his new purchase, a highchair which clipped onto the table. "So she can sit with us. I saw the one in your house, and thought it was a great idea." Helen thought this new vantage point was great, and was chattering away, banging a spoon off the table.

After dinner we repaired, as usual, to the huge, comfortable sofas. I fed Helen, and changed her, and she settled for a doze.

Rory began looking less than his usual comfortable self. He seemed jumpy, pouring me more tea, for example, when I'd barely taken a sip out of my mug. Eventually, with an air of great decision, he put down his cup, and came and sat beside me.

"Grainne," he said, and stopped. Started again, visibly nervous. "Grainne," and then he cupped the back of my head, and lowered his own face to mine. "Can I kiss you?" he whispered.

I gazed at him, the leonine head of him, the kind eyes, his mouth. His mouth was smooth and full, and I realised with a shock how erotic it was, framed as it was by beard and moustache. I was heart-stoppingly aware of his teeth, his tongue. He said, "I was going to just kiss you, sweep you off your feet, but given what happened to you, I wanted to show you that I'm as far from that man as possible, so I'm asking. But I would love to kiss you, have wanted to for months."

He stopped, and an anxious expression came into his fine eyes. I reached my mouth for his, in answer, and we kissed. His kiss was expert, soft and hard at the same time, his tongue probed me and caressed my own. I felt my breathing quicken, and he tightened his grip on the back of my head in answer to my response, and kissed me harder. I waited for panic to arise, but it didn't. I'm so safe with this man, I felt, nothing can harm me.

We slid so that we were half-lying on the sofa, his weight pressing into me. But he must have been supporting some of his own weight, because it was erotic and comfortable, not oppressive. I felt my own arousal, and his. He breathed deeply, and I was aware of his heart thudding.

At last we came up for air. "Oh Grainne, you're so beautiful," he whispered. "I wonder would you be my lady? I can't propose marriage, under the circumstances, but we could be officially together. I'd honour you and protect you and love you – and Helen too. You could live here, with me, if you wanted, or," he added quickly, "if that's moving too quickly for you, live in your own house for as long as you wanted."

I was moved. He was offering me his world. To live here, in this simple safe cottage, to be protected by this kind, good man. I'd never know fear again. Helen would have a loving father, would grow up secure and confident.

I could see the years ahead of us, a soft gentle life. Not much drama, but I'd had plenty enough of that, thank you. Both of us working at our respective jobs, sharing the minding of Helen. And maybe, even, another baby at some stage.

It sounded wonderful. I opened my mouth to tell him all this, but instead I found myself saying, "Rory, I can't. Not yet anyway. The story with Patrick isn't finished. As I told you, we're neither together nor apart. Let me talk to him, find out what he wants, long-term, and well, we'll see then."

"So it's all depending on whether Patrick still wants you?" he said sadly. "You'll take me, if he doesn't? Is that it?"

"Yes, no, I don't know," I said. "I can't think right now." I put on an exaggerated voice, saying, "La, sir, this is so unexpected!" But it fell flat.

"You must have known," he said, "all this time together, having such a nice time with each other. You must have known we were heading for this."

"I think," I said slowly, thinking it out as much for myself as for him, "that I didn't want to know. I didn't let myself realise. Yes, I should have known, I didn't mean to play with your emotions. But I was just living for the minute, enjoying your company, not thinking of the future at all. And it's not a case of choosing Patrick over you, if he'll have me, it's just a case of sorting things out with him first."

Was this true, I wondered as I was saying it, but I carried on quickly, not wanting to answer that thought. "I can't go with one man when I'm still tied, in any way, to another. I just need to clarify things, that's all. If he releases me from the marriage," my mind shook at this prospect, "then I'll be able to come to you with a clear conscience, and we can sort out the paperwork afterwards. I don't need to be legally free, just morally."

He was quiet for a minute, and then he said, "I can

see that. I'm disappointed, obviously. But I understand."

I said quietly, "I'd better go now. I'll talk to Patrick, and I'll, well, I'll let you know."

I stood in the doorway of his cottage, preparatory to running through the rain to the car with a sleeping Helen in my arms.

He said, "He'd be mad to let you go, but by God, I hope he does."

We gazed deep into each other's eyes, then I opened the door and ran to the car.

When I got home, I cradled my sleeping daughter, and I thought and thought. I realised: I don't love Rory. I still love Patrick, with all my heart and soul. But if Patrick doesn't want me, I could be happy with Rory. I thought again of what I'd imagined when he made his proposal, of days and months and years, happy together in the cottage, safe always. I'd tell him, I decided, I'd tell him I still love Patrick, but that I could love him in a gentle way, and if he wants me on those terms, then great. I won't be dishonest.

But what of me and Patrick?

I had no idea what he was thinking of our relationship – indeed, if he even was. I had no idea what he was doing in his life. It was Patrick I wanted, I knew that, I'd always known that.

I'd throw myself on his mercy, I decided, and ask him to come back to me, to give our love another chance. To get to know Helen – she's just herself, I'd tell him, there's no haunting. I'd tell him I loved him, and ask him if we could start again.

And if he said no, I'd ask if it was truly over, and if it was, then I could go to Rory with a clear conscience. With a heavy heart, mind you, but a clear conscience. And I'd be happy with Rory, I knew I would. Happy enough, anyway. And being with Rory would have the added advantage that, if Brogan ever did take me to court, I'd have a father for Helen, to present to the judge.

Then, shaking, my hands literally trembling, I dialled the number of the flat in which Patrick lived. The answerphone clicked in, and I left a message, my voice carefully neutral, "Hi, Patrick, it's me. Grainne," I added, in case he'd forgotten my voice. "I'd appreciate it if you'd ring me as soon as you can. It's nothing bad," I added quickly, "I'm not in trouble or anything, but I do need to speak to you. Bye."

I agonised about where he was, who he was with, and tormented myself with images of him embracing some woman. I decided against ringing his mobile – the conversation I needed to have was not to be conducted over the shouts and roars of some Sunday evening pub. Or worse, from some woman's bed.

I spent a sleepless night, knowing I'd be ringing him in the morning at work. At least he had his own office. So I rang his work number the next day. I got through only to his voice mail, and left another message.

And spent the whole day clinging to my phone, waiting for him to ring. But the phone only rang once, towards evening. It was Rory. "Well?" he asked, his voice hoarse.

"Oh, Rory, I'm afraid I've no news, I've been trying to reach him and I can't. I'll keep trying, and I'll let you know as soon as I can, I promise."

"Thank you," he said. "I'll talk to you soon then, bye."

He hung up, and my heart ached for this gentle, kind man whose whole future was bound up in another man's decision, who also had the agony of waiting but without the meagre consolation which I had, of knowing what was going on.

At least, I knew what was going on my end, but I didn't know anything else. On that Monday evening I tried Patrick's flat again. Still no answer. Tried our own house, in case he'd moved back there. No answer. I left messages in both places.

And then, thinking I'd crack up with the tension, I rang his mobile. I got a recorded announcement telling me that the caller was either out of range, or had his phone switched off.

And that was all I could do for that evening.

On Tuesday morning I rang his office again. Voice mail again. Another message.

Towards the end of that long, long day, I rang Jim and Moira's. Patrick wasn't there, they said, he'd gone away for the week. I didn't ask, and they didn't volunteer, as to where he'd gone. And more importantly, who with.

I rang Rory, and updated him. He sounded miserable. He said, "Would you like to come up here on Wednesday?"

"Oh, Rory," I said, "better not. I'll talk to you as soon as I know anything, I promise."

The week dragged on and on, with still no word from Patrick. He mustn't be checking his messages, I thought, but then why would he? And tormented myself with visions of a hotel's hot sweaty bed.

Chapter 29

I was sitting there on Friday evening, muscles poised to answer the phone should it ring, when there was a knock on the door. I went to answer it and there, standing outside, was Patrick!

"Hi," he said simply.

"Hi," I said, and just stood there. I didn't know what to do, or say. I drank in the sight of him, as tall and handsome as ever – and, I belatedly realised, getting wet. It was raining, I hadn't noticed.

"Come in," I said eventually, standing back.

He did. And stood awkwardly in the sitting-room.

"Can I take your coat?" I asked in my best society-hostess manner. He shrugged off his jacket and placed it over the arm of the sofa.

And then he took a deep breath, and I thought, oh God, he's going to ask for a separation, for a divorce in time. At least he's had the courtesy to do it to my face.

But then he spoke, and it sounded like a prepared speech, which he had rehearsed over and over, and he said, "Grainne, I am so sorry, can you ever forgive me? I have treated you dreadfully, leaving you on your own when you most needed me. I can only say, it's not an excuse, I know, but I was hurting badly, and confused about the whole thing. And then a couple of days after I moved out, Sinead rang and invited me – no, commanded me – to meet her for a drink. I was nervous, I can tell you – I've seen Sinead in a raging torrent before." We grinned a little at each other in appreciation of how Sinead can be. "But she was very kind, very gentle. She told me she knew how much I'd been hurting, had seen how I was left behind with my own wounds while everyone was dealing with you. She said I needed to get myself sorted out before going back to you. She told me, what I knew anyway, that we were meant to be together. For me, Grainne, it's only ever been you."

Hope was dawning in my heart.

"And so, I've been going to – to counselling," he confessed embarrassedly, as if admitting to something shameful. "Sinead gave me the name of someone truly good. And it's helped, I've worked through all my stuff about the rape, about the baby, everything. And I've just spent the past week away, alone, sorting through the final stuff, and I've come to ask you is there any way you can take me back? Or have I left it too late?"

I gazed at him in joy – I couldn't believe it. But I had to ask, nervous to ruin it all, even at this stage, "But Patrick, what about the baby, what about Helen?"

He smiled at me, that warm slow smile I loved so much, said, "Well, I am her father, so says the birth cert. But seriously, well, I'm going to make a go of it, accept her as my daughter, put in time with her to create a relationship with her, to be her father. It'll be difficult, I know, but I'm going to do it. It hit me, when you explained, that day in our house before I brought you here, that you would have left your heart behind with her. I couldn't react then, but the truth of it hit me, and I talked it through with the counsellor. She has three children, and she was able to explain to me just how strong the connection between mother and baby is. It helped. I'll try," he said again, "I will try."

We stood and looked at each other, deep into each other's eyes, and there was joy in us both. I said, "Come upstairs with me," and brought him to where Helen was sleeping in the bed. Shyly, softly, I said, "Here she is," and he looked at her, his face inscrutable.

Then he said, "She's very, very pretty. She's like you." He touched his hand gently to her sleeping forehead, and whispered, "Hello, Helen. I'm your daddy, come to claim you, to mind you and protect you and rear you as best as I can." And it was like a promise, a solemn vow.

We went downstairs again, and I hovered, suddenly uncertain.

I mentally asked him, what are you waiting for? Isn't this the bit where you grasp me to your manly bosom, and carry me off in a mixture of romantic music, soft focus and passion?

But he just stood looking at me, smiling softly, his arms hanging loosely by his side, relaxed.

And I realised, and I remembered. He had promised me that he would wait for me to come to him when I was ready, that he would not make any sexual advances to me.

I gulped. It was up to me then. And I was scared. But I seriously wanted him, wanted his hard gentle body against me, in me. Wanted to touch the soft skin over the hard muscles.

So I moved towards him, slowly, tentatively. Reached up my face and kissed him. Both our arms were hanging loosely, our bodies were not touching at all, except for our mouths. I kissed him softly and gently, he accepted it passively.

I kissed him harder then, and he opened his mouth, and allowed me to explore him. Oh, the softness of his tongue, his mouth, the warmth of it, the sweet taste! He kissed me back, moving his tongue slowly, gently, tantalisingly. But he did not move his tongue into my mouth.

It was so sensuous, so erotic, that slow, slow, kiss. As we weren't touching elsewhere my brain could concentrate on experiencing the pleasure of the kiss, with no distractions. The kiss went on for ages, and dimly, beyond the rushing sound in my ears, I heard him groan, desire and hunger expressed in that most primeval way. But still he did not move.

I reached up, put my arms around his neck, and pulled his head close to me. I moved my fingers through his hair, relishing the soft springiness of it, the silk over the hardness of his skull. I caressed his neck, and played with the lobes of his ears, and he groaned again.

I took that tiny, huge, step towards him, so that we touched along the lengths of our bodies. The thought occurred to me, one small step for a woman, one huge step for rape victim. Ex-rape victim, I told myself proudly: rape survivor.

As we leant gently against each other I could feel his erection pressing against my belly, and I welcomed the sensation, the power I had to excite him, the hardness of it coiled against me. And if there was any ghost of Brogan it was faint, like a mist which could be ignored.

And still he didn't move, letting me control the whole situation.

I released my arms from around his neck long enough to seize his arms, and wrap them around my waist. He gladly took this permission, and held me close, his large strong hands caressing me.

I moved my mouth away from his, and began nuzzling his neck, kissing and biting gently in his most sensitive spots there. He groaned again, breathed, "Grainne," and the word was a sigh of longing and desire and love.

I moved my hands down, around his waist, tugged his shirt out of his trousers, and moved my hands underneath, onto his bare skin. There was a shock of remembering, of coming home, as I caressed him, the breadth of his back, the muscles strong and defined, the skin smooth. And around, slowly, teasingly, to his front, and, still under the shirt, feathered my fingers over his body. He took a sharp breath inwards. I slowly began to unbuckle his belt. Except that I couldn't! Not when I was so out of practice, and unable to see what I was doing as it was still under his shirt and jumper.

I started laughing, little snickering laughs to myself, as I fumbled and fumbled, and Patrick gave a little laugh, which set me off more, which set off a chain reaction in us both, until we were both guffawing hugely – laughter of humour and love and relief and joy.

And the realisation came to me, really truly deeply came to me, in the most central core of my being, that this is what made lovemaking with Patrick so different from enforced sex with Brogan: the laughter. The autonomy, sure, the power of choice. But to be able to share laughter, it was a powerful gift.

And as we laughed, we gazed into each other's eyes, and his eyes were dark and hooded with desire for me, and gentle with love for me, and creased with laughter. And as he bent his head to me, I whispered, "It's okay now, everything's okay now," and this time when we kissed he did invade my mouth, with assurance and confidence and gentleness. And I drank in the taste and sensation of him, and greedily took more.

He whispered to me, "I love you. I love you so much. I've missed you so much."

I whispered, "Take off your jumper," and he did.

And I slowly unbuttoned his shirt, my mouth

following each opened button, as I nuzzled and nibbled my way down his torso, down to the delicious thin line of hair, which led like an arrow to his jeans button. And his hands clenched my shoulders, and his breathing was fast and loud. When his shirt was open, I slowly pushed it off his shoulders, and onto the floor, and my hands were caressing the newly revealed skin.

And I stood back for a second and gazed at the beauty of him, newly revealed. The broad shoulders, the well-muscled arms, the slight curve of his pectoral muscles, moving now with his laboured breathing, leading to his flat stomach.

I moved back towards him, drunk with my own power, and I unbuckled his belt, easily now that I could see it. And I opened his jean button. And I slowly pulled his zip down. And is there anywhere a more delicious, arousing sound than that of a man's fly-zip being opened? I looked into his eyes as I slipped my hand under the waistband of his shorts, and slowly eased my hand down. He groaned again, and closed his eyes, and his head fell back, and his throat was strong and smooth and golden in the firelight.

I moved my hand slightly, and he groaned again, whispered, "Grainne, don't stop." But I released him then, he groaned in disappointment, opened his eyes. And as I watched him watching me, I undressed myself. A bit shyly, a bit nervously, but I did it. And his eyes feasted on me. He reached out his hands, gently hefted my breasts.

Then he said, "Come, lay down with me," and we

lay on the floor, cushioned by our discarded clothes, before the caressing heat of the stove.

We embraced and touched and kissed each other, hungry beyond famine for each other, our bodies both so familiar and so new. Our arousal grew and grew.

But he didn't enter me, he was still letting me set the pace, and I thought I would die for the lack of him. And so I pushed him gently onto his back, and climbed on top of him. And slowly I lowered myself onto him, and slid down the long, solid length of him. And we both exhaled gently in a groan of connection and joy and completion and further desire. I had expected to feel fear, at this first sexual encounter since Brogan, but I didn't. It just felt right, like coming home, it had no connection, no resonance at all of that time with Brogan.

For moments I sat still, savouring the feeling of having Patrick within me, and I looked down into his eyes, and smiled. And his hands cupped my bottom, and he smiled at me.

I rocked slightly, in a tiny movement, and he said, "Oh God," and his eyes closed, and his grip tightened on me.

I wanted to make it last, wanted to move slowly and slowly. But despite myself my movements grew quicker, stronger. And Patrick was saying over and over, "Oh God, oh God, it's so good!" And then he muttered, "Grainne, I'm sorry, it's been so long, I won't be able to –" and he began to thrust upwards, meeting my downward thrusts, breathing even more quickly and heavily, until he came, hugely and loudly.

I didn't come, too busy enjoying the look of him, and the nearness of him, and the sheer reality of him. And too busy relishing those words – 'it's been so long'. Even though he could mean anything by 'long', and it didn't mean he had been celibate, I hoped it did mean this, and rejoiced.

After a few minutes he lifted himself off me, and lay beside me, close, still breathing heavily. I put my hand on his chest, and could feel his heart racing. After a while, when both his breathing and his heart had calmed he said, "That was wonderful, that was truly . . ." He shook his head in exasperation at not being able to find a word big enough.

He said then, "I truly am so sorry about all these past months. I'll never be able to make it up to you."

"You don't need to," I said, "I understand. I've understood for a while now. It was explained to me by a wonderful woman called Magda. She's my friend here, she's been so good to me, let me tell you."

And I told him all about Magda, how she had forced me to release my anger, and gave me back my joy in my life, and gave me the space to forgive him, Patrick, and to have him back in my life too.

"Wow, that's great," he said dazedly. "I was so nervous coming here, you've no idea. For all I knew you were so angry with me you'd slam the door in my face. I don't know how I'd have dealt with that. Or maybe you'd found someone else – a woman as wonderful as you wouldn't be short of suitors – what is it?" He had seen my expression.

Rory. For those blissful moments I'd forgotten him.

"Patrick," I said, "I did meet someone else, a kind wonderful man, who's been so good to me and Helen. His only fault was not to be you. But he offered me a future, and I'd told him I'd need to sort things out with you first. I've left tons of messages for you, everywhere I could, asking you to ring. And what I was going to say was, that I wanted to ask you to come back to me. I've only ever loved you. I would only have gone to him if you hadn't wanted me. But I promised him I'd ask you if you still did want me, and tell him, as soon as I could. I'd better do that now – it's been a long week for him, waiting."

I got up, picked up my mobile phone from the table, and then realised, "Oh, the battery's flat, I'll connect the charger and use the mains electricity."

"Oh, here," he said, "use mine. And he reached over to his jacket, fished his phone out of the pocket, and handed it to me.

"I'll ring upstairs, for his – Rory's privacy."

Patrick nodded in understanding. I went upstairs and dialled Rory's number. He answered quickly.

I said, "Rory . . .Rory."

It must have been in my voice, because he knew instantly. "You're back with Patrick, aren't you?"

I nodded, forgetting he couldn't see me. I said, "Oh Rory, I'm so sorry. I –"

"Don't be sorry. It is the right ending. I knew you still loved him, that I would have only had part of you. I would have been happy with that, but would you? I want you to be happy, and I'm glad," he said bravely, "that it's worked out like this. I hope you'll both be very happy." And Rory, that kind, gentle, blessed man, managed to say it with perfect sincerity. "Keep in touch, I don't want to lose your friendship."

"I will, I will," I said. "Goodbye."

While I was at it I rang Sinead. Our call was brief. When she answered I said, on a squeal, "Sinead!"

She said, and there was a huge smile in her voice, "He's come back to you then? I am so glad. I hoped for it so much."

"I'll talk to you soon,"I said, "I'm just ringing quickly. Will you ring Stephen and tell him?"

She assured me that she would, sent me love and kisses down the phone, and asked me to give Patrick her best wishes.

When I went downstairs to him, I felt suddenly shy. I was still naked, and while it was one thing to be undressed with him during passion, to just walk in front of him, although I'd done it a million times before, seemed difficult. But I forced myself to do it, knowing that we had to get back to normality as soon as possible.

He was still lying in front of the fire, looking beautiful. The flickering light played purple shadows on his dark skin. He was lying on his side, head supported in his hand, and he smiled when he saw me.

"You're so beautiful," he said, and his eyes drank me in.

I forced myself to hold myself straight, and smiled back at him. "You're not so bad yourself!" His long, lean body looked like poetry in the semi-darkness, and the love and tenderness and desire in his eyes flowed over me in joy. As I stood there, at the bottom of the stairs, I saw his penis quiver, and begin to grow again.

"Come here," he said roughly, and reached out towards me. Smiling, laughing inside with joy, I went towards him, lay down beside him, and drank in his beauty, his power, his love, his essence. This time I lost myself in the sensation, and climaxed gloriously. Patrick laughed, deep and throaty, with joy and, possibly, pride, at my all-encompassing orgasm, and kept moving within me, as I rode wave upon wave of sensation.

Afterwards we lay in silence. I thought of the journey to Cilltubber with him, how I ached to touch him, but didn't have permission. Now that I did have that permission, I took full advantage of it. I touched him sexually, sure, glorying in the hefty weight of his testicles, his sigh as I stroked gently. But I also touched him affectionately over and over, caressing his face, gazing into his eyes, stroking his soft springy hair. He gazed at me, a half-smile on his face and love and repletion in his eyes.

I said, "I was just thinking of when you brought me here – I couldn't take my eyes off you in the car, I ached to touch you. I was so aware of every time you changed gear, your hand coming so near to my leg, but not touching."

"Were you?" he asked in surprise.

"Sure. And you were so cool, not a bit aware of me at all."

He put his head back, and laughed hugely, and then said, "You're joking, of course. I was so, so aware of you. The curve of your cheek, of your breasts, your leg when I changed gear, the gentle scent of your perfume and fresh hair. I was so hot for you, I had a semi-erection during the whole journey, and it was only by a huge effort of willpower that it remained only a semi version."

I said wonderingly, "I never knew. You hid it well."

"So did you, after all. Anyway, it wasn't the time, was it? Not when we still had the problems with Brogan – both the practical problems of his stalking you, and the memories of the rape messing us up. But when we were here, God, I was so tempted. And when you invited me to stay the night, God," he groaned at the memory, "I really wanted to stay. But I knew that if I did, it wouldn't be in the other room. And it still wasn't time. I tell you what though, during that long journey back, I thought of nothing but you, I ached for you, I cursed myself for having left you. And every day since then, I've thought of you always. But I didn't contact you, I felt that I had to sort myself out first. I had nothing to offer you, before now. Only more of the same, and that hadn't worked the first time, had it? But I missed you so much."

I dared to ask, my heart thumping in my chest, "And did you . . . have you?"

"No," he said, understanding me, "there was nobody else. I was tempted, God knows, I wasn't used to celibacy. But I didn't want anybody but you, and I felt that I couldn't, in all honesty, act as a single man until I was – which I hoped I wouldn't be. I tell you what though, I was so nervous coming down here. I didn't know if my career as a single man was going to start abruptly with you slamming the door in my face. Did you wonder why I was so wet, tonight when I arrived? It wasn't raining that hard after all."

"I hadn't thought of it, but now that you say it . . ."

He gave a short laugh. "It was because I'd spent literally ten minutes outside the door, raising my hand to knock, and lowering it again. I knew that this was it, and while I wanted so much to be reconciled with you, as soon as possible, I felt that I didn't want the moment to come when it was over between us."

He looked at me to see how I was taking it. It was, after all, a fairly vulnerable statement to make. But I was touched, and proud of him that he could say this to me, and proud of myself that he trusted me this much.

I said then, "Let's go to bed." We gathered up our clothes, and made our way up the stairs. When we got to the bedroom I stopped. "Ah," I said.

"What?"

"I've been sleeping with Helen. I've no cot for her. Will we all fit in?"

"I might roll on her," he said, worried.

"No," I answered confidently, "you wouldn't. But I'm concerned that she'd be too near the edge if she was on the outside, and too hot if she was in between us.

He laughed. "Well, I do know that parenthood changes things, and here's one. I'll sleep in the other room tonight, and tomorrow we'll move one of the single beds in here, put it beside the double bed." He surveyed the room. "It'll be a squash, that chest-of-drawers will need to go into the other room, but it should work."

And so we spent the first night of our reconciliation sleeping apart. Parenthood does change things. But I went to sleep, snuggled up with Helen, buzzing with the joy of his return, and the lovemaking we'd shared and especially, his willingness to accommodate Helen's needs. He hadn't even suggested that she sleep in the other room, which he could have done. This was his first act as her father, putting her needs before his own, and my heart sang with happiness.

Chapter 30

Next morning she woke early, nuzzling for a feed, and as I nursed her the connecting door opened.

"I was listening for you to wake," he said, coming into the room, and climbing into the space recently vacated by the baby.

She jerked her head up, feed abandoned, at this unexpected voice. She sat up and, safe from the vantage point of my lap, stared at him. She didn't reach out to him – why should she, he was a total stranger to her? But neither did she 'make strange'. After a moment or two, she turned and resumed her feed with gusto.

Patrick laughed, a little nervously. "Well, that's the first hurdle over. I'll take it slowly with her, not overwhelm her or anything. Hey, I'll have to learn how to change nappies. That'll be a new skill for me. And give her baths." He seemed pleased with the prospect.

We sat together in the bed, and chatted while Helen nursed.

"How has it been, living here in Cilltubber? I felt so sorry for you, you looked so forlorn when I was leaving you here."

"I was forlorn and I was very lonely, and you know how I hate – hated – to be alone. But –" and I brought him up to date on the last months of my life, how I had learned so much, and grown so much from the experience, how I was busy painting and selling my pictures, and was an accepted member of the community now. "I'm very happy here," I finished, "and now that I have you back with me, well, everything is perfect."

He said sombrely, "I've missed so much, of your life, of hers," and he gestured towards Helen.

"It wasn't your fault, it was circumstances, Patrick. We've both learned so much, and grown so much these past months. Maybe we can view this time as a positive experience for us both, rather than regretting it. We can regret it had to happen, but now that it has, and is over, let's consider all we've gained, rather than the time we've lost."

He nodded in agreement. "I've certainly learned so much. Like how much I loved you – I hadn't realised the depth of it before. And to appreciate love so much more, knowing how easily things can change. And to live more in the moment, relishing each one. And I've learned that you can experience such pain you didn't know existed, but yet can survive."

Eventually hunger drove us downstairs, and we ate breakfast. Patrick talked of his job, his colleagues and other light-hearted stuff.

And then he said, with wonder and relief, looking at Helen, "You're right, you know, she's her. Herself, I mean. And we can love her for herself. Her conception is a tiny, irrelevant detail. I don't see Brogan when I look at her, I just see images of you, but mostly I see just her. And she's dotey."

Joy leapt in my heart, and I went to him where he sat at the table, and we hugged tight.

"Will we go for a walk?" I asked. "I want to show you Cilltubber. Oh, I know you know it, but I want to show you my Cilltubber, the life I've made here."

So after we showered and dressed, we strapped Helen into her buggy and went out.

As we went along I pointed out landmarks to him. Places that before had only been buildings, but now held a wealth of memories. Houses where my fellow-crafters and friends lived: "That's Aine's house, and look, that pink one up there, that's Sarah's." We met Mary, coming out of her house, and I introduced them.

We then went into Magda's shop. Magda moved towards me with her usual grace, hugged me.

I said, and I was surprised to find that my voice was breaking slightly, "Magda, I'd like to introduce you to my husband, Patrick. And Patrick, this is my dear and good friend, Magda."

She picked up the situation in an instant, and her face lit up.

"Patrick, I am so, so happy to meet you," and to his surprise, she embraced him in a big hug. But I understood. She was so happy for me, and I felt a sense of awe at her generosity. There were no second chances for her and her husband, but she was totally delighted in my second chance. She didn't say anything more, she didn't need to.

In my excitement I said, "And will you come around this evening? And get to know Patrick properly?"

She laughed. "Hardly! But if you're going to be here for any length of time?" and she looked enquiringly at Patrick.

"A week," he confirmed, "until next Sunday."

"Great," she said. "Well, I'll come down later in the week. I promise."

My re-charged mobile phone rang then. I fished it out of my bag and answered it. It was Stephen, his voice bubbling over with excitement.

"Sinead told me the news! I'm delighted for you, I really am. But listen, Grainne, I've just this minute got off the phone from John Murphy – you know, the owner of Paintings Art Gallery." Wow, only the most prestigious art gallery in Dublin, in the whole of Ireland! Brilliant, Stephen must have got some of his sculptures in there!

But Stephen was going on, "I'd showed him your work, and he loves it. Absolutely loves it! And he's going to exhibit them, once I give him your permission. And Grainne," Stephen's voice was high with excitement, "he's going to charge between €500 and €1,000 per painting! And he wants to see any other work you have!"

I was suddenly breathless. "What, what? Are you sure?"

"I'm sure, I'm sure! Isn't this wonderful?"

"Oh, God, it's beyond wonderful! Oh, thank you, Stephen, thank you! I'd never have thought of doing anything with those paintings, they were only experiments really. Wow, I can't take it in! Listen, I'll talk to you later, I need to sit down and have a stiff brandy!"

Stephen laughed with delight, said, "Richard sends his hugs and congratulations too. I'll talk to you soon. Byyyeee!"

I switched off the phone, and turned to Patrick, my face shining. "Patrick,"I said, and my voice was squeaking, "John Murphy, of Paintings Art Gallery, is going to exhibit my paintings. At huge money! I can't believe it – Paintings Art Gallery! "

Patrick gave a whoop of delight, and grabbed me around the waist, and spun me around – narrowly missing an elderly lady who was walking past, who smiled at us indulgently.

Of course, we had to rush back into the shop and tell Magda the news. She gave a great cheer, and there were hugs and kisses all around. She said, "I knew it, I knew it all along, that you had great talent in you. I'm so happy for you."

"I'll still paint for the shop, I promise!"

And she smiled fondly, and said, "We'll see. For now just enjoy your good news."

The morning sped by, as we walked through the town, stopping to talk to people, introducing with pride "my husband, Patrick Quinn" to everyone.

Eventually, Patrick asked "Are you hungry? Because I'm starving."

"Gosh, so am I – I hadn't noticed."

"Tell you what – let's go to Flanagan's. Do they still do that lovely pub food?"

"They do," I said, with regret in my voice, "but Patrick, we can't really go there, not with Helen, it would be far too smoky for her. I used to eat there quite a lot during the summer, when I could sit outside in their courtyard, but it's too cold for that now. What about the hotel?"

"Grand," he agreed easily, and we turned and walked back down the street towards the hotel.

The most beautiful woman I've ever seen was sitting behind reception. She had long smooth hair of the richest bronze colour. Her features were classical, her neck long and elegant. She was slender but shapely, from what I could see, and although she was sitting down, it seemed she was tall.

"Wow! Is that you?" she said when she saw us, confusing me mightily. "God, I haven't seen you in years. And is this your wife? And baby?"

Oh, she was talking to Patrick. How did he know such an amazing woman? And why did he marry me when he knew such a beauty?

"Hi, Laura," said Patrick, in tones of great delight. "How are you? I didn't realise you worked here."

He turned to me. "I used to play with Laura, when

we were children, along with her two sisters. But I haven't seen her in – what?" He turned and asked her, "Must be over twenty years anyway?"

It finally dawned on me who she was – the daughter of the shopkeeper Dympna Doran, and therefore the sister of Imelda, and of Claire my solicitor.

"And are you staying long in Cilltubber?" she asked him.

"Em, I'm not sure," he said, looking sideways at me, "a week for sure, and then we'll see."

Once we'd sat in the restaurant, and ordered lunch, I found myself asking, "Patrick, what do we do now?"

He said wickedly, "Eat our lunch, I suppose."

"No, I mean about our future. After this week's holidays."

"I knew that! Well, the main thing is that we're back together. The rest is only logistics, isn't it?"

"Yes. But logistics we have to consider."

"I know." He sighed deeply. "The continuing problem with Brogan really limits our choices. You certainly can't come back and live in our house. And Kevin is due back from Zurich very soon, so I'll have to find somewhere else to live.

"What's the story with our house? Who's living there now?"

He shook his head. "Nobody. I thought about renting it out, but I didn't feel it was fair to let anybody live there, with a crazy guy on the loose and ready to arrive at the doorstep any moment. I suppose we could rent somewhere else in Dublin to live. A waste of money, with a perfectly good house sitting empty, but we can't have you in that house, vulnerable."

God, no. I shook at the thought.

"In fact, anywhere in Dublin might be a problem," I said. "You know how small it is, Sod's Law I'd meet him on the street sometime. I'd always be worried about it. And even if he doesn't physically harm me, I don't even want him to be able to get a court order for a DNA sample, you know, to try to get shared custody of Helen. In fact," I took a deep breath, "Patrick, is there any chance we could live here? In Cilltubber? I really feel so at home here, I don't want to go back to Dublin. Could you get a job in Cork city, maybe? Would you even want to? Move down here, I mean."

"Wow," he said, "now there's a thought."

He was silent for some time, thinking. Our starters came, and I thanked the waitress, as Patrick nodded absent-minded thanks at her.

"Okay," he said at last. "Here's what I think. I would be happy to live here, if that's what you want. I could certainly look for a job in Cork. Or – what I'd really like to do, Grainne, is to become self-employed. To set myself up as a consultant. My current company might well give me work, which I could do from here. Get myself set up with a computer and dedicated phone line. Do work for other companies too. I've thought about it before, but it was just never the right time. I suppose I was putting it off, not wanting to give up the permanent secure job for the uncertainty of self-employment. But we could try it, couldn't we? Maybe this situation is the impetus I need. I'm sure Dad would let us continue to live in Fisherman's Cottage for free. It's a bit small, but it would do us for now. And you're earning money from painting – that would feed us. It's a pity we can't rent out the house in Ranelagh, it would provide a good regular income. That really would make the difference, financially."

"Maybe you – we - could rent it out to men only," I wondered. "Maybe male medical students – your dad would be able to talk to the university professors and see who's reliable."

"Maybe," Patrick frowned, "I just don't like the idea of students. Especially medical students – you should hear the stories my father comes home with. But look, let's agree, yes, in principle, we'll stay here. I'll put some feelers out this week, maybe go into Cork and see a few people."

"Oh thank you, Patrick!" I said in delight, and went around to his side of the table and put my arms around him, kissing his cheek. "I've felt so at home here, I'm so glad that I don't have to make a choice between living here, and having you."

We spent a wonderful four or five days together, rediscovering each other. Patrick went into Cork city, dropped into several companies he knew, and got good feedback from them with regard to consultancy work, so it was looking as if it was going to be possible to put into place our plan to stay in Cilltubber.

Oh, I do love happy endings.

Chapter 31

And then, on Thursday morning, Sergeant Farrell knocked on the door. What did he want? Had I parked illegally anywhere?

Nervously I invited him in. He came into the room, nodded formally at Patrick. I introduced them, and they shook hands, said hello.

Sergeant Farrell then said, "Mrs Quinn, I've just had a call from Sergeant Reilly in Dublin, and it's a bit strange, but I've said I'll pass on the message. She's asked me to ask you, on no account to use your mobile phone for the moment. She's on her way from Dublin now, she said she was leaving as soon as she'd spoken to me, and she'll explain as soon she gets here. She couldn't ring you herself, because of the mobile phone thing, which is why she asked me to call down to you."

Patrick and I looked at each other, confused.

Sergeant Farrell caught the look, shrugged and said,

"I'm none the wiser myself, but I'm sure she has good reason for asking."

"Yes, of course," said Patrick, "and we'll do what she said. We weren't really planning to phone anybody anyway, and we can always use mine if we need."

After he'd left I said, "I wonder why they don't want us to use my phone."

Patrick said hesitantly, as though he didn't want to burden me with what he was saying, "It might – just possibly – be because Brogan has somehow got hold of your number. I hope that's not right, but it's the only thing I can think of."

"Oh God," I breathed, "I thought that was all finished with."

Patrick shrugged. "Either way, we'll just have to wait until Sergeant Reilly gets here."

Eventually, after about five long hours, there was a knock on the door. Patrick answered it, and stood back to let the visitor in. It was Ger Reilly, looking unfamiliar in plain clothes, followed by two giants of male gardaí. I got to my feet and Ger and I hugged.

Her face was sombre, though, and she spoke abruptly, "Grainne, Brogan's raped again. Just last night."

"Oh, no," I breathed, and my heart twisted for this unknown woman.

"Thing is, he wasn't so clever this time: he was caught on security camera. The image shows his face clearly, there's no way any jury would acquit him."

"That's great!"

"Yes, and no. The problem is that he noticed the

camera, it clearly shows him registering this, and putting up his hand to shield his face from view. And in the length of time it took us to identify him, he's fled. We searched his flat, and there's clear evidence of a hasty departure. He could be anywhere."

"That's not so great."

"No," she agreed drily. "But there's worse – in his flat we found evidence that he's been listening to your mobile phone calls: the receipt for the equipment and a copy of your mobile phone bill, which of course has your number on it – God knows how he got that."

I gasped. "Can you do that? Listen in on mobiles calls?"

"Oh, yes," she nodded, "if you have the right equipment. It's expensive, but he obviously thought it was worth it."

I felt devastated, almost as if I'd been raped all over again, that he'd been listening into all my conversations without me knowing. "How long has he had this?"

"The receipt for the equipment's dated about two months ago."

I tried to think of calls I might have made over that time. Had I said anything he could use? Had I ever mentioned Cilltubber? Or West Cork? Obviously not, or he'd have acted on that information before now. I had told everyone where I was just after I had arrived – there had been no occasion to say the name of Cilltubber after that. And I thanked God for that.

"So," she went on, "he's on the run, and we need to catch him. We don't want to put his picture out on the television, for fear of panicking him – the last thing we want is him going to England, and maybe even trying to fly abroad from there. He broke the camera afterwards but obviously he must suspect the already-recorded stuff was safe. But he doesn't know that for sure, that we know it was him. And we don't want to confirm that we do. We will if we have to, but we're hoping it won't come to that. We were wondering –" She paused, took a deep breath and went on, "Thing is, I know it's an awful lot to ask, but we were wondering if you'd phone somebody and let slip, as it were, where you are. And we'd hope he'd come here as he's obviously obsessed with you. You'd be perfectly safe," she added hastily. "Eoin and Dan here," she indicated them, and we all nodded hellos, "will help. One can stay in the house, and the other keep the house under surveillance outside with me. He wouldn't be able to touch you."

"No," said Patrick, "I won't risk her – I won't have her used as bait."

But, "Yes!" I said at the same time. "Yes. I want him caught. It's bad enough that he's done what he's done to me, but now to some other poor woman – I want him stopped."

"No," said Patrick again.

"Patrick, I know why you're saying this, you're scared for me. But look, I'll be perfectly safe, Ger has just said so."

He turned to Ger, "What if Grainne and Helen go somewhere else, to a friend's house maybe? We could just have gardaí in the house. But I have to be here."

"No," I said. "What if he rings here, or something? It would scare him off if someone else answered the phone."

I was scared to have to face him again. But my point was valid. And also I *wanted* to do it – I felt that it would be the final piece of my healing, to be pro-active in helping to bring Brogan down.

Patrick stared at me for an age, while we all waited for his verdict. And maybe he realised my real reason, and decided any risk to me was worth it, to honour this need. In any case, at last he said, "Okay. I still don't like it. But I can see what you," he looked at Ger, "are saying, and also what you mean, Grainne. Okay, we'll do it. But we have to get Helen out of the house."

"Absolutely," I said. "I'll ask Magda to mind her. I'll ring her now, on your mobile."

"No," said Patrick, "who's to say that he hasn't got my number too? Here's what we'll do. I'll bring Helen up to Magda's, tell her the situation, ask her to mind the baby. I'll ring Sinead from Magda's land-line, explain to her what's going on, and tell her that she'll be getting this call from you, so she'll know how to react."

And so that was what happened. Once Helen was safely at Magda's and Patrick was back, confirming that Sinead was waiting for my call, I picked up my mobile phone. My hand was shaking slightly, and I realised that all the experience I'd ever had as the am-dram queen of Ranelagh was now going to be called upon. I hoped Sinead was up to it. I hoped I was up to it. I grinned queasily at the others.

I dialled her number, and she answered it quickly.

"Hi, Sinead," I sang, enthusiasm in my voice, "listen, I've got great news!"

"What's that?" asked Sinead.

"They've set up a website here, mostly for tourists, but also to sell the art and craft work. And I've just heard that I've made my first on-line sale! To a woman in Philadelphia who was here a few years ago on holiday!"

"That's great! Listen, what's the website address? I'll look it up. I might even buy something off it myself," she said in a teasing voice.

"Oh, do! They've got great paintings! Okay: it's www.cilltubber.ie. Spelt: c-i-l-l-t-u-b-b-e-r." Why not make it easy for him?

"Grand, I've got that! C-i-l-l-t-u-b-b-e-r. Right? I'll have a look at the website soon, I promise. Congratulations again!"

"Thanks, Sinead, I'll talk to you soon!"

I hung up and looked questioningly at the assembled crew.

"Brilliant!" said Patrick. "Oscar-winning stuff."

"Well done," said Ger. "Now we wait. We have no idea if he even heard that – maybe being on the run doesn't give him the luxury of listening in. I'm guessing that he might be though, that listening to you is important to him since, even in his hurry, he took the equipment with him. And of course, we don't know how long until he gets here, seeing as we've no idea where he's starting from. So, we wait."

And that's what we did. Ger and Dan left to set up surveillance outside and Eoin sat with us. All through the rest of that afternoon and evening we waited. In silence mostly. The tension grew. Despite my brave words to Patrick, I was scared. This was a dangerous man, and here I was, sitting and waiting for him to come and try to get me. At least Helen was safely out of the way.

Six long hours passed in this way and we began to feel he would not come that day. Perhaps he had not picked up the call after all and our waiting was in vain? Or maybe he was waiting for nightfall . . .

After we had discussed these possibilities for the hundredth time, Eoin got to his feet. "I'd love a cigarette," he said, "but I don't want to go out the front, in case Brogan chooses that moment to come past, and sees me. Is there a back yard?"

"Yes," I said, "There's a little yard through that door – it's surrounded by a wall so he won't see you – you can smoke there."

"Okay," he said, and he turned the key in the door and went out.

A few moments later we heard a small bang, and then a louder thud.

My heart leapt into my throat.

Patrick moved cautiously towards the window, but before he had time to do more than glance outside, the back door opened again and in walked Brogan. Grinning. Carrying a knife.

Patrick lunged forward, but before he could make

contact, Brogan had reached me where I sat, and had touched the point of the knife to my throat. I could feel the cold of the metal, and a delicate pain.

Patrick froze.

"That's right," said Brogan. "Now, careful – don't try anything. Move over there," and he gestured to the far side of the room.

Patrick reluctantly moved over and stood beside the stairs.

Brogan then said to me, "Stand up, you!"

He moved the knife away from my throat a few inches. Shaking, I did what he said. He grabbed my shoulder and manouvered me around so that I had my back to him, and circled me with his arm so that the knife was now in front of me, its length gently against my throat. He moved a pace forward so that his body was next to mine. I didn't dare move, but inwardly I shuddered. I had thought never again to be in a position where Brogan could make physical contact with me. My bravado at playing a part in bringing him down didn't seem such a great idea now. I could feel his hot breath on my ear and neck.

"Hi, all," said Brogan then, cheerfully, "that's some welcoming committee, outside! He's well taken care of now though. Handy enough that he came out – I was outside waiting for my chance to break in, but this is much easier."

"What have you done to him?" I asked, struggling to stay calm.

"I've done what was necessary," Brogan sneered.

"Now – I want you and the baby to come with me. We can go back over that wall outside, the way I came in, and be gone before anyone's any the wiser. You," he said to Patrick, "won't tell those gardaí so carefully hidden outside, will you? Not when you know that Grainne's with me. Safe with me. And you'll want her to stay that way, won't you?"

"How did you know I was here?" I gasped. Anything to delay him.

"Oh," and there was delight at his own cleverness in his voice, "I've been listening to your mobile phone calls for ages. I was waiting outside your house, did a lot of that. I didn't really know what else to do. But I knew I had to see you again. You, and the baby. And I was hoping you might underestimate me, and think it was safe to come back there. But you never did." Now he sounded petulant, cross that I'd thwarted him. His grip on the knife tightened, and I could feel the steel harder against my neck.

Patrick and I were staring intently at each other from across the width of the room. I was trying with all my might to show my love for him, in case these were to be our last moments together. His face was hard, expressionless, and then his eyes left my gaze and he watched Brogan carefully.

Brogan continued, caught up in the relaying of the story of his own brilliance. "And then one morning I saw the postman walking along, and I had a stroke of genius, although I say it myself. I timed it just right, reached the gate just before he did, and made as if to walk up it like I owned the place. And then, as if I'd just thought of it, I turned back to him, and I said casually, 'Anything for Quinn?'. And he just handed me the letters he had, and I thanked him, and walked up the path to the door. I hid in the porch until he'd gone out of sight, and then I left. I might still have been unlucky – the post might have been nothing but junk mail. But no!" he said triumphantly. "It was all working out for me. As if it was meant. Because your mobile phone bill came that day! And once I had your number, well, it was a simple matter to get listening equipment. Expensive, mind you," he said begrudgingly, "but simple. And I was listening in to your calls. For all the good it did me – you never once mentioned where you were." He gave a laugh then. "Until today! That was a bit silly," he said reprovingly, "telling your friend the name of the website. But lucky for me that you did."

Delay, delay, I told myself frantically, maybe the cavalry will come. Even though, I knew in my heart of hearts, that there was nothing to alert Ger and Dan that there was anything wrong. "That was clever," I said, and tried to put some sort of admiration into my voice, "but how did you manage to find me when you got here? All you knew was the name of the village!"

"That was easy! Once I got here, all I had to do was to drive around looking for your car. And those stupid guards outside didn't recognise the car I was driving, because it's not mine!"

His attention turned then to Patrick. "I'm surprised to see you here. Grand reunion, was it?"

"Divorce arrangements," said Patrick shortly.

"Really?" he said cynically. "You two looked pretty cosy for a couple about to divorce. Plus what I heard a few days ago on your phone, something about 'great news'. You must think I'm very stupid. But still, I've some information for you that might change your mind about being with her."

"What's that?" said Patrick, sounding intrigued.

"Oh, she's only been having this affair with some guy called Rory. You are such a slut," he said to me conversationally. "Being unfaithful to your husband with me, and now with this guy! I've heard her," he told Patrick, "talking on the phone with him, arranging meetings and so on."

"Have you, you bitch?" said Patrick, and there was menace in his voice. His face turned on me with disgust, "Jesus, I should have known!"

I cringed in a reflex action, even though I knew he must be acting.

"You'll be well rid of her, and the baby. Speaking of which, go and get her."

"The baby's not here, she's with a friend of mine," I said desperately, and too late realised by some narrowing of Patrick's eyes that he hadn't wanted me to say this.

But Brogan laughed cynically, "God, you really, really, underestimate me! I fell for that one once. You do not seriously think I'll believe you again!" He jerked his head at Patrick. "Go and get the baby!"

Patrick turned towards the stairs, but stopped and turned back at Brogan's voice.

"Quinn, don't try anything stupid like alerting the guards from the upstairs window, will you? Unless you want her killed. I'll have that knife in her throat as soon as either door opens, and I don't care if I do time for it. Or maybe you don't care if she dies?"

"There'll be no tricks," Patrick said wearily. "I don't want her any more after what you've told me, but we've shared a lot of years – I don't want her killed either."

He went upstairs, and Brogan and I stood silently in our unnatural embrace.

After a few moments Patrick came back downstairs carrying a swaddled bundle of clothes carefully, gently, on his arm.

"Now," said Patrick, pleasantly. "I'll give you a trade. You can have the baby, and give me her mother back."

"No, I'll have them both," said Brogan.

"If you won't let her go I'll swing the baby against the wall!" said Patrick with ferocity. "I've hated this brat of yours from the moment of its conception – it would give me the greatest pleasure to kill it! And *I* don't care either if I do time! Maybe we'll be cell-mates!"

Brogan looked confused. "I thought you didn't want this slut any more?"

It was Patrick's turn to give a cynical laugh. "I don't. Not for myself. But after what you've said she's done, I don't want her going off into the sunset with you either. I'll take her, and keep her, and make her life a misery. Nobody screws around on Patrick Quinn!"

Was Brogan really swallowing this macho bullshit? But he was so full of it himself, maybe he was. I had no idea what Patrick was planning, and I seriously hoped that he did, in fact, have some plan – that he wasn't, as I had done, just trying to spin it all out.

Brogan thought about it a second, then said, "What if she wants to come with me, once I have the baby? She's already gone through a lot to keep the child – she might choose to go with it. She might run off on you."

Patrick shrugged. "I'll take the chance."

Brogan said, "Okay. Fair deal. I can always get another woman, but a man's own child is worth having. We'll meet in the middle of the room. You'll hand me the baby, and I'll release her then."

"How can I believe you?"

Brogan shrugged. "One of us has to let go first, and I'd rather it was you. Let's not forget who's the one with the knife."

"Okay," said Patrick, with apparent reluctance.

Brogan nudged me forward, and I moved slowly, not wanting to walk into the knife. Patrick moved forward too. In a kind of bizarre shuffle we made our way towards each other.

When we were about a pace apart, Patrick said, "Okay, before I hand you the baby I want you to drop the knife from her throat. You can keep it by her side, if you want, and you'll still be left with the advantage." As he said the word 'left' he emphasised it the most infinitesimal amount, and his eyes briefly met mine, and a message flashed in his eyes.

Brogan thought about it, said, "Sure, why not, a kidney wound's as effective as the jugular." And he lowered his arm from around me, and rested the point of the knife gently against the right side of my waist.

"Okay," said Patrick, "I'm going to give you the baby now."

And then everything happened in an instant.

Patrick suddenly hefted the bundle and swung it, shouting at me, *"Left! Now!"* I let myself fall to the floor to my left, away from the deadly blade. A sharp pain went through my ankle – I ignored it and began scrambling out of the way. Brogan's eyes, exactly as Patrick had hoped, had followed the bundle being swung through the air, shocked at what Patrick was doing. The end of the bundle caught Brogan's head with a soft thud, and he swayed slightly. Patrick dropped the bundle and as it fell to the floor, unravelling, revealing the now-lampshade-less bedside light, Patrick grabbed Brogan's knife-arm with his two hands, and the two of them began a desperate struggle for possession.

I pulled myself to my feet using the bannisters. I tried to put my foot under me but my leg buckled, and I would have fallen but for my grip on the bannisters.

I watched, horrified as Brogan and Patrick wrestled for supremacy and possession of the knife as it glinted evilly in the light. Patrick had hold of Brogan's knife-arm with his own left hand, and it was wavering as he struggled to hold it with his weaker hand. With his right fist he began hitting Brogan, as best he could, in the face. At the same time he was trying to dodge, with only limited success, Brogan's free hand.

A split second only, I watched, and then I came to my senses and turned towards the front door. As I did so I was aware of Patrick suddenly lifting his leg, and kneeing Brogan in the testicles. Hard. As Brogan crumpled to his knees Patrick took the opportunity to wrestle the knife off him, and it fell to the floor.

As I hopped the few paces to the door I was aware of Patrick sharply pushing Brogan onto the floor, Brogan's legs folded awkwardly under him.

I grabbed the front door, balancing on it, and opened it, praying to God the gardaí would hear me as I shouted breathlessly, *"Ger! Dan! Brogan's here!"*

At once I heard running footsteps and they were rushing up the short path and past me into the room, as I clumsily moved out of the way. I turned to see that Patrick was now astride Brogan, kneeling on his arms, and was hitting him with passionate fury, thumping his face with clenched fists, hissing, "Do you like that, Brogan? Do you now realise what it's like to be helpless and in fear and pain, with someone stronger hurting you? *Do you?*"

Dan moved towards them, but Ger stayed him with a light touch on his arm. For some long moments we all watched as Patrick enthusiastically took our revenge. Then Ger nodded at her colleague, and they waded in, dragged Patrick off, and pulled an unsteady Brogan to his feet, briskly cuffing his hands behind him. His mouth was bleeding, and his face was nearly unrecognisable. Patrick stood swaying, breathing heavily, one eye already beginning to close, but there was a kind of victory and exultation in his expression.

Brogan began blustering, now that he was safe from Patrick. "That's assault," he said unclearly through his bruised and battered mouth, "I'm having you for assault – you're going down, mate. This pair witnessed it."

Ger Reilly turned to her colleague. "We didn't see anything, did we, Dan?"

He shook his head, said in innocent tones, "See what, guv?"

"What!" said Brogan. "You liars, you saw it all!"

"All I saw," said Ger Reilly in succinct tones, "was Mr Quinn here, restraining you, as he'd every right to do after you broke into his house."

"Oh, yeah," he sneered, "and how to you explain the state of my face then?"

The two gardaí looked at each other for a delicious moment, and then turned to him.

"Well, if you will resist arrest . . ."

He spluttered, and vowed all sorts of horrible stuff, but they just grinned.

Then Ger looked around the room and asked in alarm, "Where's Eoin?"

"Oh, God," said Patrick, moving towards the back door, "he's outside in the yard. He stepped outside and Brogan got him."

With a muttered curse Ger moved also towards the door, leaving Brogan to the tender clutches of her colleague.

A minute later later Patrick and Ger came back, supporting a groaning Eoin between them.

Ger examined his head gently under the overhead light.

"He'll be fine," she said, relief in her voice. "Brogan just clocked him one and trussed him up." And then her voice changed, "But this is nothing to what I'll do to him, once he's better, letting Brogan ambush him!"

She turned now to Brogan, and spoke in a formal voice:

"Mr Darren Brogan, I am arresting you for the rape and assault of Nora Dwyer, on the 14th of January of this year, for assault on a police offer, and for breaking and entering into the home of Mr Quinn and for armed assault on Mr Quinn. You have the right to remain silent, but anything you do say can be used in evidence against you."

"He held the knife to Grainne," said Patrick, "and was going to take her, kidnap her, and the baby too – he thought she was here."

"Right, okay, we'll have that too. Mr Brogan, I am also charging you with the crime of assault on Ms Quinn, and her attempted abduction, and the attempted abduction of Helen Quinn." And to us, "Anything else?"

I said, relief making me giddy, "You might ask him what happened to Shergar."

She grinned. "Listen, Grainne, this is over now. You're safe now. With all the evidence, for all these crimes, there's no doubt that he'll go down for a long time. Now, are you two okay?"

"My ankle . . ."

"Right, and your face, Patrick. Hang on, I'll contact Sergeant Farrell, get him to get the local GP to come down and see you both." She bent and gently felt my ankle – I felt faint with the pain. "It's only a sprain. It'll be fine in a few days – the GP will strap it up."

When arrangements were made, and we knew the GP was on his way, they took Brogan out into the night, and from the doorway we watched him being carefully placed into the back of the police car, and being whisked off to his fate.

And as we sat and waited for Magda to bring Helen down, and for the doctor, I thought about the future. We could safely rent out the Dublin house now, which would provide much-needed income. It looked like Patrick had a good chance of getting freelance work. I could keep painting, and who knew where that would lead, now that Paintings Art Gallery was exhibiting me?

And I would have days and months and years to spend with Patrick, whom I had thought I'd lost. And we'd rear Helen together.

I looked at the future, and it was looking good.

THE END